THE PEOPLE'S DETECTIVE

A Sonny Trueheart Mystery

Nicholas Louis Baham III

BOOTSTRAP PUBLICATIONS

Special discounts on bulk quantities of Bootstrap Publications books are available. For details contact:
Bootstrap Publications
Email: info@bootstrappublications.com
Website: www.bootstrappublications.com

Library of Congress Cataloging in Publications Data
Baham, N.L.
The People's Detective / N.L. Baham III
Paperback ISBN: 978-1-959220-13-8
Hardcover ISBN: 978-1-959220-15-2

Author Headshot by Robert Silver

Copyright © 2023 Nicholas Louis Baham III

All Rights Reserved. Including the right to reproduce this book or portions thereof in any form whatsoever. For information, address the publisher.

This is a work of fiction. All of the characters, names, incidents, organizations, and dialogue in this novel are either the products of the author's imagination or are used fictitiously. Any resemblance to real people or events is coincidental.

Printed in the United States of America

For Tim
Who was patient while I got it together.

For my wife Angela and my son Nick and all the love and support that you have given me.

For Liz who remembers her brother being up late at night writing stories when he should have been asleep.

For Mom who taught me how to read and nurtured my love of books and encouraged all of my dreams.

For Dad who introduced me to Oakland, California and once suggested that I would make a great detective.

For Grandma Oteal Baham who nurtured my love of mysteries, film noir, and classic detective radio and television programs.

For Honey, aka Grandma Bacon, whose vision and leadership brought our family to California. You were our ethical center and the source of our toughness.

For Grandpa Baham and Grandpa Bacon, aka Bompa, for the tall tales and the laughter and for being legends of the family who took me under your wings.

For Jeff, who holds me accountable for prioritizing my health so that I can keep writing.

For the named and unnamed who have been victimized by global sex trafficking.

TABLE OF CONTENTS

Preface 7
The People's Detective Playlist 11
1. The End of Misogynoir 15
    Transcript of Power to the People! Episode 71 25
2. The People's Detective 26
3. Cargo 36
4. Traffick 39
    Transcript of Power to the People! Episode 72 47
5. Ghost in the Machine 48
6. The Segregated Illuminati 61
7. The Onanist 70
8. Backstabbers 76
9. Aaminha 78
10. Captivity 92
    Transcript of Power to the People! Episode 73 95
11. Trouble Man 96
12. Old Man Kaz 104
13. The Young Detective 108
14. The Arrangement 117
15. Brother Malik 121
16. Afro Samurai 133
17. Trans Lives Matter 143
    Transcript of Power to the People! Episode 74 150
18. Blues and Bruise 151
19. Raising the Dead 161
20. Sexual Healing 164
21. Journalist, Councilman, and Traitor 168
22. The Mistress and the Benefactress 175
23. Follow the Drinking Gourd 186
    Transcript of Power to the People! Episode 75 193

24. Straighten Up and Fly Right 194
25. The Bardo...197
26. The Kingston 11......................................201
27. Hunger Strike 211
   Transcript of Power to the People! Episode 76 ... 214
28. Reconnaissance......................................215
29. Smoke and Mirrors................................218
30. Acrophobia 221
31. Game of Death 229
32. Black is the Color 238
   Transcript of Power to the People! Episode 77.... 240
33. Heist 241
34. Slave to the Rhythm 256
35. Gimme the Goods.................................266
36. Fight!...268
37. Wretched of the Earth 272
38. The End of Everything 278
39. Do Not Go Gentle Into That Good Night........280
   Transcript of Power to the People! Episode 78 ... 285
40. Do It Again 286
41. The Trickster 291
42. Did You Think I'd Forgotten?.....................303
Epilogue...311
GLOSSARY 319

Preface

Dear Reader,

The People's Detective is a passion project born of my admiration for the work of pioneering Black mystery and detective novelists Chester Himes, Eleanor Taylor Bland, Robert Beck (a.k.a. Iceberg Slim), Barbara Neely, Grace F. Edwards, and Walter Mosley. In the fashion of these writers, *The People's Detective* features "the blues detective" who investigates the mysteries of Black life and culture.[1] Its central characters, Sonny Trueheart and Aurora Jenkins, explore the epidemic of sex trafficking in Oakland, California and the impact of these crimes on the lives of young women of color. This is the most under-reported story in the Bay Area. This novel also takes on the legacy of white supremacy in Oakland; police violence; intra-racial class conflict; the hypocrisy of the Bay Area's post-racial rhetoric; colorism and internalized racism; gentrification; and the fentanyl drug crisis.

The People's Detective is modern Black folklore. The narrative is both starkly realistic and wildly fantastic, imitating stories told to me by my parents and grandparents of people who migrated with them from the rural South to the urban West to work on the trains and in the shipyards during World War II. These tales were full of hyperbolic situations and wild, alliterative names perfectly suited to the behaviors and flaws of their characters, and they were always subject to change upon each re-telling. They expressed great pain, beauty, and the everlasting hope for better days ahead. These stories were my first lessons in understanding the nature of the Black

---

[1] Soitos, Stephen F. *The Blues Detective: A Study of African American Detective Fiction*, University of Massachusetts Press, Amherst 1996

experience.

The People's Detective is also a love song for the city of Oakland and its people. Oakland is a beautiful and unique city. It is the unceded land and ancestral home of the Huichin, an Indigenous tribe of Ohlone speakers. It was the western terminus of the first transcontinental railroad. Pioneering Black physician Dr. William M. Watts established a hospital facility for Black migrants here in 1926. Black migrants escaped southern sharecropping, lynching and worked in the shipyards and on the railroads during World War II. Mexican laborers came to work in the wartime industry under the Bracero program. Chinese immigrants settled near the Oakland Estuary during the Gold Rush era before being relocated under the mandate of the Chinese Exclusion Act. More Asian American immigrants settled in Oakland in the wake of the 1906 San Francisco Earthquake. Vietnamese refugees created a Little Saigon business district in the aftermath of the Vietnam War. Ethiopian and Eritrean immigrants have made Oakland their home since the 1980s, leaving East Africa in the wake of political conflict and instability, and created a thriving business district in North Oakland. Oakland was also the site of a historic battle between then Alameda County District Attorney Earl Warren and the Ku Klux Klan in the 1920s. It is the birthplace of the Black Panther Party for Self-Defense, Latinos United for Justice, and the home of noted Black Lives Matter activists.

In Oakland, it's all about the culture. Oakland is the birthplace or home of many pioneering musicians in funk, soul, and hip hop including The Pointer Sisters, En Vogue, Tony! Tone! Toni!, Digital Underground, Tupac Shakur, MC Hammer, Luniz, Hieroglyphics, Del Tha Funky Homosapien, and Too $hort. During World War II, Oakland had a vibrant blues scene on 7th Avenue. Bob Geddins became the first Black man in the Bay Area to own a recording studio and record plant. Oakland is the birthplace of the Hyphy sound, street art, and sideshows. It ranks second in diversity among cities with a population over 300,000. It has the nation's largest percentage of women couples and a deep tradition of being welcoming to LGBTQIA+ families. And, in a yummy aside, Rocky Road ice cream and the Mai Tai cocktail were invented here!

Oakland is my adopted home. My wife Angela and I decided to build a life and a family here after experiencing rental discrimination in my native San Francisco. Oakland is the birthplace of my son. My father built a business here as a certified public accountant, serving Black small businesses during the 1970s and '80s. I have wonderful memories of walking along Lake Merritt with my father and buying comic books at DeLauer's and eating at Soul Brother's Kitchen. The first professional sports team that I followed were the Golden State Warriors and that 1974-75 NBA Championship year was a wonderful year of bonding with my father who took me to games at the Oakland Arena.

In *The People's Detective*, I seek to capture some of the cultural magic and history of Oakland, California. Yes, there's plenty of thrilling action here, from the opening fight scene on a BART train to an elaborate bank heist. But my primary goal is to give you, the reader, a sense of the feel and the pace of life, the spirit of its rich diversity and the beauty of its urban landscape. Even as I critique political corruption, the scandal-ridden history of the Oakland Police Department, and the gentrification that is pushing its working-class populations to the margins, I emphasize the city's abiding spirit of hope. If you've ever loved Oakland, I can only pray that I have done justice to this marvelous place.

In love and solidarity,
Nick Baham

The People's Detective Playlist

Dear Reader,

I wrote *The People's Detective* with an eye towards how the story and the landscape of Oakland, California might translate to the big screen. Foremost in this process were my considerations of a soundtrack for the novel. Every chapter was written with one or two songs that represented the main themes, characters, and action. You can listen to **The People's Detective Playlist** on **Apple music** and **Spotify**.

and play each of the selections either before, during, or immediately after reading the chapter. I trust that you will have a greater sense of my inspiration —my strange and wicked sense of humor, and my depth of feeling for this story and these characters— as the story unfolds, and that the playlist will provide a complete experience through the union of words and sound.

Nicholas Louis Baham III

1. **The End of Misogynoir** Ben Harper - "The Will to Live"
2. **The People's Detective** Anthony Hamilton - "Comin' From I'm From"
3. **Cargo** Allison Russell – "All of the Women" and The Specials – "Gangsters"
4. **Traffick** Steel Pulse - "Human Trafficking"
5. **Ghost in the Machine** The Police – "Spirits in the Material World"
6. **The Segregated Illuminati** Makaveli / Tupac Shakur – "White Man'z World"
7. **The Onanist** Chuck Berry - "My Ding-a-Ling"
8. **Backstabbers** The O'Jays – "Backstabbers"
9. **Aaminha** India Arie – "Video"
10. **Captivity** Bob Marley - "Soul Captives"
11. **Trouble Man** Marvin Gaye - "Trouble Man"
12. **Old Man Kaz** Robert Cray - "I'm A Good Man"
13. **The Young Detective** Steely Dan – "With a Gun"
14. **The Arrangement** Too $hort – "Blow the Whistle"
15. **Brother Malik** Prince – "Gigolos Get Lonely Too"
16. **Afro Samurai** Joe James - "Afro Samurai"
17. **Trans Lives Matter** Jorja Smith - "Bussdown"
18. **Blues and Bruise** Amy Winehouse - "You Know That I'm No Good"
19. **Raising the Dead** Bhi Bhiman - "Guttersnipe"
20. **Sexual Healing** Marvin Gaye "Sexual Healing"
21. **Journalist, Councilman, and Traitor** The Disposable Heroes of Hiphoprisy - "Music and Politics"
22. **The Mistress and the Benefactress** The Ohio Players – "Fire"
23. **Following the Drinking Gourd** Ritchie Havens - "Follow the Drinking Gourd"
24. **Straighten Up and Fly Right** Nat King Cole – "Straighten Up and Fly Right"
25. **The Bardo** Isley Brothers – "Footsteps in the Dark"
26. **The Kingston 11** Bob Marley & The Wailers – Burnin' and Lootin'
27. **Hunger Strike** The Temptations – "Message from a Black Man"
28. **Reconnaissance** O'Jays – "For the Love of Money"
29. **Smoke and Mirrors** Jimi Hendrix – "Fire" / The Specials "Ghost Town"
30. **Acrophobia** A Tribe Called Quest – "Check the Rhime"
31. **Game of Death** Carl Douglass - "Everybody Was Kung Fu Fighting;" and Sade – "Feel No Pain"
32. **Black is the Color** Nina Simone – "Black is the Color"
33. **Heist** Celly Cel – "It's Goin' Down Tonight"
34. **Slave to the Rhythm** Grace Jones – "Slave to the Rhythm;" Iggy and the Stooges- "Search and Destroy"
35. **Gimme the Goods** Boz Scaggs – "Gimme the Goods"
36. **Fight** Erykah Badu - "Soldier"
37. **Wretched of the Earth** Sade – "Soldier of Love"
38. **Exposure** The Black Tones – "The End of Everything"
39. **Do Not Go Gentle Into that Good Night** Jimi Hendrix - "1983"
40. **Do It Again** Steely Dan – "Do It Again"
41. **The Trickster** Bobby Womack – "Across 110th St." & Richie Rich - "Let's Ride"
42. **Did You Think I'd Forgotten** The Isley Brothers – "Fight the Power"
43. **Epilogue: The People's Detective (Slight Return)** Jimi Hendrix "Voodoo Chile"

THE PEOPLE'S DETECTIVE

A Sonny Trueheart Mystery

Nicholas Louis Baham III

1. The End of Misogynoir

Oakland, CA - Before the Pandemic

The heat hangs heavy and old school hyphy beats rattle the doors of passing cars. Aurora can feel the ground pulsing beneath her sandaled feet.

She ascends the escalator to the westbound platform for the BART[2] train at the West Oakland station and looks down at the streets below. People spill out into the balmy night. The air is redolent of cannabis. A sea of Raiders and Warriors jerseys and green and yellow satin A's jackets. Young women in halter tops and shorts with blinged-out smartphone cases, and brilliantly brown cocoa butter smooth skin. Their hair and nails are perfect. Young dreadlocked brothers widen their stances in sagging jeans and oversized white t-shirts looking up from under flat brimmed baseball caps cocked to the side with deep, ponderous stares. Heads turn at the developing street parade of tricked-out classic cars and the herky-jerky hydraulic rising and falling of halogen headlights.

Aurora had spent most of the day in her two-story Victorian home in West Oakland's Lower Bottoms. The walls were adorned with framed prints of Emory Douglas' posters for the Black Panther Party for Self Defense. Here, she wrote a column for the *Oakland Post*, the largest African American weekly newspaper in northern California, and hosted the *Power to The People!* podcast. Before leaving she sat in the high-backed wicker chair in her office with her knees pressed against her chest, wiggling her toes, and staring at a giant cork board pinned with images and names and documents. She was hoping that the informant she was scheduled to meet in the evening

---

[2] Bay Area Rapid Transit (BART) is the fifth busiest heavy rail system in the United States. It serves the broader San Francisco Bay Area with over 50 stations, six routes, and over 130 miles of track.

would help her to further connect the dots and unlock the secrets of the city.

She smells the waft of hot dogs wrapped in sizzling bacon being grilled by curbside vendors and is reminded of why she gave up meat. Hipsters riding fixies step off the train from San Francisco and pedal home to new condos and refurbished historic homes in her neighborhood. Plainclothes BART cops ooze on the periphery, protecting and serving the new money.

Her informant will be on the third car on the 7:35pm San Francisco-bound train.

Her mind wanders to Sonny Trueheart, the subject of her last column. She considered showing him the scattered bits of evidence and theories she'd put together. Trueheart. They called him the turncoat traitor cop of Oakland. Shot and killed two crooked cops and a notorious local gangster and then ratted out the corruption in the police department in the biggest scandal in the city's history since the Riders.[3] Lost his badge and his father's legacy. He'd been leaning heavy on the bottle ever since.

Trueheart was hard-boiled. An old school Black man in a young man's body. Off-white trench coat, comfortable footwear, black coffee, and a vintage snub nose .38 revolver that he took pride in never unholstering. The People's Detective. That was the title of her piece. Now, Sonny was just another drunk, disillusioned, shunned, and broken by the system, shadowboxing and talking to himself as he stumbled down the night streets.

But Aurora knew the real heart of the man.

She had to camp out on the doorstep of his East Oakland bungalow in the rain in order to convince him to do the interview. He was shitfaced drunk most of the time. She told him about her

---

[3] The Riders Scandal involved four veteran Oakland Police officers who were alleged in Delphine Allen et al v. City of Oakland (2000) to have kidnapped, planted evidence, and beaten citizens. In 2003 a negotiated settlement was reached, providing the 119 plaintiffs with $11 million dollars, the largest in city history.

years of training in martial arts and bodybuilding. Judo. Aikido. Capoeira. Turns out Trueheart was a 3rd Dan Black Belt in the art of aikido. He seemed to understand from their very first encounter that she was seeking the fulfillment of budo, a martial way of life. Trueheart just seemed to know people that way. And she understood the pain that he sought to dampen with whiskey, bourbon, and beer. Even on the juice she figured he was still better than most.

The story she had now was bigger than what Trueheart had ever dealt with in OPD. If Aurora had shared her initial findings with him, if she had shared with him her sources or shown him the evidence, he would have been able to help her fill in the missing pieces. He would have seen it coming. He would have volunteered to watch her back. He would have been able to tell her if it was merely paranoia or if she were really being followed. He would have made something of the relatively sparse crowd waiting for her train. He would have noticed the man hiding behind his newspaper who had been reading the same story for a good half hour. He would have noticed the gel nails with rhinestones on the woman dressed as an old lady seated at the opposite end of the bench. With her high profile in local print media, television, radio, and the podcast that fashioned her as a modern muckraking journalist of Bay Area and California politics, Aurora could easily be spotted, her backpack and all of her notes confiscated, and her story and her life suddenly put in jeopardy.

In spite of the help that Trueheart could have provided, there were secrets that she kept in her heart that she didn't know how to tell him. She feared that he might act out of self-preservation and refuse to help. That would be understandable, given all that he had been through. She also feared that his commitment to the memory of her sister, the woman that he had loved, would draw him deeper into this cause, and that unfolding events and forces would align against him as he discovered the truth, and that the truth itself might kill him. And so, she compromised and composed a confession in a letter that she mailed to him that morning along with three pictures and a flash drive containing the first draft of her story. Just in case.

The minutes moved slowly, dying like the languid heat of the day.

THE PEOPLE'S DETECTIVE

7:35pm and the San Francisco bound train was right on time. Aurora boarded the third car as instructed. Empty. That set off the first alarm in her subconscious. The door slid shut behind her. She glanced side to side as the connecting door between the third and fourth cars opened, and three men dressed as Oakland cops entered with Aurora's informant and walked toward her direction. The last through the door, the one with his knife held to the throat of her informant, removed his hat and she could see the gleaming bald head of Seven Daggers, the lead enforcer of the Black Archon, the vast criminal organization that ruled the city, and Aurora's fears were confirmed. Aurora let her backpack slip off her shoulders and prepared herself to fight. All the warning signs came to her in a flash and she asked herself why she hadn't been more aware, more present in the moment.

Fragmented thoughts ran amok in her head at a crisp staccato rhythm. In 2000, her colleague was murdered while investigating a crime syndicate operating out of a Black Muslim bakery. It also occurred to her that every American narrative begins with violence against women. And then, out of the corner of her eye she saw a billboard on the train with the face of a young Black woman murdered only last year on a BART train. She composed a spontaneous verse:

The misogynoir will end tonight

Move like a beam of light

Blindingly bright

She surmised neither assailant would have any problem beating women and probably had plenty of experience. These kinds of men measure their masculinity in terms of their ability to do violence to women. People forget that cops kill Black women too.

The two cops approached at Seven Dagger's command. She analyzed their muscularity, height, and weight. She named one cop "Big" and the other one "Slow." They would try to take her to the ground in this tight and confined space and grapple. They would fight dirty. Pure street fighters. Classic barroom brawlers. Each a full foot taller than Aurora and outweighing her by well more than eighty pounds.

Aurora had a handful of signature moves, but she knew that even in the greater space between the train car's doors she couldn't execute many aikido or judo throws. She also knew that the rollicking movement of the train could be her ally against their weight and muscularity.

Move like lightning

Blindingly bright

Aurora stood in the traditional *hanme* stance of the Japanese sword fighter but she remained dynamic and light on her feet, ready to adjust and maneuver in space. This was the first thing that became evident to her attackers.

In the split second before the fight began, she remembered a quote Sonny Trueheart gave her for the story: "The way of budo is love and the end of violence."

The first cop, "Big," lunged forward. Thick hair on his hands. Barrel-chested. Up close he had the physique of George Foreman circa past his prime. But his footwork was better than expected and he shuffled and danced and had a sweet left jab. Rumble in the Jungle all over again. But this time it wouldn't go to the 8th round.

She was centered and balanced. She heard nothing but the sound of her own breathing and the rhythm of her heartbeat as she whirled in the tight space like a tornado. Like the black hakama she wore in aikido training, her summer skirt fluttered in unison with her every movement. Her opponent appeared to move in slow motion. All time stood still.

His biceps moved like pistons, but he had limited speed.

Aurora timed her entrances perfectly. First rule: get out of the way. Second rule: enter.

She could feel the whoosh of air against the side of her face as she evaded each of the first cop's jabs. It quickly began to feel as if he was fighting a glass of water or a phantom. She deflected his blows and whirled to his blind spots and then took control of his wrists and elbows and moved him stumbling and staggering in whatever direction she chose and threw him unceremoniously against the train door or to the ground.

"Big" got up again and again and again, blood on his face, his uniform ever more rumpled, humiliated again and again and again, and came in like a charging bull, lowering his hands and giving up his balance and lunging and grabbing for Aurora's t-shirt with his left hand. He stumbled into nothingness. Again, Aurora was no longer there.

Time slowed down even more. With her movement she manipulated the clock, going back and forth through time. There was a kind of music to her movement, a new rhythm that reorganized past and present.

The second cop, "Slow," waiting with his arms folded, evaluated Aurora's body, movements, and skill.

The train entered the transbay tube, traveling under the Bay, and the car was plunged momentarily into darkness. It suddenly occurred to Aurora that once the train reached Embarcadero Station in San Francisco that it would not stop, that Seven Daggers had done more than invade this one car in his fake OPD uniform, and that the entire nine car train had been hijacked.

Darkness

A new ally

"Big" staggered. Fell. Got up again. Where was she? She feinted and pivoted. She knew exactly where he was. He threw a lazy left jab at nothing. Out of the darkness, Aurora took control of his left wrist with her left hand and with her right hand took hold of his left elbow and forced it upward, keeping the arm bent as she whirled him round. This was called *Ikkyo*. The most fundamental of aikido moves. If it was simply force against force, it wouldn't be possible. But all of Aurora's technique now went into controlling the elbow, using the cop's unbalanced force and the momentary darkness and the assistance of the moving train against him. His weight drove him headfirst against the train door. There was an audible crack as the cop's arm was dislocated from the socket. She told herself that this is not the way of peace but she pushed through it. The dislocated arm slipped from her hold. The cop tried to jam the loose arm back into the socket. But it was just another opening for Aurora.

In the darkness, Aurora jumped onto his back, wrapping her legs around the cop's torso and her right arm around his neck. She was instinctively getting into position to execute a classic judo move, the *Hadaka Jime* or *naked strangle*. She remembered Trueheart saying, "…in judo you have to go and get it."

With pressure from the edge of her right hand on the carotid artery…five seconds…the one-armed giant fell and lay unconscious with scarcely a whimper. She was merciful. Any longer and he would be dead with the same chokehold that he had used on countless of her people.

The end of misogynoir

She breathed deeply. Grateful that her skills overcame the beast and that she did not have to do him any further harm.

The light in the train came back on suddenly as she rose to her feet.

The second cop glanced nervously at Seven Daggers who grinned, handed him the knife, and pushed him forward.

"Slow" smelled of fear. A wonder he did not cut himself as he moved forward with the knife, casually and over-confidently waving it around and slashing the air. She surmised that he did not know how to use a knife. To rely on the knife showed how little confidence he had in himself. To rely on the knife and not know how to use it was perhaps a far greater sin.

The dimensions of the train car affected the movement of the knife. He moved toward her from the narrow aisle between the seats into the more open space between the doors where the body of his fallen comrade lay. He sweated and grinned nervously. Aurora danced light on her feet side to side. He was no challenge for her speed. Aurora had no time to wait beyond his initial slash and thrust. Her life depended on whether her aikido really worked.

Aurora sidestepped his initial thrust, shifting back and to the right, suffering only the slightest brush of the tip of his blade against her t-shirt, and took the left wrist with her left hand and the left elbow with her right hand as if beginning another *Ikkyo* maneuver. The killer tried to pull back from her control of the knife hand. Aurora turned the wrist a little too hard. Pumped on adrenalin. She could hear the snap followed by screaming and the dull thud of her assailant's head making contact with the pole. The knife fell quietly to the floor.

Aurora was still on her feet, shuffling and moving. The killer staggered to gain his footing, and grabbed his broken wrist. She wanted to end it quickly to spare her assailant any further pain.

Aurora stepped in and struck the cop's chin with the heel of her hand, momentarily cutting the oxygen off to his brain. He staggered back into the aisle.

Go down, she said to him, *stay down*! But he recovered again, picked up the knife now in his uninjured right hand, and came at her with the knife angled for an upward strike. Aurora again evaded the path of the knife, deflected the knife hand on the forearm, and simultaneously delivered an *Atemi* or open-handed strike to his throat. The cop's neck snapped backward against his own momentum. He recovered and staggered forward in his second reaction to the blow. Aurora's right hand grasped the back of his neck as her left hand cycled through the block, lifting his right arm backward and up. She moved his body forward like a wheel, in a move called *Kaiten Nage*. The train car shifted hard on the tracks at just the right time. "Slow" ping-ponged from the pole to the floor, twice impacting his head. He cried out twice upon each impact. Aurora briefly caught a faint smile on the face of the woman, her informant, still in Seven Dagger's grasp.

Groggy, from the prone position, the cop crawled toward her and closed the distance, desperately diving for Aurora's legs to take her down in a double leg lift.

There is no way to control violence. She felt her control slipping away. Aurora knew that now the fight would get even messier and she would have to step outside of the ethical principles of her art in order to survive.

You speak the master's language, you become a prisoner of the master's ideas.

But you bring an end to misogynoir

Aurora avoided his double leg lift, but the killer cop rose to his feet and lunged at her again. Muscling up and again reverting to her judo past, she wrapped both hands around his waist as he rose, falling straight back, clean and jerk hoisting him into the air and throwing him over her head and into the far door that connected the train cars.

Tawara Gaeshi. The Rice-Bag Reversal. Another beautiful judo move. That's gotta hurt.

But "Slow" was back on his feet and had recovered his position quickly and attempted to hit Aurora from behind with a solid right punch to the base of her skull. He merely grazed her as Aurora instinctively dropped to her knees. Felt like he grazed her with something metallic. Maybe brass knuckles. No. He had broken the glass and removed the fire extinguisher and attempted to bring it down against her head. The lengths that men will go to in order to hurt a woman. She felt invisible waves of the cop's violent energy pulsing out like a ripple against the looming blackness, warning her of his next move. No sound now. All was silent. Blood from the grazing blow trickling down the back of her neck. All that she could feel.

"Slow" rudely grabbed the collar of her t-shirt in his injured left hand and positioned himself for the killing blow.

And then it happened in the twinkling of an eye, as the fire extinguisher was raised above her head for the deathblow. Sujata

Ray, the tattooed woman, the compromised informant, screamed and scratched at the face of her captor, Seven Daggers, and pulled away into the aisle and kicked the assailant's knife towards Aurora. Aurora saw it double and guessed where it was by the faint scuttling sound. It skittered into her right hand. Instinct was all she had left. She turned on her knees to avoid the path of the blow and slashed the cop's right calf. "Slow" released his grasp of the fire extinguisher and fell into the fetal position at her feet, his hands desperately grasping the fresh gash across his calf. His mouth was opened in a primal scream, but she could hear nothing.

Aurora tried to stand. She still had the knife in her hand. Sujata Ray ran to her and lifted her upright from behind. Blood trickled down her back, and her head was ringing. Perhaps it was more than a grazing blow. Aurora thought, this is what it is to walk the path of violence. It is a beast that once unleashed cannot be controlled. But at the same time... *no more misogynoir*...she felt free.

The train emerged with a howl into San Francisco's Embarcadero Station and kept rolling past the crowds of waiting passengers. Sujata Ray, grabbing the back of Aurora's shirt, was roughly pulled away by the monstrous grasp of Seven Daggers, and then a shot slithered silently in the darkness. A sharp, piercing pain like a dagger thrust at the base of her spine sent shudders rippling through her legs. And then there was no feeling in her legs anymore. Aurora turned around and saw the tranquilizer gun in Seven Daggers' hands. The numbing rushed into her cerebral cortex. And Aurora Jenkins fell to the ground, motionless.

Power to the People!
A Podcast for the People
Broadcasting from the Lower Bottoms of West Oakland
Hosted by Aurora Jenkins

Transcript of Power to the People! Episode 71[4]

Broadcasting from the Lower Bottoms of West Oakland, it's Aurora Jenkins, your Momma, your Auntie, your Big Sister, your Play Cousin! I am a Queer Black Feminist activist, investigative community reporter, and columnist with a decade of experience for the *Oakland Post*, breaking through hegemonic, corporate, colonial narratives and bringing you the news that's meant to set your minds free!

This week's episode marks the first in a series of investigative reports about the unreported phenomenon of the kidnapping and sex trafficking of women of color in the Bay Area. Every year thousands of women are reported missing from the streets of our communities. This is an epidemic in our communities. Why have the authorities ignored this crisis? Who is responsible? What can we the people do for one another to protect our loved ones?

We are going to use this podcast to bring awareness and to help families find their missing loved ones. We are going to bring the names, lives, and stories of the missing to the forefront so that their families can find justice. As a community, we are going to use this podcast as a forum for gathering the evidence of whoever is responsible. Stay tuned!

---

[4] All *Power to the People!* podcast episodes taken from the archives of recordings produced prior to the disappearance of Aurora Jenkins

2. The People's Detective

Sonny Trueheart lay face down on the hardwood floor of his living room, smelling of whiskey and cigarettes, the faint taste of blood in his mouth and vague remembrances of a fight he'd engaged in with a bearded tech-bro at a bar on East 18th St. near Lake Merritt, a formerly blue-collar dive bar gentrified into a hang-out for Mini Cooper driving hipsters with soft hands. He remembered that the fight had been about whether Muhammad Ali could have taken Mike Tyson. Sonny had his money and his fists on Ali. Why do people forget their history? He remembered getting the better of the other man and then getting the better of his three friends. And then scaring everyone in the bar, and riding home drunk on his mysterious red sunglo Harley Davidson Fatboy.

Sonny was stocky and thickly built. Just a touch over 6 feet tall. 215 pounds. Biceps as thick as a grown man's thighs. His 15 and a half inch fists looked like meat tenderizers. But, in spite of his size, he walked with the ease and languor of a cat. He had the natural confidence of a man who could handle himself and always held his head slightly up-tilted. Old school brothers said he resembled the great heavyweight champion, Sonny Liston. His grandfather had been the first to recognize the resemblance and call him "Sonny," and then everyone took to calling him that.

Sonny was awakened at 7am by loud banging on his door. He rose, yawned and stretched. He checked his breath and removed his durag, revealing his beautifully braided cornrows. Through bleary red eyes he opened the door.

There stood a long, lean and strikingly gorgeous silver-haired sister with large golden hoop earrings, wearing a flowing yellow summer dress with abstract African patterns. She held a briefcase in her hand. She bowed slightly when Sonny opened the door and spoke with a lilting island accent.

"Good morning, Detective Trueheart. My name is Nzingha. I am a representative of the Anti-Slavery League." She produced her business card and Sonny looked it over quickly. "I have a rather urgent matter to discuss with you. May I have a moment?"

"Never heard of the Anti-Slavery League. What do you all do?"

"We are the oldest anti-slavery organization in the world. We were founded in the UK in the wake of the Slavery Abolition Act of 1833. Today we are engaged in the fight against human trafficking and modern slavery."

Sonny shrugged. "Solid work. But I'm only giving you time because I can't resist a beautiful woman with a Caribbean accent."

"I'm from the Bahamas. And if it takes your overt sexism and objectification to open the conversation, I'll accept that for now. But after you hear me out, I'll expect greater respect from you."

Sonny stepped back from the door and signaled her into his living room.

Nzingha quickly glanced around the room without giving away her disapproval and took a seat on the couch. Sonny went to the refrigerator and grabbed two bottles of beer. "I just happen to have a couple of Red Stripes in the refrigerator." He pulled a chair from the dining room and sat on the other side of the coffee table from the well-dressed stranger. "Want one?"

"It's a little early for me."

"Let me ask you a few questions. Just for shits and giggles. Isn't that what you people say?"

Nzingha smiled. "It's a British expression, but…I'm game." At last, Sonny thought, she smiled! He allowed himself a moment to look deeply into her eyes. One could get lost in the power of her penetrating gaze.

"First question. A brother's tryna hop on. Do I have a chance?"

The beer and the lingering buzz gave Sonny the courage to continue flirting.

"Depending on the circumstances, you might or might not have a chance," Nzingha shot back without taking offense. As a Caribbean woman, she had to endure plenty of sexist remarks and advances rising up through the ranks of the university system and the professional world. "But you might not have everything that *I need*. You should think about that before going any further with your flirtations."

"Touché," Sonny raised his beer.

"Perhaps later we can be friends or colleagues, Detective Trueheart. I am open to that." Nzingha said, growing impatient.

"Okay, make your pitch sister."

Nzingha opened her briefcase on the coffee table.

She withdrew a large manila envelope and tossed it into Sonny's hands. "I want to hire you detective Trueheart. $75,000. And I'll pay any additional expenses. This is quite a sacrifice for our non-profit organization."

Sonny weighed the envelope in his hands. "What do you want me to do?"

"Detective Trueheart, I believe you remember a young woman named Aurora Jenkins? She's a podcaster and a reporter for the *Oakland Post*. She came to interview you only last week."

"What about it?"

"She's gone missing, sir."

"How many hours?"

"48."

"So, call the cops."

"This is a matter that requires the kind of expertise you possess."

"You family or something?"

"I'm here because Aurora Jenkins was investigating the recent disappearances of women from the streets of Oakland. We have been experiencing a similar phenomenon in the Bahamas and throughout the Caribbean. Barbados. Trinidad. The Dominican Republic. Jamaica. It's also happening on the west coast of Africa in Ghana, Togo and Nigeria. We suspect that these young women are being caught up in international sex trafficking rings. Annually, millions of men, women, and children are trafficked around the globe. This is a multibillion-dollar industry. Every year, maybe as many as a quarter of a million young women disappear off the streets of this country and are reported missing. California leads the way. Tens of thousands of young women are taken into sexual slavery from this state alone. Black women are taken in numbers that exceed their percentage of the population."

Nzingha did what she could to hold back the tears. Her hands were visibly shaking. She continued. "I am tasked with helping to end this nightmare in the state of California and, if possible, with finding as many missing women as I can and returning them to their families. I believe that the majority of women abducted and sold into sexual slavery in California are being taken by a sex trafficking operation based here in Oakland. I will stop at nothing to find these women and bring this horror to an end. Do you understand me? You should be grateful that I've come here to ask your drunk ass for help."

"Grateful?"

"Yes, grateful. This is the case of a lifetime."

"Tell me, why does the Bahamian government care about what happens in California?"

"I don't work for the Bahamian government. As I told you, I work for the Anti-Slavery League. But I can tell you that global sex trafficking *is* a national security concern for the Bahamian government because our islands are being used as the second leg in the triangular trade. Women are abducted from America and then shipped to the Bahamas, where they are purchased in underground markets then shipped abroad."

"Have you developed any leads on your own?"

"Yes. There is one name linked to all of these countries. One man whose organization has substantial business interests in all of these countries."

"Dr. Lucius Godbold," Sonny blurted. "Right?"

"That's right, detective. Founder and CEO of The Black Archon Pharmaceutical Group. A Black-owned, Oakland-based corporation with ever-expanding international holdings including business interests in my country. Now you understand why I cannot call the cops. I must take a risk trusting you."

"I let you in, but only because you are such a beautiful sister. I'm not equipped to take this on. I'm sorry."

"You are, in fact, the perfect person to help us in our efforts to end sexual slavery in California."

"The Black Archon is a model of Black progress in Oakland," Sonny recited the tagline of the company's television and radio commercials. "The notion that they are a criminal organization is nothing but a myth. They're a legitimate Black-owned pharmaceutical company. Black innovators. They're developing cures for sickle cell anemia and epilepsy and so on. There are many on the street who claim that these rumors are the product of a white capitalist system trying to bring a good brother like Dr. Godbold down."

"No sir. With all due respect, you and I both know that the Black Archon is a criminal organization that has long pushed opioids in the Black community and, I believe, engaged in sex trafficking. As for the white capitalist system, The Black Archon is not an alternative or a threat to that system. It is, more than likely, a puppet... a 'client state,' if you will, of white capitalist interests in the Bay Area and Silicon Valley."

Sonny pondered. "Nothing but rumors, sister."

"I believe that Aurora had verifiable facts supporting these long-standing rumors."

"Tell me about the Anti-Slavery League sister. What kind of budget do you all have to fight global trade? You're gonna need billions to fight a billion-dollar industry."

"We have budgetary limitations. I'm sure you understand."

"How many people do you have working in the states right now? Ballpark figure."

"Well...there's me."

"Some outfit."

"I'm all that the organization needs."

"I like your confidence. But if you're supposed to be some big muckety muck international activist, why don't you find Aurora yourself?"

"I'll be frank with you, detective. I do not know Oakland nor can I truly come to know Oakland in the limited time that we have to find Aurora... if we expect to find her alive."

Her voice conveyed the purity of her cause. He wanted to hear more, but was torn between appreciating the seriousness of the moment and a desire to watch her lips move as she talked.

"Do you have a partnership with British intelligence? Maybe you could send for James Bond."

Nzingha continued. "Do I make you nervous, detective? Your humor is wearing thin. In fact, the Anti-Slavery League does have a relationship with the British. I have also established a branch of our organization in England so that we can address the needs of young immigrant Caribbean women. But we do not specifically collaborate with British intelligence. Sex trafficking is a matter of national security in *my* homeland. The British have no particular interest in the protection of immigrant women of color. Neither do the Americans."

"Okay. I get it. I just don't know if I'm up to the job at present." Sonny leaned back in his chair putting the half empty bottle of Red Stripe on the coffee table.

"I am offering to return you to the work that you do best."

"What do I do best?"

"You..."

"...kill people. Right?"

Sonny thought about the three people he had killed in a shootout during his last case as a homicide detective for the Oakland Police Department.

A silence hung over the room.

"You were a brilliant detective. What if I could make sure that you were able to obtain a license and earn a living as a private investigator? I can help you get back to *that*."

Sonny smiled. "You think so?"

"I've already done it. In that envelope, with the money, you will find a valid private investigator's license in your name. There are also permits for an exposed firearm and concealed carry. All legit."

"Really?"

Sonny ripped open the envelope. He flipped through the c-notes. The 75k was real. He found the license and permits at the bottom of the envelope. The license was real. The permits were real. She had used the very same picture on his OPD identification. How the hell did she get that picture of him?

"How does an international human rights worker get a private investigator's license for a washed-up ex-cop in Oakland? You're going to have to explain that witchcraft to me."

"I told you that I'm good at what I do. I also know that you need money for a property you've been thinking of purchasing to open a dojo. Since your fall from grace, the banks won't lend to you. Your settlement from OPD wasn't quite what you thought it might be. This 75k could go a long way toward making your dojo a reality."

"For your information, I used most of the settlement money to pay off my house. The rest I am using to buy enough liquor to eventually kill myself."

"Those are contradictory impulses."

"What do you mean?"

"On the one hand you take care of your future and on the other hand you prepare for your death. I wonder which impulse will win?"

"That's the life of a Black man in America. On the one hand living and on the other hand dying."

"You don't believe that."

"With all due respect sister, you don't know what I believe. And, how do you know about my dojo?"

"I told you, sir, again, I'm good at what I do."

"Why me?" Sonny threw up his hands. "I'm not in a good place right now, you know. You just said it. I've got to be the most morally compromised person you've ever met." Sonny confessed. "Bet you didn't know that I was drunk the night I shot Papi Elder and those two crooked cops."

"Drunk or not, you did it, and you probably saved countless lives in the process. I've done my research. Getting past the booze will be your first order of business, of course. Getting past self-pity will be the next step. Then, I'll need you to confirm my suspicions with your contacts on the street. And then, if my suspicions prove true about the Black Archon, you will need to find a way to get Aurora out of their clutches so that we can get a hold of her story and make this matter public. That is our best way to end this nightmare."

"Yeah well… about my drinking…what makes you think I can get sober?"

"As I said, this is the case of a lifetime. Besides, Aurora Jenkins was an aikidoka, just like you."

"She studied judo and capoeira as well. Are you saying that you expect me to be the patron saint of all Black martial artists?"

"No sir. Again, I expect you to be the great detective that I know you are. I read all about the Papi Elder case. It was brilliant detective work and a clean shoot. At the very least, detective, this case will give you a chance for redemption."

"Redemption? Look, I can try and get sober but...does it look like I need to be *redeemed*?"

"Frankly," Nzingha looked around, "...yes."

Sonny tossed the envelope with the money, the license, and the permits on the coffee table.

"Look, the money's good. The license and the permits are good too. Let's say you're right about the Black Archon..."

"You know that I am."

"Okay. But if you're wrong, you're paying me hella money to chase the Boogie Man."

"Our organization is willing to take that chance."

"If I took on this job, I'd need some serious help."

"I've already done some of the work for you. I've identified her kidnappers and told you what they want. I've even searched her place for you. You'll find my notes and pictures in a folder in the briefcase. How much more help do you need?"

Sonny shook his head. "If the rumors are correct, the Black Archon controls Oakland, from the Mayor and City Council down to the street. What I'm thinking needs to be done..."

"...would require a team," Nzingha completed his thought.

Sonny leaned forward. He looked at the sweat running down the bottle of Red Stripe. "I don't have many people I can trust."

Sonny thought about old friends. His sensei, Kaz Taketo. His old running buddy, Malik Akoto. Taketo was too old for the action, but he was still sharp and clever and possibly still connected to the yakuza family that he was born into and from which he had escaped. Akoto had never been able to get his life straight. The untimely deaths of his mother and father drove the man into dark places. Last he heard, the brother was doing time.

"What kind of skills might these friends of yours possess?"

Sonny rubbed the edge of his right hand. "Fearlessness. But mind you, none of them have much experience with a job like this. And frankly, neither do I."

"Are you still in contact with these people?"

"One is out the way, doin' time in San Quentin. Two years. He's already done most of that."

"So, if he's in prison he wouldn't be much help to our cause."

"No, but if you can get me a p.i. license like you did, and, honestly, I'm not sure how you pulled that off, maybe you can get him out of jail early."

"So, let me sum this up. You'll receive 75k. You'll get a detective license, a chance at redemption, and you'll get an old friend out of jail. In return you'll agree to find Aurora Jenkins or negotiate for her release from the Black Archon so that we can begin to shine a light on these missing women. Is that our deal?"

"Okay. Let's assume that everything you've said is accurate." Sonny shook his head. "The risk is still too high. I'm at an all-time low right now sister. Tryna do this could be the end of me."

"Would it be enough, Mr. Trueheart," Nzingha sat back, crossed her long legs and offered, "if I told you that Aurora Jenkins was the younger sister of a woman you once loved, Aaminha Toure?"

3. Cargo

Aurora was awakened by the jostling of the police van over the potholes that characterized most Oakland streets. She found herself seated beside Seven Daggers, slumped against his shoulder, experiencing the aftereffects of the tranquilizer.

"Where are we? What day is it?" Aurora wanted to rub her eyes. She felt the bandage over the cut at the base of her skull.

"You'll see," Seven Daggers grinned. He stood up, bent at the waist, easily maintaining his balance in the narrow confines.

The van turned sharply and came to a halt. Aurora could hear the driver apply the parking brake, exit the cab, and open the rear doors. A half-moon illuminated the docks at the Port of Oakland. Seven Daggers carefully exited and beckoned for Aurora to follow.

As Aurora stepped from the van, she saw that they had parked beside one of the giant white cranes. Standing almost 350 feet tall with neck-like beams and foundational legs like a giant horse, 22 of these giant cranes dotted 20 miles of the waterfront and had an iconic presence against the Oakland skyline. Aurora looked up at the long arm of a crane loading containers onto a black cargo ship labeled "Godbold Industries" that looked as long as a skyscraper lying on its side. Aurora tried to count the containers visible to her on the ship's deck but she already knew that these giant ships could carry upwards of 24,000.

Seven Daggers beckoned her to follow him towards a group of longshoremen working in the middle of the night.

"Why did you bring me here?" Aurora inquired.

"I wanted you to see how your story plays out."

As they approached the giant cargo ship, Seven Daggers looked up at the crane, now at least 100 feet above them, and whistled to the men. Aurora could see now that they were not in fact longshoremen. They were all dressed in black jumpsuits with yellow lettering on the back that read "Godbold Industries" just like the cargo ship.

"Lower it. Tell the crane operator to bring it back down."

The men did as they were ordered, communicating via long-range, high tech walkie talkies.

The giant white crane began lowering the container back down to the dock. Seven Daggers stepped back and pulled Aurora back with him as the crane lowered the container within 50-feet of where they stood. As the container came down with a metallic clang upon the surface of the dock, Seven Daggers beckoned the workmen to open it. Rotating and lifting the latches above the handles into a vertical position and then pulling the handles outwards together until they were perpendicular to the container, the doors opened. Seven Daggers grabbed Aurora by the elbow and forced her towards the open container doors. Aurora could see movement in the dark. Seven Daggers motioned for the workers to shine flashlights into the container, and several piercing LED lights illuminated 20 young women in tattered clothing, cowering in the container, covering their eyes from the glare. Silent. Afraid.

Aurora yelled, "No! God damn you, no!" and began to cry. She attempted to break free from his grasp, but Seven Daggers tightened his grip.

Seven Daggers looked at her and chuckled. "You want to know what becomes of all of those girls who disappear? Many of them wind up here. We ship them around the world. This lot is bound for Miami and then on to the Bahamas. They'll be trained properly. Some of them will make it, some won't. They'll serve rich tourists. Some of them will remain in the Bahamas and others may be sold off in secondary auctions. And, as you know, we keep some of the finest that we catch right here for home consumption."

Aurora cursed and spat at Seven Daggers, who casually wiped his chin and laughed. "They don't mean anything to anybody. Why should you care?"

His question further fueled her outrage, but she took a deep breath and focused on slowing her heartbeat. She had to continue to think rationally. She had to continue probing for information.

"Do all of those containers on the ship…"

Seven Daggers motioned for the workmen to secure the container doors again and for the crane to resume loading. "So…you're back in reporter mode. No, they don't all contain women. The rest of it is above my pay grade, innit? You'll have to wait for Dr. Godbold himself to tell you that part of the story. But I'd like to show you how this plays out on the streets. It's wicked cool, man!" Seven Daggers pointed in the direction of the van. "Now, move!"

4. Traffick

Aurora rocked back and forth in the police van. Seven Daggers sat across from her, smiling. She knew precisely what he wanted to show her, but she wanted him to show it to her all the same.

She felt the van slow down, bump hard against a curb and park. The driver opened the doors and Seven Daggers led her out by the wrists, apparently unconcerned about the public display of a woman in handcuffs. But, then again, he still wore an Oakland Police officer's uniform.

They stood in the dead of night on International Blvd. in East Oakland in a section known as "the walk" or "the blade," where sex workers strolled in pencil-thin heels and waved at passing cars. This was the central hub of sex trafficking in Oakland. Aurora began her research here. Now, she was met with nervous glances up and down the street as the young women acknowledged the presence of Seven Daggers. The boulevard reeked of fear.

"We find many of the girls that we sell abroad here, on these very streets. Many are already in 'the life.' Victims of sexual abuse. They're vulnerable."

"They're mostly women of color and poor."

Seven Daggers shrugged. "Poor, yes, but you'd be surprised. We don't discriminate. The girls we take come from all walks of life. We do take many colored girls or 'girls of color,' as you say. I admit that, and many Black girls. That's the biggest part of the trade really. But I've got plenty of poor white girls for sale too.

"As for the clients, they come from one particular demographic. A third of this city is rich, mostly white tech money. Families with well over 500 grand a year in income and millions in assets. Most of the customers down here are upper middle class and rich, mostly white men, but we have many men of color among our clientele and quite a few women customers.

"Dr. Godbold figured that we could take this whole operation to an international level and a broader audience of rich people of all colors. That's why we ship them around the world.

"He says the only color that matters is green. The rest, the whole racial game, is just an illusion used to distract the masses from pursuing what's real. And then sometimes he says, 'it's not about race, but it's all about race.' He's a funny bloke, the doc. You'll see."

Seven Daggers stepped into the street and whistled at a young Black woman across the street. She seemed to immediately recognize him, and came running awkwardly in her heels, tugging at the edges of her tight yellow skirt.

Seven Daggers made the introduction. "Diamond, I'd like for you to meet someone. This is Aurora. She's a reporter. She's been poking around in our business on these streets. Tell her how the Black Archon is taking care of you. Set her straight, you know?"

Diamond looked down at the street through her heavy lashes. She dared not make eye contact with Seven Daggers. She took a minute to get her story straight, hoping that whatever she might say would meet with his approval.

"It was my Mama's second husband." Diamond folded her arms. "I was probably about six or seven at the time. He used to be kind to me. Buy me toys and candy. He'd spend more time with me than my Mama sometimes. She was always working." She cleared her throat. "He had this idea about making money. He said I was so pretty. And so, he wanted to make these movies with me. My Mama knew. She knew everything. She would just tell me, 'Look pretty, baby. Smile for the camera.' And pretty soon there were other men that Mama's husband would bring over."

Diamond looked up at Aurora and forced a smile. "But the Black Archon came to save me. They practically raised me and taught me the real game, the real hustle. And, pretty soon, they gonna send me overseas to one of those fancy resort type places where I can make even more money. Have a place all my own by the sea. So…I owe them everything."

Seven Daggers dismissed her with a wave. "We got you Diamond. Your time is coming soon. We've got something real special set up for you, girl. Now you go on, leg it and do your thing."

Diamond's heels scraped the asphalt as she turned and scampered back across the street.

"Want to speak to another one?"

"You drug them and make them believe that you are their savior."

"It's a game on top of a game. That's all, innit?"

Seven Daggers signaled another young woman approaching them on the boulevard. "Come here, girl." Young, wiry thin and bearing the track marks of a heroin addict on her arms and popping her chewing gum, a Latina with short jet-black bangs, made her way towards them. "Aurora, this is Chiclet. Chiclet, why don't you tell this reporter here a little bit of your story and what the Black Archon has done for you."

Keeping her eyes focused on the ground, Chiclet spoke. "I actually went to college, you know?" She smiled, still popping her gum and vigorously chewing as she spoke in Seven Daggers' presence. "I didn't finish. I only got through a semester when mi mamá died, and there was no one to support me. I met a man and he introduced me to the life. I just said 'yes' because I needed money to continue my education and to support myself, you know? I just said yes. And I loved him too. But, when I was working, you know, I would have to separate who I really am from who I am when I'm working. Over time, he was just manipulating me. Got me using. And then…" she pointed at Seven Daggers… "this good man, mi cuate Seven Daggers, came and rescued me from that pinche cabrón. The Black Archon bought me from him. They showed me a way. They got me on these new drugs to help me kick heroin. I know… I fall back from time to time. Pero, no me chingues. I'm sure trying." She looked up through dilated pupils into Aurora's eyes. "With everything that the Black Archon has done for me…I should eventually be able to finish my education. Maybe rise up in the ranks of the organization. That's what's up."

"Yes indeed," Seven Daggers smiled. "I can see Chiclet in management one day. She's got the smarts for it." And again, with a wave, he dismissed Chiclet. "Crack on, girl."

"More trickery and mind control."

"Get back in the van. I got something else to show you."

They drove further on into the night. As they arrived at their destination, the driver nudged the curb, reversed, straightened out and came to a stop. Seven Daggers got up and led a handcuffed Aurora from the van and down the street towards a massage parlor. Aurora guessed that she was somewhere on the edge of Chinatown as they approached an establishment advertising Asian Massage.

"We've made a deal with the Chinese mafia. We provide them with a broader diversification of talent." The shopkeeper's bell rang as Seven Daggers opened the door, and they were greeted by an elderly woman who emerged into the dim red light in the foyer. "Miss Jade, this is Aurora. She's a nosy reporter, the one who threatened to expose our entire operation. Mind if I show her around the premises?"

"Our shop is your shop. Show her whatever you want." Miss Jade pinched Aurora's cheek. "She looks healthy and strong. You thinking about putting her to work? We would be glad to take her."

Seven Daggers smiled. "The good doctor has other plans for her, but I'll let you know if anything changes."

Seven Daggers ushered her up the steps and through a narrow second floor hallway. There were no doors on any of the rooms. Privacy was maintained by multi-colored beaded curtains. Seven Daggers stopped and parted the curtains at every room, allowing Aurora a peek at the activities within. In each room Aurora could see their tired and weary faces. She could smell the stench of sweat, cum and liquor. She tried to guess the ages of the girls she saw as they peeked out from underneath the flabby white flesh that pumped and groaned.

They came down to the end of the hallway and Seven Daggers parted the curtain. It appeared to be a lounge area. Couch. Couple of worn recliners. Coffee table. Television with the sound turned off. The carpet was even more worn than in the hallway, and it was sticky. There was drug paraphernalia, cigarettes, condoms and half-finished glasses of cheap liquor arranged around a lava lamp on the coffee table.

Seven Daggers directed Aurora to sit down on the torn vinyl couch. She stared at the moving, morphing blobs in the lava lamp.

"This is a break room. Girls can come in here and chill. One of them should be finished shortly and we can all have a little chat." Seven Daggers wandered around the room, hands on his hips, when a young woman walked in on cue.

She tossed her long black hair. Aurora could see that she was an Indigenous woman.

Seven Daggers made the introduction and encouraged her to take a seat in one of the recliners across the coffee table from Aurora. "This is Linda. Linda, this is the reporter who tried to expose our operation. I want you to tell her about your experiences and how the Black Archon saved you."

Aurora could see that Linda was exhausted. She was a beautiful young woman, but the fatigue left deep impressions on her face. There were dark circles under her eyes that Aurora could make out even in the dark red lighting. She fell down into the recliner and sighed heavily. She seemed resigned to the eternal hell in which she was living.

Linda reached for a cigarette on the coffee table. Seven Daggers offered her a light. Only after her first deep draw from the cigarette did she look up and make eye contact with Aurora.

"Whaddya wanna know, shitass?"

"I already know. He's just making a point. I know what they're putting you through."

Linda leaned forward. "You do? You don't know nothing, shitass. You aint know shit."

"You from here, Linda?"

"Oklahoma."

"You Chicasaw?"

"Comanche. That enough of the game of twenty questions, shitass?"

"Yeah."

Linda took another long draw at her cigarette. "You wanna know how it is?" She rubbed her eyes and yawned, the cigarette smoke flowing out of her nostrils. "I'll tell you how it is. How it is…yeah… my father got shot up and killed by federal police. You know how it is for us on the reservation. So… I came out here, looking to escape, go to beautiful, sunny California and live that motherfucking dream. You know what I mean? I ran away. You know, I just ran away. I was just 15. And when I landed, I went to this church because they were feeding people and taking care of the homeless. And I met this religious couple. They seemed so supportive and everything. Like real Christians. Hired me to be their babysitter. Let me live with them in a little au pair they had on their property. They showed me the good life too. Took me around in all their expensive cars. Bought me nice clothes and stuff. I had a smartphone and a laptop computer. I thought I was becoming a real person in the world.

"But things changed quickly. They began to change, you know? They got more aggressive with me. Started accusing me of doing things like stealing from them. And they punished me. One day, they chained me to the bed in my room. Then they came and took me to some fancy club, even though I was underage, where people were all tied up and flogging one another and stuff and there were a lot of drugs and they had me drinking and doing coke with them and then they revealed to me who they really were. Not good Christian folks, or maybe that's how all white Christians are, you know, with that white Jesus stuff and all. They ran an escort service, you see, and they wanted me to work for them. They said they'd help me finish high school and that I'd make enough money to pay for college, if I wanted to go, and set myself up real good and be independent and live that dream.

"At first, they had me answering phones and posting ads online for their service. Maintaining schedules for the escorts. Sometimes I would do hair and make-up for the girls. I can do hair and make-up pretty good, you know? But if I messed something up, they would ask me to go on the date in place of the original girl." Linda laughed uncomfortably. "The first time I did it, I forgot to ask for the money. And I got punished for that. The husband would pin me down and punch me. Broke my nose a couple times. He would tell me that I didn't have a mind of my own, or that they didn't need me for my mind. Just my body. I was forced to do more dates. It was like...every time I fucked up I was in debt to them, and the only way I could pay it back was by taking on more dates. Sometimes it made me sick to my stomach. I would throw up a lot. And whenever I would ask to just go back to answering phones and posting ads, they would tell me that everyone out there was doing it for free, so I might as well get paid. And then I got hooked on the coke, you know?

"Well... in the end, they got busted. And because I posted all those ads, the judge held me accountable as an accomplice, and that was enough to land me in prison. 20-year sentence. I mean, *I* was the victim, but the damned judge put *me* in jail and he put *me* on the sex offender registry, if you can believe that." Linda shook her head and took another drag of her cigarette. "And that's where the Black Archon came in. I guess they heard about my case. Sent me a good lawyer and put together an appeal. I didn't do more than two months at Chowchilla before I was out on the streets again. And this man," Linda pointed to Seven Daggers, "well, he saved my life. And yeah, things might not look so great right now, especially to someone like you, but I aint forced to do nothin' and one day, I'm gonna own this place or a place like it and have my own stake in the world. I'm gonna be a Madam. That shit's been promised to me by the Black Archon."

Linda stretched out her legs and arms, imagining that she was the Madam of the house, showing off a luxurious outfit. Then Aurora saw the smile disappear from her face and saw the distant, vacant look in her eyes return. Linda looked up at Aurora again and asked, "…that all you wanna know, shitass?"

Seven Daggers came up from behind Linda and patted her on the shoulder. "Good girl. Good girl." He walked towards the curtain while Aurora and Linda stared at one another across the coffee table. Aurora could see a tear gently flowing down Linda's cheek.

Seven Daggers parted the curtain slightly and glanced down the hallway. "You got another customer, girl." He clapped his hands. "Now, go and get after it."

Linda wiped her eyes and rose from the recliner. She grabbed a chain of attached condoms from the coffee table. She shuffled her bare feet as she parted the beaded curtain and stepped out into the hallway, dragging the chain of condoms across the threadbare carpet.

Power to the People!
A Podcast for the People
Broadcasting from the Lower Bottoms of West Oakland
Hosted by Aurora Jenkins

Transcript of Power to the People! Episode 72

Broadcasting from the Lower Bottoms of West Oakland, it's Aurora Jenkins, your Momma, your Auntie, your Big Sister, your Play Cousin! I am a Queer Black Feminist activist, investigative community reporter, and columnist with a decade of experience for the *Oakland Post*, breaking through hegemonic, corporate, colonial narratives and bringing you the news that's meant to set your minds free!

An epidemic is occurring in our midst. More than 1,500 women disappeared from the streets. More than 400 of these are young Black women.

This week, I want to talk to you about a recent disappearance, one like so many others. Her name is Mazzy Hinton, and she was abducted on Lakeshore Blvd. at gunpoint by three men driving a black sedan.

Mazzy was an honor's student at Oakland Tech High School in the Engineering Academy. She was the starting point guard on the Oakland Tech Women's Basketball team. She sang in her church choir and donated her time helping the unhoused at Operation Dignity. Mazzy had dreams of attending the University of California, Berkeley for Engineering.

Maybe we've grown accustomed to hearing stories like this. But Mazzy isn't a statistic. She's a whole living, breathing person. In this podcast, I want to make Mazzy and others fully visible to you. That's the only way that we can ever begin to hope to find them. Stay tuned!

5. Ghost in the Machine

The big man bathed in the hot stage lights and the warm reception of a live audience at KTVU Studio A in Jack London Square. As he entered from behind the curtain stage left, the crowd roared and rose to their feet in applause for the man who had cured sickle cell anemia, hypertension, and epilepsy and kept his pharmaceutical industries in Oakland, employing many thousands of everyday Oaklanders. He had become as big a force in the Bay Area economy as any giant biomedical or biotech firm. He was here today for a friendly forum hosted by KTVU news anchor Pam Booth to answer questions about his medical discoveries and his plans for expansion.

"Ladies and gentlemen," Ms. Booth clapped, "...please welcome the great Dr. Lucius Godbold!"

Godbold gracefully bowed before taking his seat.

This was Dr. Lucius Godbold. Accomplished biochemist. Entrepreneur. Few people knew that he was the descendant of the man who betrayed Denmark Vesey's revolutionary plot in 1822. Vesey, a free Black pastor of an African Methodist Episcopal Church in Charleston, South Carolina, who had purchased his freedom after winning a $1,500 city lottery, plotted what would have been the largest revolt of enslaved Africans in America. His revolt would have involved thousands of enslaved Africans in the city and nearby plantations and, after killing their slave masters, setting fire to their homes, obtaining arms from the Charleston Meeting Street Arsenal, and commandeering ships from the harbor, Vesey would have led the liberated to safe refuge in Haiti.

The uprising failed only because of the testimonies of two enslaved men who opposed Vesey's revolt. One of them, George

Godbold, a mixed-race man with an unimpeachable loyalty to his master, was the great-great grandfather of Dr. Lucius Godbold. The apple didn't fall far from the tree and most of George's descendants were centrally involved in historic betrayals against their own people. Whether it was the Tuskegee Experiment or the Red Summer of 1919, there was a Godbold present, conspiring against his own people and cheerfully accepting the *lagniappe* or scraps from his master's table in exchange. And so, Godbold was the son of generations of Black collaborators through slavery and Jim Crow. Men who sold out Black liberators for warm coats and extra pork.

His legitimate work in pharmaceutical cures for sickle cell anemia, hypertension, and epilepsy was motivated by the loss of his wife some 30 years ago. Evangeline Fabre. They were young and idealistic, two starry-eyed creole-identified, high-yellow, near-white-passing teens with "good hair," freckles and gray-blue eyes born and raised in the elite Black neighborhood of Grier Heights in Charlotte, North Carolina who'd managed to maximize their educational experience, and earned scholarships from North Carolina A&T. They were married hastily after completing their college degrees and then went on to medical school together at Wake Forest until she was taken away from him during the years of their residency after a violent epileptic attack. If only he had been there. She was with her closest friends. Drinking. Dancing. Ladies' night out. And, not one of them knew the emergency protocols for dealing with a seizure.

Naturally he blamed them all for her death. And in the course of the next five years, each one of them died mysteriously. This was where Lucius Godbold developed his taste and affinity for killing. When he ordered one of his underlings to kill, he would always say, "balance the books" because he called himself killing the "unworthy" in the name of preserving the "worthy". This had been the divine principle that had long motivated his ancestors.

Godbold had a large and sickly pale, freckled face with slick, wavy salt and pepper hair. He was dressed for the televised forum in a white linen suit with white silk socks and white alligator shoes. His head was enormous, with sweating jowls, low-slung and distended enough to conceal his neck, and deeply set gray-blue eyes that glimmered like bright halogen lamps beneath bushy, unkempt gray eyebrows. His body, by all accounts, was equally matched to his head, and he stood well over 7 feet in height. He was built like an elephant, and moved with slow and purposeful steps, tilting his head back and extending his broad, barrel-shaped chest. He was immensely strong. He wore rings with bright gemstones on each finger of his massive hands: a sapphire, the luminescent color of his eyes; the greenest emerald; and the reddest ruby. And there was a tattoo on his neck, a Haitian vodun symbol, or Veve, for the god of fire and war, Ogun.

The applause slowly subsided and the standing crowd settled back into their seats. Dr. Godbold maintained the rehearsed smile on his face. Pam Booth began her line of questions.

"Dr. Godbold," she began with characteristic charm, "our audience would like to hear a little about the biography of the man who discovered cures for sickle cell anemia, epilepsy, and hypertension. What motivated you to make these breakthrough discoveries?"

"The answer to these questions lies in the naming of the drugs that we have developed." Dr. Godbold spoke with an affected white southern accent, the accent of the planter aristocracy, rather than the Black North Carolina accent that was his birthright. Pam Booth seemed to pick up on that immediately. "Evangeline, the cure we have developed for epilepsy, is named for my sweet, dear departed wife who succumbed to epilepsy while completing her residency at WakeMed North Hospital. I developed this drug in honor of her so that no more would die of seizures and no more would suffer as I have since the loss of my beloved." Godbold affected a downward gaze and a solemnity that seemed genuinely felt.

Thunderous applause.

Pam Booth gave him a minute to compose himself and for the applause to die down. When Dr. Godbold lifted his head again and looked into her eyes she resumed. "And your hypertension and sickle cell cures?"

"The sickle cell cure is aptly named after Paul Williams, one of the original members of the Temptations, who suffered with sickle cell anemia and died tragically by suicide and after a history of alcohol abuse. So, we call this cure P-Will. As for our cure for hypertension, this is our most recent development and we have aptly named the drug after the great director John Singleton who quietly struggled with high blood pressure and died of a stroke. We call it The Singleton Remedy."

The crowd cheered, understanding the importance of honoring the ancestors.

"And of course," Godbold continued, "We are working on a vaccine that will inoculate the world of HIV-AIDS. I call it 'Tuskegee,' for the memory of those who were killed in that horrific eugenicist experiment on untreated syphilis. We also call it this to inspire people that our vaccine will be safe."

"But don't you think that calling it 'Tuskegee' only reminds us of the horror of that incident?"

"On the contrary. It honors the dead and celebrates the century and a half of good work done by Tuskegee University."

Pam Booth continued. "Hmm. Well, you are originally from North Carolina, is that correct?"

"That is correct."

"What was your life like as a boy?"

"I came from an educated family that spared no expense in helping me obtain my education. I come from four generations of college graduates, a legacy at North Carolina A&T."

"And yet, in spite of your privileged status, you have been moved to dedicate your life to ending the suffering of others?"

"My privilege and that of my family are relative. We are still Black, and therefore enjoy far less privilege by comparison to whites who lived in neighborhoods from which we were segregated."

"And because of the racism that you experienced you have been motivated by social justice concerns. Is that fair to say?"

Dr. Godbold extended his bejeweled hands to the audience and smiled. "I want to always be a man of the people." And once again the crowd rose to its feet and showered him with thunderous applause.

It went on like this for another half hour. More questions from Pam Booth and then random questions from everyday citizens in the audience. People wanted to know if he would consider running for mayor. No. Did he support the re-election campaign of current Mayor Freddy Pendergast? Yes. Were the rumors true about his possible buyout of Kaiser Permanente? No, but there was a wink and nod. Would he consider starting a new NFL expansion franchise in the wake of the Raiders exodus to Las Vegas? Another wink and a nod.

There was a 1946 Rolls Royce Silver Wraith waiting for him outside of the KTVU studios. Dressed in a shiny black suit and wearing white gloves was his able bodyguard and top enforcer, Adro "Seven Daggers" Onzi. Seven Daggers held the rear passenger side door of the Silver Wraith open for Dr. Godbold as he stepped outside of the facility. "You were fantastic, sir," Seven Daggers said and bowed slightly.

Dr. Godbold breathed heavily, annoyed by a speck of blood on Seven Daggers' white collar. He wet his finger and wiped at it as he stood looking down on the man. "I trust that you have something to report?"

"I do sir."

Adro Onzi, known in criminal circles as "Seven Daggers" because he favored using the knife, was a Black Brit, whose family fled to England from Zaire in the wake of the death and ouster of Mobutu Sese Seko, when he was a child. His father, also a criminal sociopath, served as a general in the then Zairian army and secret police, and was responsible for hundreds of politically motivated executions. He named his only son "Adro," a child produced by the rape of a

Lugbara woman, signifying the Lugbara god of death, as a commemoration of the family's legacy of blood. In Lugbara legend, Adro has the ability to transform into a snake and appears to people who are about to die. Adro is also the possessor of young women and is known to eat people. "Onzi" is the Lugbara word for "bad."

Upon the untimely death of his father in a tragic car accident, Adro "Seven Daggers" Onzi was bounced through a series of foster parents and orphanages. Did time as a juvenile offender. He was a big man, about 6'3" and a solid wall of muscle at 240 pounds. A legendary street fighter, Seven Daggers was recruited and eventually became a general for a group of British football hooligans who were known for having members of various ethnic backgrounds, as much as for a series of infamous violent clashes with supporters of rival clubs.

Arrested and tried as an adult for his involvement in football riots and diagnosed by the British criminal court as a sociopath, Adro "Seven Daggers" Onzi came to the attention of Dr. Godbold who was at that time engaged in a business venture in England. Always on the lookout for lost boys and toughs, he was plucked from behind bars, emigrated to America, and trained by the Black Archon. With them he saw an opportunity and the possibility of belonging. He was a quick study.

What qualified Seven Daggers to serve as Papi Elder's replacement and hence the Black Archon's Number 1 Enforcer was not his physical stature nor his impressive resume of murder and mayhem by the age of 27, but his off-the-charts IQ and familiarity with the technologies of weaponry and surveillance. But the Black Archon had long underestimated his value. They only saw him as muscle or a 'chav,' as they called the hooligans in England. They couldn't see through his physique and gruff ways and his Black British working-class accent. He had had little opportunity to demonstrate the full range of his skills.

"Are we prepared for tonight's shipment?" the big man queried as Seven Daggers closed the door for him and then walked around to the driver's seat and pulled the Silver Wraith away from the television studios and on to the road. The heavy car barely jostled as it moved over the train tracks on 2nd St.

"Yes sir. We have exceeded our quota. Our shipment goes out this evening."

"What about the reporter? Did she talk?"

"Yes sir." Seven Daggers nodded. "Plenty." He didn't dare look the big man in the eyes in the rearview mirror. He had had a more informal relationship with the late Papi Elder. In the big man's presence, he kept his gaze fixed on the road.

"What do we know?"

"I have the story itself. It was on the hard drive of her laptop that we recovered when we grabbed her. Of course, I also have her informant, one of Mistress Celestine's slave women, Sujata Ray. Mistress Celestine will sell Sujata off in the next auction, but right now she's being introduced to fentanyl. I see an overdose in her future. I learned in the interrogation that I intercepted Aurora before she had a chance to share the story with either the city editor at the *Tribune*, Valerie Ogwu, or Mayor Pendergast's rival, that up-start Councilmember Andre Chidozie. Good thing I got to her first, innit? It's one thing for her to publish the story in the *Oakland Post*. Only Black folks in the community read that. With the *Tribune*, the story would have a much bigger impact. And if the story had gotten into Chidozie's hands, it could have ended Pendergast's hopes for re-election."

"Is there anything else?" Godbold showed no emotion on the matter.

Seven Daggers grinned. "I took her well past the breaking point. She started muttering a name. A familiar name."

"Whose name?"

"Sonny Trueheart. The tosser that killed Papi Elder and testified against his fellow boys in blue."

Godbold paused. Ruminated. "Interesting."

"What, boss?" Seven Daggers asked in the tone of a faithful lackey.

The big man remained silent. The machinery was fast at work in his twisted brain. "We may have an opportunity."

"Opportunity sir?"

"An opportunity to balance the books. I want you to keep a close eye on Sonny Trueheart. Let's have some fun. This Sonny Trueheart likes to play the hero, right? We should anticipate that he'll come after us once he learns about the abduction of Ms. Jenkins. Be ready. This will be an important test for you. In the meantime, string Aurora out on fentanyl, and kill both Councilmember Chidozie and the Trib editor Valerie Ogwu just in case. Bonus points if you kill both Ogwu and Chidozie and pin the murders on Trueheart. I can see the headlines now. 'Hero Cop Gone Bad.' Let's have some fun with this, okay?" He snapped his fingers. "Make it so."

"Yes sir."

Godbold turned his attention to the streets around Jack London Square as they crossed under the I-880 freeway and into Oakland's historic district and then Uptown. He sat examining people on the streets through the heavily tinted windows of the Silver Wraith. His eyes were drawn to what he called the "hustlers" and the "streetwalkers" and the homeless encampments. He suppressed an impulse to order Seven Daggers to stop the car so that he could step out on the streets and take a life and rid the community of what he viewed as "the worthless."

"Mr. Daggers…"

"Yes sir?"

"Handle this correctly and you may well find yourself receiving an overdue promotion."

"I want more." Seven Daggers certainly did not want to look back in the mirror at the doctor's eyes now.

The big man was briefly taken aback. He knew the man's value, but he was suspicious that his ambition might compromise his effectiveness. "Justify this request."

"I'm more competent than Papi Elder could have ever dreamed of being. My technological expertise. My ability to manage a team. And the job comes with certain risks. Longevity is an issue, innit?"

"Your technological expertise is duly noted. Frankly, your value to me and the organization is that you are a sadist, a man who is given to violent excess like a duck to water. But what I need to see from you is greater loyalty. After everything I have done for you, I need to see less of this willful attitude that you persistently cling to. The Black Archon relies on the absolute loyalty of its members in order to function. Do we understand one another?"

"Yes. Yes sir."

"Hmm."

Absolute loyalty? Seven Daggers tossed the words around inside of his head. He wanted to ask the good doctor, "but are you being *absolutely* loyal to the organization with your wild fantasies of global expansion?" But he thought better of it and restrained himself.

As for Dr. Godbold having called him a sadist…well, Seven Daggers approved. Yes, it gave him pleasure to hurt the woman. He admired Aurora's skills, her quickness, her ability to dispatch two men of far greater stature and power than she, fighting effectively within the confines of a moving commuter train. Doing her best not to unduly harm even those that would kill her. If it had been up to him, he would not have tranquilized her immediately but would have preferred leaving her alone in the wake of her victory, giving her due respect as a fellow warrior. However, just as he had admired her then, he also enjoyed torturing her and would enjoy filling her veins with fentanyl.

The big man considered Seven Daggers' request. "What is it that you seek, young man?"

Seven Daggers did not hesitate. "I want to be the Number Two man in the organization."

Dr. Godbold nodded and smiled faintly. A criminal sociopath with ambition. Godbold admitted to himself that he held great admiration for the man's sense of self-worth. "You wish to take Mayor Pendergast's place? Well…I hear you. Let me say this to you: make this happen and you will be rewarded beyond your wildest imagination."

Dr. Godbold did not want to respond to the petty details of this matter. There were larger issues at hand. He knew that Seven Daggers was the more competent and able replacement for the late Papi Elder. Elder could not have handled the matter of Aurora Jenkins with ease. He would have found himself fielding a frantic phone call from Papi Elder, full of much hand wringing and indecision. The Black Archon relies on the decisiveness of its underlings. Popular as he was, Papi Elder did not fit the profile. Seven Daggers was certainly an improvement, and still there were things he didn't quite like or trust about the man. "Too ambitious," he thought to himself. "That boy is too ambitious."

The Silver Wraith approached Dr. Godbold's residence. Dr. Godbold kept two residences in Oakland. His mansion in the Oakland hills was for entertaining. It was where the Black Archon hosted slave auctions of kidnapped women for their rich guests. Godbold spent most of his days and nights in his lavish private penthouse on the 28th floor of the Black Archon Center in Oakland. From a secret office he monitored the activities of his underlings by tapping into each of their smartphones, tablets, and computers and projecting images and video onto monitors that lined the walls of his office. He conducted most of his business meetings from a glass-encased booth that shifted between two conference rooms on the 27th floor.

The Black Archon Center was a 28-story structure adjacent to Lake Merritt. In 1960 it was Oakland's tallest building and one of the first California structures to feature a rooftop garden, inspired by the design of the Rockefeller Center in New York City. The building used to house the executive offices of one of the nation's largest healthcare providers and the largest Oakland-based corporations. But Godbold bought everyone out and maintained complete control of the entire building. Only the California American Bank was allowed to remain in the lobby –as long as it maintained a special relationship with Godbold Industries– and it housed one of the most secure vaults in northern California. The penthouse was once the residence of an industrialist who became the father of American shipbuilding and established the Oakland shipyard which built Liberty Ships during World War II, and later aluminum and steel.

Godbold slept during the day. He believed that limited exposure to sunlight was the key to longevity. He came out at sunset, tended to his rooftop plants and spent long nights in his secret basement laboratories. He had no particular interests in art or music. His penthouse was Spartan with modern furnishings, high ceilings and windows covered by dark drapes that obscured the gorgeous view of Lake Merritt. He preferred to be chauffeured by darker-skinned hirelings in his Rolls Royce whenever he went out at night. He did not drink. He did not smoke. He did not participate in the pleasures of the Slave Auctions he held in his Oakland hills mansion as fundraisers for his criminal organization. He always left after his grandiose introductions. He appeared to have few vices. Many of his underlings believed that he spent all of his waking time consumed with the pursuit of money and power, and what little time was left was engaged in perfecting the research on genetic engineering that he had initiated as a younger man and which he hoped to unveil to the world soon. But this was only part of the truth.

Seven Daggers drove the Silver Wraith into the gated garage of the Black Archon Center. He parked in a wide stall beside a private elevator and opened the door for Dr. Godbold. Together they boarded the elevator and rode up to Godbold's penthouse dwelling. When the elevator door opened, they walked past the greenhouse to his residence where Dr. Godbold was greeted by the sight of Aurora Jenkins, barely conscious, constrained by leather straps to a chair and chained by the ankle to an authentic 18th century slave auction block in Godbold's living room.

Godbold stood before Aurora, holding her by the chin as she slowly opened her eyes. Seven Daggers stood slightly behind him and to his right. "My friend here," Dr. Godbold nodded towards Seven Daggers, "enjoys hurting young women like you."

"Your friend is a monster," Aurora spat upon Godbold's pristine white alligator shoes. "And so are you!"

Godbold stepped back and laughed heartily. His enormous body quivered with uncontrollable laughter. Seven Daggers knelt and wiped Aurora's spit from Godbold's shoes.

"Quite the contrary my dear," Godbold grinned. "I am the savior of Oakland."

Aurora breathed heavily, her heart racing. "You profit from selling your own people into slavery!" Aurora cried.

Dr. Godbold again laughed, but this time, controlled and brief. "Oh...*those* women. Is this all that you know about me?" Godbold caressed her moist skin, squeezed her biceps and muscular thighs. "I am not the first. Certainly, as a student of our history, you should know that. And I will not be the last to betray his people."

While the two spoke, Seven Daggers pulled a slim case from the inside pocket of his jacket. It contained a syringe of fentanyl. He squirted out an initial drop of the poison and then handed the syringe to Dr. Godbold who administered the injection to a clean vein in Aurora's left arm. A few choice veins were available without the need of a tourniquet.

Dr. Godbold held the syringe, waiting for the effect of the drug to overcome her. "Do you have any other names you would like to call me before we move on with the evening?"

Aurora was silent, glaring with all the blood fury that she could muster in her eyes before the drug took effect.

"Nothing? Why don't you add drug pusher to the list," Godbold laughed again.

Aurora cursed as the drug rushed into her system. She felt the rush as the drug bound itself to the opioid receptors in her brain. A warm flushing of the skin. A heaviness in her extremities and slowing of her pulse and breathing. Dryness in her mouth. Her eyes rolled back in her head.

Dr. Godbold handed the syringe back to Seven Daggers.

Seven Daggers placed the syringe back in the case. He watched as Dr. Godbold undid the leather straps that bound Aurora to the chair. He watched her fall from the chair to the surface of the auction block, constrained around the ankle by a length of chain secured to a mooring bollard at the right corner of the auction block.

"You have work to do tonight and I have a board meeting," Godbold spoke without turning around to face the man. "Clean her up and then go look after tonight's shipment. In the meantime, I will amuse myself as best as I can."

6. The Segregated Illuminati

Godbold took his elevator down one flight to the executive conference rooms. He went into a private entrance that led to a mobile raised platform encased in dark bulletproof glass that shifted between two conference rooms. The platform was positioned above the long tables where the Black and white chiefs of the Black Archon gathered separately.

The Black Council of 13 were all respected leaders in Oakland's Black communities. The Mayor, who was the true second-in-command in the Black Archon. District Attorney. Chief of Police. Pastors. Superintendent of Schools. City Councilmembers. Business owners. In spite of their status within the Black community, they were merely the middle managers of the organization, the overseers calling the shots for the illicit street operations. The fact that they never interfaced with the White Council of 13 who sat separated from them in the adjacent conference room, spoke volumes about their place in the hierarchy of power.

Although their organization was called the Black Archon, the true ruling council were all white men and women. Corporate moguls. CEO's. Venture capitalists. Silicon Valley tycoons. With Godbold seated on high, it appeared that the White Council were his subordinates. In fact, they were his backers. White men and women who had long used Black faces as fronts for their illegal enterprises while they bathed in public adoration as upstanding civic leaders and philanthropists. The system worked because of the pretense of equality. The whole of the Bay Area was driven by this pretense. The White Council allowed Godbold his pretense of authority and Godbold gave proper deference when necessary. Everyone knew which direction the wind blew.

Godbold could not be seen in either conference room through the dark bulletproof glass –although he could see both the White Council and the Black Council as the glass-encased platform shifted– and he projected images from his computer that he wanted to share on giant screens that hung above the center of the conference tables and his voice could be heard over loudspeakers attached to these screens.

Godbold first convened the White Council. He sat back in a leather chair and powered up his computer. The conference room went dark and the screens flickered on and Godbold shared video taken from the capture of Aurora Jenkins.

When the video of the fight ended, Godbold spoke. "We have captured the journalist, Aurora Jenkins. She is in our custody and the draft of her story is in our possession."

The conference room remained dark. All of their meetings were held in the dark in order to avoid any possibility of video incrimination from a member gone rogue. A red light flashed the number "6" on the conference table.

"Yes, Archon 6. What is your question?"

"I do not have a question. I have a statement to make. I wish to reiterate again publicly that we are grateful for the services that you have provided to us and our families. But we are aware of changes that you have made to our street operations and our core business of trafficking. We have also learned of your plans for expansion abroad. In West Africa, I believe. You must think of yourself as some version of Lord Jim. I would caution you that your hubris could bring us all down."

"I will certainly take that into consideration, Archon 6."

The light in front of Archon 12 came on.

"What Archon 6 expressed are not merely words of caution. If I were you, I would interpret them as orders to terminate your little side project."

"Thank you, Archon 12."

The light in front of Archon 7 came on. He wanted to change the subject.

"How much does the journalist know? What will become of her?"

"Her information on our human trafficking operation was considerable. She will be killed, as will those with whom she wanted to share her findings."

The light in front of Archon 6's seat flashed again. In the darkness, Archon 6 grumbled, expressing his annoyance at his colleague's off-topic question. "Is she aware of the diversion of our funds to your African project?"

Dr. Godbold folded his hands. "I do so appreciate your concern. All of you. I want to assure you that I understand my sacred role. But what you are referring to is a private investment. It has nothing to do with our organization."

The light in front of Archon 3 lit up, followed by 4, then 8, and, finally, 13. Their voices came one after the other like horns blaring in rush hour traffic.

"We live by a strict set of rules…"

"There is no such thing as *private business* in our organization…"

"It appears that your loyalties are divided…"

"By our calculations, at least $100 million dollars are currently unaccounted for."

Dr. Godbold was defiant. "Frankly, I don't see what the problem is. I have made some changes, this is true. However, none of our operations have been compromised."

Archon 2 banged her fist on the conference table. "The problem is that *you* are compromised. You've taken your position for granted, Dr. Godbold. Don't you think we can find another Black face to serve as a figurehead for our business?"

Dr. Godbold smiled. "With all due respect, I am not just another Black face."

There was silence, followed by the sounds of each of the 13 rising from their seats.

Archon 1, who had remained silent, now looked toward the dark glass around the raised bulletproof platform where Dr. Godbold sat. "The Slave Auction gala will be held in a few days. We expect that you will have returned the misappropriated funds and be able to demonstrate your loyalty to this organization by then." He formed the shape of a pistol with his left hand and aimed at Godbold behind the dark glass. "Make no mistake, you are an easily replaceable asset."

Godbold genuflected behind the dark glass and watched the other members of the White Council nod their approval of White Archon 1's gesture.

Godbold then manipulated the controls and the glass-encased platform shifted to the neighboring conference room where the Black Council waited.

***

In the room where the Black Council gathered, there were no pretensions of numbers instead of names or sitting in the dark and using lights to signal their questions. Here, the Black Council gathered as if in a convivial fraternity meeting. There was music, and food and liquor on the table –provided by councilmember and high-end soul food restaurateur Lamar Rhodes– and smoke from Cuban cigars wafted to the ceiling. As Godbold's platform shifted, he could hear their laughter.

He went through the same routine with the Black Council: showing the video of the abduction of Aurora Jenkins and assuring the group that the matter had been resolved.

Reverend Jolly of the Greater Mount Sinai Temple of the Risen God raised his hand first. "Is she dead?"

"No. She is still useful to us. We are still extracting information from her."

Oakland Superintendent of Schools Nevaeh Moore Jackson was next. "I don't want to talk about the woman, if you don't mind. I want to talk about these moves that you're making, Dr. Godbold. I'm not sure that I'm 100% on board."

Oakland Chief of Police Helmsley Aimes nodded in agreement and the nodding and signifying was infectious, as each member of the Black Council agreed with Nevaeh Moore Jackson's concerns.

Mayor Freddy Pendergast then noted, "The move to the darknet has been productive. Brilliant strategy on your part, Dr. Godbold. But we're seeing a lighter share than normal, and it's clear…according to our accountants…that as we continue our shift from the street to MambaNet, a significant amount of cash is not being transferred over to our joint accounts. We want to know where that money is going."

"*Your* accountants?" Godbold chuckled. "*Your* accountants? Let me remind you that *I* am the leader of this organization. *I* decide its ultimate direction."

Pendergast folded his hands and leaned back in his chair, taking in the rebuke. "Word on the street is that there's some kind of African project that you're working on. Is this a part of your master plan? Why are we being kept in the dark about it? What's our stake in the project?"

"Let's assume that your information is correct. Let's assume that I have been…shall we say…collecting a higher than usual tax and converting cash on the street to cryptocurrency for the purposes of building an *African Project*, as you call it. Why do you think I might want to build my very own state in Africa, gentlemen?"

District Attorney Layla Riles was next to speak. "You're chasing the dream of Marcus Garvey. You're building a new Black nation."

"Precisely, Mrs. Riles."

Reverend Jolly, who went back to the early days of small-time petty theft and street corner crack cocaine operations before he found Jesus, voiced his concern. "I don't want to live in no Africa. This here, this here is my home."

"You lack vision my friend. This is the reason why we have not spoken of this project."

"How do the white folks feel about this?" Reverend Jolly asked, gesturing towards the conference room on the other side of the wall behind him.

"This project represents a chance for us to escape their control. Now…do you understand what I am doing?"

DA Riles tapped ashes from her Cuban cigar onto the floor and ground out the embers on the carpet with her red bottom shoes. "I aint goin' to no motherfuckin' Africa. I want things to go back to the way they were before."

"Again, Madam DA Riles, you lack vision. In Africa, we have land, we have natural resources, access to oil reserves and precious metals. And I am building an army to defend our kingdom."

DA Riles wouldn't give in. She raised her hand. "I'd like to see the details."

"Very well."

The lights went dark and the giant screen above the conference table flickered on. Pictures of a rebel compound in the Borno State of northeastern Nigeria, flashed on the screen.

"Gentlemen and ladies, this is territory controlled by Boko Haram, the Islamic State of West Africa. The money that I have drawn in taxes has been directed toward the acquisition of this property. In conjunction with the Nigerian military and the governments of Benin, Chad, Niger, and Ghana, I have funded a counter-insurgency, an army of private soldiers led by this man…" Godbold presented video of a wiry thin man in glasses and military fatigues as he stood behind a row of kneeling Boko Haram soldiers, methodically slashing each man's throat with a combat knife. "This is General Lucky Ochuko, former Nigerian warlord, known as the Rumuekpa Ripper for his preference for edged weapons and the atrocities that he committed on behalf of oil companies in the Niger Delta. I have purchased his services and his allegiance. He now leads a growing force of soldiers who are driving Boko Haram out of northeastern Nigeria. The price for our services is control of these lands, where we will build a separate nation. We have a broad agreement from the Nigerian government itself. They are grateful for our services in removing this Islamic scourge. And they are willing to do anything to ensure their removal. This is where we will build our new nation."

There was a prolonged silence in the room as the lights abruptly came back on and the screen flickered dark.

"Shall we take a vote on it?"

"Fine with me," Pendergast agreed. And nods of agreement went around the table.

"By a show of hands, who is on board with the African Project?"

Members of the Black Council looked at one another in silence. No one raised their hands.

"I'm disappointed. Perhaps my vision is too esoteric for your comprehension."

Mayor Pendergast spoke for the group. "You're an outsider Dr. Godbold. You weren't born and raised here. You're a southern man. You don't understand. This is our home. You can go to Africa and build your new nation there. But we want a return to the old ways of doing business."

Chief of Police Helmsley Aimes was inspired by the sudden courage of Pendergast. "Go with our blessing, Dr. Godbold, but not with our cash."

DA Riles agreed. "We would like to see some of the so-called taxes that you have taken returned to us, so that we may continue business as usual."

Reverend Jolly spoke next. "And we would like for you to relinquish control of MambaNet to us."

Godbold folded his hands across his broad belly. "I see." He paused, as the Black Council waited for his response. "I see now that you lack vision. I see that you lack an understanding of how the world works. But let me, in my infinite capacity for charity, clearly explain things to you. First of all, you are but the grocery clerks and errand boys of this organization. Whether you conduct business on MambaNet or on the streets, you only do so with the blessing of those who control a white power structure. Do you not understand that your entire existence is predicated upon the grace and largesse of those who control this system of racial capitalism? We will never dismantle this system. But we can master its intricacies. We can have our slice of the pie. We can overcome the prison of our race. What I have presented here to you, hoping that you would understand, is a real path to power. And, because of your lack of vision, you will always be left behind."

Godbold pressed a button that produced an audible locking sound of the only entrance and exit to the conference room. Godbold watched the Black Council react in panic. "This is why they developed a philosophy and a means of euthanizing the inferior races. I now see, more clearly than ever before, the logic of Eugenics and Racial Genocide. It all makes perfect sense to me now."

Godbold watched the members of the Black Council race towards the door and futilely attempt to open it. Godbold pressed another button on the control panel. A yellow-green gas emanated from the air vents. Godbold watched as they first recognized the smell of bleach and then began to rub their irritated eyes and then to cough uncontrollably and then he muted the sounds of their screams and watched their frightened movements and gestures as they fell to their knees, grabbing their throats and writhing in pain as the irritation became death. Only when the last of them stopped moving and lay still with mouths agape and eyes wide open with horror did Godbold stop the flow of gas and initiate the vacuum that would suck the yellow-green poison back.

Godbold crossed his legs and rested his hands upon his belly. He laughed and reached for his smartphone and dialed Seven Daggers.

"Sir?"

"Now we are free."

There was a momentary silence.

"Did you..."

"Yes. I used the chlorine gas." Godbold leaned back in his chair and reflected. "You know, killing those who get out of hand is a family tradition." He leaned forward again, refocusing on the task at hand. "I'll need you to dump the bodies."

"Done. Upton's Cleaners can handle the biohazard cleanup."

"Make it happen, Adro."

"Sir...if I may...the White Council will likely object. If they come after us, there will be no refuge."

"Not to worry. They have assured me that all these Black faces are replaceable."

7. The Onanist

Aurora awoke. Dressed in a simple pink gown. Waxed. Cleaned and oiled. Her afro now hot-combed straight. Chained by the right ankle to the slave block. Godbold sat in a tall-backed wicker chair, caressing himself under his silk smoking jacket, his eyes focused intently on hers as she awoke.

"What are you doing? Does that make you feel good?"

Godbold removed his hand from under his smoking jacket and shrugged. "Money makes me feel powerful, and you have interfered with my money." He spoke with a thick North Carolina accent. It seemed to Aurora's ears to be more of a white southerner's accent than what she had been accustomed to expect from Black southerners.

Godbold rose and brought her a silver tray with a bowl of soup and a plate with protein. "The soup du jour," he said, "is a corn chowder with bacon bits. The very finest. And for the entrée you will enjoy confit de canard."

"I'm a vegetarian."

"You will adapt or you will starve. You are also now a junkie. Presumably you have never been that before either."

Aurora knew that she must eat to build up her strength and fight the fentanyl that now spoke to her, begging her for more. Godbold provided no utensils so she ate with her hands, raising the bowl of soup to her lips and roughly dismembering the duck on her plate. She ate angrily, staring at him throughout, and when she finished, she wiped her mouth. "What's for dessert?"

"Fentanyl!" Godbold smiled. He sat back in his wicker chair. "And perhaps some ice cream. Fentanyl addicts love ice cream. Or is that heroin addicts? I can't remember!" Godbold was momentarily amused by his remark. He continued. "Have you noticed that this chair upon which I sit is the very chair that the late great Dr. Huey P. Newton sat upon in that iconic picture."

"I suppose you are going to tell me that you were once a Black Panther."

Godbold again burst out into laughter. "Good heavens no! Quite the opposite. I worked with the authorities during that era to guarantee the assassinations, exiles, and imprisonment of many Black radicals. Their philosophies were flawed."

"You must hate yourself."

"Hate myself? Quite the contrary! I am absolutely in love with myself!"

"You advertise yourself as some kind of Black Savior."

"I have fooled everyone."

"Then what are you?"

"In reality I am a descendant of the bastard children of miscegenation that took place so many hundreds of years ago. I am a man in search of getting back to his core, essential whiteness, embracing the spirit of the great colonizer who yet resides in my veins. I am blessed with enough white blood to ensure my greatness and my place of honor in this society, but yet not enough to pass."

"Is that how you justify selling your own people into sexual slavery?"

Godbold shrugged and smiled. "Of course."

"You're pretty clever. You have everyone in Oakland fooled. They all hail you like a conquering Black hero but you're just another hateful white man."

Godbold nodded. "The thing is...I'm both!"

"I'll judge you by your actions."

"Okay," Godbold chuckled. "I can accept that. As far as that's concerned...there's more. So much more than what you were able to uncover." Godbold knelt to undo the chain that bound her to the slave block. "Let me show you."

They approached a great green door. Godbold waved his index finger and the door slid open, revealing a circular room with walls lined by screens monitoring every one of the 35 police beats in Oakland. "It will amuse me to show you all that you missed in your intrepid reporting."

Godbold approached the control panel in the center of the room. He instructed Aurora to sit as he manipulated the controls. "Look at the center screen. Number one."

"I know that Seven Daggers exposed you to a small slice of our global enterprise. Let me show you how extensive our operation is." He pointed to the center screen, the largest in the room. It monitored the Black Archon's activities at the Port of Oakland. Aurora could see armed Black Archon soldiers leading groups of Black women chained to one another from trucks onto the loading dock of a cargo ship. "You saw the ship bound for Miami. From there it will sail to the Bahamas. This video is from last week. This ship you see here carries cargo for Saudi elites." Godbold swung the chair around and leaned into Aurora. "Every year there are almost 10,000 Black women alone missing from the streets of this country. Oakland is but the first point of departure in the vast global skin trade that I alone control. We obtain the women from the streets. We train them in the sexual arts for which they are desired. And then we sell them abroad." Godbold stood up and adjusted himself in his smoking jacket. "So, you see, this is a far greater operation than you ever imagined."

"Where else do you send these women?"

"As I said, this is a global trade, and there is literally nowhere in the world where the sweet dark berry of young Black women is not in demand, although we cater to a wide variety of tastes. The Bahamas is an important hub, a center of the trade, where we gather women from the United States, the Caribbean, and Central and South America. Our largest customers are in Europe, of course, and Russian oligarchs are a close second. By comparison, Saudi Arabia and other oil rich Middle Eastern elites are a distant third, but only because of a competing slave trade that they support and patronize within eastern Africa. But that…brings me to my next point."

Godbold spun Aurora around again to face the central screen. Again, he manipulated the controls. The central screen now cycled through images of a vast compound in the motherland.

Godbold continued. "I am building a new nation. What you are seeing here are scenes from my compound. We are building an army and an infrastructure here that will allow us to grow our operation and dominate our competitors in East Africa."

"What about your drugs?" Aurora had always suspected something. This was not a man who possessed a shred of benevolence in his heart, although his talents alone had already benefited millions.

"Yes, the drugs." Godbold ruminated. "The drugs. You mean the cures for sickle cell anemia, epilepsy, and hypertension? Perhaps you think that my pharmaceutical research and development is contrary to my criminal endeavors."

"You are a man who is at odds with himself, Godbold."

"Yes, I am a man of many contradictions. Aren't we all? However, I do not see contradiction as conflict. Contradiction produces points of tension from which my creativity flows. For example, what happens when good and evil collide? I'll tell you what happens. A new world is born."

"What other drugs have you developed?"

"The drugs. Yes, the drugs. I think that there are some secrets that I still wish to keep. Perhaps as we get to know one another better…"

"Why hold back now?"

Godbold ignored her question. He paced the room, surveying the city. "You're smart, so I want to ask you for *your* counsel."

"You're kidding, right?"

"No. I am quite serious. Before joining you tonight, I did something so completely unthinkable."

"That seems to be your style."

Godbold looked into her eyes. "I killed all 13 members of my governing board tonight."

"Who are these people?"

"The most influential Black people in this city."

"You're done. You've written your own death sentence."

"I think not. The world won't notice that they are missing for many days, perhaps even weeks. It simply narrows the window for implementing my vision. By the time the world becomes aware of their disappearances, I will have already left to take my rightful seat as the absolute ruler of a new nation."

"You're completely insane."

Godbold stood and shook his head. "I think you're smarter than merely stating the obvious. Of course, I'm stark raving mad! I'm a visionary! All visionaries dance with madness!"

"Then it should also be obvious that you're already a dead man."

Godbold raised his head, allowing the light to catch his features. "At this point, I am beyond life and death. Life and death are the most fundamental contradictory experiences. It is only because of the tension between life and death that our lives have meaning. If I have to die, then let it be at the hands of someone greater than myself. I can accept death. I simply cannot accept death at the hands of an inferior."

"Sonny Trueheart is a better man than you. I'd like to see him kill you."

"Aaah! Sonny Trueheart. The People's Detective! Let's talk about

Sonny Trueheart. Tell me more about this person. I read your story. What else can you offer?"

"He will kill you once he finds out that you have abducted me. He will kill you as surely as he killed Papi Elder and those crooked white cops. He is probably already looking for me."

"I don't think so. I suspect that Mister Trueheart is in some seedy bar somewhere in East Oakland working on his fourth or fifth shot of whiskey."

"Drunk or not, he's still the better man."

"Trueheart is not my equal. Far from it. I fear no man, certainly not him."

"He will kill you. And he will be a symbol of liberation for the people of Oakland."

"He will die a most unpleasant death and there will be no one but you to mourn him and you will be a junkie offering fellatio for 20-dollars a turn in dark, garbage strewn alleys in exchange for more fentanyl. You overestimate yourself and your hero cop, my dear."

"He will kill you and if he doesn't…I will."

"I would NEVER allow a man of lesser intelligence to end my life. Not only will your hero cop fail in this regard, he will NEVER find you!"

Dr. Godbold picked up his phone and began calling Seven Daggers. His hands shook violently and his voice picked up volume as he spoke.

When Seven Daggers answered, Godbold issued new orders. "Come get the reporter. I've grown tired of her nonsense. Have your people move her around the city. A different location every night. Understood?"

Godbold ended the call and stared murderously at Aurora Jenkins. "What you fail to understand is that *I* and *I* alone control Oakland. Oakland is *my* city!!" Godbold balled up his fists and screamed. "This is *my* city!"

8. Backstabbers

While Dr. Godbold was preoccupied with Aurora Jenkins, Seven Daggers opened the door to the conference room where the White Council remained. He turned on the lights and held a canister of chlorine gas in his hands. He confirmed that the members of the Black Council had been murdered.

Archon 1 was the first to speak as Seven Daggers entered the room. "You were right. He's gone mad."

Seven Daggers juggled the canister of chlorine gas. "I'm sure glad that I switched out the chlorine gas for a harmless condensed water vapor in this room." Seven Daggers pointed to a light projector in a corner of the conference room that was invisible to Dr. Godbold's view. "And if Dr. Godbold had also decided to kill you, the yellow-green pin light I placed in the corner would have given the appearance of chlorine."

Archon 3 spoke: "He would not have dared."

"He might have," Seven Daggers said. "He might well have. You have no idea how obsessed the man is with this…Africa Project."

Archon 6 loosened his tie and spoke. "So, the question now is…what's next?"

Archon 1 provided the answer. "He must die." He looked at Seven Daggers. "And Adro Onzi will take his place."

Archon 3 asked, "Should we put it to a vote?"

Archon 6 nodded in agreement. "I doubt that there will be any dissent."

All 13 members of the White Council raised their hands.

"I am honored, dear sirs," Seven Daggers genuflected. "How shall he die?"

"Sonny Trueheart, the People's Detective…he should kill him," White Archon 6 responded. "It should also appear that the Black Archon has been destroyed by the People's Detective. Aurora Jenkins' story should be made public, but it should attribute all criminal activity to Dr. Godbold, including the murders of the mayor, chief of police, superintendent of schools, pastors, and Black business leaders. There should be no mention of this council, nor of any white involvement. We should blame it all on the Blacks. This will be presented to the public as the result of Black in-fighting, Black-on-Black violence, and the result of a power grab by Dr. Godbold. Detective Trueheart will be the hero. It will be a symbolic victory for the people of Oakland. We can go to ground and reform our business model."

One after another, every member of the White Council nodded their approval.

Archon 1 rose from the table and made the "Okay" symbol with his right hand against his heart. "All is well. The Archon Reign Supreme!"

Seven Daggers watched as the other 12 joined Archon 1 in standing and making the symbol of white supremacy and shouted, "All is well! The Archon Reign Supreme!"

9. Aaminha

Sonny kept wondering how he could have missed the family resemblance between Aurora Jenkins and Aaminha Toure. How could he have missed it when she interviewed him? Was he drunk then? And then he remembered that he could not bring himself to go to Aaminha's funeral. He never had an opportunity to meet her family. Their time together was brief. Their relationship was only beginning.

His first impulse was to keep drinking. Hours went by and he thought about drinking every passing second. But it was clearly time to sober up. Aurora Jenkins was the younger sister of Aaminha Toure. Fact. Everything changed. He went to the bathroom and stuck his finger down his throat and forced himself to vomit. Woozy, weary, and weak, he went to bed and took a nap. He woke two hours later, showered, dressed, walked to the Eastmont Town Center and bought groceries at Gazzali's Supermarket. When he returned home, he pulled out the blender and made a juice of kale greens, spinach, fuji apples, blackberries, and a dose of ginger root.

He put John Coltrane's *A Love Supreme* recording on the turntable and resolved to end his dependence on the booze.

He poured all the booze in his cabinets and refrigerator down the kitchen sink. Put the bottles out for recycling. He stretched and warmed up in the fashion that so many aikidokas were taught, giving flexibility to his joints and emphasizing his breathing. He went out the side door of his 2-bedroom bungalow and practiced forms with his bokken and katana in the tall grass of his backyard.

When he came back inside, he turned on the television and watched the local news. They were reporting from the scene of a

Black Lives Matter demonstration outside of the headquarters of the Oakland Police Department in the aftermath of a new incidence of police violence against Black people. Oakland City Councilmember Andre Chidozie stood beside a woman with flowing braided extensions and a BLM t-shirt. Chidozie, the product of an Oakland Black working-class family, held a bullhorn and shouted: "No Justice, No Peace!" and both he and the woman raised their fists as Black Power advocates had done so many generations ago.

He turned off the television and read Aurora's feature article. She called him "The People's Detective." He wanted to live up to that name.

Sonny lived in the same house in the heart of East Oakland where he was born and raised. He was the only child of the city's first Black private detective and a Highland Hospital emergency ward nurse. His house was right on the edge of police beat 27Y, one of the city's highest crime areas. But the Havenscourt was also a place of colorful little bungalows with beautiful lawns and friendly, working-class neighbors hoping for a better world for their children. It was a modest property with 800 square feet, 2 bedrooms, and one bath. Like so many others in the neighborhood, it was originally a 1920's vacation home built for wealthy San Franciscans seeking warmer climates in the summer.

The strongest memory he had of his mother, Rena Trueheart, was when she took him to work one day and let him sit with the emergency ward intake staff. He watched from behind the glass the screaming and the chaos and saw his mother's calm and gentle heart soothe the sick and suffering. They had lunch in the commissary and Sonny noticed a drop of blood on the sleeve of her crisp white uniform. She came and got him when her shift was over, and he held her hand tight and gazed up in awe at her.

The strongest memory he had of his father was the day he took him to his office along Grand Ave. by Lake Merritt, talked to him about his cases, and let him hold his revolver. They drove into Berkeley, had hot dogs at Top Dog on Durant, walked down the street and played pinball at Silverball, then went to a James Bond movie at a revival theater. Sonny noticed there was an African American spy in the flick, a brother with authority who took license insulting Bond. On the drive home he and his father played a game of giving the character, like so many brothers in the background of white films, a life and a backstory to go along with his name.

Tragedy interrupted an idyllic childhood. He was a troubled boy after the untimely death of his father. Full of spite and anger. His late mother took him to an aikido dojo where Kazuyoshi "Kaz" Taketo reached out to him. Kaz was like no other. The child of a Jamaican Rastafarian immigrant to Japan and a Yakuza enforcer. He'd come to America to escape the family legacy. Kaz talked to him about the peace and calmness at the center of the martial arts. He talked about the mastery of his body and spirit. He showed him this Black warrior in a video, "36 Jo Basics." Someone that looked like him. Archie Champion was like a superhero to him. He was moved by this presence and soon also by the jo, the short wooden staff favored by Champion, its power and grace.

Sonny implored Taketo to lend him the video and he fashioned a homemade jo from an old broomstick. He implored Kaz Taketo to teach him aikido. Bokken. Jo. Tanto. Iaido and the discipline of the sword. Kaz Taketo became his surrogate father. Aikido saved him. He was hooked.

Aikido became the central focus of his life. Aikido was peace, meditation and a religious epiphany. It helped him control the violence and the feeling that he couldn't do anything but damn near cry and lose his mind.

He finished high school at Castlemont, went on to college at Cal State Hayward, graduated with a double major in Ethnic Studies and Criminal Justice and entered OPD as a patrolman earning 75 grand plus benefits. As a rule, 3 to 5 years of experience are required before a patrolman can apply for a position as a detective, but, because of his education, intelligence, and impeccable record as a patrolman, Sonny was allowed to take the detective's exam within 2 years of service. He was fulfilling his father's legacy, walking in his shoes.

No job in policing symbolizes the best and the worst parts of the career than that of the homicide detective. Sonny entered the department thinking he could make a difference and provide an alternative to the predatory policing that had long been Oakland's legacy. OPD had to do better. They had to be demilitarized. They had to be accountable to the community. There had to be oversight. Put the people back in control. Protect the public. Protect witnesses and whistleblowers.

Sonny had that fire as a homicide detective, driven to help the family members in some way. There were 175 killings in his first year, an all-time high. Sonny was lead detective in well over 30 cases, and he assisted other detectives in another 50. The worst part of the job was seeing what the relatives go through when a loved one is killed. Especially a child. And you remember the faces of every dead child. The best times are when a detective can tell relatives and the community the case has been solved and offer them continued support. It's about being able to show people that you care about their losses and you want to bring those responsible to justice.

In the end, it was a grind. He took the work home with him every night. He began turning to the booze. It was an unsustainable life. But the real reason Sonny Trueheart quit the Oakland Police Department was because of Aaminha Toure.

She was a teacher at the Umoja School of the East Oakland Kemetic Community Church and worked part-time at the church cafe and bakery. She'd seen many of the kids in the neighborhood lost to drugs. She would stand on street corners with "Stop the Violence" banners and confront young dope dealers in her neighborhood.

They killed her in broad daylight right on Foothill and Havenscourt. She was carrying a fried fish plate home from the Avenue Cafe, and berating the young men who cast dice outside of the Tasty Szechuan restaurant on the corner when they drove by and shot her. Her murder was sobering, further frightening an already frightened community.

Her murder came at him like a swift, finishing blow.

It was then that the booze took control of his life. He chased down every lead in finding Aaminha's killers and worked on his own time fighting a very private war on drugs and everything that was happening to his city. He was angry and figured to take it all on himself. He wanted blood for blood. Because of her, and the graceful way that she lived her life, he decided to do it right and by the book. But he needed the booze to suppress his urge for revenge.

He called in all favors. He shook down all of his confidential informants. He pounded the pavement, worked the neighborhood. Ballistics couldn't tell him anything. "Do you know how many 9mms are out on the streets today?" the Crime Scene Investigation Unit asked him. There was no reliable physical evidence to dig into. The OG's were the only ones who would speak with him and point him in the right direction. But even they refused to offer testimony. He needed witnesses. And, in the end, it was a child, only 10 years old, who had seen it all go down and told her grandmother and her grandmother trusted Sonny enough to tell him. The little girl knew their names. They were boys that she had seen in the neighborhood every day. They were a group of drug lord wannabees who hadn't even owned the car they were driving when they committed the shooting at the behest of Papi Elder, the man who controlled East Oakland's drug trade and the owner of a number of auto detailing businesses that he used as fronts. Papi Elder had hired teenagers instead of doing it himself, kids who rode around the neighborhood on BMX bikes that always seemed a couple sizes small, wearing white t-shirts and sagging blue jeans, selling dope for others higher up. The eldest was only 17 summers old.

Sonny knew that the kids would break under interrogation and lead him right to Papi Elder. No one would have been sorry to see Papi Elder taken off the streets. The little girl said that she had seen Papi Elder come out of the Avenue Cafe right behind Aaminha. Apparently there had been words in the restaurant. She'd seen Papi Elder give the order to his boys as they waited in their car outside of the Avenue Cafe. She'd seen the kids peel out and burn rubber and come careening around the corner, firing at Aaminha as she walked home. Bullets passing through her and pock marking the wall of the Tasty Szechuan restaurant with holes.

If only Sonny could somehow miraculously recover the very guns used to murder Aaminha by each and every one of the young men in that car. But what were the chances? He could, of course, try to plant evidence and falsify reports and give the DA an open and shut case. The community would know for certain that he had the balls to take on the real gangsters in the neighborhood. The OG's would know that Sonny meant business. It would be a major victory for the people of these streets. And after Sonny took down Papi Elder he could probably walk the streets tougher than any gang member. He would never have to worry about anyone opening fire on him, having a target on his back. They would all know. Don't mess with this one. And his superiors would reward him for reminding everyone that OPD was in fact the toughest gang on the streets.

But the indictments handed down to the cops involved in the Riders scandal were enough to scare any cop away from planting evidence. This rogue group of veteran Oakland police officers waged a fake war on drugs in an 18-month reign of terror in West Oakland in the late 1990s and were indicted in 2000. Assaulting and kidnapping innocent citizens. Planting evidence and falsifying reports. Secretly, many of Oakland's so-called "finest" wished that there was still someone out there with the balls to take the situation by the throat by whatever means necessary.

As it turned out, there was another group of rogue officers who succeeded "The Riders." Papi Elder was a key informant for this new, as of yet unnamed group. Sonny figured it out when he tailed and staked out Papi Elder one night, sitting in his car, drinking bourbon and waiting for his moment to grab Papi and force him to identify all of the shooters. The shit hit the fan in the midst of his unofficial surveillance when two police detectives snatched Papi Elder off the streets and stuffed him in the trunk of their car and drove him down to the parking lot of Golden Gate Fields racing track in Berkeley. Sonny tailed them, thinking he was witnessing a hit, parked under the freeway and went by foot into the lot with a digital camera that could capture stills and video, clicking away with a telescopic infra-red lens. He had a voice recorder in his pocket. He wore a bulletproof vest.

But it wasn't a hit.

They pulled him from the trunk with care. There were apologies for the rough treatment but appearances demanded it. Handshakes all around. One of the detectives offered Papi Elder a cigarette. There was much talking, planning, nodding of heads, a little laughter. An agreement had been reached.

Sonny switched the camera to video. He feared that he was too far away to capture sound. But their laughter echoed in the empty parking lot. Some words rang out louder than others.

The two detectives offered to take Papi Elder back in the trunk. Elder shook that off and made a call on his cell for an associate to give him a ride back to his car. The cops waited with him for his ride to arrive. They shared a smoke. More laughter.

Sonny set down the camera and kept the video running. He kept the voice recorder in the breast pocket of his shirt. He drew his service pistol from the holster. Sonny clung to the darkness, rose, and walked over to Papi Elder as he stood there waiting with the two detectives.

Seeking to pump himself up, get the adrenaline flowing, knowing this would save his life, he told himself: *They must answer for Aaminha. Remember how much you loved her. You wearing a vest? You got your backup piece? Well then, you're ready. Take these dirty cops down, Sonny.*

In the empty parking lot Papi Elder and the two dirty cops heard feet shuffling and turned. They saw Sonny's long overcoat in the darkness, then the pistol in Sonny's right hand, his badge in his left hand as he came closer to the lights of their car. Sonny stood partly shrouded in the darkness some 100 feet from them.

One of the detectives thought he recognized him. "Detective Trueheart! Is that you? I recognize you. Well, good evening! Everybody, this is young Homicide Detective Sonny Trueheart."

They were Detectives Charlie Playe and Buck Bridgewater. Southerners. Bon vivants. Big time shit talkers. Good ol' boys from Alabam' who took pleasure in busting Black skulls.

Det. Playe spoke up, moving to stand between Sonny and Papi Elder. "What have you got there, Detective Trueheart?"

Sonny gripped his police issue Glock 17. "I'm arresting all three of you. Drop your weapons. Slowly. Kick them over to me."

"Is this really necessary? I mean, we're all friends here, detective."

"Get your boy under control," Papi Elder urged Playe and Bridgewater. "You better get ahold of your boy now."

As Papi Elder spoke, the two detectives unholstered their Glocks and pointed them towards Sonny. Elder pulled a pearl handled, nickel-plated snub nose .44 revolver from his waistband. "Motherfucker!" he groused. "You gonna make us do this?"

Sonny screamed. He wanted to make sure their voices were recorded. "Are you aware that this man ordered the murder of a young Black woman, a schoolteacher?"

Both detectives shrugged. "He's done a lot of dirt. What's it to us if he helps us get the job done?"

"I'm an informer," Papi Elder gleamed.

Sonny eyed the two detectives. "You let him push his filth and kill innocents…for what?"

"You lookin' to get on the payroll?" Papi Elder queried. "Cuz…we can make that happen."

"It's good money, detective. And good police business too."

"Don't be a fool. We'll let you in on it. And you can pull down a few high-profile collars too."

"We can find somebody, somebody really bad to pin the woman's murder on. It doesn't have to be Papi. It could be somebody just as bad…or worse."

"Aaminha."

"What?"

"That was her name."

"...okay..."

"...and it'll be the name you pigs think about every day in prison."

"...aint going to prison."

Det. Playe took another step forward, raised his pistol, and fired. He aimed for Sonny's overcoat, the clearest target in the darkness.

Kicked like a mule in a shitstorm. Sonny took it point blank in the chest. The shot lifted Sonny off his feet and kicked him backward. His service pistol flew from his hands, clattering on the concrete behind him. His left shoulder banged the concrete hard but he managed to roll off his back –the aikido instincts taking over. He felt nauseous. Felt like passing out. He fought against the darkness and, as he went over and then back up to his knees, he reached into the holster attached to his left ankle and drew his backup piece and fired instinctively.

Again, with that voice inside of his head: *Lucky S.O.B.! Now, blast these fuckers!*

Sonny carried his father's vintage snub nose revolver as a backup piece. The little monster roared, and the devastating .38 hollow point load pierced Det. Playe in the gut. as he stepped out in front of his partner. The man cried out. He turned and twisted, his gun arm thrown wildly to the side, upon the impact of Sonny's bullet. Playe's finger reflexively squeezed the trigger and his next shot inadvertently hit Papi Elder as Elder prepared to shoot.

That's it!

Bridgewater, standing behind his partner, reacted quickly to the freakish wounding of his comrades and lifted his gun and fired.

Watch out for Bridgewater!!

Bridgewater's shot grazed Sonny's right cheek. Sonny felt the warm rush of blood. Sonny could hear his breathing and his heart pumping steady like a drum.

Flesh wound, just a flesh wound!

He kept his cool. Sonny fired another shot, hitting Bridgewater dead center and square in the chest, a lucky shot, sending the man hurtling backward as though he had been yanked from behind by an invisible hand. The retort from successive gunshots echoed through the vast parking lot and a high-pitched whine seared Sonny's hearing and he hallucinated that the cylinder of his revolver was spinning wildly and creating the shrill sound and he could barely hear Papi Elder scream.

Both detectives writhed in pain and struggled to regain control of their weapons. Sonny approached them slowly and fired again. Again. Again.

They can't kill me! No one can kill me!

Sonny emptied the 6-shot wheel gun. Both detectives now lay still with limbs akimbo in sick, horrid death poses.

Papi Elder screamed. "Now, whaddya do that for?"

Papi had fallen down on his butt and was furiously pressing his hand against the wound from the first cop. Kidney shot. Passed clean through him and opened a larger hole in his back. Trying to stop the bleeding. Fighting the fear. Breathing hard. Sonny kicked Elder's revolver and sent it skittering across the parking lot.

There would be crazy ballistics on this shit.

Sonny ripped open his overcoat. Damn if the vest didn't hold up. He convulsed. Bent over and puked. Wiped his mouth. He located and holstered his fallen Glock.

Sonny walked back towards Papi Elder. He put Aaminha's picture in Papi Elder's face and illuminated it for him with his flashlight. He let him know why he was dying.

Papi Elder remembered her. Explained why he had to shut her up. Never apologized. He referred to her as "bitch" as though that was her real name. What was the point of using language like that, Sonny wondered out loud? Even an album full of pictures of Papi's many victims wouldn't drive the point home and make him feel something. Papi Elder pleaded for Sonny to call an ambulance. Sonny asked for the names of the shooters he'd used and patiently scribbled them down in his notepad. This confirmed the names that had been provided to him by the little girl. Sonny told him he'd call an ambulance, but he knew he wouldn't.

"Don't you gotta call it in now? Will you call the ambulance for me, man?"

"Yeah," he lied.

"You aint gonna call the ambulance! You a lie! You gonna leave me to die! You gonna wait for me to die and then call it in! Want to finish it, man? Just finish it, motherfucker!" Papi Elder was shouting, spittle flying from his mouth. "You done crossed the line," He laughed. "Thought you was too good to be a nigga! But you aint no better than me!!" He was screaming. "What kind of nigga are you now, motherfucker?"

Sonny didn't know. Couldn't answer him.

Sonny didn't want to know what it was like to kill a man. Sonny was committed to doing his work with the tools of his mind. Logic. Reason. Deduction. Sonny didn't want to go the way of the gun. But now, as he stood there and watched Papi Elder take his final breath, and the two crooked cops that lay at his feet, there was no going back to what he had been before.

Don't worry about it. You did what you had to do.

All he could remember was Aaminha. It meant lady of peace and harmony.

He thought about that as Papi Elder took his last ugly breath.

And then Sonny just walked away.

Picked up the video camera. Walked out of the parking lot. Ripped off the overcoat and the vest. Felt the deep bruises from the shots he'd taken. Got into his car. Sonny turned on the overhead light and looked in the rearview mirror at the damage from the bullet that grazed his cheek.

Only a flesh wound. Might leave a nasty scar. That's about it.

Miracle that he had survived. He drove a few blocks. Parked. Looked for the bottle he'd tossed on the back seat. Empty. Walked into a corner liquor store and bought an ass pocket of whiskey and some breath mints. Saw his reflection in an oval mirror over the door as he walked out. Turned on the radio and listened to a rerun of Art Bell on *Coast to Coast AM* talking about conspiracy theories and paranormal phenomena. Took a few slugs from the bottle.

Just chill brother. Just chill.

Went to a payphone and called it in. Erased the audiotape and the video. There was nothing to contradict his testimony. It would come down as a clean shooting. He went back to the parking lot where now three men lay still. Heard police sirens in the distance. Sat down on the ground and took a couple breath mints to kill the smell of the liquor. Waited.

Clear your head, brother. Get your story straight.

The cops came. He gave a statement. He would have to write it up in the morning. His C.O. and Internal Affairs would want to talk to him. He told the officers on the scene that he would drive himself to the hospital.

He drove down to the Berkeley Marina. He changed the radio station to KJAZ. They were playing Charles Mingus' somber dirge "Goodbye Porkpie Hat." It would be okay, he thought, to die with that song playing. Sonny drew his father's gun, loaded one round, spun the chamber, and put the barrel to his head. It was too late for Aaminha. Was it now too late for him now too? He looked at the beast in the rearview mirror and thought of what he had just unleashed. He wanted to pull the trigger.

But...

He told himself: *It aint gonna be that easy, brother. We still got work to do.*

The next morning as the news broke about the shooting, Sonny Trueheart, his cheek now properly bandaged, told his C.O. he wanted to work the names Elder had given him as he lay dying.

No one in the station house spoke to him. He was a cop killer now. He was no longer one of them.

He got together a team of reluctant uniforms and rounded up everyone Papi Elder identified. Sonny had four kids in separate interrogation rooms. He went at them alone, going from room to room fucking with their heads like a chess master taking on multiple opponents. He had cops going back and forth between observation rooms taking notes on his techniques. It was probably the best piece of police work that he'd ever done. In less than two hours he had four confessions. Sonny Trueheart put four teenagers in jail, tried as adults for the murder of Aaminha Toure. No one got anything less than 30 years to life.

As he left the station house, four confessions under his belt, it seemed as if every eye was staring, searching for a soft spot to bury the knife.

Sonny took a few days off after that, because a workaholic like him always has sick time in the bank. And he drank his way through the next day, the next week, the next month. First it was bourbon and then it was whiskey and then it was whatever hurt the most going down. And then he walked into his C.O.'s office and surrendered his gun and badge and offered his testimony in the emerging scandal. Said he'd testify in open court about everything he knew. Hell, everyone knew, but only Sonny was willing to break the code of silence.

Hearing of the trial, Sonny Trueheart's testimony and his disillusionment and downward spiral, Kaz Taketo reached out to him. They met at Brown Sugar Kitchen on Mandela Parkway in West Oakland. Over chicken wings and collard greens and mac and cheese Sonny spoke of his dream of opening East Oakland Aikido. Sonny was in a deep downward spiral. He'd seen and lived through too much on the streets of Oakland.

Taketo told him that he could be released from his burden, that he could be redeemed. He offered to invest in East Oakland Aikido. The offer was Taketo's way of saving his life. Again. And Sonny accepted the offer. He planned to file a whistleblower lawsuit against the Oakland Police Department and repay his sensei with the settlement. There was an ideal property for sale right in his neighborhood, on Bancroft Ave., next to the church where Aaminha worshipped and within walking distance of his house. If he could make the winning bid, he could open the doors of East Oakland Aikido within months.

And now someone was threatening to take the life of Aaminha Toure's younger sister. He remembered the first night that he and Aaminha discovered and expressed feelings for one another, the tenderness and intensity of their time together, the secret that they had decided to keep from the outside world, the indeterminacy of what this could lead to, and what they had dared to yet speak. He wanted to tell her everything that he was feeling. But then it happened, and he had not told her that he loved her. In his meditation he resolved that he would never let that happen again.

10. Captivity

Seven Daggers unlocked the handcuffs. Aurora rubbed her wrists. Alone in a dimly lit, windowless room in another location. They moved her every day. Sometimes in the middle of the day, sometimes in the dark of night. They varied the routine to keep her disoriented.

Seven Daggers brought her more clothes. Draped a warm blanket over her shoulders. He spoke softly now. But the threat of his violence was ever-present. He brought her a hot vegetarian meal, allowing her to resume her diet. Ethiopian food and a bottle of Harar, a pale lager. This would be the first clue to her location. There was nothing about the windowless room in which she was being held that could help her understand where she had been taken. But Aurora knew every Ethiopian restaurant in the East Bay.

Seven Daggers sat opposite her and pushed the take-out container in her direction. Aurora opened the container and smelled the berbere sauce, onions, and garlic. She broke off a piece of the spongy injera bread and used this to grab a mouthful of mustard greens. It was a familiar taste. Enssaro restaurant. Grand Avenue. She was still in Oakland. Near Lake Merritt.

"You like that stuff, huh?"

"Yeah," Aurora said between mouthfuls.

"I don't like eating with my hands. It's for the poor. It's nasty!"

"I can think of things worse than being poor. Like selling your own people into slavery."

Seven Daggers grinned and brushed it aside. "I hear you got a new boyfriend. Sonny Trueheart. Right? Wonder if he'll try to save his precious Aurora."

"When he does, he'll come and kill you all!" She spat fire with her eyes.

"Did you tell him about your story on the Black Archon?"

"No!" She was emphatic. Seven Daggers took note. Aurora stared into his eyes. Tried to control her breathing. "I just wrote a story about him. That's all."

"Nah, that aint all." Seven Daggers laughed. "You already gave up the Trib editor Valerie Ogwu and Councilmember Andre Chidozie, right? I know you gave *them* the story. Maybe you gave it to Trueheart too."

Aurora shook her head. A chill went through her as she realized that her confession under the influence placed Ogwu and Chidozie in danger. She reiterated, "Trueheart doesn't know anything."

"So…if he doesn't know anything about us, then you just expect him to magically figure it out and come charging in here to save you? You think he cares about you? Tell you the truth, I don't think he'll come to your aid. Even if he's mister chivalry and all that. He's a boozer, you know. When he finds out we've got you…if he finds out we've got you, he'll probably just fall back into the bottle. You probably know that he lost a woman before."

So, they didn't yet know that Aaminha Toure was her sister.

Relieved, Aurora responded, "I don't know anything about that. And I don't care." The Ethiopian food and cold beer reinvigorated her. She could feel her strength coming back with every bite and sip.

"I bought you some clothes. Jeans. T-shirts. Kind of stuff you like to wear."

"What do you mean by that?"

Seven Daggers shrugged. "I mean, you're kinda mannish and all. You're good looking, I guess. I've never seen a woman like you. You got some muscles and you can fight. You don't shave or anything. You got tattoos. It's like you wanna be a man or something. That's kinda nasty."

"Again, I can think of things that are much nastier."

"Your boyfriend Trueheart must like that, huh?"

Aurora smiled at his provocation. "Even if you stop this story, the truth is going to come out at some point."

"Wanna bet? I think we'll get away with everything that we want to get away with."

"My father used to tell me that evil always loses, in the end."

"Your father was wrong. He was probably also a damn fool. You have no idea how powerful we are."

"I do," she shrugged. "Doesn't mean I'm afraid of you. Doesn't mean Trueheart will be afraid of you either. He could take all of you down all by himself. Drunk or not."

Seven Daggers roared with laughter. "I like your spirit woman! But you're a damn fool just like your father, and if Sonny Trueheart actually believes that he could take us down, he's a damn fool too."

And then, as he had done before, the light, jovial, conversational moment ended and Seven Daggers rose with red fury in his eyes, grabbed her by the forearm and forcibly administered another dose of fentanyl.

The room began to swirl and time began to fold in on itself. Seven Daggers held her face in his right hand and stared intently in her eyes. "Trueheart can't take down Dr. Godbold. Not without my help." He pushed her away from him and she fell listlessly to the cot. She heard his boots scrape the floor and heard his sick laughter as he departed.

Power to the People!
A Podcast for the People
Broadcasting from the Lower Bottoms of West Oakland
Hosted by Aurora Jenkins

Transcript of Power to the People! Episode 73

We continue our series of investigative reports about missing and kidnapped women of color in the Bay Area. Today, we are asking whether the disappearances and abductions of women of color are directly linked to the prevalence of sex trafficking in Oakland, California. We are also asking why the City Council and the Mayor have not prioritized these issues.

The community has called for a special alert and designated hotline for reported victims of sex trafficking. This year alone, we have seen over 125 cases of missing women from the streets of Oakland. There is no specific division of the Oakland Police Department that is dedicated to solving these crimes. No, the Oakland Police Department prefers to spend its budget on other priorities like terrorizing folks in the Twomps.

We are specifically asking OPD to create a VICE/Child Exploitation Unit to successfully locate and rescue women and juvenile victims of human trafficking. We are asking OPD to partner with the National Human Trafficking Hotline, ReportJohn.org and other similar organizations and police units throughout the state and country. We also want the city of Oakland to partner with community organizations to provide support and pathways to recovery for victims of human trafficking.[5] Stay tuned!

---

[5] On May 16, 2023, the Oakland City Council approved a resolution to create an "Ebony Alert" to help locate missing Black women and Black Youth.

11. Trouble Man

There was an envelope in his mailbox containing a letter, three photographs, and a flash drive sent from Aurora Jenkins and postmarked the date of her disappearance.

Det. Trueheart,

I want to apologize to you with all sincerity. The real reason that I came to interview you is because I am Aaminha Toure's younger sister and I wanted to get to know the man that loved her, the man who was willing to give up his career and put his life in peril for her, the man who brought her killers to justice.

I have been working on a story about the criminal organization that was ultimately behind my sister's murder. Please see the enclosed flash drive. You will find the draft of my story. You will also find pictures that will give you a sense of what I am working on. Until we talk again, let me just tell you that it goes way beyond Papi Elder.

This is the work of a growing criminal organization. They call themselves The Black Archon. Most people think that's the name of a legitimate pharmaceutical company. It's not. I know that this sounds like a wild conspiracy theory, but the leaders of the Black Archon, including Dr. Lucius Godbold, are the descendants of the Black folk who betrayed us many generations ago on the plantations. They are the children of those who collaborated with our slave masters and mistresses. Godbold and those in his organization are still collaborating with a largely white and racist capitalist power structure. These are the ones whose forefathers proudly wore their masters' coats and relished the leavings from their masters' plates. I believe that this organization is behind the recent disappearances of Black, Latinx, Asian American, Pacific Islander,

Indigenous, and poor white women on the streets of Oakland. I believe that they are kidnaping and trafficking these women.

I'm sharing this with you in the event that anything happens to me. I know that you'll know what to do with it. As the title of my article suggests, you are truly the People's Detective.

With gratitude,
Aurora Jenkins

There were two color and one black and white photograph with the letter. The first was a picture of Aaminha at her college graduation.

Sonny looked at the image of the woman he once loved. "I won't let you down, Aaminha," he said.

The two other photographs were held together by a paperclip and Sonny set these off to the side.

Sonny took the Harley out into the early evening and bought take-out from the buffet at Lena's Soul Food on Bancroft and 14th just before they were about to close. A fried fish dinner with red beans and rice and collard greens. He stayed up all night reading and re-reading Aurora's materials. He did not drink a drop of liquor.

He got up at the crack of dawn the next day and opened the safe that was bolted to the floor of the closet in his bedroom where he kept his father's 1975 Colt Detective Special 6-shot snub nose .38 special revolver. This was the gun that he had used to take down Papi Elder and two dirty cops. But the gun had an even more legendary origin story.

The gun had been given to Sonny's father by Franklin Mieuli, the loveable, eccentric former owner of the Golden State Warriors, who favored deerstalker caps and preferred to travel across the Bay Area on a motorcycle rather than in a limousine. Mieuli hired Sonny's father as private security during the Warriors successful 1974-75 NBA Championship run. Trailing 3-0 in the 1975 NBA Finals, the Washington Bullets were so desperate that Bullets' wing Mike Riordan concocted a wild plot to get the Golden State Warriors' best player, Rick Barry, tossed from the game. Early in the first quarter of Game 4, Riordan took a wild swing at Barry's head. Before Barry could respond, Warriors head coach Al Attles ran to his defense, confronting both Riordan and Bullets' court enforcer Wes Unseld.

The night before the game, Sonny's father was having dinner with Mieuli and Attles when they heard rumors that the Bullets were going to do something to try to get Rick out of the game. The trio concocted a plan of response and decided that Sonny's father would be responsible for rushing onto the court after Attles, protecting him from Unseld's fury, and escorting him from the on-court melee that was certain to ensue. When it all went down, the older Attles proved himself more than capable of handling the younger bully, but Sonny's father was nevertheless there to rush Attles off the court and throw a cheap shot of his own at Unseld in the process. Sonny's father was granted a long-term contract to provide security for Mieuli and the team until Mieuli sold the franchise in 1986.

As a present for his efforts, Sonny's father was given a 1975 Warriors Championship ring and a carbon steel 3rd Generation Colt Detective Special snub nose revolver. In the insular world of cops and private investigators, the gun was popularly referred to as the "Dick Special."

"This gun helps me remember how wonderful those days were," Sonny's father would say.

Sonny's father had replaced the original checkered walnut grips with longer and wider contoured cocobolo grips that contained a hidden compartment in the base for an extra bullet, effectively giving the gun a 7-shot capacity.

His father used it mainly for show and, in all of his years as a private detective, had never had to kill anyone with it. "I don't want to shoot anybody," his father would say, "but sometimes I gotta scare a fool."

Sonny hated what he had done with his father's gun and his father's legacy. But his father's gun had, after all, saved his life.

Sonny handled the piece. Its long grip felt good and familiar in his hands. Like an old friend. He opened the cylinder and spun the wheel, looking at all six empty chambers. He checked the empty hidden chamber at the base of the grip. Maybe his father's pistol would save his life again. Then again, he reflected for moments that passed like an eternity, he didn't want to ever have to kill anyone again. He knew in his heart what taking Nzingha's offer and having the gun in his possession meant. Inevitably he would have to kill for Aurora…just as surely as he had killed for Aaminha.

Sonny took a deep breath and closed his eyes.

Sonny showered, dressed and hit the road. He wanted to give himself a whole new look. In his closet were the suits and overcoats of his OPD days. He wanted to go with something different. He opted for a more casual look: blue jeans, dashikis, guaveras, and a leather motorcycle jacket. He went to Cedric's Barbershop on International Blvd. and asked him to re-braid his hair and give him a clean shave with a straight razor. He shopped at the Oakland Swap Meet along 880 near the Coliseum and kept driving north to the Albo African Gift Shop on Telegraph in North Oakland in Little Ethiopia and then the Berkeley Flea Market and found all that he needed including a couple pairs of motorcycle boots and an assortment of dashikis. He found a vintage wristwatch with a nylon wristband. Bought a laptop and a smartphone with an unlimited data plan at the Apple store on 4th St. in Berkeley.

From there he drove further north on San Pablo Avenue to a gun shop in El Cerrito and bought speed loaders and several boxes of rubber bullets and some 125-grain hollow point ammunition. He bought a suede shoulder holster that he could wear under a coat or jacket and a leather inside the waistband holster that he could drape his dashiki over on hot days.

He then drove back to Oakland and all through the day and into the night he stirred the hornets' nests, from San Antonio to Sobrante Park, the Laurel to Lakeview, the Dimond to Downtown, Fruitvale to Fremont, the Temescal to Toler Heights, Millsmont to Eastmont, the Laurel to the Lower Bottoms, Funktown to Jingletown, Grand Lake to the Glenview, Little Saigon to Koreatown, and Uptown to

Chinatown.

He was operating in plain sight, trying to get the word out that he was investigating the disappearance of Aurora Jenkins. Reacquainting himself with old contacts, friends and enemies. For most, it was the first that they had heard of her coming up missing. He was creating the notion that her possible disappearance was a political act in light of her role as an investigative journalist, but he also found clever ways of asking people about sex trafficking in Oakland and the Black Archon.

He spoke to the brothers and sisters at the East Oakland Black Dragons motorcycle club on East 14th. OG's at Famous One's Barbershop on International. Pastor Gary, the downtown street corner preacher, who stood on a milk crate outside of DeLauer's Newsstand and preached his concept of how all living things were part of one shared galactic consciousness. Pot clubs in Oaksterdam. Barbeque joints on MacArthur and taco trucks in the Fruitvale. Local merchants and hustlers. Street corner ballers at Mosswood Park.

The word went out that Sonny Trueheart was back.

For dinner he had the best burger in Oakland at Luka's Pool Room on Broadway and Grand. Childish Gambino's song "Telegraph Avenue" was playing through the restaurant's speakers while Sonny sat at the bar with his tonic water and his burger. Sonny sang the refrain out loud.

He went back out onto the night streets. He hit San Pablo Avenue in North Oakland at the Emeryville border. He hit International Blvd. in the Fruitvale and then went deeper into the Twomps or what they now call the Murder Dubs on 25th and Foothill in East Oakland as he headed homeward. These were among the usual places where sex workers toiled. Sonny carried tens and twenties and paid for bits of information that might confirm what Aurora's draft concluded about sex trafficking in Oakland.

And the words that came back to him from the street bolstered her report.

The Black Archon holds auctions for wealthy white folk who want to purchase a taste of brown sugar.

Many of the women are underage from what I hear.

Who knows where they send the women that they take off these Oakland streets.

They bring women in and they take women out like trading for coffee or tobacco or rum.

The Black Archon are nothing but a front for white corporate money.

When Sonny returned home, he concocted another healthy smoothie and put in a DVD of the Gordon Parks blaxploitation epic *Three the Hard Way* about three martial arts experts who try to stop white supremacists from poisoning the water supply in Black neighborhoods. He'd bought it back in the day at Rasputin's on Telegraph Ave. in Berkeley. Starring Jim Brown, Jim Kelly, and Fred Williamson, and featuring music from The Impressions, *Three the Hard Way* was a meditation on what determined Black folk could do to save their city.

With the film on in the background, Sonny set up his new laptop, inserted the flash drive, and scrolled through the draft of Aurora's story. Aurora was a compelling writer. She wrote with passion and detail. She was a relentless investigator. Her story gave voice to the voiceless, weaving together scraps of hard evidence with the narratives of women kidnapped and taken into the Black Archon's sex trade.

Sonny knew that this was the organization that funded and protected Papi Elder and the Riders and other crooked cops, and controlled all Black political power in the "O." Heavy hitters indeed. This was also the organization that was responsible for the murder of Aaminha Toure. Even though as a cop you knew that taking down this lot would effectively end most of the serious crime and deaths in the city, the Black Archon were largely untouchable, regarded as mere legend, and there was hardly a man, either cop or hood, who wasn't on their payroll.

Sonny knew precisely what Aurora had been on to and what Aurora had yet to uncover. Some of her informants spoke of two separate and unequal groups of leaders and advisors for the Black

Archon's criminal enterprises: one Black and the other white. And so, behind the Black Archon was an even more powerful cabal of white capitalists. She had likely been kidnapped in order to stop this phase of her investigation.

And then Sonny studied the second and third photographs that came with Aurora's letter and flash drive.

One was a vintage photograph with the year "1924" marked on the back depicting a gathering of 13 people at the Oakland Municipal Auditorium wearing white Ku Klux Klan robes.

The other was a professional portrait of a convivial black-tie gala at a mansion. The women he had just spoken to on the street confirmed such events. Black men in tight white coats holding serving trays with hors d'oeuvres and champagne flutes. At the center of the picture were 13 people wearing white Ku Klux Klan robes and hoods. Every one of the hooded revelers held a naked woman on a dog leash. The faces of these women tethered to their masters betrayed their anger and pain. Their bodies were scarred, bearing deep bruises and lacerations.

Taken together, the testimonies of victims of trafficking and the faces beneath the hoods, what did it all mean? What dark truths and traditions were concealed?

Time to throw it all against the wall and see what stuck.

Sonny remembered a large, sticky easel pad in his coat closet that he used for cases. Each sheet of paper was a good 25" x 30". He retrieved this and posted several sheets on the walls of the second bedroom in his home that he used as an office space.

On two sheets he wrote all of the names of Black officials and business persons that Aurora identified in her story. Beneath each name he wrote down the names of businesses that each person controlled in the city.

He titled the remaining sheets of paper "The White Council."

Sonny stayed up all through the evening until the sun began to rise on the new day searching on the internet for articles by investigative journalists on Bay Area corporations and whistleblowers associated with the Black Archon; company records; publicly accessible information on shareholders and board members; electronic court records; any leaked memos or information; import/export databases; and academic articles on the history of the Klan in Oakland. He was looking for older and modern corporations that had in any way been associated with Oakland's ugly past, Black Archon Pharmaceuticals or any affiliated businesses owned by the members of the Black Council.

Somewhere in all of this he was hoping to uncover hard numbers that would reveal relationships and a vast criminal services industry of lawyers, bankers, and accountants. Silent investors. Parallel sets of accounting books. Proxies, offshore banks, and fake contracts. Sonny hoped that the numbers would weave together a story of the Black and the White Council and the many voiceless victims and the 13 faces hidden beneath the hoods.

There wasn't enough time to file a freedom of information request. His investigation would be purely speculative and limited to internet searches. The most useful sites were Aleph, an index of information on the properties, bank accounts, court cases, and leaks of corporate information; ImportGenius, which tracked import/export transactions through national freedom of information laws; and PACER, which provided public access to court electronic records.

Sonny looked for patterns, recurring affiliations and associations of names of individuals and companies. And when he located a name that appeared more than twice in association with either the 1920s Ku Klux Klan, modern day Black Archon Pharmaceuticals, or a member of the Black Council, he wrote that name on the poster board.

By 8am Sonny had written 13 names.

12. Old Man Kaz

In spite of his advanced age, Kazuyoshi Taketo was still the picture of perfect health and virility. For a man of small stature who stood just a little over 5 feet 6 inches, Taketo carried himself with an upright authority, dignity, and gentlemanly composure. He wore a fantastic royal blue kimono, as was his favorite, and big, yellow-tinted glasses. His hair was now completely gray, yet it was wavy, beautifully kinky and it glimmered slickly silver and was combed back severely from his face. His skin, betraying the rich brown tones of his Jamaican mother, was smooth and youthful.

Kaz Taketo was the child of a yakuza enforcer, Kensuke Taketo of the Yamazaki family, the Ford Motor Company of organized crime in Japan. He was dispatched by the Yamazaki organization to Jamaica in the early 1950's in order to broker an international narcotics deal with members of what would later become known as the Trenchtown Yardies. The deal was blessed by the Labor Party of Jamaica, which was as deeply affiliated with the Trenchtown Yardies as the Japanese government was with the Yamazaki family.

In the course of his dealings, he met and fell in love with the stunningly beautiful Jamaican daughter of one of the Trenchtown Yardies leaders, Desdemona Collingsworth. The story was that they had fallen in love at first sight. Although the marriage was blessed by the Trenchtown Yardies, it was not greeted as enthusiastically by the Yamazaki family. Kensuke tested the limits of his power and authority by marrying Desdemona and bringing her with him back to Japan. Such was the power of Kensuke Taketo that few dared utter a racial insult either towards his bride or, later, their only child, Kazuyoshi Taketo.

But there was a group from the Shintani family who had reportedly made much of insulting Taketo's wife and child, even going so far as to send teenage thugs out to taunt the boy on his way home from school. Kensuke Taketo took care of this with blood and single-handedly waged war on a Shintani group, killing some 17 men before a formal truce could be declared, all in defense of the honor of his wife and son.

The truce held for more than a decade, and Kensuke Taketo's membership in the Japanese yakuza protected his son's racial status. But truce is always tenuous in the environment of organized crime. As an insurance policy, Kensuke Taketo sent his son to America to attend school. While studying in America, Kaz Taketo received news of the brutal gangland slaying of his father. The long truce had ended.

Taketo dealt with his grief by investing in his students. He unlocked the physical and spiritual insights of aikido and gave his students a warrior's code to live by. With Sonny, Kaz Taketo found a kindred spirit, a young man grappling with the same grief that he had grappled with. He listened with an open heart to Sonny's hopes and fears, and assumed the role of a surrogate father.

Kaz Taketo retired after a productive career as an entrepreneur and martial arts instructor to a picturesque bayside property in Marin. Everything was traditional Japanese style. Taketo embraced Sonny warmly upon his arrival.

"Very good to see you, Taketo Sensei."

"And you too, Sonny. I am sorry about this unfortunate business. We must work to make this right."

They sat in the lotus position around a Japanese table with silk placements, drinking sencha tea, reminiscing and speaking the truth about their lives.

Sonny brought him up to speed, providing the details of Aurora's story, the Black Archon, Nzingha, and the possibility of Akoto's early release. He added, "Aurora is Aaminha's sister."

Taketo was reserved as always. "I see. So, we find ourselves in trying times again. We must stick together as family, as one. Always as one." He took a sip of his tea. "What is your plan?"

"I've got no clear plan. And I'm not sure that we can do this without violence. I've dealt with these kinds of people before." He gritted his teeth "I thought about asking you if you still have contacts in the Japanese underworld. I might need some heavy hitters backing me up."

Taketo shrugged. "I would be reluctant to engage with these people again. It is a path of no return." Taketo folded his hands. "I have spent my entire life running away from my father's legacy. Why would I want my best student to find himself obligated to the Yakuza?"

"I am a man alone in this city, and I am fighting an enemy with unlimited resources."

"You are more powerful than you know. It is possible for a person of extraordinary power and gifts to bring down an organization such as the Black Archon, and end sex trafficking in Oakland. Certainly, this is the logic that Aurora followed. You must act with judgment and within the principles of a warrior. Apply everything that I have taught you. Use your aikido on a larger scale. Do not attack this enemy head on. Use their power against them. This should be the guiding principle of your new life…as a private detective."

Sonny Trueheart looked at the lights coming on along Sir Francis Drake Blvd. and the bay across the boulevard from Taketo's living room window. He allowed himself a moment to meditate on Taketo's words.

Taketo continued, "You have already assembled a capable team. We are all that you will need."

"We? Sensei…I cannot ask…"

Taketo poured more tea. The sencha fukamushi was one of Japan's most popular steamed green teas. Taketo enjoyed its balance of sweetness and bitterness.

"You will have my assistance of course. I am not much longer for this world. Let me give you what I can."

13. The Young Detective

Sonny took the Richmond-San Rafael Bridge back to the East Bay and rode down the 580 East into downtown Oakland's Historic District and enjoyed a late dinner of authentic southern Mexican cuisine at Cosecha Cafe. It was a safe space for him to retreat when he worked OPD. Here, he was outside of his district. Cops rarely frequented the market. It was a heterogeneous space filled with new and aging radicals and community activists.

He drove home and spent the remainder of the evening searching the internet for more financial information of companies affiliated with Black Archon Pharmaceuticals. He slept the sleep of people withdrawing from alcohol, waking often in the middle of the night his body sweating and his heartbeat racing. Whenever he could sleep, he dreamt of the time he first met Aaminha Toure.

***

He could see the boy who lay in a pool of his own blood. His eyes were open but there was no life behind his gaze. He wore a new pair of pleated khakis and sneakers and a short sleeve button down shirt. He sported a fresh haircut. He was only 16 and he was on his way to an interview for a summer job. His mother wailed and moaned and two beat cops held her back as other cops roped off the scene.

The shooter, a young beat cop, sat in the back of Sonny's car, hidden from view by the tinted windows, complaining about the eventuality of having to go on paid administrative leave. Sonny could hear him rambling on and on.

Sonny rode with senior detective Corey Thibadeaux. Thibadeaux, who had been gathering testimony from eyewitnesses, walked towards him, his head hung low.

"Black Lives Matter is gonna be out here in a minute. Everything is going to shit."

"You want me to drive Hamilton out of here? Back to the station house?"

"Yeah. Get that white boy outta here."

Sonny saw a group of protestors mingling with the neighborhood crowd. There was Rita Falcon, leader of the local Black Lives Matter chapter, consoling the mother of the deceased. Her people handed her a megaphone. She stepped up onto a milk crate.

"People of East Oakland, may I have your attention? OPD has taken the life of another one of our children. Look at how they have left him here to bleed out in the streets. OPD is sending us a message, people. And that is a message of fear. But we refuse to live in fear. Say it with me now, WE REFUSE TO LIVE IN FEAR!"

"Where's that goddam ambulance?" Thibadeaux wondered aloud.

Sonny got in the unmarked police car. He listened to Hamilton spew epithets and racial slurs. Sonny said nothing. Nothing could be said. The patrolman would have the backing of the union and the security of qualified immunity. The department would declare the shooting justified. The community would raise a ruckus, but the media would eventually go away, things would pass and all would eventually get back to normal until the next shooting. And then the process would start all over again.

Sonny started the engine and drove towards the station house.

Sonny glanced at Hamilton in the rearview mirror. "How about I grab you a coffee before we hit the station? Calm your nerves."

Patrolman Hamilton nodded. "If you really want to calm my nerves, you'd buy me a drink."

"Can't do it. Internal Affairs is going to have you submit to a piss test as soon as we return to headquarters. Let's stick with coffee, okay? How do you take it?"

"Black. Two sugars."

"Cool." Sonny pulled over and got out of the car and walked to a corner café. They were still in Oakland's Havenscourt neighborhood in East Oakland. Bancroft St. and 66th Ave., only a few blocks away from the shooting and the developing protest. There was a new corner café run by the East Oakland Community Church of Kemet. Proceeds from sales helped to fund the Pre K-8 Umoja School. Books and pamphlets on Kemet and the principles of Ma'at were on sale inside the café. Sonny liked the irony of buying Afrocentric coffee for the racist cop. There was a beautiful sister with wide eyes and high cheek bones behind the counter. She wore a gorgeous kente head wrap or ichafu and looked like African royalty.

"Two coffees," Sonny smiled faintly and pulled out his wallet.

The sister did not return his smile. She went about the business of pouring coffee into two compostable cups. "Cream and sugar over there," she pointed.

The sister rang him up. Sonny paid and put a generous tip in the jar. He turned to put a cream and sugar in his coffee and grabbed a little sugar for the killer cop.

"You OPD?" the sister inquired. She had spotted his gun and his badge as he reached for his wallet.

"Homicide detective."

"Word is that you killed another young Black man down the street?"

"I didn't kill him, sister."

"You work for the people who did. Did you know that boy was a straight 'A' student?" His name was Demetrius Terry. I knew him. I used to be his teacher."

"You're a teacher?"

"Second grade."

"Teaching is a noble profession."

"Being a cop sure isn't."

"Like I said, sister, I didn't kill him."

"You aint gonna go after the man who did kill him though. You all just gonna sweep it under the rug."

"I'm a cop because I want to serve my community."

"Where do you live? Are you even from Oakland?"

"Born and raised. I live right here in the Havenscourt."

"How come I've never seen you up until now?"

"I live on 68th Ave. Between Arthur and Avenal."

"But I've never seen you."

"I've seen you." Sonny smiled.

Again, she did not return the smile.

Sonny walked to the counter and handed her his card. "August Trueheart. But my friends call me Sonny. You've probably seen me plenty times when I'm off duty, riding a red Harley."

"You belong to the Black Dragons motorcycle club?"

"No. I don't belong to anybody."

"You belong to OPD, right?"

"It's my profession. But I'm my own man, sister."

"If you're your own man, why don't you bring your own man self to one of our neighborhood meetings?"

"Meetings?"

"We're tryna to put together a Citizens Committee to oversee the cops, watch the watchers. We put a proposal in front of the mayor. We have a meeting tonight at Allen Temple Baptist church. Everyone is going to be there. Christians, Muslims, Buddhists, Yoruba, atheists, and those of us who practice Kemeticism. We're going to discuss this boy's murder and what we intend to do about it. Drive your red motorcycle on over. Meeting starts at 7pm sharp. Be on time."

"I'll think about that. Thank you for the invite, Sister…"

"Aaminha. Aaminha Toure."

"Nice to meet you Sister Aaminha Toure."

"I hope I'll be able to say the same, Detective August Trueheart."

"My friends call me Sonny."

"I'm not your friend, detective."

"Perhaps that's just a matter of time."

"Perhaps."

"What if, as a friend, I told you that the patrolman I've got in the back of my car is Demetrius Terry's killer? What if I told you that he's been spouting off some racist bullshit? And what if I suggested that you come out with your smartphone and maybe get this on the evening news? I mean, if you don't want to see this go the way all the other shootings go down?"

"So, there's a reason why you stopped in my coffee shop, right?"

"Like I said, I've seen you before in the neighborhood."

"I see." Sis. Aaminha Toure removed her apron and walked from behind the counter with her smartphone.

Sonny departed and walked back to his car. Sis. Toure followed him discreetly. Her camera was on. Sonny wanted to make sure patrolman Hamilton was audible and within view of her camera. Hamilton was still yammering on and on when Sonny opened the back door. He set his coffee on the hood of the car and handed Hamilton his cup. The lid was slightly off and as Sonny handed it to him, it slipped from his hand and spilled on patrolman Hamilton's leg.

Hamilton squealed. He stepped out of the car and screamed in Sonny's face.

"You're just like the rest of these other goddam Blacks! Can't even get my freakin' coffee! Can't even do that right! How did your Black ass make detective anyway? You weren't on the streets any more than a couple of years! Goddam your Black affirmative action ass! Don't any of you people understand? You don't make any sudden movements against an officer of the law! Why don't you goddam people understand that? He made a sudden movement and I shot his Black ass! That's one less that'll wind up on welfare! I did the state of California a goddam solid!"

Hamilton caught Aaminha Toure filming him out of the corner of his eye and made a move towards her. Sonny grabbed Hamilton by the collar and forcibly slammed him head first against the trunk of his car. "Don't ever speak that way to a superior officer. You hear me?"

Hamilton cursed. He was dazed and concussed. Sonny had half a mind to drive off and leave him there on the street.

Hamilton turned and saw that the woman that had been filming him had left. "You see that woman? She got me on camera saying all that shit!"

"Yeah? Better hope it don't wind up on the evening news."

Sonny released his grip on Hamilton and retrieved his coffee where he had set it on the roof of his car. He went over to the driver's side and entered his vehicle, waiting for Hamilton to decide to re-enter the vehicle.

"Was that woman in the coffee shop?"

"No."

"I don't believe you. I'm going to go back and have a look for myself."

"No, you won't. Don't ever come back here, or I'll finish what I started. Understand?"

"You set that up, didn't you?" Hamilton screamed, red-faced and flustered.

"Me? I'm just a dumb ass affirmative action hire. Remember?"

***

The night shift was coming in at the Area 5 precinct house. Sonny ran into two senior detectives, Playe and Bridgewater, in the locker room as he was changing into his jeans, t-shirt, and leather jacket.

"Rough day on the job eh, detective?" Playe queried, a foul white southern grin on his face. Playe and Bridgewater were the last of a generation of cops specifically recruited from the South back when OPD went looking for white boys who knew how to "handle Black folk."

"Hamilton came back kinda roughed up, huh? Got a huge knot on his forehead. They beat him up out there? Or was it you?" Bridgewater asked.

"Nah. He tripped and fell."

"Really? You gonna go with that?" Bridgewater chuckled.

"Go with what?"

Playe and Bridgewater closed in on Sonny in the narrow confines of the locker room. Sonny pulled his service Glock from his shoulder holster and knelt down to withdraw his backup revolver from the ankle holster. Playe and Bridgewater stepped back. Sonny looked innocently down at his hands, his Glock in his left hand, and his backup in his right.

"What?" Sonny queried. "No worries. I aint drawin' down on you two. I can't ride my motorcycle with my guns." And Sonny placed both guns in the messenger bag he carried. He casually put on his leather jacket.

"Cute," Det. Playe laughed uncomfortably.

"If I find out you're the one who roughed up Hamilton…" Bridgewater began, "I'll…"

"You'll what?"

"You'll have to answer to me, detective."

"To both of us," Playe added.

Sonny walked between both men, the sharp edges of his shoulders and elbows making hard contact as he plowed through them on his way to the exit. He opened the door to the locker room and stopped momentarily, looking over his shoulder at Playe and Bridgewater.

"It's not my first day on the job, detectives, so I know for goddam sure that I don't answer to either of you."

Sonny walked to the parking lot, got on his motorcycle and rode off into the night.

At 7pm sharp Sonny Trueheart went to the community meeting at Allen Temple. Sonny wasn't religious, but he respected what they did here. Buying up abandoned properties in the area to prevent them from turning into drug houses. Building senior housing. Offering drug and alcohol counseling.

The event was part meeting and part religious service. Sonny arrived just in time for the greeting of visitors. Black Christians, Muslims and folk like Aaminha looking for spiritual alternatives, all engaged in interfaith dialogue, unified by what was happening in the community. There were representatives of a new organization. They called themselves Black Lives Matter. Sonny could not have agreed more. Black lives did matter.

The choir broke out into a Holy Ghost groove. Christians, dancing in the aisles, throwing up their hands to Jesus. Muslims sitting calmly and giving all respect and honor to the customs of their hosts. A young minister then preached on the violence. How Black-on-Black crime was being used by the media and the right-wing to distract from the issue of cop killings. And then the meeting was opened up for discussion moderated by Sis. Aaminha Toure.

There were young mothers with pictures of their murdered children, weeping and speaking of the circumstances that led to the murders of their children. No details were spared.

The young minister who had opened the meeting called for a closing prayer "in the manner that you are accustomed." She offered herself for any special prayers and a line formed. Sonny joined the line. Sonny asked for the anointing of oil and a special prayer and the young minister pressed her fingers to his forehead. "You're walking on an unpaved path. I see blood on the road in front of you." And with that she snapped his head backward and splashed oil on his forehead in the anointing.

Sonny was in the parking lot, astride his motorcycle, putting on his helmet when Sister Aaminha Toure approached from the sanctuary.

"Thank you for coming, detective."

"I appreciate you inviting me."

"We need someone within OPD to advise us on how to create an effective Citizen's Committee. Would you commit to that?"

"I will."

As he left the church that night, he thought about the commitment he had made and the role he could play for his community. And his memory of the voices of the choir singing warmed his heart.

Soon and very soon
We are going to see the King
Hallelujah, Hallelujah,
We are going to see the King.

14. The Arrangement

Nzginha enjoyed the cool summer breeze and the view of Old Oakland as she sipped a Mango Habanero Margarita from the rooftop bar of Oeste, a popular Afro-Latinx woman-owned restaurant and bar in the heart of the historic neighborhood. She wore a broad-brimmed yellow sun hat, yellow and black leopard print silk-blend Dolce and Gabbana pencil dress, black Tom Ford lock stiletto sandals, and black Ray-Ban Jackie Ohh sunglasses. The sound system played Carlos Santana's meditative composition "Aqua Marine," and Nzingha's thoughts drifted to memories of the clear waters of her Bahamian home. But it was a fleeting moment. Her reverie was interrupted by the heavy footsteps of two men in Florsheims trudging up the steps from the first level of Oeste to the rooftop. She opened the clasp of her clutch bag and gripped a .25 pistol.

The two men who emerged were CIA contractors. Black suits, black ties, reflective sunglasses. Two standard issue white men. Both 6 feet in height. Sculpted biceps, pectorals, and abs displayed by their fitted suits. Nzingha knew them well. Mister Love and Mister Joy. Both approached and stood with their hands clasped behind their backs.

"Good afternoon, Ms. Nzingha," both men said in unison.

"That's Senior Commander Nzingha to you. Good to see you gentlemen. Would you care to join me for a bite and a cocktail?"

"No. Thank you," said Mister Love. "We're just checking in."

"We're on schedule, gentlemen," Nzingha assured them.

"We understand that you've enlisted the help of Sonny Trueheart, is that correct?" Mister Joy asked.

"The disgraced former Oakland police detective," Mister Love added.

"And a drunk," Mister Joy said, taking it further.

"It's my case. I have broad discretion over who I enlist for assistance."

"There are always limits," Mister Love stated the obvious, "when you're working with the agency."

Nzingha cleared her throat. "To be clear, I'm not working *with* the agency. The agency has simply been informed of my activities and, at present, has no issue with my purpose. Is that still the case?"

"It is. We're aware that, given the cooperative relationship between the CIA and the Royal Bahamas Defense Force, you have been allowed to operate on your own terms on a limited basis and for a limited time in this country," Mister Joy stated blandly, as though he had memorized a script.

"So, gentlemen, you've stated the obvious," Nzingha took a sip of her drink. "Let's cut to the chase, shall we? What's the real purpose of your visit?"

Mister Love furrowed his brow. "This man Godbold has suddenly become a person of extreme interest." He pulled a slim envelope from the inside pocket of his black suit jacket and tossed it unceremoniously on the table beside Nzingha's cocktail.

Nzingha opened the envelope. One sheet of paper with black-and-white images of a military compound. Child soldiers in fatigues with Chinese rifles. A short, bespectacled man wearing the uniform of a general, brandishing a knife, and standing over prone bodies. She waved it in the cool breeze. "What's this?"

"Dr. Godbold is now using funds from his illegal enterprises to fund a separatist group in northeastern Nigeria. They are planning a takeover of Boko Haram territory and will build a nation there. Black Archon money is supporting the leader, a General Lucky Ochuko, popularly known as the Rumuekpa Ripper," Mister Love said. "You will receive a formal briefing in due time."

"The prerogatives of your mission have changed, Commander Nzingha. Your original mission involved the rescue of Bahamian women kidnapped and taken into Dr. Godbold's sex trafficking operation. That was all that you were allowed to do. And you were asked to preserve Godbold's organization, The Black Archon. Now, Commander Nzingha, the Black Archon must be destroyed and Dr. Godbold must be terminated," Mister Joy said, matter of factly.

"*Senior* Commander," Nzingha crossed her legs and took another sip of her margarita. "*Senior Commander.* So, the big white money behind Godbold has decided to abandon him?"

Behind their reflective sunglasses, neither Mister Love nor Mister Joy responded directly.

"What happens if Sonny Trueheart gets too close to the big white corporate money and decides to expose them as well?"

"Confine your efforts to the Black criminal involvement," Mister Love advised.

"I see that even crime is segregated in America," Nzingha quipped.

"Do you see the child soldiers in the pictures?" Mister Love asked. "This phenomenon is related to your interest in sex trafficking, is it not? Focus on that."

"So, let me get this straight. I had an agreement with you to operate on my own terms, but now I have to confine myself to the Black criminal underworld. You care about Black child soldiers today and yesterday you cared about women of color being sold into sexual slavery. You now see them as related phenomena. And you care enough about these Black child soldiers, that you now want me to go for the full monty and kill Godbold. But yesterday, you didn't want me to kill Godbold over missing and trafficked Black women. There are too many mixed messages here, gentlemen. Maybe you neither care for Black child soldiers nor women of color being sold into sexual slavery. Perhaps there's another reason…shall we say…*national interest?* Perhaps it's no longer in the national interest for a Black man to become as powerful as Dr. Lucius Godbold?"

"Would you have a problem with that?" Mister Love inquired.

Nzingha shrugged. "RBDF's bargain with the CIA for recognition and protection came with a price. The role you've carved out for us involves Black people killing other Black people. That's all we're doing here. There is no other principle involved in this transaction."

"All you need to know, *Senior Commander*," Mister Joy said, "is that the agency is removing the original restraints of your arrangement."

Nzingha pondered as Santana played his soaring guitar solo for "Aqua Marine." "You want this Rumuekpa Ripper pretty bad, don't you?"

"Do you accept the modifications of the agreement?"

"I do," Nzingha nodded. "But, with a few conditions."

"Name it," Mister Love and Mister Joy spoke in unison.

"Number one: I need you to get someone out of jail in order for me to complete my mission here. Number two: if Sonny Trueheart should step outside of the color line and get close to the big white money, let the chips fall where they may. Big white money has a way of taking care of itself. Big white justice will surely offer a plea deal for greater cooperation. One hand washes the other. Number three: if Sonny and his people should benefit financially or in any other way from this operation, the government must look the other way. Number four: when I'm done, when we've taken down Godbold and the Black Archon, you're going to come and ask me to lead the mission to bring down this…" she waved the paper she had been handed, "…Rumuekpa Ripper. But, I want to do it my way. No conditions, restrictions, or modifications."

"Agreed," Mister Love and Mister Joy once again spoke in unison, "*Senior Commander* Nzingha."

The two men bowed slightly, turned, and departed.

15. Brother Malik

The ring of his smartphone awoke him in the morning. It was Nzingha.

"This is a new phone. How'd you get this number so fast?"

"It's what I do, Detective Trueheart."

"What's up?"

"Your good friend, Malik Akoto is being released early into your custody. I have made all the arrangements. You can pick him up this afternoon."

"You're good."

"You'll never know just how good, Detective Trueheart."

"I mean, I just talked to you about Brother Malik a couple days ago."

"I'll let you in on a secret. I've been working on this for a little while now."

"You knew I'd take the job, didn't you?"

"I wanted to hire you even before Aurora began her story, but I didn't think I could get to you. After Aurora was kidnapped, I knew I could convince you to resurrect your career."

"Were you working behind the scenes to help Aurora gather evidence?"

"Perhaps."

"Can you give me a straight answer?"

"Perhaps."

Sonny took to the streets. People in the neighborhood waved as he went by. Trueheart felt the summer heat and perspired under his helmet. He waved at a group of young women from the neighborhood wearing tank tops and short shorts as they walked back from the nail salon, comparing colorful designs. My people are so beautiful, he thought.

Sonny rode out to the airport where he rented a luxury sedan. He raced out toward the North Bay and crossed the Richmond – San Rafael Bridge and picked up Brother Malik Akoto at San Quentin.

Akoto was a native San Franciscan. Like many of San Francisco's Black population, his family struggled to survive in the midst of aggressive gentrification aided by the forced evictions of the Redevelopment Agency and predatory policing that set the stage for the devaluation of Black properties.

Akoto's mother was a Bahamian who could trace her roots through her mother's line back to the Ashanti clan of Akoto. His father, Emile Baptiste, was from New Orleans, a member of one of the major Mardi Gras Black Indian krewes. They met while Emile was on holiday in Nassau, and Emile brought his love to New Orleans where they lived for a short period of time before migrating westward to escape the conservative and racist politics of the American South. Akoto's mother was a true free spirit and, like so many thousands before, envisioned a fully liberated life on the west coast. Akoto was born in their new home in San Francisco within two years of their relocation.

By his account, Akoto had a blissful childhood until the untimely death of his parents in a tragic car accident when he was 12 years old. Brother Malik was bounced through a series of foster homes and orphanages. Did time as a juvenile offender. Earned degrees in the school of hard knocks. Found a way for himself in the businesses of violence and sex where positions are always available for the underclass.

Tall, lean, and rangy. Malik Akoto had wide and inviting almond-shaped eyes and full lips, resembling the Benin bronze of an Oba.

His hair was burnt red like that of Malcolm X. He looked like a man who was born to lead other men. But he was a bit of a Jekyll and Hyde character.

Malik Akoto was an unrepentant hedonist, a sensualist who would have been at home on the streets of Montmartre in the 1920s, Times Square in the 1970s, or amidst the brothels of Amsterdam. He carried the scent of testosterone and hard liquor. He was a foul-mouthed brawler who haunted seedy bars, pool halls and strip clubs. He was known to lurk in the shadows at upscale sex clubs. He favored a spot on Hegenberger near the Oakland Airport. The Black Bottom. The Black Bottom was a two-story industrial affair amongst the high-priced lofts in Jack London Square with eight themed rooms for participants and voyeurs. Akoto could be found fully clad in skin-tight black leather, and often worked the Cuckold Room. This was the specialty of The Black Bottom Club. The club's regular customers included wealthy European-American couples seeking to fulfill racial fantasies of domination at the hands of dominant Black men and women.

He was also a deeply spiritual man who had studied traditions as wide-ranging as Buddhism and Rastafarianism. He was a student of Shotokan-Ryu Karate before coming to Taketo Sensei's dojo, and had been trained in this system to develop a powerful, single debilitating blow with his fists. He did not fetishize weapons, considering them merely a means to an end, although he favored the nunchaku, popularized by Bruce Lee and was capable with a knife.

The brother had changed. He was 6'3" but he had always been a little lanky and lean, although he was wiry strong and quick on his feet.

Now, after a stretch in prison, he had bulked up substantially.

As a final humiliation the guards made Malik change into his street clothes in front of Sonny. One of the white guards made a comment about Malik's penis. Malik resisted responding. Sonny could not help but notice his musculature. He had the body of a Mike Tyson at his prime. Sonny watched him change from the orange jumpsuit into the polyester performance fabric black suit and purple shirt that he had been wearing when he was arrested. Malik's suit no longer fit his bulk. He was busting at the seams. Even his neck had swollen. His hair now flowed in gorgeous burnt red dreadlocks. He had a long, mangy red beard. He smiled when he saw Sonny Trueheart and the two men embraced.

"It was *you* who got me outta here, brother?"

"It took me some time, but when I saw a way, I took it. But there's a catch."

"Catch?"

"We gotta do a job."

"Did you make a deal with the white devil? Cause if you did, I'd just as soon go back in and finish my sentence."

"Nah. I made a deal with a sister who works with a human rights organization. I think she's from the Bahamas."

"Come again?"

"That's right. Thought about you the minute she walked through my door."

"So, you're looking for an ally."

"One good soldier. Taketo Sensei assures me that you're all that I'll need."

"True. True. I've always loved the old man for his confidence in me but I keep letting him down. Tell me more."

"I'll fill you in later. For now, let's just get you back in stride."

Akoto asked that Sonny first take him to San Francisco. They crossed the Golden Gate Bridge, slicing through the fog and brisk winds in the heavy sedan, and Akoto directed him to the home that his mother and father once owned on Lincoln Way, across the street from Golden Gate Park in the Sunset District.

The Sunset had never been a traditional Black neighborhood. Real estate agents steered Black clients toward the Western Addition, Bayview-Hunter's Point, and sometimes the Hayes Valley. But

Akoto's parents had purchased the two flats on Lincoln Way while the home's previous white owners had been on vacation and the sellers had mistaken the last name Akoto for Japanese.

Sonny slowed the car down to a smooth stop. "Who lives here now?"

Akoto disembarked and looked up at the living room windows in both flats. "Not sure."

Sonny looked out across the busy four lane street at the majestic Blue Gum Eucalyptus and Redwood trees of Golden Gate Park. The two men stood outside under the sun.

"I'm going to get this house back one day," Akoto said. "I just have to get the money together."

"How much do you figure?"

"My parents bought it back in the day for around 50k. Nowadays it's gotta be going for upwards of 1.5 mil I figure."

The two men silently pondered the odds of coming into that much cash.

"One day," Akoto dreamed.

"Do you have some money saved up somewhere?"

"I'm doing good. You want to know what I did to make that money? So yeah, I acted in a couple high end porn flicks and I had a steady gig at a dungeon. I made a little money doing that. But the real money I earned came from rich white couples. White guys wanted to see their wives or woman friends make it with a Black dude. They called me their Black Bull. My best client bought me a condo and a car, so I was able to save a lot of cash. I think I'll be living better than most ex-cons." Akoto laughed, "I wonder what my parole officer is going to say?"

"Your parole officer won't be a problem." Sonny reached into an inside pocket of his motorcycle jacket and handed Akoto an envelope. "Another thing that our Bahamian friend was able to handle."

Akoto opened the envelope and glanced at the photo of his would-be parole officer.

A shady motel room. A hidden camera. A grown man taking advantage of a juvenile offender who couldn't have been much older than sixteen or seventeen. Caught. *In flagrante delicto.*

Akoto smiled. "I get more impressed with this sister with every passing word. Really looking forward to meeting her!"

"She's looking forward to meeting you. Tell me more about these rich white folks you were working for."

"You know, that lady I spoke of who bought my place and my ride... we'd hook up sometimes without her husband knowing. She said she loved me and wanted to leave her husband, give me her money and all that to be with her. The husband found out we were getting together on the side. He beat her and he set me up for it. I'm out on the streets and the cops pull me over and drop a rape charge on me. You shoulda seen how bad he hurt her. They laid that on *me.* Husband, sicko that he was, kept a used condom with my semen from our sessions. Husband thought he had me dead to rights. And then, the wife went behind her husband's back and got me a high-priced lawyer and she gave him a video we'd made of one of our sessions. The lawyer used the video and they had to drop the rape charge because the video showed that it was all consensual and that the husband was in on it, like...'orchestrating' it, my lawyer said. So the DA dropped the rape charge, but they kept the B&E The prosecutor claimed I got angry about the relationship ending and that I came back one night uninvited and broke into their home and destroyed property. The lawyer told me to plead to the B&E and I'd get a reduced sentence. So, I entered a plea and got the minimum of two years with a chance for early parole."

"That was your first time in jail, right?"

"Yeah. I got into a few fights as a foster kid. But nothing that would have landed me a felony. So, I didn't have to suffer under that 3 strikes bullshit. But now that I'm released into your custody, I know the cops are gonna try me. The husband...I mean...he was trying to have me do some serious time, so I know he won't let that slide. This guy...I mean, these folks...they *own* the police Sonny. You know?"

"You've bulked up pretty good inside. Did you continue training?"

"Yeah. Guys in there wanted to study martial arts. I was training Jamaicans and the Muslim brothers. The warden gave me a space and bought some mats so that we could practice.

"And I didn't just train my body. I trained my mind too. I had this spiritual moment, you know? I saw a vision of my deceased mother one night. You know, she was an island woman. From the Bahamas. She said she would come to me from time to time in my dreams.

"The main thing was that I needed to get my life straight. All these brothers were talking to me about God and Haile Selassie and Allah and all this stuff. I wanted to explore my mother's heritage, you know, and find out about her spirituality. She was a Christian and she called her Jesus 'Black Jesus' and she said that Black Jesus was a revolutionary for the people who fought the Roman colonial establishment, that's why they killed him. She said white folks were worshiping 'White Jesus,' the god of money. But you know, we shouldn't have to say that because Jesus really was Black."

"That's real stuff my brother."

"Yeah. Real shit."

"Right."

"Hey, this sister we're working for...I just wanna meet her. I love them island sisters man! I gotta get a haircut and a shave so I can make a good impression!"

The two men laughed.

Akoto continued, "Hey, let's get back to the East Bay. You can tell me more about the case. Maybe you can ask that sister to join us!"

The two men stood and embraced for a moment before entering the car and heading back towards the East Bay.

***

Malik Akoto lived in a 3-story live/work condo on 28th St. and Mandela Parkway in West Oakland owned by a former patron of his Black Bull services. The West End Commons was a community of stand-alone townhomes grouped along five private, gated lanes and connected footpaths that gave the area an urban neighborhood vibe right in the center of an old, industrialized section of the city. Malik had a 1-bedroom unit with high ceilings and windows on the 3rd floor with a great view across the freeway of the Bay and the bridge with a tiny outdoor patio.

Unlike so many thousands of displaced Black San Franciscans, Malik Akoto had landed on his feet. Whatever he had done, it had been enough for someone to gift him prime Oakland real estate. Condos in the West End Commons ranged upward of $600,000.

In the common garage Sonny pulled up at Akoto's command to a vehicle draped in cloth. Akoto removed the cover and beneath was a white Dodge Challenger SXT, an all-wheel drive 3.6-liter V6 muscle car with 303 horsepower, 268 pound-feet of torque, and an 8-speed automatic transmission.

"*Vanishing Point?*" Sonny asked, referring to the 1970s cult film classic that featured the white Dodge Challenger.

"You got it!"

"Another gift from your benefactress?"

"You know it, baby. But the car's in my name. She still holds the deed for the condo." Akoto opened the trunk with a key in a tiny magnetic box mounted to the undercarriage of the car. He lifted the panel for the spare tire and found another key. This was the key to the condo.

Malik instructed Sonny to park the car in an available guest spot and the two men took the elevator up. They rode the elevator up to the 3rd floor and entered Akoto's spacious condo.

Akoto's condo was modern. Spartan. Full of light. The furnishings were African and Caribbean from the rugs to the tablecloths, and there were giant reproductions of paintings in Jacob Lawrence's Toussaint L'Ouverture and the Haitian Revolution series in the living room.

Malik pressed a button on a bank of light switches and the reproduction of Toussaint at Ennery, with the great general riding a white horse and leading the charge, slid to the left, revealing a wall safe. Malik withdrew a laptop, a smartphone, and something that looked like a silver credit card. Sonny could also see a fighting knife and a vintage automatic pistol buried in the back of the safe next to a pair of red oak nunchaku. Akoto then placed the laptop, smartphone, and the credit card on the coffee table as Sonny took a seat on the sofa. He powered up the laptop and smartphone.

Malik pointed to the safe and then the items on the coffee table. "I have loud weapons, and I have quiet weapons. Crypto is my quiet weapon. I buy, sell, and trade off my laptop and smartphone. This thing that looks like a credit card is an advanced cold storage wallet that lets me trade, swap, and store my assets. I can make purchases with it as well. Biometrics enabled. 3-factor authentication. Probably the most secure way for me to store my crypto."

"How much do you hold in crypto?"

Akoto accessed the app for his cold wallet on his smartphone. After going through the authentication process, including facial recognition, a fingerprint scan and an 8-digit code, he slid the phone across the coffee table and Sonny could see values for Bitcoin, Ethereum, and Dogecoin in the neighborhood of 500k in U.S. dollars.

"I got in the game early," Akoto smiled. "I'm going to get out early too, well before the game comes crashing down."

Sonny was immediately impressed. "Sex work sure is profitable."

"No. It isn't. For most, it's just survival work. But I know how to save my money. I know how to hide my shit from the authorities. I connect with most of my clients in sex work over the dark net. I get paid in crypto. It's all adding up. Told you I'm gonna buy back my family's house one day."

"Hmm. You ready to talk about the job?"

"We been talking about the job. Black Archon fam, that's serious business." Akoto pointed to the bulge under Sonny's left armpit where he carried the snub nose revolver, "You're not going to beat them in a shootout. I can tell you that."

"I'm tryna do this without killing."

"I'm with that. I feel you. But if you carry a gun, you're bound to use it. And it's the innocents that get caught in the crossfire. Once the shooting starts, you can never be sure where stray bullets will land. And there will be strays for sure. Bet on that."

"I don't want to, but I don't know if I have an alternative."

"I'm not against a gun in a Black person's hands, as you can see." Akoto pointed to the pistol in the wall safe. "Ida B. Wells once said that every Black home in America needed a Winchester rifle to guarantee justice where the law wouldn't provide. To be Black in America is to be born into violence. But, we must be judicious in how we use it. Because we are limited in number, stealth is our best option. For that, we have to use quiet weapons that we are familiar with." Akoto again pointed to his laptop, smartphone, and the crypto cold wallet.

"What are you talking about?"

Akoto nodded. "Have you been listening to me...my brother?"

"I heard you. I just don't think you understand what we're up against."

"On the contrary. I understand better than you do."

"Do tell."

"It's not like I don't know about the Black Archon, my man. Folks inside have been talking about how they've been shutting down safehouses where they store cash, moving money from the street, moving away from the traditional places where they launder money. You've told me that the Black Archon kidnapped a prominent journalist who was putting together a story about all of these women coming up missing on the streets. Put it *all* together. These folks are *making moves*."

"Making moves?"

Akoto opened a dark net browser on his laptop. "They call this MambaNet." He pulled up a digital marketplace for illicit sex and turned the laptop around in Sonny's direction so that he could see.

Sonny saw a listing of women. Faces of young women. Women identified by their age and ethnicity. Black, Brown, Asian, Pacific Islander, Filipina, Indigenous and white. Most 17 to 25 years of age. Missing women from Oakland for purchase. Values ranging from $25,000 to $250,000 with younger and less experienced women going for the highest rates. Sonny scanned pages and pages of lost faces.

"This is slavery. How is this possible? Why don't the authorities shut this down?"

"It's the darknet. Lots of illegal activity is happening here. Murder for hire. Drug sales. Terrorism. You name it. Law enforcement doesn't have people on the payroll who can hack it. There's probably only a handful of people in this world who have that level of skill. That's why it's been such a safe space for criminal activity."

"It isn't just about the alt right wackos then?"

"Sure, they're on the dark web pursuing their conspiracies and organizing hate. But they're not on MambaNet. That's owned and maintained by the Black Archon."

"Goddam."

"They're bigger than you think they are. Aurora probably figured that out. They created MambaNet a few years back, right after all that shit with you and Papi Elder went down. Back then they began moving all their street operations onto the network. They've got global exposure on MambaNet. They and other affiliated criminal organizations can buy and sell anything here, including underage women of color. It's much bigger than the Oakland street operations you were dealing with when you were a cop. That's why you can't get any real information on the streets. The real action isn't happening on the streets. It's happening on the darknet. Paid for anonymously with crypto. Godbold understands the growth and power of crypto and he's shutting down and laundering any and all lingering cash operations and moving that into crypto."

"I'm studying up about that stuff now, but I've got a lot of catching up to do. I'm tryna put the pieces together."

"All you have to know is that the process of moving from cash to crypto is underway. Somewhere, there's a hoard of cash money that's being transferred to crypto as Godbold shuts down street operations."

"Maybe it *would* be easier if I just kill him."

Malik Akoto understood the full weight of the burden that Sonny carried since killing Papi Elder and those two cops. "Violence is only a half measure. You know that better than anyone."

"What would you consider to be a full measure?"

"Steal the *money*."

16. Afro Samurai

In spite of what he had told Sonny, Kaz Taketo placed calls to several of his Yamazaki and Trenchtown Yardies contacts within the Japanese and Jamaican underworld and inquired about the global reach of the Black Archon, Dr. Godbold, and Seven Daggers. He wanted to make certain that Sonny's attacks on the Black Archon would not violate any agreements with either the Yakuza or the Jamaicans, in effect potentially making Sonny a target for either of those organizations. In response to his inquiries, Taketo received a call and directions to visit contacts at a Japanese bath house and restaurant on the edge of San Francisco's dangerous Tenderloin district.

Taketo drove all the way to the West Oakland BART station, parked, and took the train through the tunnel beneath the Bay into San Francisco, disembarking at San Francisco's Civic Center. He walked five blocks through the Tenderloin and its open-air drug market atmosphere littered with used syringes and shattered glass pipes. Fentanyl addicts slept on the sidewalks that reeked of urine and human fecal matter. Christian worshippers from Glide Memorial Church, doing the real work of the Gospels, formed harm reduction teams that ministered to the addict population, saving lives with nasal spray bottles of Narcan.

Amidst the apocalyptic terrain were funky art and concert venues, independent community theaters and upscale trendy restaurants and bars styled as speakeasies for millennial crowds and the businesses of San Francisco's Little Saigon. Taketo turned the corner onto Eddy St. and came to the Onsen Bath and Restaurant, a Japanese bath house and sake bar that served what San Franciscans called "Japanese tapas," where his contacts waited.

He was immediately greeted outside the door by a stocky man with neck tattoos wearing dark sunglasses and a black suit with the noticeable bulge of a pistol under his left armpit. Taketo noticed that the man was missing the tip of his half pinky finger. Taketo identified himself and the security guard bowed and opened the door. "Your father was a legend," the man said. "Respect."

A beautiful older woman in a long-sleeved floral silk kimono stood in the foyer, her hair styled in one of the traditional nihongami styles, with two wings at the sides of her head curving up and towards the back of her head to form a topknot. She bowed and greeted Kaz Taketo.

"*Irasshaimase*," she said, welcoming him.

"*Dou itashimashite*," Kaz Taketo bowed and followed the hostess as she led him through the empty facility with its black-tiled floors, brick walls, and beautiful hanging paper cranes.

"No customers today?" Taketo asked.

"Your friends have booked a private party."

The hostess led him to the communal bath where two young men soaked naked, enjoying the frothing sauna jets, resplendent in the colorful tattoos that adorned their muscular bodies. One was a representative of the Trenchtown Yardies. The other was a representative of the Yamazaki clan.

"Bunny Ricketts," the dreadlocked Trenchtown Yardies enforcer introduced himself. "Make yourself comfortable, Taketo Sensei. Join us. We will talk and feast afterwards." Taketo admired the wonderful tattoo on his left shoulder of the great Bob Marley smoking a blunt.

"Ren Watanabe," the young Yakuza enforcer introduced himself. "I have great respect for the son of Kensuke Taketo." Ren's full body tattoos depicted koi fish swimming over waterfalls and against the tide. In Japanese legends, the koi fish symbolize good luck, strength, and perseverance.

"Much appreciated. I am grateful for the kindness and generosity that my father's friends have shown me."

"Your mother was special too," Bunny gave a nod to Taketo's Jamaican ancestry. Bunny knew that in spite of the reverence for Kensuke Taketo, the Yakuza would never have fully embraced the half-breed Taketo. "You could have been a leader for Trenchtown Yardies."

"My heart chose another path, but I am deeply appreciative of the respect and deference that I have from both of your families."

The hostess arrived in time to bring three wooden trays of sake flights for each man. In a traditional Sento, or Japanese bath house, neither alcohol nor male customers with tattoos would be allowed. But the Onsen Bath and Restaurant was considered neutral territory and its only requirement was that weapons were not allowed. She set the sake flights around the edge of the bath and then helped Taketo disrobe, taking his clothes and finding a hanger and hook beside the clothes of Bunny and Ren.

Taketo entered the warm, frothy water. The sake flight that was set before him offered Junmai-shu, Ginjo-shu, Daiginjo-shu, Honjozo-shu, and Namazake varieties. Taketo tried the Junmai-shu with its acidic, full-body flavor born of a high percentage of milled rice.

"Shall we talk business, Taketo Sensei?" Ren Watanabe asked.

"Let's."

Bunny Ricketts cut straight to the heart of the matter. "We understand that your people, Sonny Trueheart and dat ragamuffin Malik Akoto, will be going after the Black Archon organization and Dr. Godbold himself. Correct?"

"Yes. That is what we have planned."

"Because of the kidnapped reporter?" Ren asked.

"Yes. Do you know where they are holding her?"

"Godbold is moving her around different safehouse locations," Bunny offered. "But we're not sure where she is at any given moment."

"Sonny's going to do everything in his power to get her back."

"Will violence be involved?" Ren Watanabe inquired.

"We are hoping to minimize casualties."

"Trenchtown Yardies has a neutrality agreement with Dr. Godbold. But his organization may have violated the terms by including captured Jamaican women in his sex-trafficking ring. We are not happy about someone coming into our territory to steal our young women."

"Same," Ren Watanabe offered. "We have no particular business conflicts with Godbold and the Black Archon. However, it would not disturb us in the least if he were to suddenly…disappear."

"So, we have your permission to proceed?"

Bunny and Ren spoke in unison: "Yes."

"That's good to hear, gentlemen. Good to hear."

"What's Sonny's plan?" Ren asked.

"I think we're going to rob a bank," Taketo confessed matter of factly. "I believe that Sonny will decide to rob the Black Archon and then use that money as ransom to secure the return of Aurora Jenkins."

Bunny and Ren looked at one another.

"No one robs banks anymore," Bunny suppressed a laugh. "It's a lost art. But I've got mad respect for this Sonny Trueheart."

"You'll need backup," Ren added. "You're bound to set off an alarm and have the entire Oakland Police Department after you."

"Can you be there, in the shadows, without Sonny knowing? Sonny must never know."

"Sonny will never know that we were around," Ren assured him, "but, whatever moves you make, we'll be watching."

"We'll have your back," Bunny added.

"Do you know where I can find Seven Daggers?" Taketo asked.

Ren smiled. "I'd like a piece of that *ketsu no ana*."

Taketo acknowledged with a smile. The best English approximation of the term that Ren used was "asshole."

"He holds regular meetings at a downtown Oakland restaurant. Suya Broadway. They serve African and Caribbean food," Bunny said. "And I'd like a piece of *dat batty hole* too. We understand that he may be plotting against Godbold. We have noticed that he is engaged in private conversations with the corporate boys who serve on the White Council."

"White Council?"

Bunny took a sip from the fruity Namazake sake, straightened his back, and code switched into the tone and mannerisms of the corporate boardroom. "The Black Archon uses Black faces to front its operations. Dr. Godbold is its current leader in name only. There are two governing boards that Godbold must consult with. One is made up of Oakland's elite Black citizens. Mayor. District Attorney. City Council members. Chief of Police. Business owners. All Black. The other governing board is all-white. There's more money and influence on this board, and because of that, they are silent partners. They don't even have any public affiliations with the pharmaceutical front operations of the Black Archon. They represent a lot of corporate interests that prey on Black communities. Private prisons. Payday lending. Fast food. Liquor. Members of these two boards are segregated officially, although they sometimes mingle at private functions."

"How do we get to the real power, this White Council?"

"You don't," Ren admitted. "If your people go after that white corporate money, you'll either wind up dead or in jail. All of you. But if, as we think, the white money is backing off of Godbold…you will have everyone's blessing to go after *him*."

Bunny relaxed and sank down to his chin in the water. "You can literally go in there and steal everything you want and walk out without so much as a misdemeanor. You can be the *duppy conqueror* and pro'ly even get away with killing Godbold and Seven Daggers.

You know how it is. Da man is *always* good with us killing one another."

"But, if we *insist* on going after the White Council, how do we untangle it?"

"You'll need a black hat computer hacker," Ren offered. "I got a guy for you. He's family. Unaffiliated like you, but he's fam nonetheless."

***

With the information provided to him by Bunny Ricketts and Ren Watanabe, Kaz Taketo arranged a meeting with the computer hacker at Suya Broadway at 6pm. Taketo figured he could kill two birds with one stone, given the urgency of Sonny's mission.

Suya Broadway in downtown Oakland was a spot where Seven Daggers often conducted business and met with his underlings. It was also one of the only places in the Bay Area where he could enjoy his childhood favorite beef suya, a dish his mother made often. Essentially a spicy beef shish kabob, beef suya is a traditional dish of the Hausa people of Nigeria, Cameroon, Niger, Ghana, and the Sudan where thinly sliced beef or ram or chicken is marinated in peanut cake, salt, and vegetable oil and then barbecued and served with dried peppers and onions.

Tonight, Seven Daggers came alone and parked his black Jaguar F-type coupe in a disabled spot in the front of the restaurant. Taketo noticed that a parking cop approached Seven Daggers' car but upon recognizing the license plate, moved on without issuing a ticket. He watched Seven Daggers enter the restaurant and take a table near the rear exit but remain within view of the door looking out onto his car.

Presently Kaz Taketo was joined by a young dreadlocked brother of mixed Jamaican and Japanese ancestry, who had been referred to him by Bunny Ricketts. The brother was young, early 30s, a graduate student at U.C. Berkeley. He reminded Kaz of himself when he was young, particularly given their shared mixed ancestry.

When they spoke on the phone, Taketo asked him to look for his car and join him in the passenger seat. As Taketo saw the young man approach, he unlocked his car door and waited for the young man to enter and get comfortable in the leather seat. The two shook hands.

"Orpheus Anderson," the young brother introduced himself.

"You come highly recommended by our friends in Japan and Jamaica," Kaz Taketo commented. "Have you ever had Nigerian food?"

"No. Can't say that I have."

"Let's conduct our interview over a good meal," Kaz Taketo said, "you okay with this?"

The young man nodded his approval.

Suya Broadway had that safe-for-white-millennials feel that everything now had in Oakland in the midst of gentrification and a white return to the urban centers. Brick wall. Sparse furnishings. Only a handful of tables in the narrow space. Grilled West African and Caribbean street food served by beautiful young sistas with African jewelry and natural hair styles.

Kaz and his new friend sat at a table by the main door and ordered beef suya and ginger beer. Kaz sat so that he could see Seven Daggers over Orpheus' shoulder. As they waited for their food and drinks two men walked into the restaurant, a slightly built gray-haired brother and his younger and substantially bulked up companion. They approached Seven Daggers' table, politely acknowledging him and even bowing. Seven Daggers waved his hand and invited them to sit. They order a couple of beers but nothing to eat. They spoke in hushed tones and Taketo struggled to make it out over the musings of his lunch companion.

Orpheus was in the midst of telling Taketo that he was a computer science grad student working toward his doctorate.

"But I'm struggling right now, and I could use the work."

"How is that possible?"

"I lost my grant. I've been advanced to candidacy and am trying to begin my research for the dissertation. I just need to find another source of funding. What I'm going through is only temporary. I hope."

"My understanding is that you're not in 'the life.' You're a civilian. Although you have family who are...affiliated."

"That's correct. Same as you?"

"My father was a top man. I did not seek to inherit his throne." Taketo smiled. "I like to tell myself that I took a more honorable path."

"Perhaps that is true."

Taketo nodded. "Perhaps. But...here we are."

Kaz Taketo excused himself briefly and walked towards the restroom. As he walked past Seven Daggers' table, the muted chatter of the three men ceased. Taketo feigned stumbling and instinctively Seven Daggers moved to support him. The young cashier gave a tiny scream, providing a brief distraction. Kaz grabbed the edge of the cool metal table where Seven Daggers and his party sat. He deftly attached a listening device under the table. Only 2 inches in length and ¼ inch in height, 32 GB of capacity, noise canceling, and only one key required to start the recording. Taketo had attached a strip of double-sided adhesive to the tiny black recorder and it stuck effortlessly under the table.

"Take care of yourself old man," Seven Daggers said, as Kaz Taketo righted himself. And the young cashier asked, "Are you all right sir?"

Taketo nodded. "I'm fine. Thank you," and walked towards the restroom.

Kaz Taketo made sure that he was alone in the bathroom before he opened an app on his phone that allowed him to listen and record from the tiny device he planted under their table. The muted chatter of the three men continued:

"*...it's draining the resources of the organization...*"

"... *this is his dream...the fulfillment of everything for him...*"

"...*they say that his new country is to be called Godland...*"

"...*aint that somethin'...*"

"...*it's our people he's taking down...*"

"...*with him out of the way we can get back to the real business...*"

"...*reason number one why we take the power back...*"

"...*I'm ready for us to make that move...*"

Taketo returned to his table. The muted chatter ceased again as he walked past. Taketo acknowledged Seven Daggers and thanked him once again. Seven Daggers finished his meal and his companions finished their drinks and, as Taketo took his seat opposite Orpheus, Seven Daggers and his companions rose and departed from the restaurant.

As the food was finally delivered to their table, Orpheus motioned towards the front door and the recently departed trio. "These the guys you're spying on?"

"Yeah. Ever seen either of those men?"

"They're Black Archon."

"How do you know?"

Orpheus pointed to his wrist. "They all have a small tattoo that signifies their membership. Head of a Black Mamba snake."

"What would you say if I was willing to offer you substantial payment for some...computer consulting?

Orpheus nodded. "That's why I'm here."

"Tell me, what do you know about the darknet?"

Orpheus shrugged. "Plenty, I suppose. I see people on the streets out here buying fentanyl from pushers who are getting their supply off the dark net."

"Do you know how to hack into a dark network?"

"Are you talking about hacking MambaNet?"

"Precisely."

"Do you want information, do you want to spy on them, or do you want to destroy the network?"

"All of the above."

"Hypothetically speaking, you'll want someone with expertise in breaking through the kind of firewalls and content filters that the MambaNet team maintain. Someone who could both obtain information and plant spyware and some kind of ransomware in their system and hold MambaNet and the Black Archon hostage." Orpheus stared intently into Taketo's eyes. "It would be expensive."

"How expensive?"

"Mmm. It would have to be enough to disappear into the ether and lay low. Any hacker who would do this would also understand the power and the reach of the Black Archon. They would need enough money to disappear, possibly for years."

"Would *you* do it if it meant hurting the Black Archon?"

"Hypothetically? Yes."

"We have an agreement then." Taketo and Orpheus shook hands and Taketo handed him an envelope of bills from money Sonny had been given by Nzingha. "Just a down payment. There's much more to come. You'll earn a percentage of the take. It could be sizable." He handed Orpheus a burner phone. "I'll call you and I'll introduce you to the rest of the group." Taketo excused himself for a moment so that he could retrieve the listening device he had attached under Seven Daggers' table. As they stepped out onto the street and parted ways, Taketo said, "You're family now."

17. Trans Lives Matter

The notes were the same but the rhythm varied from day to day. Transport from one safehouse to another. Interrogations. Fentanyl injections. The application of Narcan whenever her breathing would slow to the point of death. Hours alone in the dark with excruciatingly painful withdrawal symptoms. A brief respite and revival of her spirit with vegetarian meals and strong cups of coffee. Light banter laced with homophobic and misogynistic remarks from Seven Daggers as he daily inspected her body and mannerisms and expressed disdain.

But there was no discernable order or regular pattern to any of it. She might be moved in the dead of night or the crack of dawn. They might inject her with fentanyl at 8am in the morning or 3pm, only to return within minutes and either inject or apply the nasal spray of Narcan as she teetered toward the edge of death. She might have her biggest meal at midnight or late afternoon. Seven Daggers might lead her to a shower and present her with a change of clothing and leer menacingly at her body in the morning or noon or sunset.

Perhaps they thought this would throw her off and that her disorientation would yield valuable information. But her resolve was strong and in the midst of every fentanyl high, she dreamed the same dream where Trueheart would come to her and assure her that he was out there, working to set her free. "*Hold on,*" he would say to her in the dream. "*Stay strong. Stay alive.*" Sonny Trueheart came to her every day in her dreams, and she used his visits to anchor her in time.

There had been no fentanyl today. The pattern of daily injections was broken, and Aurora shivered and screamed and experienced night sweats in her cell. When Seven Daggers came to bring her meal, she kicked the tray, spilling to-go containers of edamame and vegetable tempura. She stood and faced him, screaming at the top of her lungs, demanding the drug, cursing his name, and throwing wild blows at his torso until he grabbed her by the wrists, handcuffed her, and led her from the room into the police van that they used to move her around the city.

"I'm taking you to a special place," he said as they sat across from one another in the police van. "There's something you didn't write about, and I want you to know everything."

She cursed under her breath. "I *need* the drug." Seven Daggers could see that her pupils were constricted. "Give me the drug or just kill me and get it over with," she whispered.

"Of course." Seven Daggers withdrew the black metal case that contained the syringe. He knelt before her, injected her and waited and watched as her eyes rolled around in her head and her head fell back and her mouth opened and her body shook.

She did not know how many minutes or hours she lay there, experiencing a dreamtime conversation with Sonny Trueheart. Her heartbeat slowed to a stop and then she was jolted back to life by the Narcan spray. She was shaken by firm hands grasping her shoulders, and then led handcuffed out of the van.

Warm summer winds blew the swaying blue gum eucalyptus and Monterey pine trees. Tudor mansions hidden from the street by well-manicured hedges lined the steep hills.

Seven Daggers took Aurora by the hand and led her uphill towards a towering estate with open windows and high exposed wood ceilings. Even as she fought off the effects of the drug, Aurora could tell that they were in the hills of Montclair.

Seven Daggers opened the tall, natural wooden gate and pushed Aurora forward as she stared at the formally dressed revelers in the living room. Seven Daggers led her past a central fountain and along a cobblestone pathway that encircled the perimeter and they arrived at an expansive deck above a deep canyon and a view overlooking the city and the bay.

Aurora saw a crowd encircling three naked dancers illuminated only by a quarter moon. A waiter dressed in a tuxedo and wearing white gloves approached Seven Daggers and Aurora with a tray of champagne. Another waiter approached with hors d'oeuvres. Aurora waived off both as Seven Daggers ate greedily and consumed the champagne in one gulp.

Aurora watched the three naked young women dancing. Their bodies were slick with oil and sweat. They began to touch one another. To kiss and caress. And then they lay down on the deck and began having sex as the crowd watched.

"They're trans," Aurora said.

Seven Daggers wiped his lips with his forearm. "I've brought you to an exclusive party. We provide trans girls for special events. Trutrans, you know? This is the home of Neil Bello. Know who that is?"

"No."

"He's some big banking executive."

"He works for the Black Archon?"

"The Black Archon is controlled by rich white folks like him. Godbold's just a gaffer, you know, a front man."

"You gonna let me speak to Bello?"

"Sure." Seven Daggers grabbed Aurora by the wrist and led her into the spacious house. Through the sliding glass door, past the kitchen with marble countertops, by an island in the center with bar stools for seating and into a living room with vaulted ceilings. Aurora looked up and struggled to keep her balance. Seven Daggers waved to a nondescript, slender, middle-aged man who stood beside his much younger wife, speaking loudly and bragging about investment opportunities that he had shared with his clients. Seven Daggers turned to Aurora. "Behave yourself with Mr. Bello and I'll also let you talk to the girls we have working here."

Neil Bello excused himself from his audience and walked towards Seven Daggers and Aurora. He pointed, "In the kitchen."

They turned and walked together into the kitchen and Aurora leaned against the island.

"Why did you bring her *here*?" Bello asked.

"She's an investigative journalist, yeah? So, before I kill her, I figured I'd let her see everything she was investigating." Seven Daggers cupped Aurora's chin in his left hand. "She aint gonna be alive much longer anyway. I'm fulfilling her last wish. That's all, innit?"

Aurora shook her head free of Seven Daggers' grasp and cleared her throat. "You one of the white folks that really run the show?"

"*White folks?* No." Bello bristled at the term. "But I work for the people who do. And…" Bello pointed to the three young trans women making love in the midst of the circle of onlookers. "…I get a few perks for my efforts."

"I bet you bought this house with Black Archon blood money too. Right?"

"I don't have to answer to you."

Aurora leaned forward and hissed, forcing Bello to step back. "Oh, you'll answer to me. You'll answer for your crimes."

Seven Daggers blocked Aurora's further progress with his left arm. "Now, I told you to behave yourself. Understand? Behave yourself and I'll let you speak to the girls outside."

Bello began retreating back to the living room with his guests. "Get her out of the house. When the girls are finished, I'll send them out to your car. I'll have the waiters send you food and drink. Just get her out of my house."

Seven Daggers acknowledged with a nod and led Aurora from the house back to the van. They waited as waiters brought plates of food and bottles of champagne. Aurora again refused her portion and watched Seven Daggers satisfy himself.

Presently the three young transwomen arrived, knocking on the door of the van, and were let in by Seven Daggers. They were barefoot and dressed in silk kimonos, and body glitter gleamed against their skin. They sat opposite Aurora and Seven Daggers and introduced themselves. Kimi, a Filipinx transwoman originally from Stockton, aged 19. Carla, a Black transwoman and Oakland native, aged 23. And Aimee, a mixed-race Afro-Latinx transwoman from Sacramento, aged 20.

Carla spoke first. "You want to know my story? So yes, it's like everybody else's. I was sexually abused. When I told my mother, she did nothing, and I never felt like I had a safe place. My mother used to say I was born with a sign on my back that said 'just made for sex,' because that's all I knew. She said that me being a woman inside but having the parts of a man would make me special. More valuable than other girls. And so, because there are so few opportunities for us, and because I wanted money for the surgery, I went into sex work. I have done some films, but mainly I visit clients in private residences like this one.

"You have to understand that my mother did not protect me. I loved her. May she rest in peace. But after I left home, I reached out to her and I told her I was doing sex work and that I wanted help and she said to me, 'If you're doing sex work, why haven't you sent me any money?'

"If you want to know how I ended up working for the Black Archon, well...I had a bad date one night. I was in a client's room. He was very soft and sweet to me at first and told me how special I was. And then, after he came, he beat me. He was ashamed of himself for what he desired." She looked away from Aurora and caressed her face. "He broke my jaw. And then the door got kicked open and I saw the badges and all the guns and then I knew I had walked into a raid.

"It was the Black Archon." Carla pointed at Seven Daggers. "It was this man who got me out of jail. Paid my bail and for a good attorney and my medical bills. In return, I work exclusively for them and for the clients that they bring to me. It's very good money and it's safe because I have their protection. No one beats me anymore because they know that they will suffer."

Kimi was the next to speak. "Like my friend here, I've been beaten, I've been abused, I've been molested. So many of us are kicked out of the house and disowned by our families. I was homeless for a while, doing survival sex work, you know. I was not really much of a streetwalker." She pointed to Seven Daggers. "This man literally found me, sleeping on the streets. And he took me in. Cleaned me up. Showed me how to do this work so that I could make real money. I would not be alive without his assistance."

Aimee spoke last. "It's like everybody already said. From the transwomen that I know personally, all of them have engaged in survival sex work, at some point in their lives. There are no other jobs for us out there in this world. My story is a little different though. I come from a super religious family. They tried to 'pray the gay away,'" Aimee said as she performed air quotes with her long fingers and their immaculate neon yellow nails, "and they considered me being a woman inside to be a sin. So, they spoke with the pastor of our church and he came to our house and talked with me and then told my parents that I was possessed by a demon. They tried some kind of ceremony, like an exorcism. But it didn't work, of course. And then, eventually, my parents told me to leave and never come back. They disowned me. Like Kimi, I spent many months on the street, homeless. Doing survival sex work. I found a trick who wanted me to do internet porn and so I did this for a while. I lived in his garage. After a while, he wouldn't let me leave his garage. Had me chained to a post. He started making me do more extreme stuff on camera." She shrugged. "I guess the Black Archon found out about me. They took care of this guy who was holding me as his sex slave. Seven Daggers here messed him up real good. And now, like Carla and Kimi, I work only for the Black Archon. They don't hurt me. They don't abuse me or chain me up at night. I have their protection, and I have a real family now with these girls and others. So yeah, I have a much better life now with the Black Archon than I ever had before."

Seven Daggers rose, prompting Carla, Kimi, and Aimee to rise and bow slightly to him. Aimee came forward and embraced him, and, as Seven Daggers leaned forward to receive her, she kissed him on the cheek. Seven Daggers waved as the three departed and then sat across from Aurora.

"We keep going over this territory…" Aurora said, "the Black Archon is the champion of all oppressed women. It rescues women from predators and exploiters and provides them with protection and opportunities for a clean living. Right?"

"That's the story you should have written, innit?"

"The story that I wrote should have addressed brainwashing and the culture of fear created by the Black Archon."

Seven Daggers' laughter rang throughout the confined space within the van. He pounded on the sides, prompting the driver to start it up and drive to the next safe house.

Power to the People!
A Podcast for the People
Broadcasting from the Lower Bottoms of West Oakland
Hosted by Aurora Jenkins

Transcript of Power to the People! Episode 74

It's Aurora Jenkins, your Momma, your Auntie, your Big Sister, your Play Cousin! Your Friendly Neighborhood Queer Black Feminist activist, investigative community reporter, and columnist. I want to focus our attention today on the story of Juliana Adams. Juliana was a 16-year-old student at Skyline High School when she was reported missing. That was two years ago. Juliana Adams has recently been found. We want to celebrate that, we want to celebrate that Juliana is still alive. But we have to draw attention to what happened to her and how the system treats Black women. It turns out Juliana was arrested several times under false names for sex work by the Oakland Police Department. She faced minor prison sentences and fines as a sex worker. She is now facing significant prison time for murdering her captor and pimp in self-defense. Keep in mind that she is a victim of the larger crime of sex trafficking. It probably doesn't surprise anyone in this audience that Black women represent a significant majority of women who face some form of incarceration as a direct result of their status as victims of sex trafficking.

We have to use this podcast to change the law and put pressure on local authorities to provide assistance rather than incarceration.

Say her name. Juliana Adams. Wasn't her so-called "crime" an act of resistance, and an attempt to escape her victimization? She has been effectively criminalized simply for resisting and existing.

18. Blues and Bruise

At night Sonny rode into the Lower Bottoms in West Oakland to Johnnie's Rocket Room, a known Papi Elder money laundering spot back in the day, strategically located near the freeway, the port, the West Oakland BART station, and Oakland's Main Post Office.

Johnnie's used to be the place to go and find out everything going down on the streets of Oakland. In a tiny underground room in the bowels of this kitschy corner blues bar —bearing the legend of a Black cowboy riding on top of a flying saucer— all the weed, coke and meth cash was counted and then dispersed throughout the city in the early days of the Black Archon when Papi Elder was king. It was no secret that many a crooked cop who worked West Oakland used to collect payoffs there. If you wanted to know anything about anything in Oakland, you had to be here. But rumor on the streets was that the Black Archon had been moving money out of the traditional spots. The order of things was changing. The old friends were no longer required.

A Mr. Johnnie Boudreaux ran the operation. More than just a bag man, Boudreaux had long been West Oakland's Black conservative voice from the hood, a man who'd already twice run for political office in the city with the promise of being, according to him, the only man who could reverse the ravages of the American welfare state and the radical, progressive agenda that had held Blacks back since slavery.

At the behest of the Black Archon, Boudreaux had his people working against Occupy and the 99% Movement during the Great Recession. Inciting riots and violence. Posing as anarchists. Dragging down the good name of the movement. But, even as effective as he had been, there were rumors that Boudreaux had been abandoned by his friends in the Black Archon.

As for the blues music scene at Johnnie's, Oakland had a ton of great blues artists. But it was nothing like in the glory days of the '50s on the 7th St. Corridor. Or so the old-timers said. Legends like Lowell Fulson, Sugar Pie DeSanto, and Saunders King. There was a local band Sonny had never heard of on the bandstand. He waited on his motorcycle through the last of their set. Tonight, the band had the crowd roaring with Robert Cray's "Smoking Gun." The band kept it funky and let the bass rumble down. The guitar player was in the zone, manipulating the feedback from his amp and wailing with a buttery smooth vibrato.

As the band finished its last number, Sonny waited for the crowd to disperse and the band to pack up their matte black van. He waited until only Boudreaux and the bartender, Earl Dukes remained.

Boudreaux was a burly, bowlegged, and balding brother about 50 in a fine 4-button pin-striped tailored suit and Italian leather shoes wearing a gleaming gold Rolex and monogrammed cufflinks. His grandfathers would have called him a creole. He dressed like a Black Pentecostal preacher with a brass handle and tipped cane. In spite of Boudreaux's importance in the street operations of the Black Archon, none of the usual heavies were present. This may have been a further sign of rumors that the Black Archon was closing down its street operations.

Boudreaux wasn't happy to see Sonny Trueheart walk through the door and take a seat at his bar.

Trueheart stared at the array of bottles behind the bar and ordered a Coke. "Well...look who's back from the old days!" Boudreaux grinned. "Sure, you don't want a real drink, detective?"

There was a moment of profound silence. You could hear the BART train rolling across the elevated tracks outside and down through the tube beneath the bay and into San Francisco.

Boudreaux looked Sonny hard in the eyes and the look that came back to him was not one that he remembered. Boudreaux thought he seemed different. Sonny was no longer a cop. And now, he was no longer a broken-hearted drunk. He looked like a man with a purpose.

Maintaining his stare at Boudreaux, Sonny pulled up his dashiki and drew his revolver. The polished blued steel cylinder gleamed under the bar lights. "I'm here about the kidnapping of a journalist."

Boudreaux stuttered. "You were a hella good detective, Sonny Trueheart. What you been up to?"

"Spare me the pleasantries, Boudreaux. Aurora Jenkins. Know her?"

"Sure. I've heard of her." Boudreaux shrugged. "But, what's she got to do with me?"

Sonny maintained his stare.

"Okay. W… w… well…how about we talk this out like civilized men?" Boudreaux stuttered.

"Just talk, Boudreaux!"

"You h…h… hungry?" Boudreaux inquired.

On cue, the bartender, Earl Dukes, a disabled Afghan war veteran who'd experienced massive hearing loss and a consequent loss of equilibrium fighting for a country that never fought for him, shakily set a generous basket of just barely warm chicken wings on the bar. Dukes handed Boudreaux a shot of whiskey. Boudreaux raised his whiskey in a glass marred by dishwater spots. Sonny could see Boudreaux's hand shaking as he raised the glass to his lips. Dukes kept his head down and went back to cleaning.

Boudreaux whined. "You kill me, you aint got no assurance they return her to you." He took the whiskey down hard. That was his shot of courage. "You know me. I don't want to start no trouble. I just want to live to see another day. Those are the facts, as far as I see them." Boudreaux sipped at his glass of whiskey again, this time with his pinky extended so that you could glimpse the diamond ring on that finger.

"You're no longer important to the Black Archon. So, let's get down to it. What do you know?"

"You caint do this, you know. You used to be a cop. A good cop. You used to try to do good for the people in this city. They call you the People's Detective in the papers. Cause that's what you are."

"I aint a cop no more."

"Really? Y...y...you really gonna kill ol' Boudreaux? "You're just jawsin' me, right? You got hella funnies today, Sonny."

Sonny reached across the bar, over the basket of chicken wings, grabbing Boudreaux by the collar. "I'm finna ask you a few questions. You're finna to give me straight answers. If you lie to me, I'll know it, and I'll do much worse than kill you."

"If I tell you anything, *they'll* kill me." Boudreaux's knees sagged. "Look, it's bigger than Papi Elder ever used to be. It's bigger."

"Do tell."

"Word is the woman ran afoul of folks at the highest level."

"Know where they're holding her?"

"Hell if I know."

"Got a name?"

"Yeah, sure. I mean...maybe."

"Spit it out." It was like Boudreaux was stalling for time, but there would be no bell to sound the end of the round and the retreat to neutral corners.

"s...sss...Seven Daggers."

"Whose that?" Sonny feigned ignorance.

"Top boy in the organization. Replaced Papi Elder. He shoulda been there that night you shot them cops and killed Papi. But he wasn't and he inherited the throne. He's more respected by the top boys in the Black Archon than Papi ever was. This one aint no small-time pimp or drug dealer. He's trained. He's ... tactical. Organized. Smart dude." Boudreaux pointed to his head. "And big and strong too. Ruthless. Committed. You caint take him down like you did Papi."

"I'll be the judge of that."

"You caint beat everybody Sonny. Good as you might be or *might have been*, you caint beat everybody."

"Watch me."

Boudreaux remained silent for a minute, lowering his gaze. "You know, I used to wash money for the Black Archon, but we on the way out. We aint gonna be a part of their operation anymore. Or haven't you heard? The Black Archon is pulling money off the streets of Oakland and into this internet thing they runnin' now."

"MambaNet?"

"Yeah. That's it."

"Take me downstairs, where you keep the money. Let's go. Now."

Sonny knew there was a trap door in the back office that led down to a subterranean storage space that Boudreaux had turned into a secret vault.

Sonny forced Boudreaux back into his office, where Boudreaux promptly opened the trap door. Dukes kept about his business. Just a veteran, trying to get his job on. He had nothing to do with the money laundering operation Boudreaux had been running for decades. Boudreaux descended the stairs first. Sonny ordered him to turn on the lights.

In the tight space, three walls were covered by computer screens and television monitors. Baseball games. Horse racing around the world. Live streams of Texas Hold 'Em Poker. International stock market and crypto activity. Machines for counting money on a raised work table with two stools in the center of the room. There was a tall safe against the wall behind the only desk in the room.

Sonny forced Boudreaux into a chair.

Sonny waved at the office safe with his revolver. "Open it."

"There aint much more Archon money in that safe, Sonny... I mean, Detective Trueheart. Aint no need of you strippin' me. Told you they taking all this street cash and moving it to MambaNet and crypto currency. I'm telling you the honest to God's truth."

Sonny pulled the hammer back on his revolver.

Boudreaux dropped from the chair to his knees and crawled toward the safe. He stood up, leaned against the safe, and his hands, slick with sweat, trembled as he tried to turn the dial.

Not much money indeed! Sonny inspected the opened safe and thumbed through stacks of bills in boxes on five shelves. Nearly a good hundred and fifty grand, but according to the usual Black Archon standards, this was little more than petty cash. But what also interested Sonny was a ledger Boudreaux kept of financial transactions and laundered money and envelopes addressed to departments in the Oakland city government.

"I aint got much money. I done told you," Boudreaux affirmed.

"Yeah. You done told me." Sonny lowered the hammer and holstered his weapon. He waved the ledger in Boudreaux's face. "What's this?"

"Ledger."

Sonny opened the book. A couple of old photographs fell from between the pages. Sonny bent down to gather them. "What are these?"

"Old pictures."

Sonny flipped through the pages of the ledger. "I see some familiar names in the ledger. Are these payoffs?"

Boudreaux shrugged. "Man, they gonna kill me if that gets out." He tapped his head with his index finger. "I'm gettin' too old to keep it all in my head."

Sonny glanced at the photographs. They were drugstore printouts of smartphone pictures of street signs and monuments and stone pillars marking the entrances to neighborhoods in the Oakland hills. "What you got here, Boudreaux?"

"I like to study history. It's all 'round us. It's on the street names and the statues and stuff."

"What's all around us? What are you talking about?"

"The history of the city, man. The old, ugly history of the city."

Sonny was confused. "Okay. Whatever you say."

Boudreaux tried to explain. "You know that Jack London was a white supremacist, right?"

"Yeah. He hated the Chinese, right?"

"Right. So why do they still have a place called Jack London Square? And it aint too far from Chinatown. Why? Ought to name it after Bobby Seale."

"Okay. Got it. So, you have an interest in local history. Cool. Why is this stuff in the ledger?"

Boudreaux grinned. "If you gonna take it, look it up, man. Look up Duncan McDuffie who created the Claremont neighborhood or Joseph and John Le Conte in Berkeley. Look it up. That old, ugly history is all around us, everywhere."

"Appreciate the history lesson, Boudreaux. Now, let's get back to the matter at hand. Where they keeping the rest of the money?"

"With the white folks, of course," Boudreaux grinned. "They keep everything now in the California American Bank vault in the Black Archon Center. You know, that's they headquarters man. The big man lives there too. Word is they pulling it all together and turning it into crypto for some expansion project."

"What do you mean? The Black Archon already owns everything. The chiva, the bo, thizzies, cream, and now the fentanyl and the meth. Legitimate and illegitimate business. Marijuana. Banks. Counterfeiting. Prostitution. You name it. Expansion? Where?"

"…overseas man…overseas…"

"Sexual slavery overseas? Is the Black Archon kidnapping these young women off the streets of Oakland and selling them overseas?"

"No, ... yes...no...yes." Boudreaux lowered his head. "Look, I don't know no specifics."

"Tell me more."

"They call it *The Operation*. Remember *The French Connection*? Remember that movie? Well, it's like that, but only in Africa."

"Who's running the Black Archon now that Papi Elder is dead?"

"Papi Elder never ran the Black Archon. He was just the face of the Archon on the streets. You don't wanna know...you don't wanna go up that far. They'll kill me just for speaking his name."

Sonny reached for his revolver. "Who?"

"Dr. Lucius Godbold. Ever heard of him?"

"No. Should I?" Sonny lied.

"One never hears of the Devil until it's too late."

Sonny kicked the safe. "How much you figure is being stored in the California American Bank safe?"

"Whole lots of money, man. Gotta be millions. But it's Archon money. You take that,...and we all dead. You can't strip that place no how, detective."

"Why do you say that? I didn't say anything about robbing a bank."

Boudreaux smiled. "I can see that idea rattling around in your head, man. But that might be the most secure vault in all of northern California. They say there's 10 levels of security. Magnetic and seismic alarms. All of that. No way you could ever pull that off."

"Let me be the judge of that."

"Man, what's happened to you? You used to be a straight-laced cop. You goin' bad now?"

"Hear me. I'm finna find Aurora Jenkins and then I'm finna find out what's happening to all these beautiful sisters disappearing off our streets and then I'm a deal with this Godbold and his boy Seven Daggers and rid this city of the Black Archon. By any means necessary."

"Over a journalist? Man, just move on!"

"She is the younger sister of Aaminha Toure. Remember her?"

"Yeah. I remember her. That was your big case. I remember her. So…it's the principle of the thing?"

"Yeah. It's the principle of the thing."

Boudreaux shook his head. "Aint no principles involved here man. You wanna beat the Archon, you're going to have to become somebody that you aint never been, aint never been prepared to be. In order to beat the devil, you're going to have to be a devil yourself. And there won't be no coming back."

"Thanks for the advice. Now, here's some advice for you. Bag up the cash and the ledger for me and run. Get yourself and your people tucked off…now."

***

Within minutes of Sonny's departure, Seven Daggers made his appearance at Johnnie's Rocket Room. Dukes offered him the uneaten basket of chicken wings and a shot of rum while he sat at the bar in conversation with Johnnie Boudreaux.

"What does he know?"

"He knows about the sex trafficking. He knows about MambaNet. But he doesn't know the names of all the players. He doesn't know about the white folks on the council."

"Did he take the money?"

"Yeah. Although I aint sure why you'd want to…"

Seven Daggers patted Boudreaux on the forearm. "Leverage. He's our leverage, fam. We should fund his efforts, particularly if it will pay dividends in the future. Understood?"

Boudreaux nodded. "Did you know that Aurora Jenkins was the sister of Aaminha Toure?"

Seven Daggers put a finger to his lips and whispered, "Hush." He reached for a chicken wing. "Did he take the ledger."

"Yeah. Not sure why you want him to have all that information either."

"Rest easy, my friend. We have a master plan. The ledger links your street operation to the good doctor."

"But it implicates me too." Boudreaux poked himself in the chest.

Seven Daggers leaned forward. "He's not interested in you, Boudreaux. He wants the big man. We're just helping him put together the pieces and fill in the gaps from Aurora's story. And remember, everything you're doing now buys you a seat on the new council I'll be putting together."

"You really think we're gonna need to break free of Dr. Godbold?"

Seven Daggers crudely wiped the excess hot sauce from his lips with the back of his giant hand. "Most definitely, fam. It's gonna have to go down that way, innit?"

***

When Seven Daggers departed, Earl Dukes approached his boss and asked, "You didn't tell him about everything you told Trueheart, now did you?"

Boudreaux wiped his brow. "Our survival rests on the shoulders of that drunk. Sonny's gonna rob Godbold's bank and then, he's gonna have to kill Godbold *and* Seven Daggers, and I gave him a way to get to the white folks after that. If he does all of that, we'll be free of everybody."

19. Raising the Dead

On the way home, Sonny bought a half pint of whiskey at a liquor store around the corner. Looking at all of those bottles behind the bar at Johnnie's Rocket Room had filled his mind with longing. He bought a bunch of cut roses from an elderly Latina sister who was packing up her flower stand. He resisted the temptation to open the bottle and begin drinking. Instead, upon arriving home, he put Christian Scott aTunde Adjuah's *Anthem* album on the turntable and listened to the opening composition "Litany Against Fear" and counted the cash. Almost 150k from Johnnie's Rocket Room. Mostly Franklins and Grants.

He carefully went through Boudreaux's ledger that he had stashed in his saddle bags. Of the host of documents that Sonny carried out of Johnnie's Rocket Room, the most important was the ledger and correspondence tucked within its pages marked "Official" with City of Oakland and Alameda county seals. Oddly sensitive papers to leave around in an underground safe under a blues joint in West Oakland. It was almost as if someone wanted him to see this.

Only the names of the Black members of the Council were in the ledger. Evidence of the criminality behind Dr. Godbold's "benevolence," confirming all of Aurora's investigative work. The Mayor. District Attorney. Chief of Police. Oakland Superintendent of Schools. Black business leaders. A megachurch pastor whose members marshaled foot soldiers every election season. The ledger not only confirmed their control and revenue drawn from illicit operations from drugs to sex trafficking, but it also paid testimony to the rumored transformation of the organization from cash to cryptocurrency and the advent of MambaNet.

This was an enormous criminal organization, perhaps not as large as the present-day Mexican cartels or Chinese or Italian or Irish or Russian mafia. But they had shipping, small banks, construction, cannabis, local media, and local police. These people were involved at every level, from the streets to the Chamber of Commerce and the office of the Mayor and City Council. Sonny had no beef with Black power. Lord knows, he thought it was long overdue. But any Black power in Oakland had to be fully accountable to the people and needed to be in the hands of the right people, chosen by the community. How many generations of failed Black leadership had Oakland already endured? It was long past time for a reckoning. What Oakland needed was a real Black democracy.

The real problem was that, in the ledger, all roads led to Dr. Lucius Godbold and a corrupt Black elite. The data went no farther.

Sonny knew that it had been far too easy to shake down Boudreaux and obtain the ledger. He had been practically spoonfed enough information for indictments. Someone wanted him to see a ledger that isolated only the names of members of the Black Council.

Sonny paced around his home office, looking over the names of those he believed were members of the White Council that he had written on poster board. All roads logically led to a higher ground of invisible white billionaire corporate tycoons who were playing their game of Monopoly on the streets of Oakland. And with each passing day, Sonny was identifying patterns in the data available online, including a set of three shell companies used for payments to formation agents that also appeared on import/export databases.

He was getting close, asking the right questions. But he needed a break, a whistleblower or another piece of hard data to confirm and clarify. Sometimes the job required a little luck.

He looked at the photographs of street signs and monuments that Boudreaux tucked in the pages of the ledger. What was Boudreaux trying to tell him?

He then went to his laptop and searched for street signs, monuments, and statues of the people Boudreaux had mentioned,

McDuffie and the LeConte brothers. They were all noted California environmentalists, but McDuffie was involved in racist zoning laws and the LeConte brothers built weapons for the Confederacy and opposed the end of slavery.

Sonny had an idea. He paid for a membership to a website that helped people search for public records of their ancestors. He entered the names of people he suspected were on the White Council of the Black Archon. He again worked through the night and well into twilight until his legs were numb from sitting.

When he had finished, he got up and wrote notes on the poster board sheets on the walls of his office. He walked around his house and opened the bottle of whiskey in the kitchen and put it on the nightstand beside his bed. He could smell the liquor wafting in the room. He stared at the bottle. He raised his bedroom window and poured the contents out onto the grass. He pulled two of the best roses that he had bought and put them in the empty bottle. He sat on his bed, looking at the flowers and meditating. His heart rate steadied and his mind cleared. When he later fell fast asleep, he dreamt of the first and only time he made love to Aaminha Toure.

20. Sexual Healing

Sonny dreamt of his first date with Aaminha Toure. It happened one mid-September night after a planning meeting for the community-police relations board. It had been a lively meeting, made perhaps even more lively by Sonny's presence and his attempts at answering questions from the community.

"If you're such a conscious brother, how do you square that with being a cop?"

"Do you face any discrimination in the workplace?"

"Why are so many Black cops unwilling to call out all of these racist white cops?"

"Does the code of blue supersede being a Black man in America?"

Sonny did his level best to answer all of the questions directed at him in the wake of several recent police killings in East Oakland, but they were right to question him. What was he doing working for an organization with a profoundly racist history? He ran it all down with Aaminha as they walked to his motorcycle.

"Pretty rough in there," she said. "But they need to build trust with you. So, you have to keep coming. Let them see that you're for real."

"They asked all the right questions. Why am I a cop? The real answer is that it's the family business. My father was a licensed private investigator. My grandfather did the same work but they didn't allow a Black man to get a license in the South during the height of segregation. He couldn't call it 'detective work,' it was all unofficial…but he 'fixed' things for folks. Sometimes that involved getting into some pretty dangerous situations with white folks."

"Did either of them tell you any stories about their work?"

"Yeah, I've got plenty stories from both of them. My grandfather, his name was Mohawk Baronet, told me this one story about a case he worked on in Louisiana. He had been tasked with rescuing the grandson of a prominent church pastor from a lynching. The young man had been accepted to Xavier University and was destined for greater things. The lynching party came after him on a rape allegation. Of course, the real motivation was his bright future. My grandfather had a couple handguns, a rifle and his courage. He snuck up on a lynching party of thirty or so angry white folks. Not just men in hoods, but wives and children gathered under burning crosses at night dragging a badly beaten young man from a truck bed to the tree and lowering the noose around his neck. They stripped him naked and were preparing to cut off his penis and vivisect him. My grandfather set fire to the surrounding woods in order to stop it. Came into the confusion firing shots at the scattering crowd. Said he wasn't sure who he hit and that he didn't care. Managed to rescue the young man and get him back to his people. He knew that if those ofays ever found out he had started that fire and shot at them and rescued that young man that they'd come after him too. So, he put his young wife, my grandmother, in the car and they decided to start their lives over. In California my grandfather changed his name to 'Trueheart.' He kept doing the same kind of work, 'fixing' things for people in the community."

"Sounds like you come from a lineage of heroes."

Sonny shrugged. "My grandfather simply did the right thing. He was the biggest and baddest man in his community and people relied on him. He often had to take on white people and long odds. But he always believed in doing the right thing."

"Are you going to do the right thing?"

Sonny stopped as they came up to his motorcycle. He looked into Aaminha's gorgeous almond shaped eyes. She was so incredibly beautiful. High cheekbones. An enticing smile that reminded him of pictures he had seen of Dahomean royalty. She sparkled. "I'll do right by you," he said and then he kissed her.

"And I'll do right by you too," she replied. "So, I guess we're a thing now, huh?" And they laughed, hugged, and kissed again.

Aaminha was willing to ride on the back seat of his motorcycle and to wear the helmet he had purchased specifically for her. She removed her ichafu and shook her tiny coil afro. Sonny was pleased to see that the helmet fit comfortably. He took her all the way across the city to the Lake Merritt area and they ate at Café Romanat and enjoyed Ethiopian cuisine. Gomen. Kik Alicha. Misir Wat. Mushroom Tibs. Sonny drank honey wine and Aaminha enjoyed a flaxseed smoothie. She spoke with him about plant-based medicines and how you had to return the body to homeostasis. She said she was studying nutrition and acupuncture. She used medicinal marijuana to help her with anxiety and insomnia. She practiced yoga, meditated, and took edibles at night before sleeping and sometimes took a little CBD before these community meetings to relax her mind and nerves. She said her ultimate dream was to open a wellness clinic in East Oakland.

They ate and talked until closing. As the night developed, their trust blossomed and she told tales of her sexual exploits, her bisexuality, and secret trysts with other sisters and brothers in the Church of Kemet. Sonny confided to her about the difficulties of finding someone to love as a cop and the dark places he had gone for sex.

He brought her to his house. They moved from his couch to his bedroom and sat illuminated by the colorful shapes swirling in a lava lamp on his nightstand. He played a Coltrane and Johnny Hartman record, they smoked herb, undressed and began to touch.

There are fleeting moments of bliss in this life. When the moment comes, you have to welcome it in.

They communicated in the stillness through touch. There was only the sound of their deep breathing and the connection of their bodies. In the dark she understood that he wanted to know her and to love her and she trusted him deep into the long hours of the night.

He caressed her thighs, grabbing the edge of the boy-shorts she wore, pulling them down to her ankles so she could kick them off. He felt the slick sweat on her thighs and trailed his hands up to the thick, moist hair. He was alternately rough and soft with her, gripping his huge hands on her thighs as his soft lips and tongue trailed down the length of her body until he tasted her sweetness. She responded to his deliberate unfolding of her pleasure, as he slowly kissed and licked from her outer labia to her clitoris, one layer after the other until she was completely his. He pulled her t-shirt up and over her head with his long reach. He grabbed her breasts and sensed the developing hardness of her nipples responding to his rough play. She placed her hand at the back of his head and kissed him, forcing her lips against his, holding him tight, wrapping her legs around his torso, and began grinding her hips, bucking and undulating, as she felt his erection entering her, bringing waves of shuddering pleasure in steady succession.

He closed his eyes and moaned, his body joined to hers, feeling the rush of becoming more than he had been before, as if his essence was floating and joining hers, breaking and reforming. And as they rose to the upper room of consciousness on the herb, his bedroom became filled with florescent swirls, glowing faintly, and he thrust his hands forward to touch the swirling colors as they formed around the shape of her body that frolicked in a forest of light and she enveloped him with her warm caresses and he sucked her hard brown nipples, sensing the softness and suppleness of her skin and her firm grasp, heard her hushed and excited tones, tasted sweet apricots on her tongue, and caressed her buttocks as she massaged his shoulders and bucked to the rhythm of his strokes as they became fully intertwined and his body grew higher than the highest heights of the swirling forest of lights until his head scraped the night skies, the stars burned in his eyes and they cried, becoming aware of everything that was living and the rhythm and pulse of life and that here, in that sacred sweet moment life, was eternal and infinite, and then their hearts exploded together into a million bits of stardust.

21. Journalist, Councilman, and Traitor

Valerie Ogwu, City Politics editor for the *Oakland Tribune,* was a classic workaholic. Unmarried. No children. Most of her family still lived in Nigeria. Valerie came to America as an international exchange student. Earned a Bachelor's degree in Journalism at Howard University. Obtained her Master's in Communications at U.C. Berkeley. Became a citizen. Worked her way up the food chain and came to prominence with her stories about the Oakland Police Department's Riders scandal.

Kaz Taketo was relaxing on her comfortable suede sofa in her cute little apartment in North Berkeley when Valerie entered. She was not surprised to see him sitting there, nor to see her cat laid out luxuriously beside him.

"I figured it was a matter of time until they sent somebody," she said. Setting down her bag and joining him in the living room. She poured a glass of single malt Scotch neat and took a healthy swig.

"They?"

"The Black Archon. Isn't that who you represent?"

"No. I represent the man who is going to take down the Black Archon and liberate the city of Oakland. My name is Kaz Taketo. I work for Sonny Trueheart. The People's Detective." Taketo rose and extended a hand to Ms. Ogwu who received it suspiciously.

Taketo explained, "Ms. Ogwu, you received a draft of a story from Aurora Jenkins. Because you received that story, members of the Black Archon will ultimately seek to remove you, fearing that you might publish whatever you have. I'm here to urge you to leave the country immediately. Are we clear? It is a life and death situation for you. Do you understand?"

"I understand, but I've never run from anyone and I've been threatened plenty of times."

Taketo spoke clearly and forcefully. He properly enunciated all of his words. "It would be *most prudent* in this case to leave. We should have completed the bulk of our work within the next two weeks. It will then be safe to return."

"Yes." Valerie rose and began to walk towards her study. "I'm just going to the study. I'll bring you everything that she gave me. And then I'll pack."

"Wise decision Ms. Ogwu. Wise decision."

Valerie Ogwu retreated to her study and retrieved the backpack of materials Aurora had left with her. She brought the backpack out to the living room and waited patiently as Taketo went through it.

He rifled through the photocopies of her notes. There was also a portable flash drive containing the final draft. "Looks good," Taketo said.

Valerie went into her bedroom and momentarily sat shaking on the edge of her bed. "I hope you are who you say you are Mister Taketo."

"I am."

"If you're not, you needn't have gone to all this trouble. The *Oakland Tribune* will run its last edition by the end of the year. We've been purchased by a New York media group that will consolidate several major newspapers in the Bay Area. It's possible that Aurora's story gets lost in the shuffle."

"We are going to make certain that Aurora's story gets the attention it deserves."

"Where am I to go, and how will I pay for my travel and lodgings?"

Taketo remembered. He pulled an envelope of the cash Sonny had taken from the safe at Johnnie's Rocket Room. He walked into her bedroom, stopping at the threshold to ask her permission to enter. "10,000 dollars. Should be enough to go far away and stay someplace nice. Wherever you go, don't tell me. If I am captured and tortured, I do not want to have any information that might threaten your safety."

"Understood."

"And I will wait while you pack and take you to the airport."

"What about my cat?"

Taketo smiled. "Yes, we became fast friends while I waited for you. She can stay with me while you are away. I promise to take great care of her."

***

Councilmember Andre Chidozie, a charismatic young Black reformer, was having dinner with colleagues at Oakland's posh Black-owned southern restaurant, Picán's on Broadway and Grand. He was enjoying the sorghum glazed duck breast with collard greens, garlic buttered turnips and carrots, and a hickory smoked tomato aioli. He washed it down with an excellent small batch bourbon. Taketo enjoyed the same from the bar, waiting for a moment to speak with the Councilmember alone. And then right before the dessert of bread pudding arrived and after his second bourbon, Chidozie strolled to the men's room. Taketo followed and locked the door behind them. He knelt and peeked underneath the stalls. The two men were alone.

Taketo laid a leather briefcase flat on the floor and pushed it beneath the door of the bathroom stall that Chidozie had entered.

"Campaign contribution," Taketo said. "How's the campaign going, by the way?"

Chidozie paused and opened the briefcase. He stared at the cash and tried to roughly count the amount. "It's going nicely. Beyond our expectations. Mayor Pendergast seems to have disappeared, actually. The same with the Chief of Police, the District Attorney, and the Superintendent of Schools. Really quite mysterious, don't you think? Perhaps they're all away plotting somewhere. By the way, who are you?"

"A messenger."

Chidozie closed the briefcase, pulled up his pants, flushed and stepped from the stall. His hands were shaking as he approached the sink. He barely looked at Kaz Taketo and seemed entirely engulfed in fear. "A messenger with 25k in cash? You with the Black Archon? Figured you guys would get around to buying me *out* of the mayor's race."

Taketo raised his hands, palms open. "I represent a man known as the People's Detective. In two weeks-time, we guarantee that we will have taken down the Black Archon and cleared your path toward a mayoral victory. We will be calling on you at that time for a number of initiatives that might truly help the people of Oakland. I am here today to ensure your safety."

"My safety?"

"You are in the possession of documents that you obtained from Aurora Jenkins. You planned to use these documents to smear Mayor Pendergast. These documents specifically allege that Pendergast is a member of the Black Archon and that the Black Archon is a criminal organization. Possession of these documents places your life in jeopardy. You will leave the country tonight. Tomorrow morning you will have your people call a press conference and officially suspend your campaign for personal or health reasons. I assure you, Pendergast will not win reelection. You will be able to resume your campaign in two weeks, and by that time, Pendergast will be an indicted co-conspirator in crimes against the people of Oakland. You can either consider the contents of this briefcase an initial contribution for the resumption of your campaign in two weeks or as vacation funds. But, if you value your life and safety as well as that of your family, you must leave the country tonight. Understood?"

"Understood," Chidozie paused, "...but tell me this...are the allegations provided by Ms. Jenkins true?"

"Yes."

Chidozie studied the resolution in Taketo's eyes and body language. "You're not afraid of them, are you?" Chidozie was incredulous. It was hard for him to believe that there was anyone in the city who didn't fear the Black Archon. "You're really not afraid of what the Black Archon will do to you?"

"My father was a top man in the Yakuza. So, I've seen death before. I've grown accustomed to its presence in my life. This is all foreign territory for you. You have able bodyguards. Have them travel with you."

Chidozie washed and rinsed his hands. "Where should I go, Mister Taketo?"

"I cannot know where you are going. If I am captured and tortured, I could end up providing information regarding your whereabouts. You should remain as discreet as possible wherever you go. There will be breaking news in the coming weeks and you should pay attention to that in order to plan your return. Otherwise, you will not hear from us while you are abroad."

"Thank you, Mister..."

"When this is all over you can thank Sonny Trueheart. You will be the next Mayor of Oakland thanks to your friend Sonny Trueheart."

"The People's Detective huh?"

Kaz Taketo nodded. "You're a reformer. So is Sonny Trueheart. If he's the People's Detective, you can be the People's Mayor."

"That's what I'm trying to do."

"Good, because we will hold you accountable." Taketo took a step towards the councilmember and looked deeply into his eyes. "There are powerful forces running this city. Just make certain that you don't succumb to their corruption. Understand?"

"I understand. Should I walk out now? Get back to dinner?"

"Yes, of course. I'll walk out a few minutes after you?"

"Because you don't want us to be seen together?"

"No," Taketo grinned, "because I need to take a piss."

***

Seven Daggers sat quietly in the driver's seat of his black Jaguar F-type just down the street from Pican's. He observed Councilmember Chidozie nervously departing with his usual coterie of bodyguards. He waited a few minutes and watched the old aikidoka Kaz Taketo depart moments later. He had also observed Taketo's comings and goings after leaving Suya Broadway, and at Valerie Ogwu's house. He followed Taketo and Ogwu to Oakland International Airport.

Seven Daggers drew the marijuana deeply into his lungs. He'd spent months planning this out. Godbold was mad. A criminal genius no doubt, but absolutely stark raving mad. All that money sitting there and destined to be wasted on some fantasy project in Africa. *The Operation*, Godbold called it —although folks in the Black Archon called it *The African Project*. What a joke!

What would Papi Elder have said? Seven Daggers remembered that Papi Elder, his former organizational mentor, was no more than a simple-minded pimp caught within the spell of the great Dr. Lucius Godbold. Seven Daggers laughed as he recalled the events that led up to Elder's death. There was a reason he had been late to pick Papi Elder up from his meeting with Bridgewater and Playe. There was a reason he had fed tips to Detective Trueheart through other sources. There was a reason he had advised Papi Elder to order the death of Aaminha Toure. Doing so had, predictably, resulted in Papi Elder's death. And here he was, now only one step away from glory. All thanks to Sonny Trueheart.

Seven Daggers knew men like Trueheart. Good men. Deep down, good men. Trueheart had his faults but his name rang true to his personality. He was a truly good man, committed to helping the community. Seven Daggers delighted in the thought of using him, manipulating him like a chess piece on his board. And now he would use Sonny Trueheart to help him ascend to the throne.

Seven Daggers picked up his ringing smartphone. His ringtone was Buju Banton's homophobic song "Boom Bye Bye."

"Dr. Godbold…"

"Did you kill Valerie Ogwu and Councilmember Chidozie?"

"No sir," Seven Daggers regrettably confessed. "Trueheart must have convinced them to flee. I got to them too late."

"I see." There was a long pause from Godbold.

Seven Daggers took a long pull on the joint. He liked hurting people at the behest of Dr. Godbold. But an independent spirit was evolving within him. What did it matter if Ogwu and Chidozie were all on the run? The organization and its vast resources would soon be his.

Godbold breathed heavily into the phone. "Earn your promotion, son. Do you understand me?"

"Yes sir."

And then, silence.

22. The Mistress and the Benefactress

Malik Akoto suspected that his long-time benefactress might continue to haunt the Black Bottom dungeon in search of able-bodied Black men to fulfill her needs. He knew the danger. Messing around with her had put him in jail. But, after a shave, a haircut and that first good meal of Salt Fish and Ackee on the outside with a few shots of Trinidadian rum at Miss Ollie's on 9th and Washington, he journeyed to the Black Bottom, a BDSM dungeon within a two-story loft in the Jack London Square area. He observed all the necessary protocols by announcing his presence and first seeking a quick word with its owner, his former employer, Mistress Celestine.

Akoto was led from the main door to Mistress Celestine's office by her imposing bodyguard, the always mute Mungiki. Mungiki did not search him but was surely experienced enough to notice the bulge of the pistol under his left armpit. His attitude suggested that he did not consider Malik, a former employee, a threat.

Akoto admired Mungiki's long black leather coat as they walked through the dungeon and past a shibari rope demonstration taking place in the main hall.

"That's a mighty fine coat there, my man. A mighty fine coat."

Mungiki remained mute. His eyes were deep set and as black and impenetrable as the coat.

"What size you wear brother? I bet that coat would look mighty fine on me."

Silence.

Minutes before Akoto drove up to the dungeon and parked down the street, Mistress Celestine received a call from Seven Daggers, whose employer, Dr. Godbold, had provided the initial seed money for her dungeon.

"You used to employ a bloke named Malik Akoto, innit?"

"Yes. He was a good employee. He kept his mouth shut."

"Did you know he's Trueheart's mate, the copper who killed Papi Elder?"

"I was reading about that in the paper today. I remember all of that. I didn't know they were friends."

"Malik Akoto was released from the nick this morning and is in the custody of Sonny Trueheart. We are trying to determine who made this arrangement. In the meantime, I want to inform you that this man is on his way to your dungeon. I want you to report back to me about everything that this man says and does."

"Do you think he's working with Sonny Trueheart?"

"Boss man is gonna be pretty brassed off if that's the case, innit? It looks bait, but it could just be coincidence. From what I hear, this Malik Akoto's got the bottle. Big fucker. He's well fit, yeah? Keep your hair on and report back to me, luv. Understood?"

"Understood."

Mistress Celestine ended the call as Malik Akoto entered her office. She tossed her phone on her desk and rose from her throne.

"The prodigal son returns!"

Mistress Celestine was 6 feet 2 inches with attitude. She wore thigh-high patent leather boots, a chain mail skirt and blouse, and she was equipped with a gleaming .380 caliber stainless steel automatic pistol strapped to her thigh. She was bald and had the most pronounced and elegant of features, like the sister on the cover of The Ohio Player's *Pain, Pleasure,* and *Orgasm* albums. Large hoop earrings accentuated her sharp jawline. She spoke in a lilting and musical N'awlins accent. In recent years, she had become the most powerful resource of the Black Archon, and the one who properly trained captive girls who were the most resistant to the organization's indoctrination.

She approached Akoto as he entered and they warmly embraced. This was the woman who brought him into the sex industry, trained him as a dominant, marketed him to couples seeking interracial cuckold fantasy, and set him up with bondage film shoots.

They kissed. Friendly. The spark from the relationship they had begun and ended so many years ago was no longer there. They were now simply former business associates.

Behind her desk was a wall of television screens where she could observe the activities taking place in each of the private rooms in her dungeon. There was a masked woman suspended from the ceiling near her desk. Akoto stared. She asked him to have a seat and offered him a puff from her vaporizer pen. Akoto accepted. She took the first puff from the vaporizer pen and then handed it to him with the mark of her lipstick. Typical domme move. The indica dominant herb burned smoothly.

Mungiki remained in the office and stood quietly by the door in his long black leather jacket.

The masked woman was stripped naked to the waist. Her arms were bound to lengths of chain suspended from the ceiling. Her feet were bound in chains to a floor anchor. Her flesh was raw from the severe whipping she had just suffered. Her breathing was labored. Sweat ran down her body. There was a tattoo of the Buddha on her left shoulder. The name "Sujata" was tattooed on her right arm. Akoto could see fresh needle marks on her left arm.

Mistress Celestine gestured towards the suspended woman. "You're curious about this one, huh? Let's just say she needed a little reinforcement of her training."

"She doped up?"

"What do you care?"

"It's not how you trained me."

"There are always exceptions to the rule."

Akoto shook his head. He disagreed, but now was not the time to get into it. "Well, I'm out. I'm a free man once again."

"Let's try to keep you out this time. You looking for work?"

"I'm looking for Laura Bello."

"These older, rich, white women will be the death of you, Malik."

"But she remains a valuable client of yours, right, as are so many other rich white women? I mean, you let her back into the club even after she did me wrong like that."

"I figured when she paid for your lawyer that everything was straight between the two of you. So why should I carry the grudge?"

"True that. But *I* need to speak with her. *I* need to square it."

"You're in luck. She's here today. She came for the shibari demonstration."

Akoto got up to leave. "Great. Mind if I speak with her?"

Mistress Celestine threw up her hands. "I can't stop you. Just don't cause a scene if she's not as happy to see you as I am."

They embraced. Mistress Celestine kissed him again full on the lips. "I'll have work for you if you need it. I'd love to have my top boy back on the payroll."

Akoto looked at the woman chained beside Mistress Celestine's desk. "Do me another favor, okay? Let this sister loose. This aint the way we should be doing things."

Mistress Celestine sighed but agreed and unchained the woman. Akoto took her in his arms as she fell from the chains.

Mungiki opened the door to lead them out.

"You sure you won't sell me that coat? It'd fit just right." Akoto opened his wallet and flashed five c-notes.

Mungiki silently considered the money being waved in his face in the dim light. He pulled a 9mm pistol from the right pocket of his leather coat and stroked the slide.

Akoto stepped back. "I'll take that as a 'no,'" and he draped the woman with his own jacket. Shivering, she acknowledged Akoto's help as they walked from the office.

Mungiki replaced the gun in his pocket and silently glared at Akoto as he led the young woman away.

As they approached the main hall, the woman he had taken from Mistress Celestine's office slowly regained her strength and footing and handed Akoto his coat. "I'm okay," she said, speaking through the leather mask. "Thank you." And then she walked away to the private dressing rooms.

Mrs. Laura Bello stood alone at the very back of the crowd as the shibari demonstration continued. Tall with long, lean legs accentuated by black pumps, wearing a white leather skirt and sleeveless leather blouse. Her hair was gothic black and cut Bettie Page style. She played the part, as always, of the trophy wife. She saw Malik Akoto out of the corner of her eye as he approached and stood next to her but made no move to face him.

"Your husband here?" Akoto whispered.

"No, but he has people watching me all the time now. We no longer play like we used to."

"Sorry to hear that."

Laura directed him to step back from the onlookers. They spoke in hushed tones.

"I heard about your early release." Laura stepped forward and wrapped her arms lovingly around him. "I was hoping you would come here tonight. How did you get out early?"

"Good behavior."

"I miss you, Malik."

Akoto smirked. "You don't miss me, Laura. You miss what you think I represent."

"I'm sorry I couldn't visit you in jail this time."

"I got your letters. And your photos. Probably the least you could do after stabbing me in the back like that."

"I had someone look after the condo and the car. Water the plants."

"Thank you."

"Now that you're out, maybe I can lose my husband's bodyguards for one night and visit you at the condo."

"It's probably not a good idea for either of us. I aint tryna to go back to jail."

"You're beautiful." She caressed his arms and leaned against him. "I do love you."

"You're incapable of loving me. Truth is, I lost a little bit of my soul every moment I spent with you and your husband."

"That's not true, Malik. I just don't know how to express myself to you."

"I don't think either of us were ever honest with one another."

"I fell in love with a Black boy when I was 12. I didn't know anything about race. But when I told my mother and I introduced her to him after school, she took me home and beat me and told me never to bring a Black boy home. It didn't discourage me. It only made me want that boy more, made me want every beautiful Black man I've seen ever since."

"What does that have to do with me? I'm not that person that you fell in love with when you were 12. I just *represent* that person to you because we're both Black. But it has nothing to do with *me*."

"I understand."

"Do you?" Akoto stepped back from her. "You know what I saw when I first met you?"

"What?"

"Money. Power. Privilege. Things I don't have, might never have, and certainly will never have like you do. Things you take for granted. I wanted to know what it was like to feel that money and power on your body, to taste it, and roll in the bed with it."

"That sounds very angry, Malik. Did you really feel all of that when you were with me?"

"Yeah. But my anger didn't prevent me from feeling your vulnerability, your fear, and through you I came to know how fragile whiteness is and how some of you fear us and want us at the same time."

"You felt all that in me?"

Akoto nodded. "And I also felt how afraid you are of your husband. We were both his playthings. The only thing is that because you're white, or...because *you think* you're white...you deluded yourself into thinking that I was the only plaything in the room. You do know that he used both of us to act out his fantasies, don't you? It wasn't about you and your needs. And it certainly had nothing to do with my needs. I was simply the hired help."

"I know that now. But I told myself certain lies to avoid that reality. When I was first with you, I imagined that I was reunited with the boy I had a crush on when I was twelve and I understood when I was with you why my mother beat me so."

"Why?"

"She wanted me to keep all the colors in the lines. Remain in control. Know where the boundaries lie."

"I'm sorry that happened to you, but my mother might have beat me for the very same offense."

"What did you mean when you said *I think I'm white*? What did you mean by that?"

Akoto smiled. "You want to be real? Okay... you do know that I know your secret. Right?"

"My secret?"

"You're not really white at all. You've been passing for white since the minute you came out of the womb. If that story about your mother is true, it's a sign of how much your mother was in on the game of making sure that you passed without detection and got a real chance in this country."

Laura blushed. "How do you know that?"

"I just know."

"Okay. It's true." Laura breathed deeply and felt the tension leaving her body. "Been so long that I don't know how to be anything else."

"Leave the husband and I'll show you."

"I can't. You know that. He owns me. He has me trapped."

"If I find you a way out, you gonna take it?"

She leaned against him. He could smell her perfume. Chanel No. 5. She could smell the coconut butter that he massaged into his skin and she could feel the gun hanging from the shoulder holster under his left armpit. "I should have just asked you to kill him for me."

"Hurting Neil was never an option. We both needed his money."

"He still uses his money to bring me playmates. He can't get off without seeing me do it with another man or woman."

"Woman?"

"He hasn't hired another man since you. Of course, he's paying Black women now."

"Really?"

For the first time she turned and looked him in the eyes. Looked him up and down. "Can you meet me outside? In the alley?"

"Let's try the all gender restroom in five minutes instead." Akoto knew that that was the one place where Mistress Celestine didn't put her cameras. Not for the sake of respecting privacy, but because the violet lighting in the bathrooms resulted in poor digital video quality.

"Mmm hmm."

Mrs. Laura Bello quietly excused herself. Akoto continued pretending that he was watching the shibari demonstration and then five minutes later excused himself and found Laura. She stood naked in the middle of the immaculate restroom as he entered. Laura's lithe and small-breasted body bore fresh scars, and purple bruises on her torso and breasts. Akoto locked the bathroom door and approached her and examined her body in the violet light. There were also belt marks across her buttocks.

"What has he done to you?"

"I told you. He has forbidden me from being with any man since you. That's why he only wants to see me with women now. He beats me for even thinking about a man." She reached out and caressed his chest and began to unbutton his linen shirt. "You've gotten bigger since you went inside."

"I need some information, Laura."

"You can have that too, lover."

"I want to know more about these women that your husband is hiring for you to play with."

"If I give you the information you seek, can I have you again?"

Akoto nodded. "Maybe. I'll take it into consideration, how's that?"

"Yes. Thank you."

"Laura, where is your husband getting these women from?"

"Mistress Celestine provides them. They're women that the Archon brings in."

"You know about the Black Archon?" Akoto realized that he had never heard Laura mention the name of the Black Archon.

"I know about the Archon. There's two of them, you know? Many of my husband's business associates belong to this group. It's like a business fraternity."

"I think it's much more than that."

"I know. I know that people say that they do criminal things."

"And you never had a problem with this?"

"My husband is in control, I told you. You know this."

"What you're describing might be part of an international sexual slavery ring."

"If my husband is involved, can you help send him to jail?"

"I'll do everything in my power to make that happen. But I'll need evidence. Something with banking transactions that link your husband and his associates to the sex trafficking operations of the Black Archon."

"I'll give you all the information you need, darling."

Akoto was intrigued. "What do you have?"

"I can get you into Neil's office at the Bush federal building and you can see *everything* you want to see on his computer. Access to *hard* evidence."

Akoto took off his jacket and removed his unbuttoned shirt. "Do tell."

***

Although Mistress Celestine had not installed cameras in the bathrooms in her dungeon, Seven Daggers had. He sat in his coupe watching the poorly lit video of Malik Akoto making love to Laura Bello. Mungiki sat beside him in the passenger seat. Seven Daggers grunted occasionally throughout the viewing.

"We should report this to Dr. Godbold, right?" Mungiki asked.

"I'll handle that," Seven Daggers reminded him of the chain of command. "That's my job."

"Should we also report this to her husband, Neil Bello?"

Seven Daggers turned and looked Mungiki in the eyes. "What did I tell you? Are you bloody daft? I'll handle all of that. Do we have a problem?"

"No sir."

"Good. Then belt up about what you've seen and heard here. This is between the two of us. If I hear otherwise, you will be held accountable. Do you understand?"

"Yes sir."

"I have plans for this Malik Akoto."

"Yes sir."

Seven Daggers motioned toward the door. "Now, you can sod off and get back to your job. I'll contact you when I need you to do something. But for now, what I need you to do is absolutely nothing. Don't cock it up. You will find that I value discretion."

Mungiki nodded and departed the vehicle. As Mungiki re-entered the dungeon, Seven Daggers continued viewing Malik Akoto's bathroom encounter with Laura Bello. He laughed aloud and nodded his approval.

23. Follow the Drinking Gourd

Aurora began to notice a pattern every time Seven Daggers moved her to another location or took her out on the streets to visit sex workers controlled by the Black Archon. For the past several days, he had waited until they brought her to the police van before administering the fentanyl injection. He would inject her and then order the driver to take them to the next location as she fell into a zombie-like stupor. He would carefully watch over her as the van rumbled over the potholes of Oakland and administer the Narcan when she began to display symptoms of overdose. When the van pulled into its location, he would leave her for a half hour while she recovered.

The Narcan only worked in her body for 30 to 90 minutes. Aurora knew that the half hour when Seven Daggers left her alone to recover might be her only opportunity to escape, and, in the 30 to 90-minute window before the effects of the overdose or the hunger for the drug returned, she would need to have effectively escaped and secured a safe location.

And so, the evening's routine began. Aurora was removed from the safehouse and ushered into the van around midnight. The van rumbled to life and Seven Daggers pulled the syringe from the metal case that he carried in his inside breast pocket. He grabbed Aurora's forearm and injected the drug and waited for it to take effect.

Within minutes Aurora's body began to shake and then stiffen and then shake again, as though she were experiencing a seizure. Her lips turned gray. Foam formed at the corners of her mouth. She could hear Seven Daggers calling her name, but she was unresponsive until he administered the Narcan nasal spray. As she came back to full awareness, Aurora curled up in a fetal position on the hard metal bench in the van.

Seven Daggers patted her on the shoulder. "You gonna be okay?"

Aurora moaned. "One of these days you won't be able to bring me back."

"You're right. One of these days, the boss man will order me to let you die." And with that, Aurora felt the van easing into a stop and Seven Daggers exited.

Aurora counted to 50. She sat up, her bare feet chilled by the cold metal van floor, looked at the doors, and wondered if it was possible, if it just might be possible to escape.

A typical police van —what they used to call a "paddy wagon"— is 10 feet deep inside, 4 feet in height, and 5 feet wide. There's room for 5 prisoners on each side, with a solid metal partition down the center and seatbelts for each prisoner. The metal partition had been removed at Seven Daggers' request, providing Aurora with a little more space to maneuver. A typical police van usually has two sets of rear doors: one metal set of split rear doors and another set of exterior split rear doors. Seven Daggers had also, for some reason, removed the metal split rear doors.

At present, Aurora was the only one in the van aside from the driver, and Seven Daggers had never used the seatbelts to restrain her. There was lighting along the upper wall, but it had been switched off. It was sufficiently dark and Aurora could see the back of the driver through a chain link partition. He sat there at the wheel, ignoring her and watching something on his phone while he waited. However, even with his ear pods, Aurora knew that as soon as the soles of her bare feet struck the metal doors, the driver would certainly be alerted, and she would have to be prepared to deal with him swiftly and decisively.

Realizing that the driver might stand in her way, Aurora pulled at one of the seatbelts, one with a thick metal buckle on the end. Glancing at the driver, who remained engrossed, Aurora knelt and bit at the fabric of the seatbelt, attempting to tear at it with her sharp canines, feeling the hard fabric bruise and cut her gums and the warmth of blood in her mouth. She was unable to create even the slightest tear in the fabric as she furiously bit and chewed. She looked up and noticed that the bolt that secured the seatbelt to the wall of the van was loose, and she was easily able to spin the washer beneath the bolt. With all of her fentanyl-drained strength she pulled, trying to use the rough edges of the spiral groove of the screw to cut the fabric, and was finally able to create a significant tear. Jerking and pulling the seat belt from side to side against the spiral groove, she was able to increase the tear until the fabric was ripped free and the makeshift weapon was now in her hands.

There had been minimal noise. She glanced again at the driver. Still engrossed in his phone.

Because the rear doors could not be unlocked from inside, Aurora's plan rested on the possibility that an over-confident Seven Daggers had not locked them from outside and that a strong kick, one that she had long trained for in the martial arts, would be sufficient. If Seven Daggers had locked them, she might not be able to escape. She had to take the chance. Aurora lay down on her back and positioned her legs to kick open the exterior rear doors with maximum power. She braced herself against one of the benches and, with one powerful kick from a prone position with her muscled thighs, the very same muscled thighs that Seven Daggers had disparaged as "unladylike," the unlocked exterior doors burst open. Aurora could hear the driver asking "What's up in there?" as she ran out into the Oakland night.

As she emerged from the van, feeling the cold asphalt under her bare feet, the driver rushed out and around the van to stop her. He was met with a hard metal buckle to his face as Aurora whipped the torn seat belt. And then she ran, the seatbelt weapon still in her right hand.

She found herself on the streets of Jack London Square, in front of the Home of Chicken and Waffles that was adjacent to the train tracks that ran along Embarcadero West. Seven Daggers had likely retreated there for his late-night meal, and the restaurant kept the latest hours in the city. There were no trains running at this time of night. That would have been a miracle and Aurora might have been able to stow away on a passing train. Instead, Aurora ran in her bare feet across the tracks, anesthetized from the pain by the fear of being caught, and towards the shops and restaurants on the Jack London Square Marina. She ran towards the slips where a number of recreational boats were moored, trying to keep in the shadows and avoid the limited number of people who still wandered near the water.

Breathing heavily, her heart pounding, she came to the docks and quickly surveyed the boats that tossed in their moorings. She spied a bowrider with a V-hull and an outboard engine. The boat was 25 feet in length and used for day cruising on the bay. Remembering as much as she could in the moment from the years that she and her sister Aaminha would spend aboard their grandfather's fishing boat in Clearlake catching bluegills and crappies, she ran down the pier and jumped into the empty boat. She braced herself against the edge of the boat and pulled up the Danforth anchor that was dug into the hard sand and mud at the bottom of the bay, pulling the 16-pound anchor by the chain hand over hand. And when she had brought it up and out of the water and into the boat, she then went to the four lines from each of the stern cleats on the boat that were crossed to the dock cleats. This system was used to secure the boat in each direction and allow enough line for the boat to rise and fall in the tide. Aurora quickly undid each of the four lines and the bowrider began to drift from the dock.

Aurora remembered one time when her grandfather had to hotwire an outboard motor for a friend, but she did not have the pigtail connector or any other tools that he had used. She found a flashlight in an unlocked cabinet that also contained a flare pistol, life vests, and a toolbox. She donned the life vest and went to the main ignition assembly and tried to gain access to its wiring. Her mind was racing. Perhaps, she thought, this might work the same way that it used to work with older cars, where she could link a wire from the ignition switch's start terminal to the battery's positive terminal and another wire from the battery's negative terminal to the ground wire on the ignition switch. She had learned how to do this from an ex-girlfriend who ran an automotive repair shop in West Oakland.

She then located the battery, but this was in the back of the boat and the ignition switch was located on the front starboard side near the steering wheel. She scoured through the tool box that she had found in the unlocked cabinet and found a tangle of short wires. Maybe there was enough to create two longer wires that could run between the battery and the ignition assembly. With her teeth she stripped bare the ends of these wires and twisted them together until she had fashioned two longer wires.

She attempted to connect the positive and negative ends of the battery to the ignition assembly. The makeshift wire from the battery's positive terminal was long enough, but the wire needed to connect the battery's negative terminal to the ground wire on the ignition switch wasn't.

She heard sirens and the sound of an approaching police helicopter. There was no time to think about it. She knew there was only one solution: she had to complete the connection from the shorter wire with her hand. She said a prayer, clenched her teeth, and made the connection, one end of the short wire wrapped around the thumb of her left hand and the open ground wire on the ignition wrapped around the pinky of her right hand. And then she extended her right leg and pressed the button with her big toe.

Sparks flew and singed her hands and her body violently spasmed and her fingers closed into fists and her toes curled as her muscles contracted and the shock threw her body from the wheel towards the port side edge of the boat as the voltage from the marine battery coursed through her body. 50 volts might have been enough to kill her, but 12.7 only made her stronger, further jolting her heart and her senses from the fentanyl. And then the outboard motor rumbled and came to life, churning the shallow water by the dock into a froth, and Aurora laughed and wiped the drool from the edges of her mouth and cursed with joy.

Her body still tingling, Aurora crawled back to the wheel, propped herself up into the captain's chair, sat at the helm and eased the boat away from the dock and into the bay, increasing speed as she came into deeper water until she could fully advance the throttle and reach a maximum speed of 45 miles per hour. She ran dark into the night and headed for the lights on the San Francisco Embarcadero.

The wind and spray splashed her face. Aurora dared a momentary smile until she saw the searchlight of a police helicopter in pursuit. She cursed and urged the craft forward. The Bay Bridge and San Francisco were in view. And then she was enveloped in the search light and she stood up and raised a middle finger to her pursuers. A shower of automatic rifle fire rained down upon the craft, ripping the stern and the water behind her. They were trying to take out the outboard motor!!!

Aurora maneuvered the wheel, taking sharp turns from left to right, moving like a snake across the choppy waters, the craft hitting the waves hard and bouncing wildly into the air. The gunfire from the helicopter was relentless and a volley of shots eventually found their mark, ripping through the outboard motor which caught fire and emitted black smoke as the bowrider stalled in the violent waters of the bay.

Aurora reached for the flare pistol and aimed for the helicopter. The searchlight was blinding, but she tried to shield her eyes and aim. She pulled the trigger and watched the arc of the red flare. Her aim was true and the flare entered the helicopter's cabin, igniting a fire and causing confusion, and Aurora could see the helicopter spinning and she could hear the screams of the pilot losing control as it drifted further out over the bay and descended sharply in altitude until it hit the unyielding waters hard and fire spread across the bay.

Aurora sat back at the helm and sighed as the boat drifted in circles. She then saw the searchlights of three approaching police fast boats. She rose and resolved that she would rather die than surrender. She wanted to die just as her ancestors had died during the Middle Passage, resisting their fate at the hands of white slavers and diving into the waters to rejoin their ancestors. Aurora removed her life vest and dove into the water and began to knife downwards towards death and freedom.

The ice-cold waters were a shock to her system. But she pushed through it and fought a losing battle against the undertow to descend deeper as the fast boats approached above. And then she heard his laughter. That sick laughter that she had been subjected to every night. As one of the fast boats cut its speed and drifted above her, she heard his laughter carry below the waves when he dove in after her and she felt his powerful grasp on her shirt. She furiously attempted to undo her shirt and tried to scream underwater, "Let me die!" But Seven Daggers easily managed pulling her back up to the surface and onboard the fast boat, restraining her as she writhed in fury and spat in his face.

As her spittle rolled down his cheek, Seven Daggers held her wrists in a vice grip while a police officer came behind her and administered an injection of fentanyl into an exposed vein on her left forearm. He screamed, "You're more trouble than you're worth! You want to die? I'll do worse!" And the drug rushed into her system, propelled that much quicker through her bloodstream by her fast-beating heart and she slipped away into oblivion.

Power to the People!
A Podcast for the People
Broadcasting from the Lower Bottoms of West Oakland
Hosted by Aurora Jenkins

Transcript of Power to the People! Episode 75

It's your Momma, your Auntie, your Big Sister, your Play Cousin, your Friendly Neighborhood Queer Black Feminist activist, investigative community reporter! Today, dear listeners, I want to shine the light on the disappearances of American Indian women. We are often unaware of communities of Indigenous people living amongst us in our cities and towns. We are unaware of the fact that Indigenous people face higher rates of police murders than Black and Brown folks. It is the same with the disappearances of Indigenous women. The numbers are staggering. The silence, even more deafening.

I want to report on the case of a Yokuts woman from the South Bay, Josie Rivercombe, who disappeared over two weeks ago near the Tachi Yokuts reservation in Porterville, some 4 hours' drive south of Oakland. Josie began experiencing addiction and mental health struggles in her late 20s, allegedly setting fire to a hardware store on the reservation. Her family hoped that her arrest would lead to treatment and recovery. Instead, she was released by the tribal authorities on her own recognizance against the wishes of her family. Josie was an accomplished traditional dancer and had interest in traditional medicine. She was last seen at the far western edge of the reservation where the road borders the woods. Over the past two decades, there have been nine instances of Indigenous women disappearing in this area. The tribe has issued an emergency declaration and has been a part of broader California tribal efforts to draw attention to these disappearances.

24. Straighten Up and Fly Right

In the morning Sonny was roused from his meditation by the invasive knocking of the Oakland Police Department at his door. His old boss flashed his badge, pushed the door further open and entered without invitation. If it had not been for the color of his skin, his former Sergeant, now Captain Larry Gibson would already have been named Chief of Police. He was, after all, just as corrupt as any other police administrator. Making himself feel right at home, Gibson, with his salt and pepper horseshoe of hair, went to the refrigerator to find a beer. Finding none, he settled for a bottle of water.

"You stop drinking or something, Sonny?"

Sonny stepped outside for a minute and glanced up and down the block. There were no other cop cars outside.

"Sonny, I gotta ask you. Were you anywhere near Johnnie's Rocket Room a couple nights ago? You steal anything from them?"

"Johnnie's? Haven't been there in a long time, Captain."

"I've got eyewitnesses who identified your motorcycle."

"Plenty of Harleys all over Oakland, Captain. You've got nothing on me."

"How about Councilmember Chidozie and *Oakland Tribune* editor Valerie Ogwu? Have you been in contact with either of them in the past couple of days?"

Sonny shrugged. "I don't know them, Captain. How about the disappearance of Aurora Jenkins?"

Gibson smirked. "She hates law enforcement."

Sonny disagreed. "No, she hates pigs."

Gibson stiffened. "You think because you somehow managed to get a p.i. license that you're immune? That it? I told you to get out of town after you killed Playe and Bridgewater and testified. For the longest time, *I* was the only thing keeping you alive. You got no more friends in Oakland."

"I thought *you* were my friend and my role model, Captain."

"You making fun of me, Sonny?"

"I'm always making fun of you, Captain."

"You know I really am your friend, Sonny. That's why they sent me."

"Who sent you?"

"You know who sent me. Did you hear about that boat chase on the bay last night?"

"Was that Aurora?"

"She tried to escape. Made it to the Embarcadero at Jack London Square. Managed to hotwire a fishing boat. She didn't make it very far."

"Do you know if she's all right?"

"They've got her doped up. They've been trying to get information out of her. See how much she knows and who she tried to communicate it to. That's all I know. They called us in when she escaped. I know that she's alive and that she tried to escape. I also know that she's made herself more of a problem than she's worth. She put two good cops in the hospital. Critical condition. That and all of your poking around and meddling and stealing..."

"That mean that they're ready to deal?"

"Tonight. 5:00pm. Bardo Lounge on Lakeshore. Maybe you can work something out with them."

"How long have they had you on the payroll Captain?"

"It's been a while."

"The Black Archon is on the endangered species list, Captain. Your dirty money gravy train is finna end."

Gibson shrugged. "I'm good. I got mine." He pulled a sealed business envelope from his uniform pocket and tossed it at Sonny.

"You were good police Sonny. Maybe the best man who ever served under my command. But you're a goddam Black Panther in a police uniform. I get it. At the end of the day, I'm a Black man too." Captain Gibson pointed to the envelope. "Look, I've been holding that for a rainy day. Digital recordings of my conversations with Dr. Godbold's main boy, Seven Daggers. These recordings go back to when you killed Papi Elder. It's all there. Seven Daggers is looking to make a move on his man. He's been thinking about it for some time. Maybe you can make something of that when you meet with him."

Sonny looked at Captain Gibson and waved the envelope in his face. "Were you on the payroll when they killed Aaminha Toure?"

Captain Gibson remained silent.

"You could have warned me that they had a hit out on her, Captain. You could have helped me save her life."

"What can I tell you, Sonny? I'm a coward and a self-interested actor. I had to look out for mine."

"Neither Godbold nor his top boy will make it through the summer. Neither will you, Captain."

An impenetrable silence lingered between the two men.

"You gonna make the meeting, Sonny?"

"I'll think about it. Tell your slave masters that you did your job."

"Fuck you, Sonny."

"Fuck you too, Captain."

25. The Bardo

At 5pm sharp Sonny showed up at the Bardo Lounge and Supper Club on Lakeshore with its aged red brick walls and mid-century modern furnishings. The beautiful, well-stocked bar was tempting, but he breathed through it, stayed focused and ascended the stairs to the formal dining area that looked down on the ground floor cocktail lounge.

Seven Daggers sat at a table against the wall dressed in a smart black suit with black shirt and black tie, eating a plate of oxtail ragout with spaghetti squash, lobster, cocoa nibs, and sunchokes. He spotted Sonny in his dashiki and cornrows immediately. Seven Daggers was alone on the upper level. As Sonny approached his table and took a seat, he set down his glass of Bordeaux and placed his signature lean 7-inch stiletto knife beside his plate.

Seven Daggers grinned. "Want anything to drink, detective?"

Sonny refused to take the bait. Instead, he withdrew his revolver and placed it on the table.

Seven Daggers smirked. "Never bring a knife to a gun fight, right?"

"Something like that."

"So, I'm going to assume that Valerie Ogwu is in the wind?"

"Assume all you want."

"Councilmember Chidozie too?"

"Could be." Sonny shrugged.

"What do you want, detective?"

"Aurora Jenkins."

"Who?"

"You got jokes now?" Sonny shook his head. "Look, you called the goddam meeting. What's your price?"

"I'm no tiger kidnapper, detective. And if I was, it would take heaps of dosh, more than you could afford."

"Give me a number."

"This isn't about money, copper. I don't even care about the bread you stole from Johnnie's."

"Everything's about money."

"You think so?"

"If it aint about money, it's about power or it's about sex or it's about all three."

"If you've read the draft of her story, then you know this isn't about any of those things, detective." Seven Daggers continued eating his oxtail ragout. "And none of those will get you Aurora Jenkins. It's about the future of the race. You see, for some people Dr. Godbold is the genius behind ending all diseases that plague Black America. But those of us that work closely with him know the truth."

Sonny gestured. "Get on with it."

"Those cures for sickle cell and high blood pressure...with all of that scientific knowledge in his head...do you really think that those are the only drugs that he has developed, copper?"

"Hell if I know."

Seven Daggers hissed through clenched teeth. "Some bluebottle you are. I guess you'll learn in time. Damn, you are daft my brother! But for now, let's just say that my motives are pure. I'm strictly criminal. I am not the one with the grand visions of global domination like the good doctor that I serve."

"What do you want for Aurora's release?"

"Maybe if you did me a favor. Something special, just for me."

"Spit it out."

Seven Daggers had come prepared. In the chair beside him was a slim file folder that he now placed on the table and shoved in Sonny's direction. Sonny holstered his revolver and opened the folder. There were the original architectural plans for the Black Archon Center. and a host of alarm codes and the names and routines of security guards. Sonny knew instantly what Seven Daggers wanted him to do in exchange for the release of Aurora Jenkins.

Sonny looked up into the eyes of the man who would dare betray Dr. Lucius Godbold. "I'll need proof of life."

Seven Daggers grinned and sipped his wine. "Of course." He reached into his jacket pocket and withdrew his smartphone. "I've got your girl working off her debt to the Oakland Police Department, so I'll have to see if she's free to talk."

"What do you mean...*working off her debt?*"

"She tried to escape, and she had to be punished. Two police officers lie in critical condition because of her nonsense. So...the coppers got arsey and demanded *reparations.*" Seven Daggers chuckled. "Perhaps you heard about her little escape attempt last night? The police helicopter crash over the bay? I've got the bird all pretty and dolled up in sexy garms and ready to service the boys in blue. I'm gonna make her work off her debt. It's fair, innit?"

"You're way outta pocket here. You'll have to stop punishing her. That's a necessary condition for me to do what you're asking me to do."

Seven Daggers shook his head. "You'll make no such demands. You'll do as you're told and then, and only then, only after you've completed your task, will I release Aurora into your custody."

"Stop punishing her or no deal."

"You'd rather that she die, detective?"

"I *know* that she'd rather die."

Seven Daggers nodded. "So be it, copper. You drive a hard

bargain." He reached for his smartphone and dialed a saved number. "Give her the phone," Seven Daggers ordered, and then slid the phone across the dinner table to Sonny.

Sonny slid the phone back across the table. "Tell them to keep those damn cops away from her."

Seven Daggers took the phone back and smirked. "We won't be working her tonight. Keep her stashed." And he slid the phone back to Sonny.

Sonny put the phone to his ear. "Aurora?"

"Detective Trueheart?"

"Yes."

"Oh, thank God."

"I'm negotiating for your release."

"These people…they're never going to let me go."

"I promise you, I'll get you out."

"I'll never see the sun or walk along Lake Merritt or drink Ethiopian coffee on Telegraph or hang out with my people at the Black Joy Parade ever again." She sounded forced, but she was sending him a message.

"I'm coming, Aurora. I'm not going to let you down."

"You know, you didn't let my sister down. You don't have to live with that guilt."

Sonny closed his eyes and was silent for a minute. Seven Daggers reached across the table and snatched the phone.

"There's your proof of life. And I've agreed to suspend her punishment. If you break this deal of ours, your precious Aurora Jenkins will have hell to pay for it. Do we have an understanding?"

Sonny looked at the envelope on the table, and then turned his gaze towards Seven Daggers. "I'll keep my end of the deal. You keep yours. If you do any further harm to Aurora, it'll be you who will have hell to pay for it."

26. The Kingston 11

Nzingha was the last to confirm, but the group got together at the Kingston 11 towards the end of dinner hours. The Kingston 11 was a Jamaican restaurant and bar with live reggae music on Telegraph Ave. near downtown Oakland. The oxtail stew was legendary.

Sonny drove straight from his meeting with Seven Daggers at the Bardo. His path took him by the Grand Lake Theater, along Lake Merritt, and past the Cathedral of Christ the Light until he stopped at a red light by the Black Archon Center on Lakeside Drive. He looked up at the 18-story structure where Dr. Lucius Godbold resided, and whispered, "Soon."

Sonny arrived at the Kingston 11 with a leather motorcycle messenger bag full of materials that he wished to share with the group. Sonny had reserved a private room at the back of the restaurant for special parties.

The reggae was thumping when Sonny entered. The bar was full. Every table was occupied. People were throwing their heads back and dancing to the syncopated beats. The scene gave you a view of the strength of Oakland's Jamaican community. It gave Sonny a feeling of being on the islands, but he struggled with the temptation of the signature house cocktail, the Kingston Smash, with bourbon, falernum, sage molasses, and fresh tangerine juice.

Within twenty minutes of Sonny's arrival, Malik Akoto oozed with catlike steps into the restaurant against the backdrop of heavy reggae rhythms. He was clean-shaven and had trimmed his red baby dreadlocks. He wore a tan linen suit, fitted white shirt, and Italian sandals. He carried a slim leather briefcase.

Sonny embraced him as he entered the private room and could

feel a shoulder holster under his left armpit concealing the pistol he carried beneath the suit jacket. Sonny declined to comment on the matter.

Akoto smiled, with that free and open way of his, fearless in his provocation, a glint of expectation for the fight that lay ahead in his eyes. He knew his role in the drama that would unfold.

Taketo was the next to arrive and he brought with him the young hacker, Orpheus Anderson. Akoto bowed and warmly embraced Taketo as the quartet waited for Nzingha.

"It's good to see you, my son," Taketo said.

Akoto whispered into Taketo's ear. "Thank you for continuing to believe in me, Sensei."

Nzingha strolled in fashionably late, decked out in a red leather outfit. Her silver hair gleamed under the lights of the Kingston 11.

After introductions and Akoto's flirtations with Nzingha, Sonny directed the group to share all recent developments. "Let's talk about what we know and what we're going to do."

Taketo played back the recording of Seven Daggers at Suya. Sonny shared the information he had gathered at Johnnie's, played a snippet of the audio recording he had been given by Captain Gibson, shared information from his meeting with Seven Daggers, and spoke of his phone conversation with Aurora. From his motorcycle bag he produced copies of a *Wired* magazine article about an elaborate bank heist in Antwerp, Belgium and passed this around the table.

"Any questions?" Sonny asked.

"Is Aurora alive?" Nzingha leaned in.

"Yes. Aurora is alive. Seven Daggers provided proof of life. He let me speak with her briefly. She let me know that they are moving her around the city at night. I believe that they've held her in various locations including near the lake, North Oakland, even downtown."

"So," Nzingha offered, "a direct rescue is impossible."

"Right. But there's another route. Seven Daggers provided the plans to the Black Archon Center. I'm supposed to get in and get to the penthouse level and kill Dr. Godbold there."

"All the cash that Godbold is taking off the streets and converting to crypto-currency is likely to be in the vault at the California American Bank," Akoto added.

"Precisely," Sonny smiled.

Kaz Taketo cleared his throat, "I've been observing the comings and goings around the California American Bank. Trucks coming in and out of there every day. Back and forth between safehouses and the bank. Something's going on."

Sonny folded his arms and leaned back in his chair. "Right. Instead of breaking into the Black Archon building to kill Godbold, we are going to break into the California American Bank in the lobby, steal his money and use it to deal for Aurora's life."

There was quiet in the room but Kaz Taketo beamed.

The room remained silent until Akoto howled with laughter and slapped the table. "Full measure! Hell yeah! I'm hyped!"

Nzingha looked at Sonny with incredulity. "You do know that nobody robs banks anymore?"

Sonny shook his head. "Read the *Wired* article. It provides the details of an elaborate diamond heist in Antwerp in 2007." Sonny leaned forward. "The vault used by the Antwerp Diamond Center was successfully robbed of over $100 million in gold and jewels. The authorities only managed to arrest one person on circumstantial evidence. The robbery was widely referred to as the crime of the century. *Wired* used testimony from the one guy they caught. He lays out all of the details in the article. We will study these and follow them to the letter."

"It simply cannot be done." Nzingha repeated.

"It can be done," Sonny countered. "The California American Bank vault has a similar design. 3-ton steel vault door. Multiple levels of security. On the vault door itself there's a 0-99 combination dial that requires four numbers to be opened thus generating 100 million possible combinations; a locked steel gate; a magnetic sensor; and inside the vault there's a heat and motion sensor. The vault doesn't have a seismic sensor for some reason. Perhaps because of the frequency of tremors in the Bay Area. The loot will be stored in safe deposit boxes, each of which is likely made of steel and copper with both a key lock and a combination with over 17,000 permutations. Seven Daggers has given us a way to get into the building through the service entrance. He's given us info on shift changes for the guards in the building. We will need to find a way to evade the city's security cams on the streets, cut the power on several floors, take out at least two night guards, disable motion and heat sensors, obtain the codes for the vault itself, quickly break into as many safe deposit boxes as we can, and somehow get away with the loot."

"How do you know all of this," Nzingha asked.

"When I was a patrolman for the Oakland Police Department, I backed-up on a shooting at the bank. Some desperate idiot with a shotgun thought he could hold the place up. Didn't get far. The job gave me the chance to talk with bank security."

Nzingha remained silent. Shaking her head.

"I'll need someone to plant a camera in the vault so that we can obtain the access codes. I'll need the equipment laid out in this article in order to disable the magnetic sensor outside of the vault and the heat and motion sensor inside the vault. Just in case, I'd like everyone armed. Our way in will involve hijacking the building's cleaning crew. I'll need muscle for that and I'll need muscle once we're inside to overpower the guards."

Orpheus spoke for the first time. "I can get the vault codes if you can somehow get me access to Black Archon computer servers. The bank will have its own cameras inside of the antechamber to the vault. If Godbold and the Archon are using the vault as their own private bank, they'll have access to that video feed."

"Where are those located?" Taketo inquired.

"San Francisco. George Bush Federal Building," Akoto offered.

"Godbold has servers and access to security video in the penthouse. But the White Council also has their own special access. We all know that the Black Archon is a front for corporate players who keep their distance from the street. But they still like to keep a watchful eye on Godbold. I have a source who tells me that they have access to MambaNet on servers in the Bush Building and they have a video feed for all the cameras in the Black Archon Center. I'm guessing that they have a view of the vault."

Nzingha objected. "You're talking about robbing a bank and breaking into a federal building. Dramatically expanding the scope of our mission. Breaking federal laws. Do you know who and what you're dealing with?"

"Let me tell you something," Sonny spoke emphatically, "we're not going to end sex trafficking in Oakland just because of one newspaper story. Aurora only meant for her investigation to be the opening act. Let's hurt the Black Archon where it counts. Let's get everyone's attention." Sonny paused. "I know *exactly* who I'm dealing with."

Akoto smiled. "I like the plan." He flipped through the article Sonny provided.

"Agreed." Taketo chimed in.

Orpheus nodded his agreement.

Sonny looked around the table until he got to Nzingha. "You in or not?"

Nzingha stared Sonny down hard. "This better fucking work."

"It will work. But we're going to have to move quickly. Word on the street is that Godbold is urgently moving money out of Oakland, leaving the Black criminal underworld behind, and betraying his corporate backers. This presents a great opportunity for us to seize cash and shut down the very network that they rely upon. But we have to get to that cash before they can effectively launder it, turn it into crypto-currency, and take it abroad."

Akoto smiled. "The time is right. The Black Archon is divided.

Godbold has alienated the streets and the boardroom."

"So, you're thinking we can exploit this division?" Nzingha asked.

"You're goddam right," Sonny nodded.

Nzingha shook her head. She turned her gaze from Sonny and looked at Akoto, investigating the confidence in his eyes. "And, how do *you* know this? Who's your source?"

Akoto turned to Nzingha. "I used to be involved with a white couple who work for the Archon. Turns out, the husband is the one that's been entrusted with maintaining the computer servers that run all their operations."

"That's altogether too convenient," Nzingha smirked.

"What do you think you'll find when you hack the network?" Sonny asked.

Akoto smiled broadly. "Everything. The servers should contain all the information we need to end the Black Archon."

"The vault codes are the priority. But I'll need you to look for evidence that might link the members of the White Council to the Black Archon's sex trafficking operations," Sonny implored. He reached into his bag and withdrew a copy of the speculative chart of members of the White Council pasted to the walls of his office. "Focus on these names and businesses."

"How can you even be sure that the servers are there? How can you be sure that she's not setting you up?" Nzingha returned to the primary concern. "It's just too much of a coincidence that her husband controls these servers."

Akoto smiled. "I know because she's *my* lady, not his."

"*How* do you get in?" Orpheus was intrigued.

"Laura tells me that the security is crazy tight," Akoto acknowledged.

"If you can't get in, that doesn't help, does it?" Nzingha smirked.

Akoto laughed. "I said it was impossible to get in, yeah, but not for me. I can do it."

"So…we've accounted for two buildings that we have to break into. What about the third?" Taketo asked.

"The third?" Nzingha asked.

"The third one's just for you," Akoto replied. "We have an opportunity to rescue some of the women before they're transported out of the state. There will be a party held at Godbold's mansion in the Oakland hills on the very night that we've planned the heist. They auction the kidnapped women and girls. They do it right out in the open."

"Also heavily guarded?" Nzingha inquired.

"Probably," Akoto shrugged. "But we can get two people in, no problem. Laura will give me authentic invitations."

"The beautiful thing," Sonny smiled, "is that Godbold will be at the party when we rob the bank, and back at the Black Archon Center when we rob the party."

Orpheus Anderson thought the matter over. "So, we have to commit three robberies in one day if we are going to have any chance of rescuing Aurora. Do I have that right?"

"You won't be involved in any of the break-ins. But yes, this is our best path to a bloodless coup." Sonny turned to Orpheus. "The level of difficulty increases with three break-ins. No doubt. But the odds are still better than us shooting it out in the streets with the Black Archon."

Orpheus shook his head. "I know that I'm new to the group and, believe me, I respect what you are trying to do. But why are you assuming that this man Seven Daggers is on the up and up? What if the police are waiting for you once you enter the Black Archon Center? What if it's a move to gain even greater favor from his boss? I'm a numbers guy. The way things add up to me, Seven Daggers sets you up, destroys the legend of the People's Detective, gains even greater favor from his boss, moves even further up the corporate ladder."

Sonny reminded Orpheus of the conversation Taketo heard at Suya Broadway and the recordings that Captain Gibson brought to his attention.

Orpheus continued to think on it. "What if this Captain Gibson is in on it? And Mister Akoto, what if your source is in on it too, in spite of your powers of romantic persuasion?"

Malik scoffed at the suggestion.

Sonny appreciated the advice. "Yeah, there's a lot to take on faith here. But time's running out for Aurora. We're going to have to throw caution to the wind. If anyone wants to back out, now would be a good time…"

"It's not as I would have wished but I hired you for a reason and I have to trust my judgment," Nzingha admitted.

Taketo had been thinking about the logistics of the impending bank robbery. "How did you say the thieves got past the magnetic field sensors inside the Amsterdam vault?"

"They used aluminum slabs to reposition the magnetic field away from the vault door," Sonny responded.

"How about the heat and motion sensor?" Nzingha asked.

"Women's hair spray."

The group broke out in raucous laughter, releasing the tension.

Nzingha waved her hand, struggling to suppress her amusement. "Okay, okay! I'm committed! But none of us have any experience in this."

"There's a fine line between cop and criminal," Akoto offered. "Isn't that right, Sonny?"

Sonny nodded. "There's more than a grain of truth to that."

"Of course, one of us has more experience than she's let on," Taketo leaned back in his chair, folded his arms, and stared at Nzingha.

"Why are you looking at me, Mister Taketo?"

"You *say* that you are a human rights activist. In fact, you are no such thing," Kaz Taketo spoke definitively. "You are a spy. You work for the Royal Bahamian Defense Forces. Your human rights organization is real, but you don't work for them. You are using the Anti-Slavery League as cover. You're here on the orders of your government to retrieve the Bahamian women who have been caught up in this affair."

Sonny winked at Nzingha. "Sounds like Sensei put out feelers among his connections in the Yakuza and Trenchtown Yardies. Seems they know a thing or two about the RBDF."

Taketo shrugged, feigning innocence.

Nzingha relented, reaching across the table to shake Sonny's hand. "Touché, Detective Trueheart. If I had been straight with you, you would never have agreed to work with me."

"You're a spy?" Malik smiled. "I suppose we all have our demons."

Nzingha clenched her fists. "The demons are out there, and they are real. I want to take them all down. The Black Council and the White Council. And I want the big man who runs the Black Archon first. His lineage is steeped in traitors and slave chasers. He comes and exploits his own people here in Oakland. If we can take down the head of the snake, we can discourage other such people in our communities from making the same deal with the devil." Nzingha was feeling the impact of the Kingston Smash.

Malik Akoto understood and felt her tone. She reminded him so much of his mother.

There came a knock on the door to the private room. Five servings of the oxtail stew came in on a tray carried by a dreadlocked sister with arms bearing tattoos of the Lion of Judah, Haile Selassie, and Bob Marley. Another Kingston Smash for Akoto.

Sonny eyed Akoto's drink longingly, still fighting the urge. He took a healthy pull from his sparkling water.

Akoto caught Sonny's glance. "All this and you have to keep off the booze."

"Rest assured, I can handle myself."

***

Seven Daggers sat outside of the Kingston 11, watching Sonny Trueheart and his people. He had followed Sonny from the Bardo. Although the group were smart enough to enter separately, Sonny's crew made the mistake of leaving together. A thin, gray-haired sister. The aging Kaz Taketo with slicked back gray hair and a sporty silver BMW roadster. A rangy young man with a grad student vibe who had been Taketo's dining companion at Suya Broadway. Malik Akoto. Sonny Trueheart.

Seven Daggers picked up his ringing smartphone.

"Sir?"

"Yes. What do you have to report?"

"Sonny Trueheart is working alone."

"Are you sure of that?"

"Yes. He has no allies. I have not ascertained by whom he is being paid or even if he is being paid. He may be doing this because Aurora Jenkins wrote a favorable story about him."

"Be serious. You're better than that. He's doing it because Aurora Jenkins is the younger sister of Aaminha Toure."

"I did not know that sir."

"How could you not know that after endless hours of questioning? I am beginning to have my doubts about your abilities."

"Please sir…it's just an oversight on my part."

"We cannot afford oversights. We simply cannot tolerate mistakes. Understood?" And then silence.

27. Hunger Strike

Aurora sat on the edge of a dirty bed in a cramped and filthy room on the third floor of a rundown motel on International Blvd. The windows were boarded up. The carpet was threadbare. The bathroom reeked of mold. The bedsheets were stained and smelled of cum.

Seven Daggers paced in front of her, inspecting her body, the leather skirt, halter top blouse, fishnet stockings, gold-plated hoop earrings, and red pumps that he had dressed her in so that she might be more appealing to the cops who were scheduled to exact their revenge upon her body. "You're butters, even in fresh garms. I can't make you look like a proper sket, can I?"

She had lost a great deal of weight during her captivity. The fentanyl had taken its toll. But what was most concerning now were her refusals to eat or drink in the aftermath of her failed escape. There was an undisturbed tray of food and an unopened bottle of water on the bed.

"I was gassed to put you to work in order to pay off your debt to the coppers," Seven Daggers rubbed his chin. "But I made a deal with your boyfriend, that damn Sonny Trueheart."

"Sonny wouldn't deal with you."

"Bollocks! You havin' a laugh? He's done precisely that. Yeah, he's proper moist. He's agreed to perform a service for me in exchange for your return. And, in the meantime, I've also agreed not to put you to work servicing Oakland's finest. But…if he fails to complete his task…all bets are off, innit?"

"If you're trying to give me hope so that I'll eat, you're doing a poor job of it."

Seven Daggers knelt before her and placed a hand on her thigh. "I really didn't want to put you out there for the coppers to tear you apart. But they've asked for reparations for the two copter fuzz you put into intensive care and I won't be able to hold them off much longer. If bruv can complete his task, I'll return you to his custody and square things with the coppers. It's all up to him, really. So…" Seven Daggers held Aurora's chin in his right hand. "…there is *real* hope for you. And you should eat and keep up your strength."

Aurora screamed at him, spittle flying from her mouth as she cursed his name. "I won't eat! I'm taking back *my* body! I'm going to take back my body from them and from you! If you bring the cops in here to rape and brutalize me, they'll find nothing but my dead, emaciated body!"

Seven Daggers rose and wiped his face. "Yeah. You got plenty spirit, girl. Plenty spirit."

"I'm not a girl or a female! I'm a woman!" Aurora stood and met Seven Daggers' stare. "Maybe we should just handle this, mano a mano, you and me." Aurora assumed a fighting posture.

"I'd kill you, luv!"

Aurora pushed Seven Daggers back and raised her fists. "Isn't that what you want to do anyway? Well then, let's get it on!"

Seven Daggers stepped back and smiled. "Yeah, that's why I like you, girl. You've got the bottle. Look, I aint gonna fight you. Right now, you're my ace in the hole. If your boyfriend plays it straight, you'll be back in his arms in no time. So there aint no need for fighting right now. And…" Seven Daggers pointed to the tray of food, "…there aint no need in starving yourself."

Aurora waved her hands in frustration. "Aint no need? Look at how you got me dressed, threatening to put me before cops who are going to violate my body and my soul. You and all the horror that you've shown me, selling me this bullshit idea about the Black

Archon being the savior of all sex workers. *Saving?* More like brainwashing." She pressed her index finger against her temple. She stepped closer and glared at him. "I damn sure don't want you saving me now only to kill me later. And, even if Sonny made a deal with you, I'm taking matters into my own hands. I'm taking my life back. I'm in control now, you understand?"

Power to the People!
A Podcast for the People
Broadcasting from the Lower Bottoms of West Oakland
Hosted by Aurora Jenkins

Transcript of Power to the People! Episode 76

It's your Momma, your Auntie, your Big Sister, your Play Cousin! Your Friendly Neighborhood Queer Black Feminist. On today's broadcast I am calling on the community to help provide information that might lead to the discovery of a missing teenager. 16-year-old Annabelle Villafuerte was last seen this past weekend. She is described as a Latina standing a little over 5 feet tall, weighing 90 pounds, dark brown hair with blonde highlights and dark brown eyes. She was last seen wearing a pink sweatshirt and faded, ripped blue jeans. She is described as being in good mental and physical condition, however, she is considered at risk because of her age.

It has been reported that she has been estranged from her family and living away from home with a close friend. The family, however, disputes these claims, emphasizing that Annabelle is very close to her family and to her Abuelita. Annabelle is a loving and kind young woman who wants to go to college and become a veterinarian.

It's important, when we report on missing persons in our communities, for us to provide details that fully humanize and help us understand the total person. These are real people with real lives and real hopes and dreams and people who love them. If you have any further details or information, please reach out to this program and the family as well as the Police Department's Missing Persons Unit.

28. Reconnaissance

There is no formula for pulling off a bank heist. No *YouTube* video, no *Bank Robbery for Dummies* and no *TedTalks* for Bank Robbers. There is certainly no formula for five novice bank robbers breaking into the most secure vault in northern California and making away with the blood money of the largest criminal organization in Oakland. The mission was, in Sonny's estimation, reasonably doomed to fail. And yet, it was certainly the best and seemingly least violent option for bringing the Black Archon to the table for the release of Aurora Jenkins.

There was a quixotic romanticism about the whole thing and a camaraderie that developed amongst the conspirators. The heist reunited best friends and dojo mates, a master teacher with his two best pupils, and introduced new people and a new world into the original trio. And yes, it offered Sonny an opportunity to redeem himself, as Nzingha had suggested.

Sonny assigned tasks for each of the team members to complete. They would have a mere 24 hours to complete their tasks. The bank heist would have to take place within 48 hours. Even that was pushing it. Aurora's life was hanging in the balance.

Akoto and Orpheus were assigned the tasks of breaking into the George Bush building, obtaining the vault codes, and planting a virus on the MambaNet servers. Given Orpheus's civilian status and Akoto's understanding that the man's presence would only slow him down, they agreed that Akoto would be the only one to physically break into the server room and that once in, he would communicate with Orpheus via burner phones.

Nzingha was assigned further surveillance within the bank vault.

She accomplished this relatively easily by shopping for a safe-deposit box in disguise and under a fake passport –she had many– and flirting with the bank manager, effectively distracting him as she shot video from her smartphone. Amazing what you can do by playing to the male ego.

Taketo was assigned reconnaissance of Upton's Uptown Cleaners, the company licensed to clean the Black Archon Center. Security was used to seeing their vans and they regularly appeared on the video feed provided by the building's external cameras and Oakland's traffic cameras. The crew would take their trucks and their uniforms. Taketo also acquired nose pullers from a West Oakland locksmithing company. They would need these to break open each of the safe deposit boxes in the vault.

Sonny held another meeting with Seven Daggers at the Bardo. He confirmed his schedule for assassinating Dr. Godbold. Sonny had Seven Daggers expecting that the job would be done in three days, even as he planned the bank heist to occur in the next two.

Sonny also assigned himself the task of obtaining weapons and finding an anesthetic that could render the guards in the bank unconscious. He called a night meeting at the Harley Davidson dealership on Hegenberger with the owner and former lead mechanic for the Black Panther Party for Self Defense known as "The Blacksmith," who still repaired vehicles and dealt weapons for anyone involved in what he called "The Resistance." He operated under the Black Archon's radar. The Blacksmith had sold Sonny his beloved mysterious red sunglo Fatboy back in the day. Sonny asked The Blacksmith to provide heavy weapons for the crew and had in mind four M4 semi-automatic rifles. However, on short notice, The Blacksmith could only produce four unmarked and untraceable compact polymer 9mm pistols for the crew, including a subcompact 9mm for Nzingha. These would be dumped into the Bay following the completion of their crimes.

The Blacksmith's most valuable contributions were several syringes of a drug called Midazolam, a powerful anesthetic used before surgical procedures. The drug would slow down brain activity and produce a loss of consciousness and memory. If used improperly, it could stop breathing and lead to permanent brain damage. Or, as The Blacksmith remarked, "You better make sure a motherfucker don't die on you."

The crew checked in with one another at Sonny's house the night before the robbery. Everyone confirmed the completion of their assignments. Sonny went over the plan once more with precise detail, making certain that each person fully understood their role.

The next day at noon, Akoto would break into the George W. Bush Federal Building. In the evening, at 9 pm, they would break into the California American Bank vault in the Black Archon Center. Near the midnight hour they would raid a Black Archon party. Quite a full schedule.

Sonny encouraged everyone to get 8 hours of sleep and to be mentally and physically prepared for the next day.

After everyone departed, Sonny sat in meditation, listening to jazz guitarist Jim Hall's version of "Concierto de Aranjuez," with the graceful improvisations of Paul Desmond, who had been diagnosed with cancer by the time of this session, the sweet lyricism of Chet Baker, and the spare and beautiful solo expressions of Jim Hall.

Sonny initiated his meditation with a deep breath and focused on the steady rhythmic pulse of bassist Ron Carter which took him to a state of higher consciousness. Sonny saw the immediate future. He saw the robbery unfold amidst a sepia haze, as though he were witnessing a vision through a glass darkly. As he opened his eyes and took a deep breath coming out of his meditation, he felt a greater clarity of purpose and was secure in knowing that the success of his mission was ordained.

29. Smoke and Mirrors

An act of God happened that confirmed Sonny's vision. A series of wildfires erupted across the northernmost part of California in Butte County, creating what would become America's deadliest wildfires on record since 1918. Ignited by a faulty PG&E electric transmission line and fueled by a historically brutal drought season and powerful east winds driving the flames downhill, the Camp Fire, as it would be called, blew through the rural community of Concow and into the towns of Magalia and Butte Creek Canyon culminating in an urban fiasco in the foothill town of Paradise. 85 fatalities, 12 civilian injuries and 5 injured firefighters.

The powerful Diablo winds carried the disaster further south, blowing smoke and ash that carried tiny bits of aerosolized particulate matter that human lungs are incapable of filtering out, well into the Bay Area.

Oaklanders woke up to a sepia-toned sky filled with smoke and thick layers of ash on the streets. City officials urged citizens to wear breathing masks and cautioned the public to remain indoors as much as possible. Overnight, Oakland became the dystopian landscape of an Octavia Butler novel. Hospitals saw a surge of patients struggling with respiratory issues. Sonny prayed for the dead and the dying and those who would surely lose their homes further north. Perhaps some of what they would steal could go to the victims. But he also knew that the smoke would interfere with street surveillance cameras and that local first responders were being called to assist already overwhelmed fire and police departments in Shasta and Trinity counties. The Oakland streets would be a virtual ghost town at night, eerie in the smoke-filled haze that Sonny had envisioned during his meditation.

A perfect cover for their caper.

Sonny woke up at the crack of dawn and walked outside, wearing an A's baseball cap, and wiped ash from his motorcycle. He looked up and down 68th Avenue and the ash covered cars, the ash on rooftops and the black asphalt streets.

He tied a bandana around his mouth and nose and started up the Fat Boy.

He drove from his East Oakland home to downtown and drove several times around the Black Archon Center and the bank, observing security and the flow of armored trucks. Some of these were certainly carrying cash from Black Archon street operations that were increasingly being shut down and moved onto MambaNet.

He checked his watch and waited until 8am for the security shift change. He noticed four armed guards who worked the graveyard shift departing while only two entered for the morning shift. Was the security light because of the smoke? Would this hold up this evening?

Sonny continued motoring around downtown Oakland, paying close attention to security details at other banks, retail stores, jewelry stores, and pawn shops. He drove into West Oakland and Emeryville, giving a cursory examination of security at big box stores and distribution centers and warehouses. When he returned into Oakland proper he took the 580 and the offramp at Fruitvale. He parked and grabbed coffee at Peet's across the street from Farmer Joe's Market and used their internet signal to search a popular Oakland-based private security firm called East Side Watch Dogs.

Sonny looked up the street and saw the Wells Fargo Bank Fruitvale branch. "Hello, I'm with Wells Fargo. Fruitvale branch. Our regular team is a little short today. What are the chances of us being able to obtain security staff on short notice today?"

The gruff East Side Watch Dog employee on the other end of the line responded, "Not today. No chance. All our people are out on call today. City's low on cops and other first responders because of the fires. And with all this smoke, businesses all across the city are nervous about security. Means that everyone, no matter what company you call, is going to tell you the same thing. Every private security firm is gonna be maxed out. Everyone is running a little thin today because of the demand."

Sonny hung up.

He browsed the social media pages of several security firms and found pictures of the smoke-filled skies in various neighborhoods across the city and postings seeking additional help. Overtime was offered. Guidance was provided about health and safety.

When he returned home, he called each member of the crew, making certain that they were prepared for the day.

30. Acrophobia

Malik Akoto looked forward to the opportunity to visit the new Federal Building in San Francisco, but this was insane, and he loved everything about it. The entire plan was impossible: committing three separate break-ins and robberies in a single day. But, as he looked up at the sepia haze in the sky and saw the thin layer of light ash covering the streets of downtown San Francisco, he felt as Sonny felt, that the odds were suddenly in their favor. He was here at noon during the lunch break for federal workers in this building to break into Neil Bello's office on the 18th floor and obtain access to the California American Bank vault codes and the MambaNet servers. This would complete the first significant break-in and provide information for the second. Akoto had to succeed or the remainder of Sonny's plan for the day would fall through.

Akoto entered the lobby of the George W. Bush Federal Building on the corner of Mission and 7th St. with concrete walls made of blast furnace slag from Portland, perforated metal panels, faceted wood ceilings and chic paintings. It was also a naturally ventilated "green" building that consumed less than half the power of a standard office tower.

Architecture was one of Akoto's many passions. This new Federal Building was a fitting place for the white members of the Black Archon to oversee their darknet transactions. Someplace completely segregated from their Black counterparts in Oakland.

The building was aesthetically cold but practically steamy with its lack of air-conditioning. It was massively over-budget and ill-conceived in many respects, but you had to respect the architect for trying.

The new George W. Bush Federal Building had a particularly annoying feature for Malik Akoto: elevators that automatically stopped every third floor to promote employee interaction and health by encouraging walking. This could pose a significant problem if he needed to make a quick exit.

Akoto gained entry by impersonating a bicycle messenger. In the morning, Akoto took note that the "Speed Demons" courier company was favored by many of the offices in the building. He "bumped into" a bicycle carrier on the street and offered the man $200 for his uniform vest, bicycle helmet, gloves, and no questions asked. Now, at noon, Akoto walked into the George Bush Federal Building in uniform with his short red locs concealed under the helmet and the right cuff of his jeans secured crudely by a rubber band, as many cyclists do in order to prevent them from getting stuck in the gears. The security was light, and even the Federal guards were spread thin, as Sonny had anticipated. When asked by lobby security personnel to sign in, Akoto provided a false name. He carried no weapons and easily passed through the metal detector.

Once inside the building he pretended to go about his business, delivering fake documents to the offices of the U.S. Department of Labor on the 14th floor before taking the stairs to the 18th floor where he would find Neil Bello's office. Akoto carried two packages. He flirted with an administrative assistant in the Labor office and secured the code for the all-gender bathroom.

Alone in the restroom, Akoto closed his eyes and breathed deeply in and out. When he emerged from the bathroom with the packages under his arm, he looked through tall windows down at the people walking on Mission St.

He was ready to do what he had to do.

He heard voices and movement coming down the hall. Akoto moved back into the restroom. He set down the packages and pressed his ear against the door. As the voices grew louder, Akoto burst from the restroom, lunging at the first security guard, lifting him off his feet and throwing him against the wall. Moving quickly and using the principles of aikido, Akoto sidestepped the grasp of the second security guard, gaining control of the man's elbow, and used the man's momentum to carry him headfirst into the wall beside where his colleague lay. The guard slumped and fell into a deep slumber.

The first guard attempted to rise to his knees and fumbled to grab his weapon. Akoto reached down and gripped his collar with his right hand. He hooked his left arm under the guard's left arm, then stepping over the guard's head with his right leg, he hooked it around the man's neck, pulled him up by the arm and collar into the tight crook of his bent right leg, completing the choke.

Akoto released the unconscious guard, stepped back and glanced at his watch. 45 seconds tops. He dragged both men into the restroom, stripped them completely naked, and pulled four zip ties from the pocket of his uniform and bound them about the ankles and wrists. He put each man in a separate stall. He rummaged through their clothing and took keys, walkie-talkies, smartphones, and guns from both men. There was also a nice gold lighter in the breast pocket of one of the guard's uniform shirts that Akoto pocketed.

He changed into one of their uniforms —a decent fit overall— and stuffed the other uniform into a trash receptacle in the bathroom. He holstered one of the 9mm's and dismantled the other weapon, tossing its polymer parts in the trash and pocketing a spare magazine. He brought both walkie-talkies with him. He kept the leather bicycle gloves and put these in the left pocket of the pants he had stolen. He put on a pair of nitrile gloves from the pocket of the bike messenger uniform. He also carried a roll of one-hundred-dollar bills in the messenger uniform —some of this he had used to purchase the outfit from the Speed Demons messenger— and he transferred this to the right pocket of the guard's uniform.

Malik Akoto made his way to Neil Bello's office. He unlocked the door successfully after trying four different keys. He was surprised that it only required one key to enter the room, but he knew that there might be a security camera. This is why he had changed into one of the guard uniforms and left the lights off.

He smiled at the thought of committing high crimes and misdemeanors in the name of justice. He rather appreciated the opportunity.

Akoto sat down at the main desk in the room. He looked up from under the lowered brim of the guard's cap and examined the corners of the room. No cameras. Lucky. There was a narrow, rectangular LED screen and a telephone keypad embedded into the surface of the desk. A prompt came up on screen for a password. Akoto entered the name "laurabello" as the phone number "528-722-3556." A central computer whirred and came to life. A giant screen and keypad rose from the desk.

She had been right. The room's design had apparently been the brainchild of Laura's husband and, in spite of his abusive behavior toward Laura, the man was strangely sentimental.

Akoto withdrew his smartphone and dialed in Orpheus Anderson for a video chat and made certain that his camera revealed a clear view of the giant screen.

When Orpheus answered the call, Akoto asked, "Can you see it clearly?"

"Yes.'

"What should I be looking for?"

"Go to the Finder and let me see the list of all folders on the hard drive."

Akoto opened the Finder and waited as Orpheus searched programs that might contain security codes. The bank would certainly change these everyday, and perhaps even multiple times during the day. The new codes would be issued daily from this office.

Orpheus punctuated long moments of silence with the command, "keep scrolling.'" Akoto kept slowly scrolling downward, and Orpheus kept searching.

"Got it!" Orpheus exclaimed. "Look at the folder that is labeled 'All is well.' That's a popular white supremacist phrase. Click on that!"

Akoto did as he was told and found a livestream video application in the folder and cycled through the many cameras that the Black Archon and their paymasters had set up throughout the Bay Area. There were hundreds of cameras with views of bars, nightclubs, massage parlors, brothels, and street corners where trafficked women sold their bodies. The control room was a window out onto criminal spaces across the entire Bay Area.

One of the livestream feeds displayed several views of the California American Bank safe. There were hundreds of short video files. There were high-definition videos of California American Bank guards entering codes and unlocking the steel gate to the antechamber, opening the vault itself, and a camera inside of the vault that gave him a sense of how many safe deposit boxes there were.

"You think this will be enough?"

"Attach the flash drive that I provided for you directly to the server."

Akoto reached into his pocket and produced the drive. "Where do I place it?"

"There should be a bank of hard drives somewhere in the room that are connected to the computer that you are viewing."

Akoto noticed a large sliding wooden door in the room. He carried his phone with him, so that Orpheus could see everything. He walked towards it and opened the door, revealing another room with an impressive array of tall computer servers and equipment racks with cabling that extended out of the room. The room was cold from the air conditioning coming from floor vents between each server.

"It's a hot aisle/cold aisle configuration," Orpheus explained. "That means that two rows face one another and have their backs to the next row so that the hot exhaust coming from the back of one row won't be sucked into the cooling intake of the next row. Servers tend to vent front to rear, you see?"

"Not sure what any of that means. Does it mean that I am in the right area to place the drive?"

"Yes, because you are now walking down an aisle where the rows of servers face one another. There will be a port you can use on either side of you."

"Why are there so many servers?"

"It takes a lot to maintain MambaNet. I would recommend 1 DS server for every 3,500 to 5,000 computers. The amount of servers in this room gives you a sense of how vast MambaNet is. It's also possible that they are using some of these servers to mine crypto right here in a federal building."

"Depending on the cryptocurrency that they are using, they could also be laundering profits from MambaNet transactions."

"Right," Orpheus agreed. "If they use a stablecoin or a cryptocurrency tied to real world dollars, they could have both anonymity and stability and maybe route everything through an offshore exchange that violates U.S. banking rules."

"How could we find any evidence of something like this?"

"The biggest challenge is attributing the crypto transactions to specific people. Sonny gave us 13 names and asked us to look for patterns in financial transactions. At first, all we will be able to see are anonymous digital addresses."

"What can you do, Orpheus?"

"I'll have time with the spyware to do some prying. Maybe I can get enough for Sonny to present to the DA They have the software that connects crypto transactions to the real world and they have the legal authority to analyze the blockchain. It's just a digital ledger. They can determine who's sending funds. Nothing is truly anonymous. But sometimes you have to get a court order. I can only go so far."

"The easier way to go is with testimony from Neil Bello. Right?" Akoto was already considering alternatives. "Maybe I can help Sonny turn him into a witness for the prosecution."

Akoto kept waking, allowing his camera to scan the equipment on either side of him. He stopped when he heard Orpheus exclaim, "That's it! I want you to connect the flash drive right there." Akoto pointed so that his finger was visible to Orpheus. "Yes! The server you are pointing to right now has two ports on its main chassis. See that? Now, connect the drive to one of these. I'll do the rest."

After attaching the drive, Akoto went back to the desktop in the office and opened the two packages that he had held onto. One contained two mini-bar bottles of a 12-year-old blended scotch and a plastic Glencairn whisky glass and the other had a to-go container of chicken and sausage gumbo from Brenda's on Polk St.

While Akoto ate and drank, he opened another browser and stepped into the world of MambaNet. He saw the faces of the missing and the full horror of the Black Archon came to him. There were hundreds of faces as he scrolled down the page, hundreds of faces with nicknames and false bios to advertise their sexual skills and proclivities.

"Orpheus, can you download the information about the women on this site?"

"Yeah. We can help the cops return them to their families."

The walkie-talkie of the fallen security guard chirped, interrupting their conversation. "Carlos," the voice called to him, "where are you?"

"Thought I would take a break." Akoto did his best to imitate the voice that he had heard walking down the corridor before he had overtaken both guards.

"Where?"

"In the hallway on the 18th floor."

"We don't take our breaks in the hallway."

"I need some space, ese. You know things aren't going too well for me at home right now."

"Oh. Didn't know that. Sorry bro."

"It's cool."

"Where's Bryan?"

"Taking a leak."

"I'll give you some space bro."

"I owe you one ese."

Akoto breathed a sigh of relief.

"Was that the security team?" Orpheus asked.

"Yeah, I gotta make my escape pretty soon. We straight?"

"No. The flash drive is labeled 'X.' Open the icon on the desktop. You will see a program entitled 'Team Viewer.' I want you to open this program and wait for it to be installed. This will give me on-going remote access to their servers. With this I will be able to see the live feed for the codes that they enter at the end of today's shift. We will have all the up-to-date information that we need for tonight. It will also allow me to conduct some blockchain forensics, collect evidence for the DA, and plant a virus to shut down MambaNet."

Akoto did as instructed and glanced at his watch as he waited for the remote access program to download onto the servers. It took 15 minutes. Akoto signaled, "Done." Time to go. And with that he shut down the desktop, and walked out of the control room, taking the empty bottles, plastic glass, and food container, shutting the doors behind him. He dumped his trash and checked on the guards in the restroom. Stone cold slumber.

31. Game of Death

Akoto knew that there was one last hurdle. Once the guards awakened and managed to free themselves, they would signal the remaining security team to find him and take him down. They would certainly try to apprehend him on his way out of the George W. Bush Federal Building. For Malik Akoto, the challenge was now to walk down the corridors of fear and make it to the other side where he could be reunited with the people that he had grown to love.

He whistled as he descended the staircase.

Akoto loved the high ceilings and windows and the massive exoskeleton sunscreen that converted the intense sunlight coming into the building's glass façade into a passive heat pump that practically cooled the building. There was light traffic on the staircase from federal employees as he approached the 17th floor. The kind of socializing that was intended by the architects of the new Federal Building was evident. Although there were narrow corridors throughout the building, and the staircases were hardly suitable for conversation, there were a host of open meeting spaces including the Skygarden on the 11th floor where employees could congregate and socialize.

Suddenly, Akoto heard a cry coming from the steps below and then the sharp, quick steps of police officers and security scurrying up the staircase from the 15th floor.

He had been discovered!

Akoto drew the 9mm pistol and retreated back up to the 18th floor. Akoto didn't want to hurt cops. But if it came down to it…

The only alternative to the staircase were the elevators. The elevator cars were capped with glass domes and powered by hydraulic rams that pushed each car up 18 floors from below rather than through a pulley or cable system with counter-weights mounted on top of each elevator car. The hydraulic rams were long pistons driven out of hollow cylinders by pressure created by water. When the pressure of the hydraulic fluid is high enough, the force it exerts on the base of the piston exceeds the combined weight of the piston and elevator car causing upward acceleration. As the piston rises, the hydraulic fluid has more space to fill and its pressure drops. To keep the piston moving upward, a solar-powered pump draws water from a reservoir to add more pressure to the cylinder.

Akoto knew that cops were surely coming up each of the elevators and the stairs. He savagely kicked a pedestal table near the staircase door, loosening a leg of the table that he used to bar the staircase door and quickly scampered to the elevator. He was unaware of passersby scampering for cover in the corridor at the sight of a Black man —even a Black man in a guard's uniform— running with a pistol in his hand. The nearest elevator was approaching the 13th floor. Malik forced open the elevator door and looked down the yawning cavity of the elevator shaft. He saw the artful transparent dome of the roof of the elevator car ascending. The transparent domes and glass walls in each elevator allowed passengers an up-close view of the mechanical workings of adjacent elevators —you could see the hydraulic rams working— and was in step with the modern "industrial chic" of the building. He heard the wooden leg of the pedestal table that he had used to bar the staircase door as it snapped under the weight of cops bursting into the corridor from the 18th floor landing. He didn't have time to think about it.

Akoto fired the 9mm pistol down the elevator shaft, shattering the glass dome, and, without the slightest hesitation, he jumped.

Akoto looked down as he fell, knifing downwards, as the elevator slowly made its way up. He had to be perfect. The elevator stopped on the 16th floor, providing a still target for the final stage of his 2-story freefall. He shouted. Miraculously clearing any jagged glass edges, he landed hard, bending his knees to cushion the impact as he came down, crashing into the center of an elevator loaded with guards, easily breaking a man's shoulder and perhaps the collarbone of another as he came down hard upon two officers whose bodies broke his fall, and plunging the elevator into darkness. Akoto landed hard on his knees, feeling the searing agony of what must certainly have been a fractured tibia or fibula. But he didn't have the time to feel the pain nor to feel for his gun in the darkness.

There were four guards in the elevator. Two had been disabled by his fall. In the darkness there was a flash of gunfire, the shots ringing in everyone's ears. Akoto whirled, knee walking as he had learned to do when training in aikido with Sonny, his knees and shins aching with horrible pain, and pivoted toward the sound of one of the guards pulling the slide back and chambering a round in his automatic pistol. Akoto shot up from his knees and drove the crown of his head sharply upward into the guard's face, drawing a sharp cry and blood from the man's mouth as he split his chin wide open. As he rose, the guard managed to get off one shot at close range. He missed, but powder burns grazed Akoto's forehead and he saw a blinding flash and there was a spurt of blood that trickled into his left eye and he felt an incredible sting. Akoto viciously kneed the guard twice in the chest in reaction, reaching to grab him by his shirt and pull him into the thrust of his knees.

He was effectively blinded in one eye, fighting in the darkness. But there were three down now and Akoto again whirled in the darkness to the sound of the fourth guard frantically pulling the trigger of his jammed automatic pistol to no avail. "I'm lucky to be alive," he thought, as he took the man's gun arm in an *Ikkyo* move, controlling the elbow and the wrist, and drove the guard, with the assistance of his own forward momentum, face first into the glass wall of the elevator.

Akoto collapsed, leaning against the wall of the elevator. He stood over four guards, two lying still and two groaning in pain. Two guards had enough time to draw their weapons, and one had fired the shot that temporarily blinded him in one eye and the other would have killed him if it hadn't been for the fortunate misfiring of his gun.

The elevator car suddenly jerked upward and the emergency panel lights came on. Someone was trying to control the elevator remotely. Akoto stepped over a body and pressed the emergency stop button on the elevator to prevent it from reaching the 18th floor. He checked pulses. Two guards had been rendered unconscious by the impact of Akoto's fall. He'd also shot one of the guards in the anterior tibial artery – which accounted for his massive blood loss and wailing in pain– and caught another in his right shoulder, no doubt both from the shots that broke the glass dome. And then there was the guard that he head-butted in the chin and the one he slammed face-first into the elevator wall. Four severely wounded. He could never tell Sonny about the carnage. It was more blood on the Black Archon, the way Akoto saw it.

Akoto flipped the emergency stop off and banged the 11th floor button. The elevator car now reversed course. He was headed down to the 11th floor to the Skygarden.

A ray of light streamed into the elevator shaft from the cops who had managed to open the elevator door on the 18th floor above him. A cop pointed the barrel of his shotgun down at Malik until another pulled him from the breach, warning him that he might hit the guards. And the car descended slowly to the 11th floor.

An adjacent ascending elevator passed his car. It carried another four guards who looked at Malik Akoto standing over their fallen comrades with a mixture of horror and blood-boiling venom.

Akoto wiped the blood from his eyes.

The elevator doors hissed open. Akoto staggered into the corridor. In the breast pocket of the security guard's uniform that he had stolen, he found a pair of sunglasses to mask the powder burns on his face.

The 11th floor was a high open space with stunning views to the north and south of the facility. From the street on one side and from the open plaza on the other, it looked like a giant square hole in the side of the building and a dramatic break in the sunscreen that hung over the asymmetrical tower like the exo-skeleton of an insect.

He fired his gun at the ceiling, dispersing the crowd, screaming at the top of his lungs, "Stop, Security!" He snatched a scampering federal employee by the collar and screamed in her face, "Tell them I'm in pursuit of the suspect. The suspect is on elevator three on his way to the restaurant on the third floor. The suspect is holding a police officer hostage! The suspect has a bomb in his briefcase! Now run!" And he pushed the woman in the direction of the staircase.

Akoto ran the width of the Skygarden and kept announcing that he was a security guard. He screamed that there was a bomb on the elevator and screamed for everyone to drop to the ground and seek cover. There were piercing screams coming from the employees in the Skygarden now.

Akoto gave a wry smile. That would buy him the time he needed.

Now to prepare for his exit.

Akoto remembered the gold lighter that he had stolen. He knocked the lid off a recycling waste container and ignited the disposed paper. He grabbed and held the container up to the sprinkler heads at the ends of pipes running down from the high ceilings of the Skygarden. The smoke rose. The fire alarm was sounded, and the sprinklers turned on and began to shower the Skygarden.

He headed toward the Skygarden opening that looked down on the open-air plaza, removed the nitrile gloves, exchanging them for the bicycle gloves in his pocket, and quickly put them on. The bicycle gloves would protect his hands to some degree. He pocketed his gun and stepped over the railing, slowly lowering himself and seeking a firm hold on the building's sunscreen exoskeleton.

He found purchase on the thick exoskeleton. From 11 stories high, he looked out at the ash covered streets beneath the sepia-toned sky. Akoto felt the searing heat being absorbed by the material, the heat that was effectively blocked from the structure itself. It was a relatively cool day beneath the smoke of the fires, but the accumulation of the day's heat energy was already baked into the exo-skeleton. Akoto's hands would have burned as if he were grasping a hot poker if he were not using the bicycle gloves. Even these began emitting steam under the heat. He knew that his hands would still be burned and blistered if he could survive.

11 floors down. Akoto descended like a spider. No guards aiming down from the opening above. No cops arriving in the plaza. Firefighters would be on their way in response to the alarms. Certainly, more cops would be called to the Federal Building. Akoto was counting on the firefighters and emergency rescue teams to arrive first, but the smoke-filled skies blown into the Bay Area by the fires in Butte County meant that many first responders had been called out of the area to assist up north.

There were a handful of bike messengers admiring his feat. Doubtless there was someone shooting video and posting it on social media. Akoto was glad that he had the sunglasses on as he descended.

In spite of the diversion he created, he knew he was still running out of time. Precious time. Akoto decided that he had to take chances. Had to quickly reach the ground and escape across the open-air plaza and into the city beyond.

The building sloped steeply outward. If he released his grasp momentarily, he wondered if he had the strength to regain his hold and whether he would fall away from the building as he descended. He loosened his grip ever so slightly and tried to dig in his feet and began sliding ever faster down the façade. As he accelerated, he judged his speed and braked suddenly with a tighter grasp on the rungs of the exo-skeleton. He repeated this three times. The stops were painfully jarring and he felt as if his arms were being yanked from the sockets. There was no room for error. He felt that he was so close to a speed that would send him flying off the building and plummeting to the street. But there was the issue of time.

Still no cops in the plaza or the curb below. No cops above in the Skygarden opening. None of the frightened employees had seen him go over the railing. No one had thought to look. Surely, he was on a surveillance camera. Was every cop too busy tracking him down inside? Was no one manning the cameras? Was that possible? Had his decoy bomb scare worked? And there wasn't a single one of the bike messengers below that would have even considered calling the attention of the police even as they filmed his movements with their smartphones. They were the counterculture, and everyone resented the rudeness with which the Federal Building cops treated visitors.

And then Akoto heard the sound of the fire engines. His gamble —100 to one odds— paid off.

He estimated that he was 7-floors up when the fire engine arrived. The bike messengers pointed and alerted them of a man escaping down the building's façade. Several firefighters broke out the portable life net from the ladder truck while their brothers raced into the lobby of the Federal Building. Akoto knew that it took at least 10 men to hold the life net but there were only four now, holding the outside ring chest high and palms up. Malik knew that the life nets were designed to catch people falling from 3 stories and lower. He intended to work his way a little further down the netting and then jump when all hell broke loose and a cop car careened onto the plaza, siren wailing, responding to the emergency.

A young cop in a loose-fitting uniform stormed out of his car with his weapon drawn, shouting into his walkie talkie, "Requesting back-up! I have the suspect! He fits the description!" Malik Akoto saw the cop draw his pistol and aim. Rather than wait for him to descend, the cop fired, clipping Akoto on the right calf.

"Fuck all." Malik muttered to himself. And he fell.

He fell 7 stories. He fell, spinning as he came down into the dead center of the springy life net and then, with a hard bounce as the net slightly gave way under his weight and the limitations of only four firefighters, he came up and off the edge and onto the concrete, the 9mm slipping out of his waistband and clattering to the ground, and he landed on his side, instinctively slapping at the concrete to brace the shock as he fell. His head scuffed the concrete. He quickly assessed his injuries. It felt like a bruised hip, but Akoto again fought the searing pain and his body's desire to blackout and he rolled onto his other side and then stumbled into a standing position as the young cop closed on him.

Akoto remembered how Taketo used to compliment his effort. "Don't corner this dog," he would say, "you never know what he'll bring forth from the depths of his spirit."

Blind in one eye, knees and shins numb with pain, a sharp pain in his left hip area, a bullet wound to his calf, and his hands burnt and blistered from the heat of the exoskeleton, Akoto wildly rushed the young cop who fired reflexively, grazing Akoto's left shoulder as Akoto closed the distance. Akoto struck the man under the chin with a savage right uppercut. The cop dropped his gun as his head snapped backward. Akoto followed up with a hard shot to the young man's ribs and then kicked at the cop's shins, sending him to his knees on the hard concrete. Akoto grabbed the cop's pistol and stood over the man, reaching back and hitting him on the back of his head with the butt of the pistol. As the young cop face-planted on the concrete, Akoto could hear more police sirens in the distance.

The four firefighters who had only recently saved his life with the trampoline now stood indecisive before an armed and obviously dangerous man.

The bike messengers were cheering.

The firefighters stood motionless. "I don't want any problems," Akoto said to them, and dropped the police officer's gun. The four firefighters continued to stand motionless.

Malik Akoto pulled a thick roll of hundred-dollar bills from his pocket and turned to his bike messenger audience. "I want the fastest bike." And he tossed the roll to the ground in front of them.

A messenger with a red mohawk and nose-rings and skull tattoos on his arms rolled a bike in his direction and gathered the money.

"Steel frame. Fixed gear. No brakes. Can you handle it man?"

Akoto mounted the bike. "Thanks." And he awkwardly mounted the bike and began to pedal across the plaza, the still motionless firemen in his peripheral vision. Akoto pedaled gingerly over the decomposed granite surface of the plaza that allows rainwater to circulate back into the earth and prevents the city's sewers from being overloaded with runoff pollutants. He pedaled off the grounds of the Federal Building and onto 7th St. and then South of Market St. onto Mission St. where he became lost from view on the ash-covered streets amidst the sea of fentanyl junkies, sex workers, the unhoused, and the starving artists of the South of Market or SOMA District and he was gone.

32. Black is the Color

Aurora stripped and threw the leather skirt, halter top, fishnet stockings, red pumps, and hoop earrings into a corner in the filthy windowless room. She ran her hands along her naked body. She could no longer feel her ribs poking out from under her skin. Instead, she felt almost full, as if she had eaten a 4-course meal. They no longer brought trays of food. Instead, Seven Daggers would come and subdue her with fentanyl and, after administering the Narcan, he would bring in a team of male nurses who would administer an IV of sodium chloride. One night they used propofol to render her unconscious and then inserted a catheter into a vein in her chest through which they fed her intravenously.

She tried to write a story to expose them, but they kidnapped her and suppressed the story. She tried to escape, but, with the aid of the Oakland Police Department, they stopped her before she could even reach the Bay Bridge. She tried to take her body back through a hunger strike, but they subdued and force fed her.

Aurora sat on the edge of the bed with her head in her hands. What was Trueheart up to? Why was it taking so long? Had she been wrong to trust him?

Aurora looked around the small room and considered a variety of available means for ending her life. She could attempt to break the boards and throw herself out of the window. She could remove the sheets from the bed and fashion a noose and dangle from the cheap ceiling light and fan. She could break the glass on the bathroom vanity and slash her wrists. She could bash her head on the porcelain sink or drown herself in the bathtub.

But Sonny Trueheart was always there in her fentanyl-induced dreams, encouraging her to push on and remain alive.

Aurora looked at her body and her beautiful brown skin, and then the answer came to her. She would take her body back in a different way. She would take her body back in a way that would help her prepare to fight Seven Daggers. If there had been a deal between Seven Daggers and Sonny Trueheart, Seven Daggers would certainly never honor his end of the bargain. There would be a betrayal and a conflict at the moment of exchange, and she would need to be prepared.

Aurora stretched and then, once sufficiently loose, began to run in place, fighting the sluggishness and the desire for the drug that would be administered again soon. She completed 25 pushups and 25 sit ups. She shadow-boxed until she could feel the sweat dripping down her back. She practiced judo moves, using a pillow to execute leglocks, arm bars, and choke holds.

Yes! If they were going to insist that she eat, then she was going to try to regain her strength!

Power to the People!
A Podcast for the People
Broadcasting from the Lower Bottoms of West Oakland
Hosted by Aurora Jenkins

Transcript of Power to the People! Episode 77

It's Aurora Jenkins, your Momma, your Auntie, your Big Sister, your Play Cousin! Your Friendly Neighborhood Queer Black Feminist activist! I want to talk to you today about intersectionality. As women of color, everyday we face multiple, co-existing levels of bias and discrimination. We are Black and we are poor. We are immigrant women. We are disabled women of color. You can imagine how these multiple, overlapping identities might play out for those among the missing and victims of trafficking.

And so, I want to bring attention to the case of Maria LaGuerre, an intellectually disabled 13-year-old Haitian immigrant who was reported missing last week from the grounds of her Vallejo middle school campus. Maria has difficulty with communication and interaction and will present as shy.

Maria's case prompted me to investigate the stories of women facing emotional and intellectual disabilities who are kidnapped across this country. Young women with intellectual disabilities may constitute as many and 15-20 percent of all those kidnapped, particularly in younger age groups. They may constitute an even higher percentage of those classified as runaways.

The case of Maria LaGuerre can only be viewed through an intersectional lens. Young woman of color. Immigrant. Intellectually disabled. Working class family. We are praying for information leading to your safe return, Maria. And we love you.

33. Heist

Upton's Uptown Office Cleaners was a second-generation family business. Started in 1954 by George and Eunice Upton who also parlayed their savings into buying prime real estate in Oakland's Glenview and Maxwell Park neighborhoods. In the 1950's the commercial segregation in the Bay Area limited their ability to serve anything but Oakland's Black business community and in time they expanded their services to serve Black businesses in Richmond, California. This was an Oakland and a Richmond long-forgotten. Both long-time Garveyites, George and Eunice turned segregation into Black pride and, even in the wake of the Civil Rights movement, they continued focusing almost exclusively on Black business clients. Now there are but mere vestiges of the kind of Black capitalism that could sustain such a venture in either city. There are only faded signs painted on condemned buildings waiting to be torn down and turned into market rate housing, tech office space or boutique shops for millennials.

The Uptons had three children: George, Jr. and his sisters Tamala and Malia. Faithful to their parents' legacy and racial perspective, the Upton children maintained the business as best as they could as well as all three family houses in Oakland. At the first hint of gentrification and Black out-migration from the Bay Area, the Uptons turned to the Black Archon and were able to secure an exclusive contract for cleaning their business and commercial offices. And the Uptons thrived. It was not uncommon these days to see any of the Upton children driving luxury foreign cars through Glenview or Maxwell Park.

The business itself was still headquartered in George Jr.'s family home on Park Blvd. in the Glenview, the first home that George.

and Eunice purchased. George Jr.'s family was certainly the last of a few remaining Black families in the Glenview and, outside of the offices of pediatrician Dr. Jimmy Green, the only other remaining Black business in the neighborhood. Not coincidentally, Dr. Green served as the pediatrician for all of the Upton children.

The regular routine for weeknights involved Tamala and Malia joining George Jr.'s family of four for dinner and then heading out to clean the California American Bank office in downtown Oakland. The central part of their agreement with the Black Archon included the promise to never farm out the work. All three of the Uptons and only the Uptons were asked to be present at every cleaning. Because of the hold that the Black Archon had on the Black community, the Uptons never feared being robbed nor the prospect of burglars entering Archon businesses as they cleaned at night. That would have been unthinkable and the retaliation of the Black Archon would have been swift and unimaginably horrific. Dressed in their smart green and yellow outfits—an obvious nod to the colors of the Oakland Athletics— the Upton trio could be seen every weeknight at 8pm sharp, self-assuredly boarding the Upton's Uptown Cleaners vans and headed downtown under the financial and personal protection of the city and the city's preeminent Black criminal organization.

On this night, as they exited the side door and walked towards the two vans parked one behind the other on the driveway alongside George Jr.'s spacious 3-bedroom 2-bath 1920s Craftsman style home, the trio were met by Sonny Trueheart, Nzingha, Kaz Taketo, and Malik Akoto in Barack Obama masks, each holding pistols and ordering their silence. Their movements were hidden from the view of Park Ave. passersby by the vans in the driveway.

"Are you out of your mind?" George Jr. exclaimed. "Do you know who we work for?"

Akoto, who wore a bandage over his left eye beneath the mask, responded by holding his pistol closer to George Jr.'s face and pulling back the slide.

The crisp click-clack of the chambered round silenced any further discussion.

With a wave of his pistol, Sonny ordered George Jr. to unlock both vans and Akoto demanded Tamala and Malia to follow. Sonny instructed the trio to remove their cleaning equipment from both vans parked in the driveway. This included industrial vacuum cleaners, rug shampooers and buckets of cleaning supplies. The Uptons dragged these to the backyard of George's spacious home, where they would not be visible from the street. Once they had completed this task, Sonny directed the Upton trio into the lead van and told them to strip. He then deliberately and carefully gagged and blindfolded all three.

Walking gingerly because of the hard falls he had taken and the bullet that grazed his right calf, Akoto grabbed the ring of office keys that George Jr. had in the pocket of his uniform and handed these to Sonny. Nzingha had earlier treated Akoto to a fine, aged, Bahamian, single-barrel rum while she stitched up his wounds and drew him a bath with Epsom salt. The rum along with a little ibuprofen had helped to dull the edges of the pain without blunting his focus.

Sonny ordered all three to sit with their backs together and he bound the group together with a soft twisted cotton rope that he carried in his backpack. Sonny taped their mouths shut with gray duct tape. Akoto removed a case from the small backpack he carried with syringes of Midazolam and injected each of the Uptons in the muscle tissue of their biceps. He carried five syringes in the case. Three for the Uptons and two for the guards in the bank. The drug would take 10 minutes to begin working and the dose that Akoto administered would last six hours. Akoto nodded after administering the final dose of Midazolam.

As they waited for the drug to take effect on the Uptons, Sonny, Taketo, and Nzinga changed into the Upton's Uptown Cleaners overalls. Akoto was without a uniform, but because of his size, he would never have been able to wear the Upton's overalls. Instead, he had purchased an XXL pair of overalls with cash at the Ace Hardware in the Laurel District that fit perfectly. Sonny took the wheel of the van that carried the Uptons with Nzingha riding shotgun while Akoto drove the other van with Taketo riding shotgun.

Sonny pulled out onto the street, taking a right turn westward on Park Blvd., he flashed the bright lights of the van twice and the other van driven by Akoto followed and they headed towards the entrance of the 580 freeway. They rode the slow lane on the freeway from Park Blvd. to the Harrison St. exit.

Festive holiday lights were strung around Lake Merritt as the vans approached the Black Archon Center on 300 Lakeside Drive. The public plaza of the Cathedral of Light on Harrison St. was illuminated and reflected off the magnificent glass structure. There was an eeriness to the glow of lights through the dense smoke of the Camp Fire in Butte County.

Sonny remained focused on the road and cautiously pulled the lead van up to the gated service entrance of the Black Archon Center. He rolled down the driver's window, entered the six-digit code given to him by Seven Daggers, and the security gate lifted. Akoto's van followed.

The two vans parked next to the service elevator in spaces marked "Uptons," next to the now empty space marked "Godbold," where the doctor undoubtedly parked his signature Silver Wraith Rolls Royce. Sonny exited the back of the lead van and then moved to unlock the service elevator with the key that Akoto had taken from George Jr. The four entered the elevator, without saying a word. Before pressing the button for the lobby level, Sonny and Akoto hoisted Nzingha upwards and she removed the prismatic lens troffer and then each of the three low voltage reflector light bulbs, casting the elevator in complete darkness. Nzingha was lowered and Taketo pressed the button for the lobby. As the elevator rose from the garage, Sonny once again had an opportunity to view the lights strung around Lake Merritt in the darkness. Shadows of the four danced along the walls of the elevator. Sonny checked his watch and signaled the group with a nod.

The elevator opened and the quartet were met by the first of the building's two security guards as he entered the dark elevator for his regular smoke break. According to Seven Daggers' notes, the lobby guard habitually abandoned his post at the building's main desk with its view of the security cameras to feed his habit and smoke in the garage. Sonny lunged at him from the darkness, quickly throwing the man into the elevator and disabling and bringing him to his knees with a wristlock as Taketo pressed the button to close the elevator doors. Akoto administered a dose of Midazolam in the man's neck. The man shrieked as the elevator doors were closing and the quartet glanced at one another nervously, hoping that the other security guard was not within hearing distance. 10 minutes of silence until the drug began to take effect.

Taketo sighed deeply, relieved, and pressed for a return to the garage.

The quartet waited silently in the darkness as the elevator descended and the drug took effect on the guard. When the guard fell completely limp, Sonny reached into the man's pockets and took his keys, handing these to Taketo, and carried him to the van and laid him carefully down beside the Uptons. In the van, Sonny bound the guard at the wrists and ankles in the twisted cotton rope and taped his mouth with duct tape.

Now it was time for Nzingha to go to work. She would have a limited amount of time to disable the power sources for the lights, cameras, and motion sensors in the building.

The National Electric Code requires that every commercial building dedicate a specific space for electrical panels and equipment. The Black Archon Center had four such dedicated spaces that were relevant to the California American Bank. There were rooms on the first and second floors that contained electrical equipment for the offices of the executives of California American Bank on those floors. There was a room in the lobby that powered everything except the California American Bank vault. The fourth room, located within the bank itself, contained the electrical panels for the vault.

The crew would crudely disable the power in the first three of these rooms. Because they needed power from the fourth room to unlock the vault with the codes that they had stolen, the crew had to focus their efforts on "tricking" the sophisticated security.

Every other floor in the 28-story building had its own dedicated space for electrical equipment, and Godbold's penthouse had two. But these floors were irrelevant to the crew. What Nzingha learned from her reconnaissance was that the electrical panels from the lobby to the second floor were linked as a security measure for all California American Bank employees and had to be sabotaged in a particular descending sequence. The second floor had to be taken out first and then the first-floor offices and then the lobby and then the vault. If the sequence was violated it would trigger the alarms and the quartet would find the building almost immediately swarming with Oakland's finest.

Sonny and Akoto reentered the elevator with Taketo and Nzingha and the quartet rose again, this time bypassing the lobby level and first floor and moving toward the second floor. Taketo handed Nzingha the security guard's keys. The lobby security guard was entrusted with keys to each of the four control rooms and provided basic training on how to handle emergency power outages.

There would be another security guard patrolling all the offices on the first and second floors. This guard was not entrusted with keys to the control rooms, but he would have to be disabled as well. Sonny checked his watch. According to the schedule provided by Seven Daggers, the second guard would now be on the second floor.

Akoto drew the remaining syringe of Midazolam from his backpack. Sonny stepped from the elevator, turned the corner, and saw the security guard headed towards him from about 5 yards away. The guard reached for his pistol and yelled, "Hey, you!" but Sonny effectively closed the distance and tackled the man around the waist. The guard's pistol clattered to the floor as Sonny mounted the man's chest and punched him squarely in the mouth. The guard squealed, but Akoto was right behind Sonny and had already knelt, and with his knee pinning the guard's left arm, he injected the drug into his shoulder.

Sonny and Akoto looked at one another through their Obama

masks and breathed deeply as the guard slowly fell unconscious. Sonny nodded. Akoto bound the man and the pair dragged him by the ankles down the hallway toward the elevator.

As Akoto and Sonny disabled the guard, Nzingha disembarked and rushed to disable the second-floor fuse box. Sonny, Akoto, and Taketo would take the second guard down to the garage level and lay him out in the van with the other guard and the Uptons. Before disembarking, Nzingha held out both hands, signaling ten minutes. In ten minutes, she would disable the power on the second and first floors and meet the others in the lobby. She quickly found the room and tried each of the keys on the ring until she found the correct one and entered.

Nzingha knelt in front of the panels, with the exhaust duct overhead, and set to work. She withdrew her headlamp and fastened this over the Obama mask and waited for the seconds dial to hit 12 on her watch, and then shut out the power on the second floor. She then left in the darkness, with her headlamp illuminating the way, and took the elevator down to the first floor and did the same. When she took the elevator down to the lobby to meet the others, there were still 2 minutes remaining.

As she disembarked onto the marbled floor lobby, the others waited for her by the lobby's control room. Akoto had rolled up the sleeve of his uniform and was busy ripping off strips of black duct tape that he placed in a row along his left forearm. Nzingha unlocked the door and went to work, as she had on the second and first floors. By now, she had established a routine, and disabling the lobby's power took less time than she had required for the second and first floors.

The lobby was now thrust into darkness, along with the second and first floors. Motion sensors and alarms in the bank were disabled, with the exception of the vault.

The headlamps worn by the quartet now illuminated the challenge ahead.

The lobby guard's keys opened the main glass doors of the bank.

Behind the teller stations there was a steel gate that guarded the antechamber of the vault. The crew moved in silence through the dark, with their headlamps illuminating the way, working their way through the bank until they came to the gate of the antechamber.

Sonny found the camera that provided a video feed outside of the antechamber and disabled this with a strip of duct tape handed to him by Akoto. Akoto then entered the code that Orpheus saw from the video feed on the Black Archon servers at the George Bush building. He heard the satisfying click and a green light on the digital keypad. The four then entered the antechamber. Sonny led the way, found the camera that provided the video feed inside the antechamber, and covered the lens with another small strip of duct tape handed to him by Akoto. Taketo noticed a single large utility cart and wheeled this closer to the vault door. The cart would come in handy for loading the loot.

Once in the antechamber, the four stood before the 3-ton steel vault door. There was a combination wheel at the center that had numbers from 0 to 99 just like the Antwerp vault. 100 million possibilities. Only four correct numbers. Akoto received the code from Orpheus in the late afternoon, but before he could dial the numbers, they would have to disable the magnetic field.

The vault door was bracketed by metal plates that created a powerful magnetic field and if the vault door was opened before settling this issue, the vault's alarm would be triggered. Like the Antwerp vault, there was a companion foot-long key to disarm the magnetic field. Nzingha's reconnaissance had confirmed as much. There wasn't enough time nor a clear strategy for obtaining a mold of the lock and having The Blacksmith replicate the key. They would have to "trick" the magnetic field instead.

Akoto withdrew the aluminum slabs from his backpack and secured these to the metal plates that conducted the magnetic field. He used strips of double-sided tape where the surface of the slabs touched the plates. He also secured the aluminum slabs to the antechamber wall with longer strips of duct tape. Sonny learned from the *Wired* article that aluminum is not magnetic. It is a "paramagnetic" material that behaves like a very weak magnet and has unpaired electrons and molecules whose ends have opposite charges which are not lined up in the direction of the magnetic field. Their misaligned molecules can obstruct magnetic fields.

The gamble here was that the process of securing aluminum slabs to the original metal plates that conducted the magnetic field would not set off an unexpected alarm. Akoto knew that if he began to unscrew the bolts and loosen the original metal plates or drill through them in order to better secure the aluminum, he could certainly trigger an alarm. Akoto gingerly and successfully executed his maneuver in 15 minutes and the crew watched in silence and breathed in relief when he had finished.

Sonny now deftly manipulated the four-pronged handle of the combination wheel through the numbers Orpheus provided and the bolts retracted and the big 3-ton vault door opened for them.

The crew took it all in for a moment.

Sonny stood at the threshold of the vault. There was no light sensor as there had been in the Antwerp vault, so he felt free to use his headlamp. His headlamp revealed rows of safe deposit boxes on all three walls. According to Nzingha's intel, the safe deposit boxes on two of the walls contained cash, jewelry, and other valuables. The bank used the safe deposit boxes on the third wall to store portable crypto hard drives or cold storage "wallets" that could be removed and carried. The vault contained both Black Archon cash that was to be converted into crypto currency and the cold storage wallets in which the already converted crypto was being stored.

Sonny quickly spotted the camera and the heat and motion sensor in the upper left corner of the vault. This was all contained in one device, a passive infrared monitor that appeared to have two camera lenses, one clear, and the other red. The clear camera provided a live video feed. The other was the infrared camera that had two functions: detecting heat signatures and detecting motion by using temperature changes.

The addition of the livestream camera was an advancement over the technology in the Antwerp bank. It transmitted via wifi and Orpheus was stationed in Akoto's apartment, attempting to intercept that signal. Bank officials had probably gone with infrared technology for the dual heat/motion sensor instead of using ultrasonic sound waves to bounce off the walls of the vault and interpret echoes for the same reason that they had rejected a seismic sensor: to avoid false alarms given the frequency of seismic activity. The infrared device was quite a bit more sophisticated and would ignore small changes in temperature, but once triggered, would generate an alarm.

Taketo retrieved an extendable dry mop handle. Attached to the end of the handle was a Styrofoam plate. Taketo handed this to Sonny who slowly extended the dry mop handle until the Styrofoam plate covered the dual heat and motion sensor and the camera. Sonny's steady movement and heartbeat was intended to limit sudden changes in movement and heat. Sonny then looked at Akoto, signaling him to enter the vault as he tried to keep the Styrofoam device steady.

Because he was the only one tall enough to reach up to the device, Akoto was chosen to enter the vault first. He slowly walked to the left corner and reached up and stuck the nozzle of the hair spray in the slight gap between the Styrofoam cover and the sensor and liberally sprayed the sensor with the thick oily fluid of an aerosol women's hair spray.

While Sonny held the dry mop handle steady, Akoto reached up above the sensor and attached a small piece of duct tape over the top part of the sensor where the live feed camera was located, making sure that his hands never brushed against the device. The sticky tape now covered the lens. Akoto grabbed another and longer strip of tape and carefully separated the Styrofoam cover from the end of the dry mop and firmly secured it against the two devices, anchoring the tape to the wall.

It was unclear how long the trick would last. But, between the combination of the disabling hair spray and the Styrofoam cover, they should be clear for some time.

Nzingha and Akoto were next into the vault. They threw two dozen large black duffel bags into the dark space. There were a total of 150 safe deposit boxes, 50 on each wall, in two distinct sizes: 3" x 5" x 21" and 10.5" x 10.5" x 21." They had no idea how many safe deposit boxes were owned by Dr. Godbold, nor how they would distinguish these from those owned by ordinary citizens. Bank officials had informed Nzingha of the paucity of available safe deposit boxes, citing primary ownership of most of the contents of the vault by Godbold Industries. It seemed that Godbold was using the California American Bank vault as his primary private secure storage. The two dozen duffel bags that Sonny's crew brought certainly indicated that they were prepared to rob a majority of the 150 safe deposit boxes in the vault.

Sonny, Nzingha and Akoto withdrew the nose pullers. These were made of wrought iron and bar steel and designed to pull out a lock core from a safe deposit door. Each member of the team simply mounted the device to the face of each safe deposit door, turned the screw into the center of the core's keyway as an anchor, slipped a spacer block into place, and then tightened by turning the knurled knob clockwise, very slowly and gradually until the entire core keyway was drawn out with a loud popping sound. Each box was made of steel and copper and only accessible with a key. With the nose pullers, it took about 2 minutes for each member of the team to break open a safe deposit door once they got going.

Each member of the team worked a separate wall of safe deposit boxes and Sonny instructed them to begin with the larger boxes at the bottom and work their way up. Sonny popped the first lock on the wall that contained the crypto cold storage drives and he pulled out the box and opened the lid. He found scattered lumps of cold storage wallets covered by a black cloth that read "Godbold Industries."

Sonny waved the black cloth, silently alerting the crew that these would help them distinguish Black Archon assets.

Nzingha and Akoto now furiously broke the locks of the large boxes on the walls to which they had been assigned. They saw the black cloths and hurriedly yanked the contents of the safe deposit boxes, largely cash, into the duffel bags. But as they proceeded, there were diamonds and other valuable jewels and the crew took these as well.

As Sonny labored, he confirmed that the majority of the safe deposit boxes on his wall contained the Black Archon's cold storage crypto wallets. The Black Archon was using the most up-to-date technology, and many of the cold storage wallets were not much bigger than a portable flash drive. There were fifty to sixty of them in each safe deposit box, each likely allotted to captains of the Black Archon street teams for converting cash.

Sonny could see a process happening here in the vault. In the beginning, street captains were given the simple order to deposit cash and stolen valuables that Godbold would convert into crypto. And then there was a transition where street captains were trained to convert cash and goods into crypto in order to speed up the process. This would leave Godbold with only the task of loading the crypto on hundreds of small wallets onto a larger device.

It took an hour for each member to open 30 safe deposit boxes. 90 total on the three walls. 24 of the opened boxes on each wall contained black cloths labeled 'Godbold Industries' covering the loot. In total, 72 of the boxes that the crew had opened in the vault were owned by Dr. Godbold.

Nzingha signaled for them to load up and depart, but Sonny pressed their luck, calling for another hour of work. Sonny was adamant, and he pushed the crew forward. Another hour of work would mean close to a total of 3 hours in the bank. Unless Orpheus could interrupt the signal, security personnel in the George Bush building across the bay would certainly periodically check the remote feed inside the vault. How long could they expect the disabled vault camera to go unnoticed? 2 hours was pushing it. 3 hours would certainly be untenable. There was also one last robbery to commit and the time was drawing near.

Taketo, who had been assisting with loading the loot into the duffel bags, stepped in front of Sonny. He shook his head and

A SONNY TRUEHEART MYSTERY

pointed to his watch. Sonny looked at his watch and raised his hands. Taketo pointed to the duffel bags that the crew had already filled. 12 duffel bags were full to bursting with cash and jewels. Wasn't that enough? Taketo tried to express this with his hands. Sonny shook his head. He motioned for them to finish drilling into any unopened box on the walls to which they were assigned. Keeping a steady pace, the crew emptied many of the remaining boxes in their assigned spaces. The 2-to-3 ratio of Godbold-to-civilian owned safe deposit boxes held up and more of the Black Archon's cash and jewels were loaded into duffel bags.

Nzingha and Akoto continued to labor and Taketo disapprovingly continued assisting with the loading. After another half hour, Taketo again signaled for him to stop. It had taken Sonny 30 minutes to open up 10 more safe deposit boxes on the third wall. There might be other boxes with more of Godbold's cold storage wallets among the remaining 10. But the crew certainly could not risk taking another half hour to discover them. Sonny understood this and finally relented, nodding in agreement. The old man was right. The crew should not press their luck any further. Sonny gave a hand signal for Nzingha and Akoto to move quickly and drag the heavy bags outside of the vault and load them on the cart outside of the steel gate.

Nzingha tossed the loaded duffel bags out of the vault to Akoto who loaded these onto the cart. When Sonny finished dumping the cold storage wallets into a duffel bag, he helped Nzingha toss the bags out of the vault and then the two stepped out to help Akoto load these onto the cart. Now there were 13 full to bursting black duffel bags piled precariously high.

Taketo stepped over the debris in the vault and exited, closing the vault door. He followed Sonny, Akoto and Nzingha who carefully pushed the loaded cart out of the antechamber and through the bank. Akoto pushed the cart from the back and Sonny and Nzingha pulled from the front, making certain that the bags did not topple. Once Taketo exited the antechamber, he rushed ahead of them to open the bank's main glass doors.

As they pushed the cart out of the bank and through the lobby and into the elevator, Taketo stopped to look at the city scene beyond the main glass doors of the building. The lights along the lake were faintly shining in the thick smoke. Traffic was sparse. He knew that his friends in the Yakuza and the Trenchtown Yardies were out there somewhere monitoring the streets. Once Taketo entered the elevator, Nzingha came up behind him and rested her hand on his shoulder, silently acknowledging the stillness and calm of the night.

They remained in their masks in the elevator. No words were spoken but they could hear each other's heavy breathing behind the thick plastic masks. When the elevator reached the garage level and the doors opened, the crew pushed the loaded cart toward the two cleaning vans. Taketo checked the van in which the Uptons and the two security guards still lay unconscious under the influence of the powerful Midazolam. The others loaded all 13 duffel bags into the other van.

Sonny had each member of the crew keep the polymer pistols he had purchased from the Blacksmith. He and Nzingha would use theirs for the next robbery.

They drove the two vans out from the garage into the silent streets and the night obscured by smoke. Once beyond the view of the building's exterior cameras, they removed their masks and breathed deeply.

Sonny and Taketo drove the van with the Uptons and the two security guards back to George Upton, Jr.'s home on Park Blvd. They parked in the driveway and waited for Akoto and Nzingha, who were following them in the second van, to arrive.

When Akoto and Nzingha arrived, they parked right behind the first van. Akoto opened the back of the van and the entire crew began unloading the black duffel bags, storing eight in the trunk of Akoto's car and four in the trunk of Taketo's smaller car and the 13th bag on the back seat.

They all walked back inside of the empty van that had stored the loot and changed out of their uniforms and back into their street clothes and walked quietly in the dark to their parked cars and then drove to Akoto's condo in West Oakland.

Within a half hour, they pulled into the garage. Orpheus Anderson came down and helped load the heavy duffel bags from the two cars onto the elevator. Once they reached the third floor, Nzingha and Taketo held the elevator doors open while the others carried the bags into Akoto's condo.

It was only when they were all reunited in Akoto's condo that they spoke. They sat around the 13 duffel bags piled high in Akoto's living room. There was no time to count or speculate how much had been stolen. But the 13 full duffel bags spoke to the damage they had surely done to Godbold's business.

Sonny smiled at Nzingha. "I told you it could be done."

Nzingha returned the smile and placed her hand over her heart.

"Without the 54-character passwords, the drives won't be of much use to us," Orpheus noted.

"At least the Black Archon won't have access to them anymore," Nzingha grabbed the bottle of rum she had earlier shared with Akoto and took a shot.

"I may be able to help you break the codes," Sonny offered and checked his watch. 12:15am. "But that's for later. We have to keep moving right now. We don't have much time to celebrate."

It was now time for the final burglary. Sonny and Nzingha quickly showered and changed into formal evening wear. Sonny donned a gray afro wig to cover his braided hair. He pasted a fake, gray mustache and goatee to his face as Nzingha drove them both in Akoto's Dodge Challenger. Akoto would need rest and recuperation and rum. In the morning, Akoto and Taketo would rent a van with false identification and a credit card provided by Nzingha. They would drive this vehicle out to the parking lot at Golden Gate Fields for the inevitable exchange of cash for Aurora Jenkins. This van would carry 13 duffel bags filled with shredded paper.

34. Slave to the Rhythm

Sonny Trueheart knew that merely robbing the California American Bank vault would neither honor the work and life of Aurora Jenkins nor satisfy Nzingha and her superiors in the Royal Bahamian Defense Force. Even though they were plainly exhausted, they would need to secure the release of some of the women being trafficked. It was now 12:45am and they would crash the Black Archon party in the Oakland Hills. Their invitations, provided by Malik Akoto's contact, bore the names of Dr. and Mrs. Jerome Daniels. Chevron chemist and his wife. It would be their first auction.

Imitating his wealthy white southern counterparts, Dr. Godbold preferred to hire Black servants for his parties, recreating the optics of the era of slavery. Black men in tight white coats and black bow ties were everywhere throughout the crowd circulating glasses of champagne and hors d'oeuvres.

Godbold's home in the hills was a mid-century mansion. There was a meticulous Japanese garden and two rear decks banking a formal fragrant rose garden with a lion sculpture-guarded swimming pool. There was the smell of eucalyptus, and a magical view from high atop the Oakland hills. The fog rolled in and gave the sense of floating on a sea of clouds.

The main hall, a two-story atrium like the Achillion Palace in Corfu, where the costumed revelers were gathered for the party, contained a massive aquarium with deeply recessed walls for huge glass tanks, brightly lit for viewing the hundreds of exotic, tropical fish and plankton species. The glass magnified their size. They looked like giants of the sea.

There were private rooms on the upper level where captive women purchased for the evening could be taken for use. Every purchase was worth two hours with an enslaved person. And within that time frame there were no limits and no liabilities.

After showing their invitations, Sonny and Nzingha were given a pair of Roman style half face masks. Sonny grabbed a glass of champagne for Nzingha and the pair mingled, looking for where the money would be collected and stored. This was a cash event. None of the revelers could afford a paper trail or record of electronic payment.

Sonny ran into a middle-aged couple. Pharmaceutical executives who lived on the bay in the exclusive homes at Point Richmond. "Welcome! What kind of woman are you looking for tonight?" the wife asked after the exchange of names and professions.

"We're looking for a woman with some experience," Nzingha responded.

"They have Mayor Pendergast's old favorite here tonight. But we're looking for something fresh and exciting. Something with a little spirit that needs to be broken in!" And Sonny faked a laugh with them as he spotted out of the corner of his eye a guard coming out of a room on the second level of the atrium with a briefcase. He noticed the lump of an automatic pistol under the armpit of the guard. Upstairs probably where the money was being collected.

Like the Achillion Palace, the hall was further decorated with statues of Achilles at various stages of his heroic life. But the heads of every statue were not those of Achilles but of the massive head of Dr. Godbold. The look of his face and the enormity of his head gave a sense of his importance, but Trueheart had to suppress his desire to laugh at the enormity of Godbold's narcissism.

There was a raised platform in the center of the hall for a slave auction block. A little person in a red top hat and tails took the stage with a microphone and called the crowd to order.

"Ladies and gentlemen…welcome to Mistress Celestine's annual slave auction! We have some excellent specimens for your purchase and your pleasure today, fresh from the streets of Oakland, from deep down in the heart of the black jungle! Taut and lithe bodies, primed and ready for the punishment you want to put them through! But before we begin, the great Dr. Lucius Godbold wishes to address you and officially open the proceedings!"

An obsequious roar came up from the crowd. The man whose giant head was on every Achilles statue took the stage and stood under the moonlight streaming down through the glass ceiling into the atrium. He was accompanied by an extraordinarily tall bald woman in a latex bodysuit and thigh-high stiletto-heeled boots. Two stories of party revelers watched the man and his silent companion with a sickeningly silent awe, the kind of respect given to dictators and cult leaders.

The crowd raised their glasses and began chanting, "Godbold! Godbold! Godbold!" as though this were a political rally.

So, this was Dr. Lucius Godbold. The putative head of the Black Archon. The man whose illicit fortune Sonny had just stolen.

He spoke in slow, measured, southern tones with a lyrical North Carolina accent. He reeked of the Old South. Slavery. Cotton fields. Mint juleps. The lash. A Black man speaking with the tones of the southern white planter class.

"Ladies and gentlemen. We have a special treat for you tonight! New slave women, many of them fresh from the very streets around us, treated with a special drug I have been working on to increase stamina and resistance to pain. So…when we say 'no limits and no liabilities,' we truly mean it!"

Another roar came up from the crowd.

"Y'all need to know that our organization is moving forward into the world! Everyday we are growing stronger and stronger! You may notice that the 13 Black Archons aren't with us tonight. That's because they are all busy working towards the next phase of our plan." Godbold made the white supremacist "okay" symbol and placed this against his heart. "They all wanted me to send their love to you tonight. All is well, my friends. All is well! And even greater days lie ahead. So, please enjoy this great night of revelry! As you know, these events help to fund a good many of our activities, so be generous with your bids!"

Godbold descended from the stage with his silent companion and into the crowd where he shook hands and shared his fake smile before exiting with a coterie of bodyguards. There was a palpable electricity in the air as he worked the crowd. He commanded them, and they were faithful to his every utterance.

The little man took the stage again, followed by a group of 10 naked women in chains.

"Here they are! A special batch just for your particular pleasures!"

Sonny and Nzingha surveyed the group. He remembered the pictures of Sujata on the flash drive. It helped that her name was tattooed to her right arm. And there she stood amongst the 10 women shackled and chained on the stage. Naked. Her body was oiled and reflecting the hot lights. Her head was down but Sonny could see that just like all the others, she was drugged and undoubtedly unaware of her circumstances.

Sujata Ray was a strikingly beautiful Bahamian sister. Petite. Lithe. Small of stature but powerful. Her gorgeous dreadlocks spilled onto her shoulders in big kinky coils, dyed blonde and bronze. But her beauty was marred by visible purple welts on her buttocks and thighs, made even more visible by the sheen of oil on her body, as though she had been horse whipped. Sonny guessed that this was how they had chosen to punish her for sharing information with Aurora.

The first woman who was put forward was introduced by the little man: "Bianca, a slave from the Havenscourt in East Oakland, a fierce young wench with pert breasts and supple thighs who just turned 18 a week ago. Though we cannot claim her virginal purity, we are reasonably assured that she will be a virgin to your kink and her fear will be genuine and her screams honest. Bid on her and be the first to put her through the paces!"

The bidding started at $5,000 and quickly accelerated to $20,000 for two hours of pleasure, as potential bidders crowded the stage and touched and squeezed her flesh. Sonny had $25,000 of Godbold's money on him and had to hope that the bidding for Sujata wouldn't exceed that amount.

The second woman, from the Berkeley flats, who was called simply "Truth," resisted being put forward by the little man and kicked at his groin and attempted to jump off the stage before she was restrained by some of the Black servers in white dinner jackets and bow ties. Sonny noticed that the middle-aged couple that he had chatted with were approaching the stage with interest. In the end, they won the bid for her services at $45,000.

Sujata Ray was next.

"This one has been put through the paces at earlier auctions. A pretty young Bahamian sister! The only one here who is not from these streets. We are going to be moving her on to other locations, so this is your last chance to get a crack at her. Yes, she's been around, but the other way of looking at it is that she's well-seasoned and really ready to go!"

The bidding for Sujata was lukewarm. Not nearly as frenzied as the first two women. It appeared as though the present crowd was more interested in fresh local meat. And Sujata didn't help her case. She was pushed forward on the stage and seemed listless, drugged, and completely disconnected, unaware of her surroundings. She was introduced as Mayor Freddy Pendergast's one-time favorite slave. They tried to sell her experience and incredibly high tolerance for pain. But the low murmurs from the crowd suggested that because she was formerly owned by Pendergast, she might better be left alone.

Sonny and Nzingha approached the stage as the little man continued verbalizing her strengths as a submissive slave.

No initial bids. Sonny waited it out.

Sujata fell to her knees. She turned and seemed to look Sonny dead in the eyes. The little man walked behind her and grabbed

Sujata by the hair and lifted her up and started caressing the welts and bruises on her body. "Oh....that feels good," he said. And he released his tightly clenched fists, opened his right hand and gave Sujata a light whack on the fatty part of her buttocks.

The crowd sighed, "oooh!"

The little man gave her more. She moaned and swayed a bit.

Sujata's body jerked from the intensity of the hand spanking. The little man raised his hand and brought it down on her with the steady rhythm of a drumbeat. Again and again, over and over. Sujata gasped, trying to catch her breath. Sweat glistened in the lights and slid down her legs. She drooled profusely. Her thighs and arms quivered involuntarily.

Sonny yelled, "Stop!!!"

The little man stopped in mid-stroke. The room was absolutely still.

"25,000. I bid 25,000." Sonny bid everything he had.

The little man wiped the sweat from his brow. "Okay! Okay. Anything higher? Anybody want to raise that price and get yourself an experienced woman tonight who can really take the pain? Going once…going twice…going thrice…" And the little man grabbed his gavel and banged the floor of the auction block upon which they stood and Sujata Ray was sold to Sonny for the evening.

Sonny and Nzingha were escorted up the grand staircase lined by the Achilles/Godbold statues to a private bedroom on the second level, where they were instructed by a burly guard to wait for their newly purchased slave to arrive. There were two such men walking the second floor, at least one in the cash room, one at the main door, and one mingling downstairs. All were armed.

The door shut behind them. Black walls. Black rubber mats on the floor. A cage. A large aluminum plated cross, an aluminum frame chair with black leather upholstery, and a V-shaped seat with armrests and cuffs. An open Gothic armoire with leather, mesh, lace, latex clothing, boots and stiletto-heeled shoes. There was an interrogation table like those Sonny used in Homicide but with a stanchion and cuffs. Sonny and Nzingha began walking around. Looking for hidden cameras. Touching the different textures in the room.

Sujata staggered in, pushed by one of the guards, completely naked shaking and sweating from the effects of the drugs and the beating she had endured. Sonny could see that her eyes were glazed and bloodshot.

"You bought me. So now, how would you like to use me, sir?"

"I'm here on behalf of Aurora," Sonny announced and walked towards her, covering her with his jacket.

Sujata gave him that drugged half smile. "Did she show you the pictures? Do you know who these people are?" And then her eyes rolled back in her head and she collapsed into his arms.

Sonny and Nzingha laid her down on the floor and knelt beside her and Nzingha rubbed Sujata down from neck to toe. She ran her hands over her markings, lovingly caressing her wounds and calling her "sister." Sujata twitched. The twitching turned to moans. Nzingha continued to soothe and rub her down, bringing her back slowly with gentle touches all over her body, reassuring her that everything was fine and that she was okay. Sujata tried to move, but she couldn't just yet.

As she began to regain consciousness and stir, Nzingha grabbed her and lifted her up to her feet and tightly hugged her. Nzingha felt Sujata's sweat against her skin. They stood there and embraced for what felt like hours.

"Where am I?" Sujata asked, as if waking from a dream. Sonny walked over to the two of them.

"Black Archon slave auction. I bought you."

"How much?"

"Twenty-five thousand."

"I usually go for much more."

"I imagine they beat you up good on account of Aurora. So, you're damaged goods to them. Just a thing. But to us, you're a human being, a life worth saving."

"Aurora? Yes, Aurora. So…you're Sonny Trueheart?"

"Right."

"And who are you," she held Nzingha tightly as if her very life depended on it.

"Nzingha. Royal Bahamian Defense Force. I've come here for you and other women from our country who have been taken by the Black Archon."

"They don't know you're here? Can we just walk out of here right now? Can anyone stop us?"

"We will be able to get out of here shortly," Sonny confirmed. "But I'm going to take another pound of flesh before we leave. I figure the auctioneer has a few hundred thousand by now."

"Stay here. Don't leave with anybody. We'll hit the safe and come back and get you."

"I set Aurora up. They made me…but I suppose that's no excuse," Sujata shed a tear.

Nzingha embraced her one final time before departing the room. "We'll get you out of here and you'll have a new beginning." And with that they left the room.

Sonny and Nzingha jumped out into the hallway. Two burly guards remained on patrol. Nzingha charged at the first guard and delivered a sharp kick to the groin that dropped the man to his knees and then a kick to the temple that turned everything to black. The other ran towards Sonny and he side-stepped the guard's charge, taking control of his wrist, placing a hand at the base of his neck, and using his momentum to fling him forward, head over heels. The move was known as *Kaiten Nage*, the Wheel Throw, and Sonny allowed himself a moment to appreciate the purity of his technique. Sonny opened the door where Sujata waited. He put a finger to his lips to encourage Sujata's silence and dragged the two bodies into the room.

"We have to get the money and take care of the guards downstairs, okay? We will be back for you."

Sonny pulled the polymer 9mm and headed for the cash room. Nzingha drew the tiny subcompact 9mm strapped to her thigh under her evening gown.

The revelers who purchased women were in their various rooms on the second floor. There were ten rooms and sounds of whips and screams came from each room except the one that Sonny had left.

Sonny and Nzingha came hard through the door of the cash room. Sonny's momentum carried him into the lone guard, and he whipped him across his face with the barrel of his pistol, sending the man flying hard across the cash table and unconscious onto the floor. Sonny and Nzingha stepped over the guard and began hurriedly loading lumps of bundled cash into an available large bank bag. The safe was open. And there was still money on the table. Sonny and Nzingha filled the bank bag and Sonny slung it over his shoulder and, as they left the room, they saw revelers on the second floor opening their doors and discovering the chaos.

At gunpoint Sonny and Nzingha ordered every one of the women out of the room and ordered the revelers back. Nzingha hurriedly gathered wallets and jewelry and smartphones. Sonny found Sujata, waiting for him just as he had asked, and he led her and nine other young women downstairs.

"Cover your ears," he told them. "It's going to get loud."

The revelers who had not made purchases were still milling on the lower level of the atrium. Some were leaving. The servants were cleaning up downstairs, waiting to come upstairs and clean the rooms once the revelers who were enjoying their purchases left.

Nzingha fired three shots from her subcompact 9mm at each of the glass aquariums on the lower atrium. Bullets bounced off the glass, resulting in mere surface cracks, but the deafening gunshots caught everyone by surprise.

Nzingha made use of the brief moment of confusion. Trained professionals wouldn't be thrown, and neither of the two guards below were. After Nzingha fired at the aquariums, she fired two quick shots in rapid succession, piercing the pistol arms of both the onrushing guards.

Amidst the screaming and horrified crowd, Sonny now guided Sujata and the other nine women downstairs and fired up into the glass ceiling of the atrium as he descended, bringing down a rain shower of glass. He fiercely grabbed a plastic trash bag from one of the servers, handed it and the bag of cash from upstairs to Sujata, and began demanding that everyone throw their wallets and jewelry into the bag.

"Wallets, keys, jewelry, phones…everything!"

Sujata was quickly joined by all nine of the other women who had been chained together, auctioned, and brutalized. They grouped together and gathered cash and valuables, working as a team until the pockets of the rich had been emptied and there was no more. Everyone got a set of keys, cash, and random bits of jewelry. Some of the women stole dresses and coats from the wealthy revelers. Car lights and horns went off up and down the street as the women ran out of the mansion.

"Who are you?" One of the revelers shouted. It was the husband of the older pharmaceutical industry couple he had spoken to before the auction began.

Sonny turned and responded to the older reveler who shouted his question.

"I am the revolution."

35. Gimme the Goods

Seven Daggers stood quietly beside Dr. Lucius Godbold in the ransacked bank vault at 4am in the early morning after the robbery. Oakland police detectives took pictures, dusted for fingerprints and marveled at the brilliance of the crew that had robbed the most secure vault in northern California.

"Who would have the audacity?" Godbold whispered. "No one robs banks anymore. It's a lost art."

"Perhaps one of our white allies," Seven Daggers surmised when they were alone. "I told you, the white folks weren't going to let you get away with killing the 13 Black Archon members."

Godbold turned to face the man. "No. Sonny Trueheart. He is the only one with the balls for such a thing."

"Sonny Trueheart?"

"He did it to secure the release of Aurora Jenkins. I imagine we will be hearing from him shortly."

"Then who hit the auction? He couldn't have been in both places at once."

"It was Trueheart. I know it. Trueheart hit both spots. Yes. Improbably, Sonny Trueheart robbed me twice in one night. And, contrary to *your* intelligence, he was certainly working with a crew. He probably had an inside man at the bank."

"I will begin questioning the employees."

"There was also a break-in at the George Bush Federal Building yesterday."

"Do you think that had anything to do with this burglary?"

"Of course it did. They were probably able to obtain the codes for the vault."

"I see."

"Why weren't you at the Slave Auction?"

"Sir, you assigned me to take care of Valerie Ogwu and Councilmember Chidozie."

"I'm getting tired of your excuses," Godbold glared. "You were trained for specific purposes and you have asked for greater responsibility. I needed you to prevent anything like this from happening. You have not lived up to expectations. What am I to do with you?"

"I do not wish to disappoint you sir. I owe you my life. You took me out of a London jail and set me on a path toward greatness with the Black Archon. I only wish to serve you as best as I can."

"Why haven't you been able to find Councilmember Chidozie and Valerie Ogwu?" Godbold shouted the question.

"I don't know. I did as you asked."

Godbold pointed. "I am having my doubts about you."

"What can I do to redeem myself in your eyes, sir?"

"Bring me this Sonny Trueheart and do it now."

Seven Daggers moved to exit the vault when the big man put his massive hand on his shoulder and stopped his progress. "This will be your last chance with me. Understand?"

"Understood sir."

36. Fight!

Nzingha drove back to Akoto's place and Sonny picked up the Fatboy and headed back home. He was still shaking. It was 4:30am and he needed sleep. He stopped the Fat Boy at the red light on the corner of Bancroft and 68th Ave. and could feel the ground pulsing beneath his feet from the rumbling engine of his motorcycle. She, too, was restless.

Sonny parked a block away from his home and walked in the dark between two houses across the street from his modest bungalow. He observed three cops in riot gear picking the lock on his front door. They entered with headlamps searching, carrying semi-automatic rifles ready to shoot at the slightest movement. Sonny proceeded from the shadows.

Time to go toes with the po po.

Sonny crossed the street and crept up the three steps to his front porch, taking a position to the right side of the front door. There were two windows on either side of the front door, but neither Sonny's body nor his shadow would be visible until the men exited his home. He heard talk and men searching his home and objects being tossed carelessly upon the floor.

After a few minutes, the first of the cops exited the front door. Wearing the visored riot helmet, his peripheral vision was obscured and he didn't notice Sonny's presence until Sonny snatched his night stick and brought it down sharply down upon his wrists, breaking bones and setting loose his pistol. Sonny followed up with a second shot like a pool cue straight into the visor. The blow detached the shatterproof visor and Sonny was able to deliver a second blow to the man's jaw.

The second cop came running out of the house and instinctively reached for his partner's night stick in Sonny's hand and Sonny deftly used it to guide the man's momentum down the steps in a modified *Shiho Nage* and the assailant flew off the porch and onto the concrete walkway.

But the third cop, doubtless the veteran of the group, had enough time to react to the attack and had already drawn and fired his gun, ripping the shoulder of Sonny's leather jacket and grazing his skin before Sonny pivoted and executed a sharp crack of the night stick against the man's helmet followed by a downward thrust into his chest.

The cop's pistol fell and clattered on the concrete surface of the porch. Unfortunately, that was all Sonny managed to accomplish against an opponent wearing a helmet and full body armor before the cop managed to catch him with a kick to the solar plexus, causing Sonny to drop his weapon and take a step back in retreat.

Sonny heard the whisper of a blade drawn from its sheath in time to sidestep the cop's initial slash. And then he took control of the elbow. *Ikkyo*. He forced the cop face first into one of the columns on his porch, detaching the visor upon initial impact, rendering him unconscious with a secondary blow, and the knife fell to the deck along with the assailant.

There were two teenagers in jeans and white t-shirts, walking past him on their way home. Seeing the three prone bodies of the feared Oakland Police Department, the boys gave Sonny silent acknowledgement with a nod of the head.

Respect. Much respect.

Sonny dragged the three prone and bleeding bodies into his home. He brought their weapons into his home as well. He took each man's wallet. OPD identifications. Keys for the police van they parked further up the block. He handcuffed each man with the zip ties that they carried.

He went to the bathroom and attended to his flesh wound and quickly packed his most essential items in a backpack he used for camping. Toiletries. Clean clothes and shoes. His laptop. The poster board sheets on the wall in his office outlining his speculations about the scandal. The Black Archon papers and documents that he had stolen from the safe at Johnnie's. Money. Credit cards. His father's revolver. He put the flash drive with Aurora's story and the three pictures she had mailed him in the inside pocket of his motorcycle jacket.

It was then, while he considered his options for flight, that flashing red lights of cop cars panned across his windows. He knew what was coming next. The windows began to pop from the rapid firing of pistols and semi-automatic rifles. Sonny hit the deck and began crawling toward a place of safety.

Here is where misery becomes good fortune. The floor furnace gave out last winter. He was awaiting a special order that would take six months at the earliest. In the winter he heated his home with the fireplace after removing the defunct furnace. It would be okay as long as it could arrive before next fall and winter. These floor furnaces were standard for the bungalow and craftsman homes in East Oakland but were relics of a bygone era. You could only get them on special order. Sonny knew that if he got to the grate he could get down in the crawlspace under his house and find a point of exit into the backyard.

Sonny crawled beneath a hail of bullets piercing the walls and windows towards the floor grate in the hallway that he had covered with a small throw rug to keep out the cold after removing the furnace. Smoke canisters were fired through the shattered windows and noxious fumes started filling the space. He quickly lifted the rug and grate, throwing the backpack under the house, before jumping down himself.

They were aiming high, unconcerned or unaware of either the cops who lay unconscious inside or the crawl space below. Sonny crawled toward the rear of the house towards the trap door where he could escape through the backyard, unnoticed into the night. Bullets now riddled the shed in the backyard and the fire seemed to be coming from above. And it was then that he heard the rumble overhead of helicopter blades and the fire of at least two automatic weapons. This was quickly followed by the sound of concussion grenades. Those would be MK3s, specifically designed for close combat and for minimizing casualties to friendly personnel. The shock waves produced by the volley of MK3s rocked Sonny where he lay in the crawl space beneath his house. They were bringing everything to bear in taking him down. The backyard shed burst under the shock of the grenades, and bits of wood exploded out across his lawn and at the back of his house, smashing glass and tearing at the back and roof. The floor buckled again and seemed to heave as if it were a mighty chest inhaling and caving in upon him as he desperately kicked at the debris and in an instant he was partially buried with only his head sticking out of the crawl space trap door.

Sonny blacked out. He couldn't tell how long. He awoke, feeling himself being pulled around his neck by huge hands from the crawl space trap door. Clear of the debris, the figure released its hold on his neck and then grabbed him under his arms, lifting him into the air, and tossing him a distance onto the grass. Sonny was unprepared for the fall, still groggy, unable to see, his ears filled with the ringing produced by gun blasts. Sonny rolled in the grass, but felt hands again on his neck, lifting him up again, dragging him from behind his house and down the driveway out to the street and slamming him hard down upon the roof of a parked car.

Sonny could barely open his eyes, but now he saw the face. Seven Daggers.

Seven Daggers screaming at him. "Your instructions were to kill Godbold, not to steal from him!"

Once again, Seven Daggers grasped him around the neck with his huge hands and pulled him off the roof of the car, propping him up against the side of the vehicle and hit him straight in the face.

Sonny had never been hit that hard before in his life. The punch reverberated throughout his entire body, putting him into shock. It felt like something broke inside his head. He fell again to the street and the darkness returned.

37. Wretched of the Earth

Sonny Trueheart woke with a jolt, his arms and legs struggling against the restraints. He found himself naked and strapped to a cold metal operating table in a windowless white laboratory so devoid of color that it was difficult to see the corners and judge the exact size and dimensions. He was bound by the wrists, ankles and neck. His head was in a vice and immobile. There was a white-hot light suspended above him. Tubes running into veins in both arms. He was hooked up to a machine that monitored his pulse and blood pressure. He saw trays of surgical instruments and syringes. There was a dirty towel over his mouth that smelled of cheap bourbon being poured down his throat. He was being water-boarded with cheap booze.

At least, thought Sonny, the bastard could have used a better bourbon.

His mind calculated the chances of survival as he fought helplessly against the sensation of drowning.

Dr. Godbold sat on a stool beside the operating table, his legs spread and his left-hand cupping and massaging his groin as he poured the burning liquor through the rag and down Sonny's throat, causing him to gag.

Godbold let up for a second on the liquor and removed the rag from Sonny's face. "It is a pleasure to make your acquaintance, Mister Sonny Trueheart." He paused, his luminescent gray-blue eyes steadily scanning. "And I guess you saw me briefly at the auction last night. So rude of you not to come up and introduce yourself.

"You might be wondering who I am, where you are and what I am gonna to do with you and these sorts of things. I do not intend in any way for this to be a mystery to you Mister Sonny. Let me begin at the beginning.

"I am Godbold. Dr. Lucius Godbold, to be precise, for I hold a doctorate in biochemistry. Later, I will tell you much more about what I do, but for now it is more important to concern yourself with my history and how it intersects with your history and why, in fact, we are here in this moment together.

"I am the descendant of enslaved Africans, just like, no doubt, yourself. Only my people…how do you say it…well, my people slept themselves out of slavery, or, they were slept with, properly speaking…raped and defiled to be precise…and after generations of racial mixing, what they used to call 'miscegenation,' a very bad word indeed, they came to claim themselves as something other than merely Black, but Creoles of color and then later…there were some with straight hair and blue eyes who became passable white persons and free persons and in time would themselves amass wealth and even, yes even slaves. Yes indeed, Mister Sonny. Some even owned slaves."

Godbold licked his lips and ran his hand across his slick, salt and pepper wavy hair. He resumed. "I am, therefore, not Black like yourself, Mister Sonny, I am a man of nobler blood, the blood of European aristocrats, and this is how I have fundamentally been able to control an empire of Black officials, businessmen, thieves and killers alike. For the colonized mind loves nothing more than the taste and the authority of vanilla. And I am about as close to that as it comes. I am like a white man in the midst of Black America.

"As for my empire, so to speak, you should understand that I control this city, from the level of common street criminals to the offices of the mayor, city council, and chambers of commerce. I have interests in all things, big and small, but mostly, Mister Sonny, I control people. Just as my most venerable ancestors did. I consider the whole of Black Oakland to be my property…well, you name any way in which the Black man or woman is exploited today in this city and my fingerprints are all over it.

"You know that saying, crabs in a barrel? Well, I am a big crab peeking out over the edge of the barrel, with one big claw over the edge, ready to leap to freedom, and the other claw swatting away my so-called brothers and sisters who would otherwise seek to keep me down. Why do I do this? Because I must avoid being dragged down into the mud by the Black race. I must avoid being dragged down like a crab in a barrel. I must avoid that at all costs.

"As for what you are doing here, ... well, you have brought significant destruction to my operations. Oakland was a base of larger operations, international operations, and a further testing ground, if you will. I have been coalescing my capital in this area and you have done damage to that endeavor. You are just another crab in the barrel, pulling me down.

"Tell me Mister Sonny, what do you think you have learned about my organization?"

Sonny coughed and spat throughout the man's dreadful soliloquy.

"If you're going to kill me, just get it on with. Kill me! I'd rather be dead than listen to your bullshit story."

Godbold calmly resumed water-boarding Sonny with bourbon.

"I know that you have a weakness for the demon liquor, don't you, Mister Trueheart?"

Godbold paused. He removed the rag over Sonny's mouth and nose. Sonny coughed and spat and cursed.

"I am more than a businessman, Mister Trueheart, I am building a government. A state. And I will be its ruler. But before I can get my hands on a state, my own terror state, I need a sizable army. And I have developed a most powerful drug I am using to transform my soldiers into super Black warriors of extraordinary ability and strength. It is similar to that drug I was giving the women sold at the auction you attended. You've witnessed the strength and stamina that drug can give a person. Those women injected with my formula can withstand extraordinary levels of pain, and that gives them greater usefulness in the fetish trade.

"But this drug has wider applications than in the field of sex. It transforms people, making them super killers, rabid dogs, frothing white foam from the mouth as they grovel, lie, steal and kill for me. So, I call the drug Rabid Fire.

"So, what am I gonna do with you? You see, Mr. Trueheart, you've nearly broken my operation here in Oakland. The money that you have stolen from me, the confidence that you have shaken in my white allies…You've fought well and inflicted heavy wounds on me and I'm impressed with your abilities, your tenacity, your will. You are truly the People's Detective.

"You know, I'm going to have to end all of this hero nonsense and hope you are giving to the people. I'm going to give you the Rabid Fire drug. I'm going to turn the People's Detective into my obedient soldier. I want to see what the people say when they see the do-gooder People's Detective in obedience to my will.

"Rabid Fire is a cocktail of 5 distinct drugs. XBD173, an anti-anxiety drug to deal with fear and post-traumatic stress. Provigil or Modafinil, which deals with narcolepsy and sleep disorder and helps you function with less sleep. Valproic acid to deal with rapid blood loss and shock. You could survive a lethal injury for hours. Select Androgen Receptor Modulators or improved anabolic steroids with concentrated testosterone for rapid muscle growth. It could transform your body almost overnight. And finally, just a pinch of Pervitin, the Nazi cocaine. Pretty self-explanatory.

"My particular twist on all of these is that I introduce them to your body at the genetic level. These drugs will be essentially permanent." Godbold beamed. "The remainder of your life will be brutal, short, and full of madness. I think that's a fitting end, don't you?"

"What do you want, Godbold?"

Godbold chuckled and shrugged. "Aurora's story only goes so far. But she was getting close to the bigger picture. We were wise to abduct her. We picked her up before she could take it any higher. And your recent breach of our properties has been unfortunate. We are now led to believe that you have involved the Royal Bahamian Defense Force in this matter.

"So, you want to know what I want. You know…treachery is the essential heart of the Black man. Don't you think? Division and treachery. Other Africans sold our ancestors to the Europeans, and the Europeans were so cunningly evil that they managed to sew the seeds of division among tribal groups. I, and my father's fathers, have known this all along. This is why we have never hesitated, never allowed ourselves to be weakened by dialogues of Black uplift and revolution. You see," he brought his face close to Sonny's and grinned, "we decided that we had to get ours and to hell with the rest.

"We are now using science to provide this kind of Black man for the world. A super soldier who will possess such incredible anger in his heart that he would kill his own mother and father in bloodlust and rage and all at my command. Some of this we already achieved through our experimentations during the crack epidemic in the 1980s and fentanyl in the modern era. But we have a much more advanced formula now. We are using prototypes on child warriors in West Africa.

"You see, the Black man has always been useful in war. But always as someone else's pawn. He will do anything, and so much more than a privileged man will do, because he is trying to prove himself to his master.

"Even you, Mister Trueheart, have willingly murdered and will doubtlessly continue murdering your own kind in the service of the white man's laws and justice.

"But *you* know this, *you* have an understanding and an analysis of how the system manipulates us and turns us against each other. *You* are actively trying to free yourself from a system that calls you to embrace the language of violence given to you by your colonizer, the language that calls you to murder your own kind and to murder your own immortal soul, day by day.

"What *you* have Detective Trueheart is the individual will of the truly free Black man, so that you truly know that *you* are not a nigger, and that there never was any such thing. You are dangerous because you are trying to decolonize your soul. We share this awareness. But what are we to do with this knowledge? I have chosen to control others, others who lack my self-awareness, my understanding of history. You want to think of yourself as some kind of liberator. You go around calling yourself, 'The People's Detective.' What sort of nonsense is that? What I seek to test here is whether a forced drug addiction will eradicate the will to freedom that is so strong in your heart. That, Mister Trueheart, is my endgame.

"Shall we now put my theory to the test?"

As Godbold raised the syringe and cleared a tiny squirt of it from the needle and prepared to inject Sonny Trueheart with the first dose of the serum, Seven Daggers suddenly burst into the room. "Sir…we have a problem."

38. The End of Everything

Seven Daggers stood in the hallway with a laptop that displayed two open browsers.

On the first browser, Godbold could see that MambaNet had been hacked and was no longer functional. The image of a laughing Sambo in blackface danced on the screen. The Sambo wore a black-and-white striped prison uniform, but the center of his uniform read "Uncle Godbold." The Sambo danced upon the image of a ransom note that read: "500 million and you get your site back!"

The second browser showed a breaking local news broadcast about the disappearances of the Mayor, District Attorney, Chief of Police, and Superintendent of Schools. Apparently, no one cared about Pastor Jolly and the others. One of the White Council members (Archon 2), a Bay Area Crypto King, held a press conference and spoke about his suspicions that these high-ranking members of Oakland city government had either been abducted or murdered by Dr. Godbold. The man was bathed in innocence as he answered questions from local reporters and spoke of the hidden evil of Dr. Lucius Godbold and the false mask that Godbold had worn of being a savior, a medical genius, and a philanthropist. They spoke of how they, and they alone, had discovered that Godbold's pharmaceutical enterprises were a cover for illegal activities including kidnapping and sex trafficking. When asked what evidence he could provide to support such outlandish accusations, Archon 2 responded, "...my lawyers have compiled substantial evidence and are making this available to the authorities...and believe me, I have great lawyers!"

Godbold stood back from Seven Daggers and swiftly backhanded the man across the face. The laptop fell from his grasp and crashed to the floor. Even with all of his bulk, Seven Daggers reeled after the blow, temporarily unsure of his footing and stunned.

"This is all because of you! You and your incompetence! I will have no more of it!" He jabbed his finger into Seven Daggers' chest. "Wait here! I will deal with you!"

And with that Godbold stormed back into the room where Sonny Trueheart lay strapped to an operating table. He took a deep breath and approached him.

In an instant his tone changed, but Sonny could see an involuntary quivering under his eyes.

"It seems that someone, perhaps one of your friends, has hacked into my network."

Sonny said nothing.

Dr. Godbold patted him on the forehead. "You have nothing to say for yourself? No matter. I'll find out who did this soon enough. So, in light of the circumstances, I now have bigger fish to fry." Godbold produced another syringe. "This is just a simple dose of fentanyl. This will keep you under wraps while I attend to other matters." Godbold pushed out the first little squirt of the drug. "Sure, it's 50 times more powerful than morphine and your body probably isn't used to opioids, and there's a good chance that you'll experience an overdose, but I'm comfortable with that." Godbold injected the poison into Sonny's veins. "Bye, bye for now, Mister *True Heart*."

39. Do Not Go Gentle Into That Good Night

Sonny lay for what felt like hours, naked and restrained on the cold table, feeling his heart rate slow, struggling to breathe as if there was a giant foot on his chest, feeling his extremities numbing, and fighting the onset of a deep sleep. Presently he sensed a figure approaching him and injecting a needle into his arm. Sonny experienced a sharp, stabbing, diffuse pain running throughout his body, awakening him with involuntary convulsions. The restraints were removed and Sonny was suddenly aware of his nakedness, feeling shame and anxiety about what might happen next. He felt the figure clothing him and then pulling him from the table and slinging him over their shoulder like a rag doll.

Sonny was moved to a dark, empty room. A black space. No windows. The perfect absence of light. Aurora called out to him. Sonny crawled through the depths of the darkness, softly calling her name and she calls his until their bodies touched and they embraced.

"They've injected you with fentanyl. That's what they've been using on me." Aurora grabbed his wrist and ran his hand over her track-marked arms.

Sonny kissed her on the cheek and held her tight in his arms. He began caressing the injection scars on her arms. "I am so sorry that this happened to you. It's my fault. It's all my fault."

"I should have come to you sooner and shared my findings with you."

"I was in no state to either receive or understand what you were working on."

"Now, we will die together because of what we have learned. Are you afraid of dying?" Aurora asked.

"It's an inevitability. It never seemed to make much sense to fear that which is inevitable. None of us are guaranteed tomorrow. None of us."

"But you have faced death before. What ran through your mind?"

"I didn't have time to think about it. I know that I was lucky to survive. You can call that whatever you want. Luck. The hand of God. Karma. Something kept me alive in that moment so that I could be here, right now, to help you get out of this mess."

"You just acted on instinct?"

"The best way I can describe this for you…it's like…fear is a door. Most of us assume that there's something terrible on the other side of that door. In the moment, I walked through that door without thinking, without hesitation or anxiety. That doesn't necessarily make me a brave man. I simply acted and did what I had to do in the moment."

"What did you find on the other side of that door?"

"I don't know. Maybe I'm still figuring that out. Truth be told, I've been drinking to numb the memory of the horror that I experienced there. But it wasn't the horror of dying, it was the horror of me becoming an instrument of death. I believe that I can face death when the time comes. What I fear most is becoming an agent of death, standing at death's door and ushering other people in."

"But these were very bad people."

"People nonetheless. I didn't want their blood on my hands, whether they were among the righteous or not. And it was not my place to judge them and render a sentence and an execution. But I did. What about you? Do you fear death?"

"I know that death will come for us all eventually, but it's the waiting that wears on me the most. Sitting here waiting for whatever judgment they render. That's why I tried to escape. Tried to starve myself too. I just wanted to take back my power."

"The truth is that life is on the other side of that door. If you open the door of fear you have to commit to staying alive and fighting the darkness from both within and without. As you begin to fight the darkness, you realize that this is what life is. Fighting the darkness. Raging against the night. That is what it means to be alive."

Moments of silence passed between them as Aurora sought to grasp an understanding of Sonny's words.

Sonny looked through the darkness in the room and whispered softly in her ear. "Don't worry. We're gonna be okay."

Aurora shivered in his arms. "How do you know?"

Sonny pointed to a dark corner of the room. "Aaminha's here."

Aurora ran her hand along the length of his arm to feel the direction that he was pointing to. She looked hard into the darkness and saw her. "She's beautiful."

They held one another in the dark, looking at the vision of Aaminha, for what seemed like an eternity until light filtered through a crack in the door.

Sonny saw only a tall, dark figure.

The voice spoke with a thick Black British accent. It was Seven Daggers. He called Aurora. "Rise. Come to me. Now."

Aurora rose and walked fearlessly towards Seven Daggers. Perhaps, after seeing a vision of her sister, she had chosen to walk through the door of fear and venture to see what might be on the other side. Perhaps she had chosen to fight and to keep on fighting. Seven Daggers cuffed her wrists and bade her to wait. He stood motionless in the doorway staring at Sonny Trueheart.

***

Seven Daggers had just taken the elevator from Dr. Godbold's penthouse residence where Godbold sat naked in the darkness admiring the view of Lake Merritt. Day had crawled submissively before him on its hands and knees and given into night. There was a naked woman slumped awkwardly on his sofa smoking a cigarette.

She was one of his regular consorts. She drank Southern Comfort neat. She did not speak much, for there was nothing for her to say. Godbold would speak to her and she would smile and that was the extent of their relationship. She was grateful only for the fact that his interest in her had saved her from the slave auctions and she had yet to be violated by his clammy hands. She knew that he would not touch her, that she was there for ornamentation and casual amusement. Godbold was impotent. His penis merely hung there like a lifeless serpent.

When Seven Daggers arrived, Godbold dismissed her with a wave of his hand and she dressed and quietly departed.

Godbold reached for his laptop and resumed reviewing the files of men and women who might replace Seven Daggers. Even though Seven Daggers had managed to bring him Sonny Trueheart, he had long been displeased with the man's performance and attitude. Seven Daggers had an independent streak and this deeply disturbed Dr. Godbold. He reviewed the resumes and reports of former Oakland homicide detectives looking for extra work. Their records were punctuated by violence and allegations of racism, questionable shootings and disturbing psychiatric reports, all of which had led to grudging dismissals by OPD.

And now, tonight, Godbold voiced his displeasure to Seven Daggers and spoke to him about possible replacements. And Seven Daggers stood quietly and took the verbal abuse as he had done many times before. Godbold told him that he was inefficient, willful, and had displayed questionable judgment in the matter of Aurora Jenkins and Sonny Trueheart that now risked his entire operation. He had seen the security footage and chastised him for not preventing Malik Akoto from crashing the George Bush Federal Building and planting a virus on the MambaNet server. Never once had Godbold recognized his ability to capture Trueheart and he had clearly lost faith in Seven Daggers' ability to correct the situation.

"If I didn't know better," Godbold screamed, "I would think that you were plotting against me, against the Black Archon! Maybe it was you that encouraged the White Council to turn against me!"

***

Now at the doorway of the dark room where Godbold kept Aurora Jenkins and Sonny Trueheart, Seven Daggers knelt and placed something from his pocket on the floor. As he stood up, he kicked the object and it skittered against Sonny's right leg. It was Sonny's revolver.

"You didn't talk," Seven Daggers noted.

"We had an agreement."

"Yeah, we had an agreement, innit? You kill the boogeyman and I return the woman. We're both going to finish what we said we would do."

"You'll release her to me?"

"Yeah. It's *my word*, innit? I'll meet you tomorrow evening. Same place you killed Papi Elder. I'll give you back the bird if you bring the money and the crypto drives that you stole."

"You'll never be able to crack the password on those drives. It's a 54-character code."

Seven Daggers smiled, "The boogeyman is a sentimental lot. I've got him and his damn passwords figured out."

Sonny reached for his revolver. "Where is he?"

"He's on the rooftop garden. 28 stories up. Take the stairs, not the elevator. Finish what you came here to do. Don't get the shakes. Just think of Aaminha Toure and pull the trigger."

Power to the People!
A Podcast for the People
Broadcasting from the Lower
Bottoms of West Oakland
Hosted by Aurora Jenkins

Transcript of Power to the People! Episode 78

This week's episode is devoted to the disappearance of a 5-year-old child, last seen in Oakland two weeks ago with her baby-sitter. You may have heard about this story on the local news. They are covering it because it also involves the disappearance and death of her mother, an emergency ward nurse at Highland Hospital. The body of Lana Fewkes, age 33, was found last night in Joaquin Miller Park in the Oakland hills. Lana had been missing for two weeks after receiving a call at the hospital from her babysitter. Lana's little girl, Bahia Fewkes, was last seen in the care of the babysitter and her boyfriend, both of whom also disappeared two weeks ago. The Oakland police are saying that the babysitter and her boyfriend are persons of interest in the murder of Lana and the disappearance of Bahia and $100,000 has been offered as a reward for any information regarding their whereabouts.

    I've read so many of the stories of the missing, and I am always taken aback by the many stories of infants and toddlers. There are stories of toddlers who wandered off, walking for miles, often accompanied by the family dog, or wandering miles from school or along the interstate before having been reported missing. Often, all too often, missing children have been abducted by a parent.

    The Oakland Police appear to have some leads in this case, and a direction to follow. But, as always, this program remains a resource for gathering any information that you might have.

40. Do It Again

Only when Sonny Trueheart emerged from the dark room did he recognize where he was. He was in a utility room in the Black Archon Center. Likely on a hidden floor between the garage and the bank in the lobby that he had just robbed. True to his word thus far, Seven Daggers had rendered unconscious all of the guards who patrolled the hallways and corridors of the building. All the lights had been knocked out except for emergency red lights in the corners of each hallway. Sonny cautiously crept through the hallways, crouching and holding his revolver close to his body. He opened the cylinder and checked. Apparently Seven Daggers had never checked to see if he was carrying real bullets. Sonny had loaded the gun with rubber bullets provided by Captain Gibson, but there was one real bullet in the base of the extended grip that his father had modified.

As Sonny crept through the hidden basement, he observed two laboratories. He tried the door on both. One was unlocked and he entered the dark lab, clinging to the walls until he stumbled across a light switch, and was able to observe machinery for synthesizing, mixing, and compounding chemical substances. There was a small modular reactor and mini centrifuges. Workbenches were lined with precision instruments like scales, pipettes, and spectrometers to ensure exact measurements and purity of compounds. Sonny's eyes glazed over the beakers, tubes, whirring of machines and the sound of circulating fluids. There were flashing computer screens and a large white board covered in formulas written in Godbold's own hand. These were all things he knew nothing about. It reminded him of Vincent Price's laboratory in the movie *Dr. Phibes*, and he remembered watching this with his father. He knew that he would need to destroy Godbold's labs in order to prevent the proliferation of the drug that Godbold called Rabid Fire. Sonny shivered. Knowing what he now knew, it was like walking through a grotesque nightmare.

Resolved, Sonny began to move in military precision. He found a fire emergency ax and smashed down the door of the other lab. Inside he found cylinders of hydrogen. Remembering a little bit from a Castlemont High School chemistry class, Sonny opened the hydrogen gas and turned the Bunsen burners to full.

Sonny dropped the ax and ran, departing the lab well in advance of a series of explosions, and staggered through the exit door and slowly began to climb the 28 flights of steps to the rooftop garden.

Sonny knew as he pushed himself up 28 grueling flights of stairs that events would force him to kill a man again. He told himself that he was fighting for Aurora and for Aaminha. He was fighting for those who would have been injected with the Rabid Fire drug. He was fighting for the countless young women abducted from the streets of their communities in Oakland and the Bay Area and sold into sexual slavery. But in his heart, he knew, it was killing all the same.

The climb was exhausting and Sonny struggled, taking a break on the 15th floor and then another at the 22nd. *Move it old man!* Sonny muttered to himself. When he reached the 28th floor he stood by the door and caught his breath. He held his revolver with both hands and then slowly opened the door with his foot.

The summer heat and humidity had given way to sudden thunderstorms. The night air crackled with electricity and a violent summer rain came down from the sepia smoke-filled sky.

Dr. Lucius Godbold stood in a shimmering white silk robe edged in gold. It fluttered in the breeze and the developing rain atop the rooftop garden. His shoulders were massive. His head seemed to eclipse the moon. He stood with his back to Sonny in the very center of the garden, holding himself and urinating on a bed of vegetable plants.

"Trueheart?" he queried. He stopped urinating abruptly. He began to turn. Sonny caught the glimmer of a .357 magnum revolver in his hand. Sonny knelt and aimed his .38 snubby. He fired.

The first rubber bullet struck Godbold's wrist and the gun was flung from his grasp into the vegetable garden. Lost amidst the tomatoes, kale, and cabbage. Godbold nursed his hand but he did not scream in reaction to the pain.

"So, he sent *you* to kill me? He couldn't do it himself? Coward! I was ready to face his treachery!"

Suddenly an explosion rippled the very foundation of the building and reverberated up 28 flights to the rooftop. Godbold absorbed the shock of the blast. "So, you've seen my lab. Lovely, lovely." He gleamed with delight and turned to stare down Sonny, who had risen from his crouch and stood with his pistol.

Godbold pointed his finger at Sonny. "You are not my equal. You cannot kill me!"

Sonny did not move a muscle. The rain picked up, the thunder cracked and boomed and Sonny saw a flash of lightning.

"Did Adro betray me?" Godbold asked. His face was red with fury. "I always knew he would betray me. He didn't have the vision for this work. And he only lusted for money, drugs and whores. He didn't have the intellectual capacity to understand what I was doing. He thought it was all a distraction. He was really no better than Papi Elder, and Papi, you know, was just a lowlife pimp. But Papi had this great skill. He could turn *any* woman out." Godbold chuckled. "We thought about getting that little chippie you fell in love with, that Aaminha Toure, and having Papi Elder turn her out and put her on the streets."

Sonny fired successive blasts from his father's .38 Colt Detective snub nose revolver.

With each shot he yelled, "Don't! Ever! Speak! Her! Name!"

The second rubber bullet struck Godbold in the gut and the impact rippled his flesh. The third pinged off his forehead. The fourth bullet grazed his left knee and he wobbled slightly. The fifth shot struck his right knee dead center and hyperextended the joint and the big man finally sagged to the ground, falling into a kneeling posture. The sixth smashed his throat and the big man put his hands around his neck and struggled to breathe.

And then Sonny dropped his father's revolver and set upon Godbold with his fists. Encircling Godbold with furious blows. One punch from his left and, as Godbold rocked to the right on his knees, another punch from his right, taking him back to his left and back and forth and back and forth from right to left with a flurry of blows until Sonny Trueheart was breathless, and his knuckles were bruised and bleeding.

Sonny beat Godbold like a human piñata. Godbold's eyes were swollen shut and his face was barely recognizable from the swelling and the cuts. Godbold dropped facedown, hard to the ground. And then Sonny stood over his prone form, watching him wheeze and spit blood.

Sonny heard the sound of the police and fire engines in the near distance. The whirring of approaching police helicopters.

Sonny grabbed Godbold by the collar of his blood speckled silk robe and with great effort dragged the big man to the edge of the building. Sonny knelt to get his weight under Godbold's massive body, clasped his arms around Godbold's waist, and propped him up against the railing, preparing to push him over the edge to plummet 28 stories down to his death.

Godbold laughed and spat blood, mocking and taunting as Sonny struggled under the weight of his massive form. Godbold grasped the railing and struggled to stand of his own accord. "You're no killer! And you're not much of a detective, either! You're just a blind dog in a meat house!"

Sonny stepped back from the edge of the rooftop and stood motionless before the man who continued mocking him. He felt the cold hard rain falling on his head and shoulders.

As he looked at Godbold, he could see the door of death opening again and beckoning him to usher Godbold across the threshold. Sonny turned his gaze away and stared blankly out at the rainy Oakland night. He wondered, how much farther was he willing to go in order to save his city?

He knew the answer and turned to look hard at Dr. Godbold.

Dr. Lucius Godbold saw the flash of resolve in the eyes of his adversary. He spat and slurred his speech and balled his fists. "I won't give you the satisfaction, detective. You're not my equal. I am Godbold! Who the hell are you?"

Sonny raised his fists and positioned himself to strike. "I'm August and Rena Trueheart's boy."

Godbold howled and lurched forward, gathering a final burst of strength fueled by rage, and threw a hard overhand left.

Sonny leaned back and dropped his head low and to the left, evading the punch, and crouching to gather strength in his legs.

And Sonny came up hard with his left hand and unleashed the wide arcing trajectory of a haymaker that connected against Dr. Lucius Godbold's grotesquely swollen cheek, sending the bigger man stumbling back and over the edge of the Black Archon Center.

Sonny leaned over the edge and watched the bloated Dr. Lucius Godbold, naked but for his ostentatious silk robe, spiral downwards, down 28 stories, down, down, down through the rain and the smoke-filled night, his mouth open in a silent scream, until he hit the pavement on Lakeside Drive.

41. The Trickster

The Oakland Police Department sent 20 police cars that formed a barricade around the burning tower and two helicopters landed on the rooftop garden. The sirens and red-light lights pierced the sepia haze of the smoke-filled night. The rain continued steadily falling. Soon, three Oakland Fire Department fire trucks rumbled onto the scene, and Oakland's bravest men and women began to fight the fire that Sonny started in the hidden basement.

When the OPD choppers landed on the rooftop, cops in riot gear jumped out and encircled Sonny with automatic rifles. With his empty revolver tucked in his waistband and blood on his hands, Sonny stood in the wind and rain and grinned, refusing to drop to his knees or raise his hands.

Sonny balled his fists, snarled and said, "Do your worst," and spat on the ground in front of the cops.

Captain Gibson broke the circle of automatic rifles and cops who remained silent behind their visors. He stood before Sonny and offered a hand in friendship. "It appears that our alliances have shifted. How does it feel to be the hero cop again, detective?"

The cops in riot gear immediately lowered their rifles and raised the visors on their helmets. To a man, they nodded their approval and respect and parted, creating a path for Sonny to pass through.

Sonny was gently escorted to one of the helicopters, where he sat alone with the pilot. As the helicopter rose, he looked at his bruised and bloody hands, the hands of a murderer, and breathed deeply taking in the vision of the summer rain and the surreal and smoky view high above Oakland and the port.

He looked up and saw a vision of Aaminha sitting across from him.

"Did I do the right thing, baby?" he asked her.

Sonny leaned back and closed his eyes, taking a moment to bask in the liminal space and reflect on where he fit in the long history of Oakland.

Oakland.

Maybe the most diverse little city in America. Fourth largest port in the world. Most American trade with the east, notably technologies, flowed through this port. A town of great irony if there ever was one. Gertrude Stein said, there's no there there. But she was only referring to the demise of her childhood home in Oakland, not the city itself. Kinda got stuck on Oakland nonetheless. And the city's main tourist attraction was named after the writer Jack London. In a thoroughly multi-ethnic society, here was a man who once warned of "the yellow peril," who urged Jim Jeffries to rescue the white man in his heavyweight bout with champion Jack Johnson, who casually used the word "nigger," and who wrote comic anti-Semitic portrayals of American Jews. But they had a statue of this guy and had named a prominent square for him.

History is merely a thing of the past for most Americans. Oaklanders are different. Oaklanders ride with ghosts, memories, and legends.

Huchiun. An Ohlone village of the Lusjan people. They were the first here. This was their ancestral land. They did not own the land, they belonged to it. Settling around Lake Merritt and Temescal Creek, which means "bathhouse" in Aztec. Claimed by Spain in 1772 and later by an independent Mexico, Oakland became the property of Luis Maria Peralta who named the area Rancho San Antonio. Peralta's sons inherited the land and opened it to white settlers, loggers, whalers, and fur traders who would steal from them. Then came the Gold Rush, the genocide of Native peoples, the American Conquest, the exploitation of Chinese workers on the railroads and then the settlement of San Francisco refugees after the 1906 earthquake and massive African American migration from Texas, Louisiana, Oklahoma, and Arkansas in the first Great Migration. By the '20s Oakland was a major manufacturing town with naval shipbuilding and automobile plants. But opportunities were limited by the brutal rule of the Klan in the 1920's. They held political power here. That power was only broken by a graft trial presided over by Alameda County District Attorney Earl Warren. Yes, the same one who would go on to serve on the Supreme Court. From the second Great Migration of southern Blacks seeking work on the railroads and ports during World War II to the late 1960's, this was a town of working-class people of color who the Klan-infiltrated police department figured to control with bullets and batons. Then the Black Panther Party for Self-Defense was born, and its success motivated Governor Reagan's racist pursuit of Black activists. Against the soundtrack of Black protest music and the hot slap and pop funk by Sly & the Family Stone, Graham Central Station, Tower of Power, and The Headhunters, the whole Bay Area was awash in the bloodletting of the '70s from the death of little Bobby Hutton to the Zodiac killings to Manson to the Symbionese Liberation Army to the Jonestown Massacre. And in came the crack epidemic of the '80s when they finally washed all the protest and activism away in a sea of Iran-Contra crack cocaine. And then it was open season again on Black people and rarely were there ever indictments for trigger-happy police. Oakland was a Black metropolis no more. The gang injunctions the cops laid down rapidly moved bodies into the system, lowered property values and made safe the road to gentrification and the ever-increasing whitening of the city.

But now, with the end of the Black Archon, as the police helicopter rode over the rain clouds and the smoky skies, Sonny saw a way for things to change. Not just here in Oakland but everywhere. Because of police violence and gentrification, the young people out here had had enough of whiteness and its lies and betrayals. Capitalism had never worked for them and previous generations. Education and health care were designed to leave them behind. There had been no application of reforms with all deliberate speed. There had only been institutional roadblocks and double speak.

Sonny was questioned by Captain Gibson for half an hour. Gibson urged Sonny to stick to the "official" story without elaboration. *Self-defense. Suicide.* Godbold was trying to murder him. Sonny defended himself. Fearing arrest and criminal conviction, as Godbold heard the police helicopters coming in the distance, *he threw himself* over the edge of the roof. He asked Sonny to repeat it back to him.

Sonny repeated the "official story" to the interim Alamada County District Attorney, Jayda Paul, a queer Black former public defender. She wasn't interested in pressing charges, but told Sonny that she would call him in for further questioning that could lead to indictments of any and all members of the Black Archon. Sonny was reassured by her presence. DA Paul had the zeal of a true reformer. Sonny felt the weight coming off a city that was relieved to rid itself from the clutches of the Black Archon.

Sonny assured the DA that he could help her bring the Black Archon's many silent partners to justice: "I'm coming after the big money. I've obtained all the evidence you'll need."

"On that matter, I would advise you to back off, detective. My office will take it from here."

"I would advise you, district attorney, to prosecute whoever I bring to your door."

As he prepared to leave Oakland Police headquarters, Captain Gibson returned Sonny's revolver and gave him a box of rubber bullets, a box of .38 hollow points, and a speedloader, and drove him back to his demolished home. "I suppose you're going to go after Seven Daggers now?" Gibson asked.

"Damn straight," Sonny replied as he loaded his revolver one round at a time. "And I haven't forgotten about you either."

When Sonny got back home, all that was left, a block away from the roped-off rubble of his modest home on 68th Ave., was his beautiful mysterious red sunglo Harley Davidson Fatboy.

Sonny drove the Fatboy hard out of the Havenscourt. He ran right into traffic surrounding an evening sideshow face-off as he traveled out of the neighborhood.

There was a crowd of about 50 people in the rain, circled around the intersection where two souped-up '70s Buicks with gaudy metallic paint jobs, white-walled tires, spinning wheels and booming sound systems rattling the metal were gunning their engines. The red Buick made the first move. Peeling out in circles. Burning its tires. The atmosphere was all about hanging out, like people taking back the streets.

Sonny watched Oakland become the sideshow capital of the hip-hop world, where kids in jacked up cars get together to compete against each other to see who has the "dopest" looking ride and the most "handles" behind the steering wheel.

On any given night in East Oakland, driving down MacArthur or Foothill, you are bound to see pimped out Chevelles, Mustangs, and Camaros with racing stripes doing doughnuts, fish tailin', burning rubber or in the parking lot locking up their tires. Oakland has been famous for "stuntin'" like this since the late 1980s when Richie Rich and the 415 rapped about it on their song "Sideshow."

There was a celebration going on and Sonny could see that someone had spray painted the center of the concrete around which cars fishtailed and burned rubber with the following words: "The Black Archon is Dead! Long Live the People's Detective!"

Sonny honked the Fatboy's horn in celebration. He was close enough to the intersection to see the cars competing through the throng of bodies. Smoke from the tires filled the air. He could hear police sirens converging on the spot, coming in stereo. People stood and looked, unsure of whether to start scurrying. A couple of onlookers with camera phones were trying to get final shots before hopping into their cars and screeching off. Ordinarily, the cops would use tear gas to disperse the crowds. But this time, a police motorcycle entered the circle, followed by a cop car, and they too began to spin around in circles, burning rubber and generating cheers from the crowd.

Sonny revved the Fatboy, his tires burning acrid white smoke on the pavement. He raised a fist and headed towards the I-880 freeway.

The end of the Black Archon and Aurora's story could change everything in Oakland.

Sonny drove the Fatboy onto north I-880 and merged onto I-80 into Albany for the exchange in the parking lot of Golden Gate Fields. The rented van was still there. Irony of ironies. It was the original scene of the crime where he had killed Papi Elder and two crooked cops. Sonny knew Seven Daggers would call the meeting here.

The wind coming off the bay was chilly and it continued raining.

Trueheart cut the ignition on the Fat Boy, removed his helmet and waited. The Detective Special revolver was tucked into the IWB holster covered by his dashiki and leather motorcycle jacket.

Fashionably late, a black limo pulled up. Parked a good 20 yards away from Trueheart. Seven Daggers emerged from the backseat. Fastened his suit jacket. Grinned. Two of Seven Daggers' thugs came out in short order. Two white heavies with short-cropped hair. Pistols drawn. A ginger killer for hire and a blonde killer for hire.

"Didn't killing Godbold satisfy you?" Seven Daggers asked. "Because it sure satisfied me. Now I'm the heir to the throne. The new king of the Black Archon, innit?"

The man was deluded. He truly believed that Godbold's white paymasters were loyal to him. Sonny ignored the remarks. "Did you bring Aurora?"

"Did you bring the money? The hard drives?"

"It's all in the van," Sonny pointed.

"Good boy!"

"Did you bring Aurora?"

Seven Daggers snapped his fingers and one of the heavies roughly pulled Aurora from the car. She was shivering, wearing only a pair of jeans, a short-sleeved t-shirt, and sandals. The ginger and blonde goons aimed their pistols. The ginger had Sonny in his sights. The blonde held his pistol against Aurora's head.

"I want the keys to the van."

Sonny reached in his pocket and tossed the keys to the ginger-headed goon.

The killer dutifully walked towards the van, opened the back and saw 13 stuffed black duffel bags. He reached for one of the bags, unzipped it, and found only shredded paper. He went through four other bags and found the same. He grabbed a wad of shredded paper and held it in the air. "There's nothing here."

Seven Daggers approached Trueheart. "I knew you'd break our deal again. Cheeky bastard. No matter. I'll track down your people and get my money in due time. After all, I've still got the backing of the White Council. So…I'm going to kill you and Aurora's going to watch before I kill her. Tonight will be all about tying up loose ends. You know, it's quite an annoying thing, this righteous and pure act of yours. *True Heart!* You're always taking the loser's path…but I appreciate your dedication to it." He spat. "Now, Mister Trueheart, give me your shooter."

Seven Daggers motioned for the gun. Sonny complied, unzipped his leather jacket and removed his revolver from the IWB holster and set it on the ground and kicked it over to Seven Daggers the same way he had given it back to him when he was in captivity.

Seven Daggers absent-mindedly opened the cylinder. Spun the wheel gun. "Cute little snubby, innit? A little like the gun you took down Papi Elder with, eh?"

Sonny Trueheart nodded. "It's the same one."

"I hate revolvers."

"Like I care."

Seven Daggers snapped back the cylinder.

"Now…I'm going to make it slow. I'm gonna use all six bullets."

"Shut up and get on with it."

Aurora screamed, "No Sonny! No!"

"You wearing a vest, Mister Trueheart?"

Sonny shook his head. He lifted the dashiki he was wearing underneath his motorcycle jacket and showed his bare chest.

"All right Mister Trueheart!" Seven Daggers nodded, satisfied that he would not be cheated of Sonny's death. "You know how to play this game! Does the dying man request a final wish?" Seven Daggers was drunk with images of revenge and the irony of killing the man right here and with his own pistol. His eyes gleamed like obsidian.

Sonny was too calm, too cool. "Let me speak to her. One last time." He zipped up his motorcycle jacket.

Seven Daggers motioned and his goons set her free. She ran to Sonny's side. They embraced. She held him the way Aaminha used to. He felt the fullness of her body and buried his face in her hair. She held him as they had held one another while they were Godbold's captives. Seven Daggers had enough manners to step back away from the sound of their whispering voices and let the man enjoy his last wish.

She whispered. "Why did you come here? What are you going to do? You can't let them do this to you! I won't let you just surrender your life."

"You got a little fight left in you?"

Aurora nodded. "Yes. But I can't let them shoot you," she implored.

"Don't worry."

"It's time," Seven Daggers yelled. "You've said your goodbyes."

Sonny released Aurora. Looked deep into her eyes, assuring her. The blonde goon came and yanked her away.

"You might find this hard to believe, Mister Trueheart," Seven Daggers smirked, "but I actually have some respect for you. You showed up here like a dutiful prisoner, right on time for your execution."

"You told me to either bring the money or prepare myself to die. In any event, you would have killed me and Aurora whether I brought the money or not."

Seven Daggers thought on it. "True," he smiled. "I probably would have. Just for shits and giggles, you know? But I'm happy at least one of us decided to play it straight!"

"Get on with it, asshole."

"Oh, Detective Trueheart!! Tsk! Tsk! Why are you in such a rush! Do you have someplace to be?"

"Shut up and fucking get on with it."

Seven Daggers walked up to Trueheart and took aim. Stood but a few yards away. Fired two shots in quick succession. Point blank range. The .38 caliber bullets ripped through the leather motorcycle jacket, opening a wound in the center of his chest.

Sonny staggered. He tasted blood in his mouth. "That the best you got?"

Seven Daggers fired again. Four more times. Gunshots echoed across the parking lot, sounding Trueheart's fate. Sonny jerked hard under the final blasts, one errant shot grazing his temple, three others hitting home and ripping through his leather jacket into his gut and finally bringing him down to his knees. He fell forward onto his face. Whispered "fuck you" and fought the darkness coming in from the edges.

"So, you see Detective Trueheart, payback is a mother, innit?"

Seven Daggers emptied the cylinder. The shells rattled on the pavement. He wiped the revolver with a pocket handkerchief and tossed it to the ground beside Sonny's still body.

Seven Daggers laughed. He walked back to the limo. He matter-of-factly ordered the goons, "Kill the woman."

Aurora fell to her knees, slipping free of the grasp of the blonde, her screams barely audible in the ringing aftermath of the gunshots. The blonde tried to reach down and grab her by the hair.

Seven Daggers unbuttoned his jacket and opened the limo. Before entering the vehicle, he looked over his shoulder and saw that Sonny had somehow gotten back to his feet, was using his teeth to open the base of the wooden grips of his gun from which a spare bullet dropped into his left hand, was loading the single round into the cylinder, and was now aiming the revolver with his right hand. Sonny pressed his left arm against the wounds across his chest and stomach. Blood was profusely running down the side of his face.

"Yeah, six shots," Sonny grinned. "Or didn't you count the spare round hidden in the grip?" And Sonny Trueheart squinted and pulled the heavy trigger.

It was a perfect shot in the darkness that rang out against the still night and Sonny saw the bullet lift Seven Daggers off his feet and open a jagged edged third eye in his forehead. He died with that glassy eyed killer's smile on his face.

The heavies panicked.

From her position Aurora took hold of an automatic pistol in the side holster of the blonde who held her hair, and fired at a downward angle, taking his left kneecap. She was blinded temporarily by the wide spark of the muzzle flash and felt his blood splash against her cheek.

Sonny quickly reached into his jacket pocket and withdrew a speed-loader and, without even looking, emptied and reloaded his revolver. He had practiced it enough over the years that he could reload his wheel gun as fast as other cops could eject and slide a new magazine into their polymer 9mm's. And Sonny fired again and again and again, catching the ginger goon twice in his chest and lifting him from his feet and unto his demise.

Aurora regained her vision and fired two more quick shots at the blonde as he bent over, grasping his knee. Both shots missed, pinging off the pavement. The man panicked for a minute, startled by the deafening gun blasts, and fumbled for another weapon with his free hand —a switchblade in his pocket— before taking Aurora's next shot to his thigh followed by a lethal shot dead-center to his chest from Sonny's gun. The force of it, the shock of it, took him in an instant.

Aurora dropped the gun and ran over to Sonny where he stood, holding his left arm against his wounds. He was faintly grinning with pride.

"You did well, Aaminha."

Aurora kept her cool in spite of the blood streaming down his face. "Aurora. It's Aurora. How are you still alive?"

He barely had any breath left in him. "Oh yeah. Aurora. I'm sorry." He unzipped and removed his jacket and ripped his dashiki open. Aurora could see that he was not bleeding in any vital areas but had deep purple welts the size of dinner plates across his chest and a severe cut on the side of his head. "Rubber rounds, except for the hollow point hidden in the base of the grip and in the speed loader," Sonny explained. "Can't believe that idiot fell for it. But I think he broke a couple of ribs." Sonny laughed until it hurt. He ripped his dashiki completely free from his body, wiped the blood from his face and wrapped his forehead tight with a strip of the garment.

He offered Aurora his tattered leather jacket.

They could hear police sirens in the distance. Captain Gibson's boys were coming to clean up after him and weave another "official story."

"One moment," Aurora said, and she ran to the prone body of Seven Daggers and searched his pockets for his smartphone. Finding this in his right pants pocket, she held the phone up to his face to unlock it and ran back to Sonny.

She guided Sonny, now naked to the waist, onto the Fat Boy and had him wrap his arms around her and hold on tight. She revved the engine and backed up from the limo.

"Where do we go from here?" she asked Sonny as she zoomed out of the parking lot and towards the freeway.

She heard him straining to speak. "I'm going to make damn sure that everyone remembers…this is our city."

42. Did You Think I'd Forgotten?

3 Months Later

Members of the White Council slowly filed into the conference room in the Black Archon Center. They were 13 of the wealthiest men and women in the Bay Area, resplendently tanned from early fall vacations on remote Caribbean islands as they laid low in the aftermath of Dr. Godbold's death. Private Prisons. Payday Lending. Fast Food. Big Pharma. Big Media. Big Gun Manufacturers. Big Tobacco. Investment bankers from too big to fail banks. Big Crypto. Big Cannabis. They were all here, and, thanks to Aurora's quick thinking when she retrieved Seven Daggers' phone, Orpheus Anderson had been able to hack it and obtain records of text messages identifying and incriminating all of them.

For the moment, members of the White Council felt safe. The big headlines had come and gone. The perp walk spectacles of Black Archon underlings and crooked cops in cuffs had long vanished from the local news. All misdeeds had been attributed to Dr. Godbold. In exchange for lighter sentences, DA Paul convinced the Archon's remaining allies to inform The White Council that Seven Daggers had cleverly faked his death, gone to ground, and would soon resurface and call a meeting. When the call was made, members of The White Council knew that it was time to begin again, to rebuild.

As Archon 1 entered the dark room he saluted the figure he presumed was seated within the glass booth. "A brilliant move, Mister Onzi. Simply brilliant. Your foresight in staging your own death will allow us the opportunity to remake you and install you as head of our new organization."

Archon 3 chimed in. "Indeed. We have access to the best plastic surgeons."

Archon 5 was giddy with excitement. "We have a whole new identity prepared for you! We are definitely looking forward to re-making you and re-making our organization."

As the 13 took their seats, Sonny Trueheart, who now sat at the controls in the glass booth, pressed a button that turned on the lights and then another button that audibly locked the conference room door. He cleared his throat and began to speak.

"Welcome ladies and gentlemen. My name is Sonny Trueheart. I think you've heard of me. They call me the People's Detective. I take that to heart. I've asked you to assemble today in order to hold you accountable to the people."

The members of the White Council stood up at the same time, hot with outrage, and pounding their fists on the conference table.

Archon 1 was the loudest. "What is this all about, Mister Trueheart? Do you know who you are dealing with?"

"I'm well aware of who I am dealing with. I've obtained hard evidence, including financial data, linking all of you to shell companies used to launder profits from the Black Archon's sex trafficking operation."

Sonny withdrew the three photographs that Aurora had given him from the inner pocket of his leather motorcycle jacket. He kissed the photograph of Aaminha and pressed it against his chest. He placed the other two photographs side by side on the desk in front of him and continued addressing his audience.

"I know who you are. Cyril Bane of the Manifest Destiny banking and loan group. Your family company has a long history of discriminatory and predatory lending in our communities. Miles Farraday of the Quick and Easy Check Cashing group that rips people off with 400 to 800% annual percentage rates. Carissa Johns of the Red Line Real Estate Development Group. Aptly titled for a group of people invested in de facto housing segregation. Janet Booth of Good Soul Hair Care and Beauty whose products contain toxic chemicals that contribute to higher rates of breast cancer, birth defects, hormone disruption and chronic illness in Black women.

Parker Jones of the Green Wonderland Cannabis Dispensaries, who has effectively lobbied state legislators to limit the application of cannabis equity legislation that prioritizes investment in small, minority owned cannabis businesses. Elliot Dover of CoolSmokes Tobacco which markets cheap and toxic vapes in our neighborhoods. Red Humboldt of CalTex Oil, with all of your refineries polluting the air and water in Richmond, California. Brooks Moran of White Hawk Media, pumping out racist conservative lies about our people, blaming the victim for being unable to overcome the economic and political impediments that you create. Aaron Cleland of the ArmorShield Project that provides police with high-tech military grade weaponry. Patricia Adams of the Benefica Pharmaceutical group and its array of addictive opioids. Gerald Portsmith of the Happy Burger and Red Rooster Chicken fast food chains, purveyor of high blood pressure, high cholesterol and diabetes. Reese Lowie of Wonder Crypto, purveyors of the latest pipe dream. And of course, Nero Jones of the Centurion Private Prison Group, profiteer of pain.

"I know all of your names and all of your deeds. I know that you're *all* responsible for much of the pain and suffering that *we*, the everyday people of Oakland, experience every day. I know that you've grown wealthy from our suffering. I know that you have used Black faces in everything from criminal justice to education to healthcare to dupe the people and promote your poisons. I know that you used me to clean house in your organization." Sonny paused and looked at his hands. "You used me to pull the trigger and kill other Black people."

"These are baseless allegations!" Patricia Adams exclaimed. "We are businesspeople. Nothing more. I am warning you that if you do not immediately release us from this room, we will have you arrested and thrown in jail for the remainder of your natural life for assault, kidnapping, and slandering our good names."

Sonny was undeterred. "I know that you are the ones who are responsible for kidnapping and trafficking all those young women. And you're responsible for killing the only woman I ever loved, Aaminha Toure."

Parker Jones was dismissive. "That's quite an elaborate conspiracy theory, detective."

"Where's your evidence? I don't think you have *anything* on us," Gerald Portsmith, the burger and chicken man chuckled and spat.

Sonny turned on the giant screen in the conference and shared screenshots of documents Orpheus Anderson found on the servers in Neil Bello's office, including a parallel accounting ledger, records of names associated with shell companies, records of payments made by these shell companies to formation agents, and offshore companies and accounts established by these formation agents. Sonny went through each document in detail. He then played an excerpt of a video recording of Neil Bello's testimony recorded by Malik Akoto in Bello's home. With encouragement, Bello was a masterful storyteller, weaving the numbers and data points into a compelling narrative.

A prolonged moment of silence hung over the room.

"What do you want from us, detective?" Brooks Moran of the conservative White Hawk Media Group cleared his throat and asked. "Surely there's something that we can…work out?"

"You assume that I would sell out my people for 30 pieces of silver."

"We can make it worth your while," Aaron Cleland of the ArmorShield Project proposed.

"I'm not here for a quid pro quo. I'm here to find justice for the women you've kidnapped and trafficked and for their families and loved ones."

Raucous laughter circulated around the table.

"Allow me to read the charges: conspiracy to commit kidnapping and sex trafficking of young women and children through force, fraud, and coercion for sexual exploitation and related crimes including cybercrime and document fraud; conspiracy in the kidnapping and attempted murder of Aurora Jenkins; and conspiracy in the murder of Aaminha Toure. Does anyone care to offer either a confession or a defense of these charges?"

"This is a white man's world, detective Trueheart," Elliot Dover offered, in a moderated and civil tone. Sonny found it interesting but not surprising that the man who peddled cancer sticks was in fact a non-smoker. "Everywhere you turn, this is a white man's world. A white man's god, a white man's dollar, a white man's justice system. None of us will ever be convicted by a jury. In all likelihood, none of us will ever see the inside of a courtroom or a jail cell. We *don't* have to confess or explain ourselves and we are not accountable to you or the so-called people. We are accountable only to ourselves."

Patricia Adams folded her arms and snickered. "He's right. We'll offer testimony in exchange for complete immunity. We all know things that the Feds will find valuable."

"What do you *really* want from us, detective?" Reese Lowie tossed his long, graying hair and inquired. "Surely even you know that this is a futile exercise."

"I want to hear you say it, admit your involvement in all of this. I want to understand *why* you did it, and what was in it for you. Don't you all have enough money? Why involve yourselves in this ugly business?" Sonny asked.

Cyril Bane scoffed. "There is no such thing as *enough* money." He looked at the others who quickly joined him in a chorus of dark laughter. He continued. "You want to know *why*? You want to know something deeper, darker, something existential perhaps?" Cyril Bane threw up his hands. "Money needs no explanation."

Bane shook his head and continued. "You know, this is all so incredibly naive on your part, Mister Trueheart. You're really not that great of a detective after all, are you? The key to understanding us is quite simple. Here you are, tracking down crypto transactions and shell companies, when the real answer is right there in front of your face. But you still can't see it, can you? You really don't understand who or what we are and you never will."

Sonny now projected digital versions of two of the photographs that he had been sent by Aurora in the beginning of his investigation side by side on the screen. The first photograph was taken at a recent Slave Auction at Godbold's mansion. The other black and white image had been taken in 1924 of 13 men in white sheets gathered in the Oakland Civic Auditorium.

"You underestimate me, Mister Bane."

"What do you have here? Just what is this meant to prove, detective?" Cyril Bane glared up at the images.

"There are 13 people pictured in Klan robes in both of these pictures. Let's first examine the color photograph. Notice that three of the 13 people in this picture are wearing women's heels. There are three women in this room: Carissa Johns, Patricia Adams, and Janet Booth. I believe that the hoods disguise the 13 of you in this room. Although I confess that the picture from 1924 is a little grainy…you can see that the 13 pictured here in the 1920's are wearing robes of eerily similar design to those in the color photograph taken in Godbold's mansion. I believe that these are the same exact robes, preserved, maintained, and handed down to succeeding generations. These are your robes, and the robes of your ancestors.

"What these two pictures tell me is that all 13 of you in this room are the descendants of 13 of the most powerful Ku Klux Klansmen who ruled Oakland in the 1920s. You see, I always knew the *why*. Your business is slavery. It always has been, and, certainly, you always hope it will be. Kidnapping and sex trafficking are the modern faces of slavery. You are all deluded by the myth of the Lost Cause and the desire to reclaim the honor and wealth of your confederate, slave-owning ancestors.

"And your forefathers weren't ordinary Klan members, even if they wore the white robes of the rank and file. No, your families owned enslaved persons, led regiments in the Civil War, migrated west, and led efforts to establish a white empire in Oakland, one fueled by racism, anti-Semitism, nativism, and political corruption.

"You're right. It was right in front of me all along. I knew who you were and who I was looking for the minute I opened the letter sent to me by Aurora Jenkins. Aurora had only just mailed the letter with the flash drive of her story and these two photographs before being kidnapped by your people. Once I saw this, I knew that Aurora had discovered that the real power behind the Black Archon and its sex trafficking operation were the descendants of the Oakland Ku Klux Klan. I knew that it wasn't just about money, Mister Bane. It was about history and avenging the prosecutions for political corruption that ended the Klan's reign of terror in Oakland. It's about returning to your family's legacy of slavery. I knew who you were and so did Aurora. All that remained was removing your hoods and revealing you to the world."

Cyril Bane shrugged and clapped weakly. "Bravo. Good for you, detective. You're right! Okay? You're right! You win! That's us, all of us, wearing those royal garments. That photo was a special event for the launch of MambaNet. We counted down to midnight and the network was born and we watched people flock to the site and the money rolled in. Yes! Of course that's us!

"And, you're right about our *real* motivations, the things that draw us to the business of human trafficking. It's about our history, our legacy, and our birthright and the secret history of this city. Bravo, detective, bravo!

"However, as it was during the War for Southern Independence, we seem to have reached a stalemate. You've come a long way for nothing, but the ball is in your hands. Decide. Either give us all the so-called 'evidence' that you have obtained in exchange for a tidy sum, or try to make something out of it, but let's all just move the hell on."

Sonny smiled broadly, toying with his adversaries. "You've led your Pickett's charge and failed. No deals. I've decided to try to make something out of it. I'll probably never have enough for a conviction. I don't know if the police will discover the robes in the picture as they search your homes today. I don't even know if the public confession of your guilt that you just offered will stand. With all of your money, you might still find a way to avoid answering for your crimes, but we'll go through the whole drama anyway. You'll have to answer to the people of Oakland. One way or the other."

"What public confession?" Cyril Bane asked.

Sonny switched the view on the giant screen to a local evening news broadcast where a livestream of the conference room was being viewed by Bay Area audiences.

Sonny Trueheart said nothing more because nothing more needed to be said.

He exited the glass booth and entered the hallway where Captain Gibson and DA Jayda Paul waited with an escort of Oakland Police officers in riot gear. DA Paul held a white robe sealed in plastic and marked "EVIDENCE" in her arms. Gibson dispatched the armed detail to the conference room to arrest the gang of 13. Sonny took the elevator down to the ground floor which housed the California American Bank branch that he had robbed only months ago, and departed the building through the tall glass doors, finding himself engulfed by a crowd of local, national and foreign press.

"Detective, what have we witnessed today? Have you been working with local law enforcement? Will these confessions hold up in a court of law? Is it true that none of these people will ever stand trial? How can we ever bring an end to sex trafficking? Can you tell us more about the history of the Ku Klux Klan in Oakland? Is there a secret Klan government running Oakland today? What do you have to say for yourself, detective?"

Sonny stopped and looked at the sea of reporters with their microphones held forward and the gathering crowd of Oaklanders behind them. He saw Rita Falcon and her contingent of Black Lives Matter activists in the distance.

Sonny stepped forward and began to speak. "Oakland deserves better leadership. Its people are great. Its history is rich. What Oaklanders teach us every day is that the people have the power. This is what the Black Panther Party for Self-Defense tried to show us. This is what Black Lives Matter is doing now. This is what Aurora Jenkins accomplished with her story. This is all that I have tried to do."

Sonny stepped back and silently raised his fist.

Epilogue: The People's Detective (slight return)

9 Months Later

Sonny Trueheart stood on the sidewalk admiring the newly opened East Oakland Aikido and The People's Detective Agency. Sonny bought the building next to the East Oakland Community Church of Kemet where Aaminha once worked. It cost a pretty penny. He created a space that could double as a dojo and a detective agency. Dojo downstairs, private detective office upstairs. There was termite damage. He had to put in new copper pipes and insulation and update all the electrical sockets. But the cash and the crypto stolen from the Black Archon –money that he had never confessed to stealing and that Nzingha had asked the Feds to ignore– more than accounted for it. It was fair to say that the new office and dojo was the prettiest building on the block.

Sonny had to take the city to court for the destruction of his home. As part of a generous settlement that paid for upgrades and new appliances, the city purchased a fully appointed, luxury Airstream Classic trailer for him to live in. He set it up in his backyard and loved how the moon reflected against its smooth metal surface at night. It was his to keep when the reconstruction of his home was complete.

On the surface, things were looking up in Oakland. But there was always trouble lurking beneath the surface.

The livestream confessions of the White Council were deemed inadmissible in court, as were the robes and the photograph of the Slave Auction. However, Neil Bello's confession and testimony, text messages on Seven Daggers' phone, and Orpheus Anderson's thorough investigation of blockchain transactions from the servers in the Bush federal building were deemed admissible and contained enough incriminating financial information to link the White Council to the sex trafficking operations of the Black Archon.

As expected, the Feds kept a watchful eye on Interim DA Paul's investigation. DA Paul referred the case to the California State Attorney General who filed criminal charges against the White Council under the California RICO statute known as the California Control of Profits of Organized Crime Act. The Feds subsequently asserted jurisdiction over the case, citing Godbold's interstate transport and shipping of trafficked women. Every member of the White Council identified by Bello offered information in exchange for complete amnesty from federal RICO prosecution.

Turns out that the Feds were more interested in information about linkages between other sex trafficking operations within the country and terrorist networks abroad. Such an investigation would bring bigger headlines than busting organized crime or white supremacist hate groups in Oakland, California. In this way, sex trafficking was effectively rendered quasi-legal, as long as a trafficker had bigger fish to offer.

Turns out that the big white money was able to take care of itself after all.

The bulk of the criminal responsibility for the disappearances of young women of color and sex trafficking on the streets of Oakland was attributed to Dr. Lucius Godbold and the Black elite who served on the council. The bodies of the Mayor, District Attorney, Chief of Police, Superintendent of Schools, Reverend Jolly and the remainder of the Black Council had been discovered, all chained to concrete blocks at the bottom of the Bay near the Emeryville pier. Godbold was affirmatively linked to these murders after a thorough crime scene investigation of the conference room where they had been killed.

And, as usual, one hand washed the other as careers were built on the discoveries and prosecutions of Black culprits involved in the scandal.

In November, Oakland chose Councilmember Andre Chidozie as its new mayor. Apparent reforms were being undertaken, the most visible of which were local community police relations boards where citizens held cops accountable and even had access to crime scenes within a half hour after the police. But, to the dedicated community activists of Oakland, Chidozie had much to do to prove himself.

Interim DA Jayda Paul was also elected in a landslide. She not only checked off all the diversity boxes, but quickly demonstrated a willingness to investigate city corruption in high places and launched a sweeping investigation into the role played by the Oakland Police Department in the Black Archon's sex trafficking operation.

The Oakland Police Commission forwarded the name of Captain Gibson to Mayor Chidozie as a nominee for Chief of Police, moving him forward because of the publicity that associated him with The People's Detective, and –after Sonny made it clear what Gibson would have to do to redeem himself– Gibson showed himself to be a reformer who was fast at work cleaning out the crooks and the bigots from the force. He implemented the Ebony Alert for missing Black girls. He had even rejected military weapons being offered by the federal government and was making steps to demilitarize the force and end the police occupation of many Black neighborhoods in East and West Oakland.

Under the direction of DA Paul and Chief Gibson, the perp walk of crooked Oakland police officers and detectives and judges was on-going. It seemed like there was one every day being loaded into the back of a police car. As the department began publicly cleansing itself, everyday Oaklanders began walking the streets without fear. Their heads held high.

As for Sonny's crew, Aurora's story was being considered for a Pulitzer. She was experiencing a rapid recovery from the influence of the fentanyl. Her fighting spirit was tremendous, but this would be a lifelong struggle. She was drawing national attention as an investigative journalist, but she turned down a lucrative offer from the *New York Times* because of her commitment to the city of Oakland. She had been offered positions as a Visiting Professor of

Journalism at several northern California universities. But she wanted something else for her life.

Because money was no longer a concern after Sonny gave her an equal split of the take, she asked Sonny if they could move forward together in service to the people of Oakland, and so, beneath the sign that said "The People's Detective" it read "Sonny Trueheart and Aurora Jenkins, Private Investigators."

Godbold and Seven Daggers were dead but Nzingha and Malik Akoto were in hot pursuit of whatever organization Godbold had built in West Africa. Nzingha offered Malik Akoto an opportunity to serve as an intelligence operative for the Special Branch of the Royal Bahamas Defense Force and receive dual American-Bahamian citizenship. Hoping to connect with his mother's heritage and find someplace that he could truly call home, the newly enlisted Able Marine Malik Akoto, flew to the Bahamas for a brief but intensive training and would later travel to Ghana and Nigeria to take down General Lucky Ochuko's operation.

Kaz Taketo was using his cut of the bank robbery to tour the world. He wasn't sure how many years he had left in the land of the living, and there were places and people he wanted to see before the final curtain was drawn. Sonny and Aurora periodically received postcards from him that he would sign, "With Love and Solidarity."

Nzingha helped to repatriate many of the women that they had rescued at the slave auction back to their island homes. She reunited them with their families. She was doubtless considering training many of them as RBDF agents as well. Sujata Ray remained in Oakland and declined Nzingha's offer to serve her country as a member of the Royal Bahamas Defense Force. Instead, she successfully completed a program of drug rehabilitation and was looking forward to beginning her aikido training at East Oakland Aikido. Akoto "encouraged" Mistress Celestine to sign over her dungeon to him and disappear in the wind. He then transferred ownership to Sujata Ray and she turned it into a health and wellness center for sex workers.

In addition to securing the testimony of Neil Bello, Akoto was also able to "purchase the freedom" of Laura Bello and force Neil to sign a divorce settlement that gave her a controlling interest in all of his businesses and assets. In return, she was gracious enough to deed Akoto the condo in West Oakland.

Orpheus Anderson managed to crack the 54-character codes on Godbold's crypto hard drives. When Sonny told him about Seven Daggers' remark about Godbold's sentimentality, they guessed that the password would contain the name of Godbold's deceased wife, Evangeline Fabre Godbold. Orpheus used the code "EvangelineFabreGod," entering it 3 times, reasoning that these 18 letters multiplied by 3 might be the 54-character code. Not only did their gambit pay off, but it turned out that all of the crypto drives that they had stolen had the exact same code. Sentimentality indeed. Because of the wild fluctuations of the more popular digital currencies like Bitcoin and Ethereum, Godbold sought to launder his money with Cardano, a blockchain developed by the co-founder of Ethereum. In spite of Cardano's 1:1 value to the dollar, Godbold made good use of its "proof-of-stake" system and profited from its "staking" rewards and annual percentage yield. This was a different practice than the White Council's use of stablecoins pegged to the dollar and gold reserves to launder their profits. However, once properly divided, this provided each member of Sonny crew with ownership of anywhere between $10,000,000 to 15,000,000 in value.

When Aurora came out with a follow-up to her original *Oakland Post* story, everybody learned the details —with the exception of the vast wealth stolen in the California American Bank heist and the Slave Auction theft— of how they had taken down the Black Archon, discovered the hidden history of the Oakland Klan, rescued some of Oakland's missing women who had been caught up in the organization's sex trafficking ring and killed Dr. Lucius Godbold and his henchman Seven Daggers. In Aurora's story, the deaths of Godbold and Seven Daggers and the ginger and blonde hirelings were labeled acts of self-defense.

Mainstream newspapers, television, and internet media spun wilder narratives, and the details of the punishment, torture and the bombing of his home that Sonny endured were exaggerated with each passing day as the stories became local legend. Some said that he was bulletproof. Some said that he had killed Dr. Lucius Godbold with one punch. Some said Trueheart ended the influence of the Black Archon by walking alone and unarmed into Black Archon street gang territories and challenging all of their toughest men to a fight. Some even said Sonny Trueheart had wings and that he could fly.

There was an inner dialogue that he continued to have with himself. He had been forced to kill again. It didn't matter to him that these were bad people. It didn't matter that all was right with the world. Killing, to him, was an absolute, and he had crossed that line now far too many times. Heck, once was enough. It always struck him as ironic and twisted the way that people celebrated his killings. Playe. Bridgewater. Papi Elder. Godbold. Seven Daggers. The two faceless, nameless ginger and blonde killers who had accompanied Seven Daggers. The Golden Gate Fields parking lot had become a private slaughterhouse for the enemies of Sonny Trueheart. How many more names would be added to that list in his new role as The People's Detective?

And yet, wherever he walked people came up to him and asked, "Aren't you that Sonny Trueheart, the one that cleaned up the streets of Oakland? The one they call 'The People's Detective?'"

And Sonny would give that wry smile of his and say, "You're goddam right."

End

Sonny Trueheart & Aurora Jenkins will return in *Sanctuary*

Malik Akoto will return in *The People's Spy*

GLOSSARY

OAKLAND SLANG TERMS

Hella or Hecka	- Very; a lot
Finna	- Fixing to or going to
Tryna Hop On	- To show romantic interest
Strippin'	- To steal
Got me bent	- To misunderstand someone
Fasho	- For Sure
Out the Way	- To be far from where you reside; in prison
Go Toes	- To fight
Gassed	- Hyped up
You Got Jokes	- You think you're funny?
Jawsin'	- Making jokes or exaggerations or telling lies
Hella Funnies	- Funny jokes
Tucked Off	- Away from the area, in prison or jail
Bo	- Codeine Cough Syrup
Thizzies	- Ecstasy
Chiva	- Heroin
Sis	- An informal, phonetic noun that is short for "sister." It originated in the U.S. between 1825 and 1835 and is derived from the Dutch word zus, which also means "sister." Sis is usually used when directly addressing someone and can also be used as a term of endearment for friends.

JAMAICAN SLANG TERMS

dat batty hole	- Asshole
duppy conqueror	- Ghost Conqueror; overcomes obstacles
Buggaman	- Slur for someone who expresses same sex desire

JAPANESE TERMS

IRASSHAIMASE	- Welcome
DOU ITASHIMASHITE	- You're Welcome
KETSU NO ANA	- Asshole

BRITISH SLANG TERMS

Shits and Giggles	-	For fun or amusement only
Innit	-	Contraction of "isn't it" or is it not
Boozer	-	Person who drinks a lot of alcohol
Trutrans	-	Derogatory expression used by people who believe that in order to be transgender a person must fall within the medical definition
Gaffer	-	Boss
Belt Up	-	Stop Talking, Shut Up
Bird	-	Young Woman
Proper Moist	-	Lack of masculinity
Bollocks	-	Testicles; Nonsense
Bait	-	Suspicious
Bottle	-	Courage
Butters	-	Ugly, unattractive
Sket	-	Promiscuous
Tiger Kidnapper	-	Kidnapping or hostage taking in order to compel another to act
Bluebottle	-	Police Officer
Tosser	-	Dumb or stupid
Dosh	-	Money, cash
Arsey	-	Irritable and argumentative

TERMS USED BY OTHER CHARACTERS

Used by Dr. Godbold

Lagniappe	-	*a little extra; something given as a bonus or gift*

Used by Linda in "Traffick"

Shitass	-	*jerk; obnoxious person*
Mi cuate	-	*buddy, friend*

Used by Chiclet in "Traffick"

Pinche Cabron	-	*fucking asshole*

Organizations that Help Families of Missing Persons

Finding missing individuals is a critical and inclusive effort, and there are organizations that work to help locate missing persons regardless of their race, ethnicity, or socioeconomic background. While it is essential to recognize the unique challenges faced by different communities, many organizations focus on providing support for all missing individuals. Here is a list of organizations that work to find missing women of diverse backgrounds:

National Center for Missing and Exploited Children (NCMEC): NCMEC is a U.S.-based nonprofit organization that assists in finding missing children regardless of their racial or ethnic background.

Black and Missing Foundation: This organization raises awareness about missing Black individuals and provides resources and support for their families.

National Missing and Unidentified Persons System (NamUs): NamUs maintains a national database of missing persons and unidentified decedents, regardless of race or ethnicity, to aid in the search for missing individuals.

Asian Americans Advancing Justice (AAJC): While not specifically focused on missing persons, AAJC advocates for the rights and well-being of Asian Americans and offers support to those facing various challenges, including helping to find missing individuals in the community.

Filipino American National Historical Society (FANHS): FANHS works to promote the understanding, recognition, and study of Filipino American history and culture. Although not a search organization, they may provide guidance and support to Filipinx families looking for missing loved ones.

The Doe Network: The Doe Network is a volunteer-driven organization that focuses on helping solve cold cases involving unidentified individuals and locating missing persons, irrespective of their background.

National Indigenous Women's Resource Center (NIWRC): NIWRC is dedicated to advocating for the safety and well-being of Indigenous women and offers support for missing Indigenous individuals.

National Association of Missing and Exploited Children and Adults (NAMEC): NAMEC is an organization that helps locate missing adults, providing resources and support regardless of background.

International Centre for Missing & Exploited Children (ICMEC): ICMEC is a global organization that works to combat child abduction, sexual exploitation, and trafficking. They provide assistance to families and law enforcement agencies worldwide in locating missing children.

Trace International: Trace International is an organization that helps reunite families separated by adoption. They assist in locating and reconnecting adoptees with their biological families.

Red Cross Family Tracing Services: The International Committee of the Red Cross offers family tracing services for individuals separated from their loved ones due to conflict, disaster, migration, or other humanitarian crises.

Befrienders Worldwide: Befrienders Worldwide is a global network of emotional support helplines. They may assist in locating missing persons and providing emotional support to families during challenging times.

Child Find of America: Child Find of America is a nonprofit organization that assists in the search for missing children in the United States. They provide support, resources, and guidance to families.

ACFE Foundation – The Association of Certified Fraud Examiners (ACFE) Foundation provides resources to help locate missing persons and reunite families separated by abduction, human trafficking, or other forms of exploitation.

Organizations that Help Victims of Sex Trafficking

Supporting victims of sex trafficking is crucial, and numerous organizations worldwide work tirelessly to provide assistance, resources, and recovery services to survivors. Here is a list of organizations that focus on helping victims of sex trafficking:

The SOAP Project is specifically focused on educating the public to increase awareness of the prevalence of human trafficking in communities across the United States and prevent teens from being victimized by domestic sex trafficking. The SOAP Project also works directly with trafficked survivors to provide restorative services.

MISSSEY (Motivating, Inspiring, Supporting, and Serving Sexually Exploited Youth): MISSSEY is a nonprofit organization that focuses on providing services and support to sexually exploited and trafficked youth in Oakland and the surrounding areas. They offer a range of services, including counseling, advocacy, and educational support.

SAGE Project: SAGE Project is a non-profit organization that works to support survivors of commercial sexual exploitation and human trafficking in the San Francisco Bay Area, including Oakland. They provide various services such as case management, counseling, and outreach.

Stand Against Trafficking (STAT): STAT is an organization that focuses on anti-trafficking efforts, including prevention and survivor support. They offer services to survivors in the Oakland area, with a focus on empowerment and recovery.

Bay Area Anti-Trafficking Coalition (BAATC): BAATC is a coalition of organizations and individuals dedicated to combating human trafficking in the Bay Area, including Oakland. They provide resources, raise awareness, and support survivors through various initiatives.

California Against Slavery: While not Oakland-specific, California Against Slavery is an organization working throughout the state to combat human trafficking. They engage in advocacy and public education efforts to raise awareness and promote legislation to combat trafficking.

Alameda County District Attorney's Office - Human Exploitation and Trafficking (H.E.A.T.) Unit: The H.E.A.T. Unit works to combat human trafficking in Alameda County, which includes Oakland. They provide support and services for survivors and work to prosecute traffickers.

Legal Aid Society of San Mateo County: This organization provides legal assistance to survivors of human trafficking, including those in Oakland and the surrounding areas.

Polaris: Polaris operates the U.S. National Human Trafficking Hotline and offers a range of services for survivors, including counseling, emergency shelter, and legal support.

ECPAT (End Child Prostitution and Trafficking): ECPAT is a global network of organizations dedicated to ending the sexual exploitation of children. They work to protect children from trafficking and provide support for survivors.

Coalition Against Trafficking in Women (CATW): CATW is an international organization that advocates for women's rights and works to combat human trafficking, including sex trafficking. They offer support services and engage in policy advocacy.

GEMS (Girls Educational and Mentoring Services): GEMS is a U.S.-based organization that assists girls and young women who have experienced commercial sexual exploitation and trafficking. They provide a range of services, including housing, counseling, and educational support.

Not For Sale: Not For Sale focuses on combating human trafficking and exploitation, including sex trafficking, through various initiatives and survivor support programs.

Coalition of Immokalee Workers (CIW): CIW is a worker-based human rights organization that addresses labor exploitation, including sex trafficking, in the agriculture industry. They provide support for survivors and advocate for fair labor practices.

Coalition to Abolish Slavery & Trafficking (CAST): CAST is a U.S.-based organization that provides comprehensive support services to survivors of human trafficking, including shelter, legal advocacy, and counseling.

Love146: Love146 focuses on ending child trafficking and exploitation and provides survivor care services, prevention programs, and education initiatives.

Apne Aap Women Worldwide: Apne Aap works to empower marginalized and exploited women and girls in India and other regions by providing support, advocacy, and education.

ECPAT International: ECPAT International is a global network of organizations dedicated to combating the sexual exploitation of children, including sex trafficking, through advocacy, research, and support services.

Restore NYC: Restore NYC serves survivors of sex trafficking in New York City by offering housing, counseling, and job training programs.

The A21 Campaign: The A21 Campaign operates globally to combat human trafficking, including sex trafficking, and provides support for survivors.

CAST LA (Coalition to Abolish Slavery & Trafficking Los Angeles): CAST LA offers services for survivors of human trafficking, including shelter, legal assistance, and advocacy.

Please note that the availability of services and the scope of support may vary by organization and location. It is important to reach out to the relevant organization to find the specific assistance needed for families of missing relatives and victims of sex trafficking.

Also by Nicholas Louis Baham III

The Coltrane Church: Apostles of Sound, Agents of Social Justice (McFarland Press 2015)

The Podcaster's Dilemma: Decolonizing Podcasters in the Era of Surveillance Capitalism
- co-author with Nolan Higdon (Wiley 2021)

When is Wakanda?: Afrofuturism and Dark Speculative Futurity
- co-author, co-editor (Journal of Futures Studies 2020)

The Media and Me: A Guide to Critical Media Literacy for Young People
- co-author (Triangle Square 2022)

A Comparative Ethnic Studies Reader: Love, Knowledge, Revolution
- co-author, co-editor (Routledge Press expected publication 2025)

Forthcoming books in the Sonny Trueheart Mystery series by Bootstrap Publications

Sanctuary
Stakes is High
Dial S for Sonny

Made in the USA
Middletown, DE
23 January 2025